SOLANGE . . . Pampered daughter of a senator, she lived the good life in New York—and jealously guarded her relationship with the one man who really loved her . . .

SAMARA . . . She dreamed of designing clothes—and modeled for the renowned Paris house of Jules LeClaire to help make her dreams come true. She was devoted only to her mother—and to David. But her devotion will be put to the test . . .

LIES

"DORIS PARMETT TRAVELS THE GLITTERY PATH FROM NEW YORK TO PARIS . . . CAPTURES THE DRAMA OF POLITICS AND THE GLAMOUR OF THE FASHION WORLD."
—Nora Roberts

"ONE OF THOSE RARE, MEATY, CAN'T-PUT-DOWN NOVELS WE ALL LOOK FORWARD TO READING. SUPERB!" —Fern Michaels

"AN ABSORBING, POIGNANT TALE OF FAMILY SECRETS AND FAMILY BONDS . . ."
—Jayne Ann Krentz

LIES

DORIS PARMETT

JOVE BOOKS, NEW YORK

LIES

A Jove Book / published by arrangement with
the author

PRINTING HISTORY
Jove edition / February 1993

ISBN: 0-515-10991-6

Jove Books are published by The Berkley Publishing Group,
200 Madison Avenue, New York, New York 10016.
The name "JOVE" and the "J" logo
are trademarks belonging to Jove Publications, Inc.

PRINTED IN THE UNITED STATES OF AMERICA

10 9 8 7 6 5 4 3 2 1

In loving memory of my parents and my daughter, Robin.
And for Dink, who exhibited patience above and beyond.

Acknowledgments

Lies couldn't have been written without the help of dedicated and talented professionals in the fields of television, fashion, medicine, and religion.

Their names follow with my gratitude: Micki Freeman; Reggie Harris; Drs. Michael Wax, Joseph E. Ritter, and Robert McConnell; Father Phong; Père De Vial, of Saint-Pierre-du-Gros-Caillon, who not only speaks English, but once lived in the arrondissement in Paris I chose for my characters Samara and David.

In Paris I met with the press officer of the Chambre Syndicale de la Couture Parisienne and with others in the couture houses on avenue Montaigne and elsewhere.

In researching Paris during World War II, I found *Is Paris Burning*, by Larry Collins and Dominique Lapierre, to afford a rich and vivid picture. For anyone, like my character Max Gold, who is interested in running for the presidency, I know there is a wealth of reading material; however, I recommend you include *The Making of the President, 1968,* by Theodore H. White.

Every writer needs writer friends who are constant in the face of craziness. Thank you for being there for me.

Cylvia Alderman and my husband, Buzz, you lived through it. I think.

My editor, Judith Stern, guided *Lies*—and me—with knowledge and kindness. Any errors are solely my own; however, I'd like to believe they are due to literary license.

Lastly I want to thank three extremely talented authors, Fern Michaels, Nora Roberts, and Jayne Ann Krentz for giving *Lies* their enthusiastic review.

Doris Parmett
Murray Hill, New Jersey

Book

One

Chapter One

Paris, 1979

Samara Bousseauc jogged down avenue Montaigne, her long platinum-blond hair whipping in the breeze. Inside her tote bag she carried the tools of her trade: makeup, hairbrush, earrings, extra stockings, a pair of high heels, her robe, plus her prized sketch pad. The popular model knew every mètre of the five hundred mètres of prestigious luxury boutiques and fashion houses along the posh parade located between the River Seine and the Champs-Élysées. "If," as a Paris guest book boasted, "paradise had an address, it would be avenue Montaigne," and the bird of paradise would be Samara.

She rarely walked if she could sprint, dash, dart, jog, or run. She once told her best friend, Mimi LeClaire, "It's cheap exercise. It saves time for my fashion designing."

Although fairly new to the profession, Samara was in demand. A call from the agency brought her prompt appearance. The lissome beauty possessed an innate ability to dazzle, to affect a special silhouette, an hauteur. She plumbed a wellspring of nature's gifts, drawing forth the exact expression, the precise mood, to showcase the designer's creation and sell outrageously expensive clothes.

She understood a mannequin's purpose—her raison d'être—was to breathe life into the creator's genius, to help extend that genius. In her bag she carried a confirmation from *Elle*'s top fashion photographer, acknowledging Jules's request for her to model an upcoming shoot.

"Is her hair gray?" people whispered. They craned their necks for second and third looks. "What color is it?"

3

Samara played tricks on the more outspoken observers, regularly recounting her naughtier escapades to Mimi, who was no slouch herself. Some of the capers they'd thought up as kids were best forgotten—especially the shenanigans they pulled on hapless David.

Her most recent prank occurred at the Café de Flore where she had sat sipping hot chocolate one rainy afternoon. A woman at a nearby table poked her companion.

"Look." Her voice carried. "The poor girl's suffered a great shock."

Using her ability to squeeze tears from her eyes—a skill she'd perfected to audition for the starring role in a school play—Samara slumped her way to the woman's table, sighing grandly, gathering startled attention. It hurt to speak. "How perceptive, madame. Pain and suffering are my companions." She lifted a weary hand. "How do I decide between marrying an impotent, rich grandpapa or a virile pauper? I love him. I love money. But how do I live without sex? You see my dilemma. Worry has turned my hair gray . . ."

Samara clutched the woman's arm, knocking over the remains of her coffee. With a trembling toss of the hair under scrutiny, the five-foot-eight prankster slouched her way to the street. Once outside, she whooped with laughter.

Women described her eye coloring as blue-green or blue or green. Men reflected romance, describing her exquisite eyes in jewellike terms: turquoise, peridot, aquamarine, opal, sapphire. One besotted admirer—Nathan—waxed euphoric. He compared her uniquely dark-lashed orbs—a word she hated!—to the variegated undulations of the Mediterranean.

"Next he'll compare me to fish," she hooted. Beneath her playful exterior, she knew exactly who and what she wanted in life: David Orchin and designing. For now she concentrated on the latter goal. David was beyond the sea, beyond her reach—for now.

The Plaza Athénée's uniformed doorman called out to her, "How do you like this weather, Samara?"

"Fabulous," she tossed back over her shoulder, sending her hair in a spray. "I'll tell Jules you said hello."

Jules LeClaire, her mentor, her second papa. David's father, Michel, was her other father. "Fashion, my darling," Jules intoned during their private lessons, "is nothing more or less than proportion and shape." Wearing the designer's traditional white smock, he pinned and unpinned fabrics on Samara.

She darted across avenue Montaigne, reaching LeClaire's. The gentle soughing leaves on the horse chestnut trees along the broad avenue fanned her face, and the sun warmed her spirit. Who wouldn't be happy to see a bright blue sky after two dreary weeks.

"*Bonjour,* my pretties," she trilled, greeting the red and white impatiens that overflowed the flower boxes, lining the inside of the wrought-iron decorative fence. Tipped by arrogant gold sentinels, the continuous fencing lent proud distinction to a block of world-renowned establishments.

She strode toward the red velvet-lined *ascenseur,* stepped inside, and tapped the button for the third floor. Exiting, she walked the familiar hallway to an unoccupied *cabine,* and changed into her robe.

"Wear these today, Samara." The voice was masculine: deep, friendly, familiar. Two Van Cleef and Arpels security men protected the five million francs of precious gems, a triple rope of flawless graduated diamonds.

Accepting the slim velvet case, she lifted the lid, putting on the temporary adornment. "Ready, boys?" She winked. She'd known both men for six months. The younger man suffered a constant erection in her presence. He'd been in love with her for months.

Her lanky stride led her to the great white salon. The rectangular room boasted tall Grecian columns and white velvet upholstered chairs. At the far end of the salon an imposing white Steinway grand stood on a raised pedestal. Samara understood that additional color distracted from the clothes.

The guards positioned themselves in front of the mullioned windows. A spring wonderland of flowers—yellow jonquils, delicate pastel-centered Salome daffodils, and florets of pink buttercups—filled the garden. The men were content to stare at the prettiest flower of all: Samara. The younger man, entranced by the silkiness of leg and thigh, puffed furiously on a borrowed Gauloise.

"Where's Mimi?" she asked him.

"Late, as usual," he answered, distracted.

"Wrong." Mimi perched a hip on the stool opposite Samara.

While Samara was tall, slender, and light-haired, Mimi was short, fighting the tendency to fat. Her cropped dark hair capped scissor-straight bangs, cut just above the rim of her LeClaire designer eyeglass frames.

Samara peered into Mimi's hazel eyes. "Did you bring it?"

She patted her purse. "Naturally. I brought our favorite lunch, too. Let's eat, then we'll play the game."

The game was their method for exchanging gossip. They played the game, a childhood leftover, with demonic intensity, the winner choosing one or both rewards. To claim victory, the news must be of such titillating import, such high value, such great consequence, that the surprise immediately registered on the loser's face. Both adhered strictly to the honor system.

Mimi handed her a plate with one slice of toast topped with her favorite, *saumon fumé Norvégien*. She squeezed droplets of lemon onto the smoked fish. Samara poured mineral water into their glasses, handing Mimi hers.

Paris chic in a concealing beige suit and black blouse—the LeClaire signature uniform—Mimi raised a censuring brow. Samara's faded paisley robe drove her crazy. No amount of threats to throw it out, or cajoling by Mimi and Jules, or Samara's mother, Lilli, could persuade her to discard it. David sent the robe from Bloomingdale's for her thirteenth birthday, almost six years ago.

"How could you wear that tattered *shmatte*? You'd think by now you'd burn it. I can't imagine what the other houses say."

"I never wear it at the other houses. They provide robes."

"Have you no concern that Comtesse Levron might see you? You'll destroy Papa's business." Mimi's admonition was lost in a hopeless chuckle as Samara pursed her lips in perfect mimicry. The girls loved the comtesse, who with her husband divided her time between the Levron ancestral chateau on the Cher River near Chenonceau in the Loire Valley and their Paris villa.

Samara took a satisfying bite of the smoked fish. "What a tragedy for the Levrons." The Levrons' daughter, their only child, died in an automobile accident on the autoroute in Clermont-Ferrand.

"The comtesse has aged so," Mimi said. "I hear the comte rarely leaves her alone for fear she might harm herself. To lose a child. Papa and Mama cried. To think Francoise was our age, her future ahead of her. I'm told Comte Levron is desperate to see his wife interested in life again."

Both sighed. Neither wished to think about mortality at their age. Especially since they were both virgins.

"Did you know Comte Levron's a distant cousin of the Bouçicauts?"

"No!" Samara responded, impressed.

In the 1850s, the Bouçicauts helped to change the way people shopped. By pricing the merchandise in the Bon Marché, they eliminated the custom of haggling. Samara and her mother lived around the corner from the famous landmark, the park that had a statue of Madame Bouçicaut.

"After I meet the comte, I'll brag I know people from two famous families."

"Don't start, Sam. Papa's relation to Maréchal Leclerc is so distant it's transparent."

Samara never knew her father. He had died before her birth. With a longing to have a father, she savored the stories of Jules's service in the Resistance, her fertile imagination picturing him with the unit that captured the German headquarters on avenue Foch.

Mimi rolled her eyes. "You're nuts, but you're in luck. The Levrons will attend tomorrow's collection."

"Then why is she coming today?"

Mimi shrugged. "Perhaps the comte insisted."

Samara shook her head. "It doesn't make sense."

"It does if you're worried about your wife. Then there's Papa. Not for anyone will he show his clothes before the appointed hour."

A strand of Samara's hair caught in the necklace. The older guard instantly offered an assisting hand. *"S'il vous plaît, mademoiselle."*

She rewarded him with a melting smile, making the man wish his wife were as pretty, instead of having to wax hair from her upper lip. The younger guard lit another cigarette.

Mimi felt sorry for him. The bulge in his pants was obscene, especially since it wasn't for her. "You even look good in your *shmatte*. Nevertheless it's ridiculous to wear that rag with a fortune in diamonds, Sam."

"I told you to quit calling my robe a rag!" Samara charged heatedly. She didn't own a more precious article of clothing,

not even the kelly-green sheer wool cape she had designed and
sewn. "It stays with me till I die—or until David buys me a
new one."

Mimi wanted to wring David's neck. Loyalty to Samara
prevented her from firing off a letter, letting him know how she
felt. The Bousseaucs and the Orchins lived in the same
apartment house on rue Chomel. His parents, Bella and Michel
Orchin, were Samara's mother's closest friends.

David, a brilliant student, won an Armand Hammer medical
scholarship to Columbia College of Physicians and Surgeons in
New York. Common sense dictated that he hardly spent his
waking hours thinking about Samara, if he spent one hour. The
man rubbed shoulders with nurses and female doctors daily; it
stood to reason he did his share of rubbing their anatomy at
night, too. The pictures his parents proudly showed of him after
their several trips to America portrayed a devilishly handsome,
six-foot-two, brown-eyed, dark-haired medical Adonis. A far-
away Adonis.

"I thought you liked him," Samara said defensively. "He
certainly treated you fairly."

"Hah! You mean he suffered while we drove him nuts, or
are you conveniently forgetting he constantly kicked us out of
his room? Sam, you've made him into some kind of a deity in
your mind to avoid facing facts."

"What facts? Why are you so hateful?"

Mimi wanted to shake her. David. As long as she could
remember, it was David. David helping Samara with her homework. David letting her tag along to the cinema. David . . .
David . . . David . . . He had taught Samara everything, even
spouting a scientific explanation of the changes her body under-
went during the menses.

She took a deep breath. Friendship sometimes meant hurting
the one you loved for her own good. "Sam, you've tramped
around in that yucky robe since you were thirteen, tripping over
the stupid hem until you grew into it. It's a frayed mess, not to
mention full of all those permanent stains."

Samara flushed. "Oh, for goodness' sake! Leave me alone,
Mimi! Haven't you saved a stuffed animal, or a favorite book,
or a present? This is the same thing. I'm sick of your
preaching."

Mimi leaned forward. "You're almost nineteen. You flit through meaningless dates."

The young men Samara dated meant nothing to her. They were friends, nothing more. Loving David the way she did, her biggest fear remained that he'd fall in love with an American, marry the awful woman, and stay in New York forever.

"I think you're afraid of men," Mimi added.

"That's preposterous!"

"Is it? What men have you been around all your life? Does Lilli date? There's another mystery. Your mother's a knockout. Papa's begged her to model any number of times. It's an opportunity to earn extra money."

"Mind your own business!" Samara bristled.

"Don't you dare get angry. Unplug your ears. Your mother doesn't just say no. Have you ever watched her face when Papa asked her to model? A curtain comes down. It's as if the very act of presenting herself in front of an audience is too much for her."

Samara was half off the seat. "How dare you!"

"I dare because I care."

"I don't want to hear this!"

"You're going to. Your mother lives a celibate life. In all the years I've known her, the only men she associates with are Michel, Jules, and her priest. Tell me if that's normal. You two could pass for sisters. Yet she chooses to live in a safe, sexless society."

"Explain your snide alliteration before I smash your face," Samara demanded in a low snarl.

"Before you hit me," Mimi hissed, looking down at Samara's clenched fist. "You know I love Lilli. You're my dearest friend, you always will be. Dear friends talk."

"Dear friends know when to shut up!" Samara shouted, oblivious to the show she was putting on for the guards.

Mimi lowered her voice. "You attended the *couvent*. I have nothing against nuns." She hastily made the sign of the cross. "Your mother's beauty parlor caters to women. Your role models were all women." She cocked her head. "Look around you, Sam. This is a couture house. More women, except for Jules."

"Thanks a lot for making me sound like an emotional

cripple. You're a fine one to talk. Who do you date? I wouldn't call your love life a roaring success.''

''Maybe not roaring, but it's sparking. You're Miss Popularity, yet you keep men at a distance. When you date, you're with a group. You ought to be going with a special someone, falling in and out of love, do all the things girls our age do. It's unhealthy to pine for David. When you fall, it'll only be harder. Take pity on Nathan. He's dying to be with you.''

''I don't want to take pity on him. I'm not interested in him,'' Samara said through clenched teeth. ''I hate when you make it sound as if Maman shortchanged me. It's not her fault my father was the great love of her life. Where's it written she has to model for Jules or remarry? Of course she sent me to the *couvent*. She attended it, too.''

Their food remained untouched on their plates.

''How come you've got your whole life mapped out?''

''You've got something to say about everything. What's wrong with that?''

''Plenty. You're a one-track record. For God's sake, since I've known you, you've known exactly what you want out of life.''

''Don't curse,'' Samara rebuked, Lilli's training deeply ingrained. ''Tell me why that irritates you? I want to be a couturier. I want to marry David. I want to have two sons. I'm not asking to be a criminal.''

''In the first place,'' Mimi charged, ''you haven't seen him in eight years.''

''Bella and Michel prefer going to America to visit him. He's busy. He can't come home.''

Mimi rolled her bottom lip. ''In the second place, Sam, you're a kid sister to him. In the third place, he's nine years older than you. In the fourth place, you've heard the expression 'Out of sight, out of mind.' In the fifth place, how could you sit there stating you're going to have sons? Two, no less!''

Samara could feel excitement whenever she thought of David. ''He can do anything. A man as fine as he will have sons. He'll have them with me.''

Mimi threw up her hands. ''Then he's going to have to impregnate you long distance. Can the great one do that, too?''

''Be quiet!'' Samara cautioned, her eyes flashing fire. The next thing Mimi would say was that he didn't write. Which was true. She was a postscript in the letters he wrote to his parents: Give my regards to *mon petit chou*.

Although Mimi was her closest confidante, she couldn't share her innermost feelings where David was concerned. She loved him. She willingly saved herself for him. When she looked at herself in the mirror, she did so with a critical eye, wondering how he would view her.

On the surface her features were arranged correctly. Eyes that were balanced. No pimples on her skin. No wen on the tip of her nose. Teeth that overlapped but weren't crooked or buck. High, firm, small breasts. A graceful neck. Decent body. Legs that wore high heels to advantage. She felt no false pride or foolish modesty.

Mimi bristled. "All right, Sam. Be a dope. Just don't come crying to me when he sends a wedding invitation from the States!" It was as far as she dared go without risking a permanent blowup. David Orchin was sacrosanct.

"You're wrong about him," Samara fumed, half from fear that he *would* send a wedding invitation. "You refuse to see the good in him."

Mimi leaned over to whisper. "Sam, with your sheltered background it's no wonder you use him as an excuse for not getting closer to men, which, considering what an absolutely wonderful, smashingly gorgeous creature you are, is nothing less than extraordinary."

"Quit playing psychologist, Mimi, or I'll start on you."

A tremulous silence ensued. Both knew they were testing the limits of their friendship. Neither wanted to lose it.

"Have you heard from him?" Mimi asked. "Is he still living at Bard Hall?"

"No, he's moved to the Towers. It's near the hospital. He writes that the buildings are three tall concrete fingers with rows of vertical eyes, sticking up into the sky, built over a road, overlooking the Hudson River." She knew that secondhand. Bella had told Lilli who told her.

Mimi, noting Samara's wistfulness, could cheerfully choke the unsuspecting David. Of course it wasn't his fault Samara dragged his old robe around, wearing it like a second skin, pining for the day he'd come home. She still wanted to throttle him. "How long until he's through with his residency?"

"Next year—a lot of good it does," Samara added glumly. "After that he's a Fellow for two years."

Mimi voiced an idea that suddenly came to her. If Samara saw him, there was a chance she'd rid herself of her idolization once and for all. "Perhaps Lilli could send you to the United States. You could tell him you're on official business for Papa."

For a moment Samara let herself hope. As quickly as she did, she squelched her spunky friend's idea. "You might as well suggest I fly to the moon. Anyway, I've never told Maman I love him. Besides, *she* needs a vacation." Lilli had taken her to celebrate Samara's tenth birthday with a visit to the Cathedral of Chartres. Lilli read many of the famous stained-glass windows, recounting various biblical stories.

"I sat in the north transept in front of the panels, listening to the Parable of the Prodigal Son."

"I can think of better ways to enjoy a birthday," Mimi said.

"Me, too, but I've never seen Maman so happy. I made a pledge to myself to be a financial success, to buy Maman a pied-à-terre in Chartres so she could read the windows to her heart's content."

"I hadn't realized you were so religious."

"I'm not, Maman is. Religion is her comfort."

"When will David come home?"

Samara shrugged. "Who knows? It takes forever to be a pediatric oncologist and hematologist—a good one anyway."

Mimi couldn't stand it. "He might be living with someone for all you know."

"Stop it!" Samara said sharply, hating Mimi for cutting right to the heart of things, bringing the pain into the open. She preferred living in hope.

"Face the possibility, Sam," Mimi suggested gently. "What harm is there if you go out with Nathan? He's here, he adores you. I'll tell you a secret. He's making you a surprise birthday party."

"Thanks for telling me," Samara commented sourly. "You've made my day."

Mimi hopped off the stool.

"Now what?" Samara asked.

"Nature call. I've got to pee." As a child, Mimi had suffered from chronic urinary tract infection and recurrent bladder problems.

From long habit, Samara asked, "Are you taking your medicine? Pushing fluids?"

Mimi threw up her hands. "Yes to both! I'm fine. But I'm about to piddle on the floor if you don't quit being a mother."

While she was gone, Samara evaluated the conversation. Though she hadn't admitted it, Mimi had a point. Whatever she and David shared in common had long since faded. They lived different lives in different worlds, even different time zones. When she did write, she sent her letters in a neat precise hand on scented lilac paper, replete with spelling errors.

She had been an immature stick when he had ushered her into his bedroom and closed the door, presumably to offer final words of advice before he left for America.

"Must you go?" she asked, failing to hold back her tears.

He took her face in his hands. "Yes, I made a promise to myself long ago when my friend Monroe died."

Her lower lip trembled. "People die."

His knuckles grazed her cheek. "Children shouldn't. They should have a chance to live a full life. I'll be gone for a long time. When I return, you will be a grown woman. I don't ever want you to allow a man to take advantage of you. Do you know what I mean?" She didn't, but she nodded anyway.

His dark serious eyes peered into her trusting blue ones, reading the truth. He smiled. "I don't think you do, *mon petit chou.*"

That's when he lowered his dark head and kissed her. It ended as fast as it began. Afterward he gripped her shoulders, piercing her with a serious look. "Don't let a man do that to you unless I approve of him."

She promised faithfully. At the time the kiss meant nothing. A few years later his kiss came crashing back in her mind. She recalled his lips, their shape and texture, but mostly she recalled the shocking moment when her mouth opened and she felt his tongue touch hers, as if it had been lying in wait for her. Nightly she would stare up at the sky outside her window, pondering the meaning of David's actions. Why did he kiss her? When they met again, would he kiss her? *Please, God, yes.*

She never told Lilli or Mimi. Maman would haul her off to

the priest for a hundred Hail Marys. Mimi would damn David for daring to deep-kiss her best friend at such a tender age. So Samara suffered through Mimi's lectures, letting her think what she pleased. She wasn't shy or prudish as Mimi suggested. There was nothing wrong with her hormones. Thoughts of David burned like molten lava. She knew with positive conviction that she wanted David, wanted him to take her over the threshold from girl to woman. She refused to settle for less. The kiss, as far as she was concerned, was a promise—a covenant. In the meantime she lived, worked, studied. And prayed. A lot.

God forgive her for her selfishness. Sins from a sinner. She hedged her bets. Wasn't the body an object of sin if the thoughts weren't pure? The priest had said so enough times. Her mind conjured up images of being locked with David so tight it would take a crowbar to separate them. Nightly she spun lustful, lewd, licentious shapes of them until she awoke drenched in sweat. In her dreams, David kissed her, kissed her everywhere: eyes, neck, breasts. Especially her breasts. He lingered over her aching breasts.

She wouldn't dare enter the confessional, admit she lay in bed wishing David were lying next to her naked, his long legs wrapped around her, taking her in his arms. telling her she was so beautiful she blinded him. David loved children. He would make a wonderful father for her children.

A sound pulled her fevered thoughts back to the present. She let her gaze go to the free-standing screen partially visible through the door leading to Jules's office. It held his fabric selections. A muslin model—a toile—hung nearby.

As a committee member of the Chambre Syndicale de la Couture Parisienne, Jules LeClaire enjoyed well-deserved fame. His name ranked with Christian Dior, Yves Saint Laurent, Karl Lagerfeld. He worked to help prevent enormous losses that designers suffer from international counterfeiters and illegal copyists. Thieves who steal a couturier's ideas, then reproduce them; a constant problem for the master couturiers of haute couture in twenty-two houses.

Jules was an unpredictable bundle of wire. He sported a pencil-thin black mustache. He had darting black eyes, lips that continuously pursed in command, incongruous shaggy eyebrows. He was a genius, a showman extraordinaire.

From the time Samara had been a child, he had had a generous spot in his heart for her, his daughter's friend. Crayon in hand, she dogged his steps, piping questions. Flattered, he mentored her training, recognizing her talent. As she grew older, he taught her to build a dress from start to finish. She learned to sketch, drape, cut, sew, make her own patterns. Time ticked by in a world of discussion and design, of color, cut, and line, of fabric and flow. Beneath his benevolent dictatorship, she created with the goal of marrying balance, proportion, and shape while making a statement to enhance beauty. He imbued · her with what he termed Parisienne taste.

Ideas sprang to life as she pinned the toile, demonstrating her growing knowledge of merging technique and theory. She preferred designing irreverent, young, sporty outfits slashed with bold palettes and hot, contrasting colors. A pragmatic Jules assigned hours of research, beginning with Charles Frederick Worth. She read about the masters, haunted the costume section of museums, studying line, color, detailing. She felt comfortable being his second daughter.

His first daughter returned and reached into her purse for two tissue-wrapped tiny cakes. Putting them on a Limoges dish, Mimi drew her stool close to Samara's and sat. Placing the dish between them, their knees formed a table.

"Let's play," she said.

Samara agreed. "It's your turn. It better be good. If I heard it before, this is mine." With a pink manicured nail she moved one of the prizes a tad closer to her side, lifting her chin defiantly. Mimi, with a blunt nail, inched the prize back dead center. Stubbornness was a trait both shared.

Mimi cocked her curly head and smirked. "Marceau's doing it with Jeannine."

Samara levitated the dish, victory written on her pretty face. "Old news. It's mine."

"No. Don't!" The childhood game assumed deadly serious proportions. "I have something." The game provided for one amendment if corrected immediately. Samara's hand hovered in flight. Fair's fair.

"What is it?" she demanded.

"Freddie Havermeyer's sleeping with Cassie Duvale. She told me herself." Mimi scored a hit.

"I didn't know that," Samara gasped. "Freddie Havermeyer's an ugly cold fish. Cassie must be desperate."

It never occurred to them to lie, for that would ruin the game. As Samara looked on enviously, Mimi reached for her prize and, with agonizing slowness, bit into the delicacy with pearly white sharp teeth. "Oh, God, I could die for these." Mimi smacked her lips, savoring the treat's essence. "I'll open a *pâtisserie* and eat to my heart's content."

"You'll be a whale," Samara groused. There was one tiny cake left on the plate. She searched her brain for a juicy tidbit of gossip, pretending as she discarded one old piece of news for another that she wasn't suffering from the sighs of delight, the oohs and aahs, the praises to the gods coming from Mimi.

"Hurry up and finish that thing. It's almost time for me to change."

Mimi slowly licked her fingers. She squashed a crumb from the plate onto her index finger, sliding it into her mouth. "Don't rush me. This is the most erotic experience I've had all week. Besides, you're not wearing the wedding dress until tomorrow. You don't need long to dress."

The bridal dress in question was constructed of priceless Mechlin lace. It was a copy of a style made popular at the court of Louis XV. Jules's creation hung in a temperature-controlled vault adjacent to his office.

"It's my museum piece," he told her.

In a special showing for the press and invited customers scheduled for the following day, Samara would glide down the runway on Jules's arm in the grande finale, an ethereal vision. On her upswept hair she'd wear a diamond tiara to complement the diamond necklace, herself a living jewel in yards and yards of heirloom lace, wearing a pale pink silk underslip to enhance the *broderie de Malines*. Her cheeks would be tinged the palest pink, her lips stroked with pink ice, and her glorious eyes lowered beneath a shelf of curling dark lashes. She would be the virgin princess, introduced by Jules to an enthralled assemblage.

If only David were in Paris, he would take one look at the grown-up Samara, fall madly in love, and beg her on bended knee to marry him. She'd hesitate a fraction just to teach him a lesson not to take her for granted.

"I'm waiting," Mimi snapped, quelling her romantic wan-derings.

Samara clicked her tongue. "I've got one." she leaned forward, ready to pounce on the pink, green, and golden marzipan, shaped like an orchid. "Marcie Reguste broke up with Christian. She's two months pregnant. Her parents will kill her."

Mimi's hand fluttered to her chest. A birdlike cry escaped her lips. She and Samara had jointly hated, envied, or despised Marcie for years.

Samara accepted her due. She'd earned it. She lifted the cake, bringing it sensuously to her lips, wafting the aroma beneath her nose. Marzipan, petit fours, and dark chocolate could easily be her downfall. She opened her mouth for a first, delightful taste.

Behind her head an anvil crashed, a hand sprinkled with dark curling hairs swept up the dish, the other manacled her wrist. Jules, his mustache wagging in cadence with his brows, bellowed, "Don't you dare swallow that! Not a bite! Not a morsel! Not a crumb! Spit! Spit! I will not have a horse model my clothes!

"And you!" He glared menacingly at his offspring. Dressed in a blue suit, white shirt, and regimental tie, he looked every inch the commander. "Mimi, you rotten influence, go home at once!"

Samara collapsed. She winked at Mimi who giggled help-lessly. Whenever she imagined how her father might have sounded, it was Jules LeClaire's voice that filled her wishful dreams.

"Papa," Mimi gasped, her wails equaling his theatrics. "I can't leave. I've got press releases to get out. Besides, you asked me to drive you home later. Samara was only smelling the sweet before offering it to me, weren't you?" Mimi smiled so innocently Samara was tempted to choke her.

Gritting her teeth, she dropped the forbidden spoils into Mimi's outstretched palm. "Be my guest," she said ungra-ciously, waiting for it to disappear into the piranha's mouth.

Mimi eased off the stool. "Here's a free item. There are rumors Phillipe and Caroline's marriage is in trouble. They're not married a month. Grace must be *plotz*ing." Mimi borrowed freely from Bella Orchin's Yiddish vocabulary. Mimi reached into her pocket for a tissue. "It's so sad," she said, holding Jules's stern eye as in a flash she transferred the sweet to Samara. With her back to him, Samara popped it into her mouth.

Before parting, Mimi said, "Spend the night at our house. As long as I'm picking you up later to go to the cinema, it makes sense to sleep over. I'll drive you here in the morning." Samara asked who was starring.

"That dream, Belmondo. Lucky us." Mimi tucked her arm through Jules's.

Nodding agreement, Samara bounced off the chair. She headed for the *cabine.* She hung up David's robe as carefully as if it were a coat of rubies, sapphires, and diamonds. She lifted her slim arms as a helper slid a shimmering black gown over her head.

"Enchanté." The woman stepped back to afford her a look at herself in the beveled mirror. "The comtesse will be entranced."

Samara barely glanced at her glamorous reflection, at her long elegant curves, the twin straps on her bare shoulders, or the fortune of diamonds sparkling about her neck. She was wishing for a magic wand to make David fall in love with her.

Chapter Two

Samara folded herself into the back seat of Mimi's two-door Renault. Jules sat in front, dreading Paris's evening rush hour with Mimi behind the wheel. "The afternoon turned out well, better than I expected," Jules commented. "Comtesse Levron ordered several outfits."

Samara tempered her disappointment at not having met the comte. "She did seem more like her old self. What an awful time for the Levrons."

Mimi patted Jules's thigh. "Brace yourself, Papa. We're off." Gunning the motor, she lurched into the stream of cars on avenue Montaigne. Leaning on her horn, she charged down the pont de l'Alma, where the Eiffel Tower loomed on their right. She zipped around four cars, projectiled across avenue Rapp, to wing left on rue Saint Dominique.

Jules's teeth rattled. "Slower. Slower." Samara leaned forward to give him a comforting squeeze.

Mindless of other cars, Mimi roared across the Esplanade des Invalides, burial place of Napoleon.

"He doesn't know how lucky he is," Jules muttered. "Mimi, child, for God's sake, be careful! Ooooooh . . ." Groaning and clutching the door handle, he squeezed his eyes shut. In the rear seat, Samara's head bounced against the cushioned headrest.

"Not a word to Maman about *Elle,*" she reminded them. "It's a surprise."

"Okay." Mimi maneuvered onto boulevard Saint Germaine, then positioned the Renault between two taxis on boulevard Raspail. A twist of her hand on the wheel brought her angling right on rue Chomel. She screeched to a halt.

Exalted, she kissed Jules's trembling cheek. "We're here, Papa, you can come out now. Had I gone slower, we'd still be at the store."

"Samara may be home," he stammered, wiping his perspiring forehead as he got out of the car to allow Samara room to leave, "but we're not. You won't be satisfied until you kill me or give me bleeding ulcers! Samara, please ask your dear mother to remember me in her prayers when she goes to St. Sulpice in the morning. Thanks to this maniac, my days are numbered. I am certain my heart stopped three blocks ago."

Samara kissed him in parting. "Maman will be happy to pray for you. She prays for everyone." Outfitted in layers, she wore a rust linen skirt, beige blouse, feather-light herringbone blazer, and black leather shoes. "I'll see you at eight o'clock, Mimi."

A glance up the street soured her mood. Frowning, her gaze took in the treeless street that she had lived on all her life. A few potted geraniums perched in window boxes on iron gratings offered scant relief to the bourgeois-gray, short city block. Her apartment house dated from 1878. From her front bedroom window—the tall shuttered windows lacked screens—she could see a school, several stores, a small hotel. One day, she vowed, she'd earn enough money to move Lilli to a house on a street with flowers and trees.

She found her mother preparing dinner. Lilli put down the stirring spoon, lifting her face to return her daughter's kiss. Mother and daughter could easily pass for sisters, although Samara was taller by four inches. They shared the same eye coloring, the same unique shade of platinum-blond hair. When they spoke, they spoke with the same inflections in their voices, and they shared a weakness for chocolate.

But Samara's style, her approach to life, differed from Lilli's. All legs and coltish bounce, her eagerness to learn, to advance her career, and to expand her horizons beyond Paris contrasted sharply with her mother's acceptance of her sheltering life-style. It would stifle Samara to live in the cloistered atmosphere populated by a beauty shop clientele and a daily routine of prayers at St. Sulpice. Mimi had correctly stated that Lilli limited male contacts to Michel, Jules, and her priest. It drove Samara crazy that her pretty mother accepted her quiet existence; she intended to change it.

The kitchen doubled as Samara's workplace. Near the

window, she kept her folding bulletin board, replete with fabric and her sketches. A small table on the patterned linoleum floor held her sketch pad, pencil, crayons, pens, and neat stacks—to please Lilli's fetish for neatness—of *Elle* and *Madame Figaro*. They couldn't do much about the street noise except to shutter the windows at night. The apartment was drafty in winter, hot in summer. All the more reason to become successful, move out.

The aroma of savory lamb stew permeated the room. Samara lifted the lid to sniff. ''Mmmm, my favorite.''

''How did everything go today?''

''Okay,'' Samara replied, dipping a spoon for a taste. ''Maman, don't you get lonely?''

''I have you, darling.'' Lilli put freshly baked baguettes in a basket, bringing it to the table.

''Suppose I marry?''

Lilli tilted her head. A smile lit up her face. ''Nathan's proposed!''

Samara shuddered. ''No, but it's natural I'll marry, isn't it?''

Lilli's face expressed mild amusement. ''Of course it is. It's what I want most in the world for you.''

Samara braced against the counter. ''Maman, are you happy?''

Lilli wiped her hands. She pushed back the hair from her face. ''What a question.''

''It's a fair one. How can you be happy when you rarely go out except to work or pray.''

''My goodness! You make me sound boring. Am I as stodgy as that, Samara? I go out all the time. What a thing to say.''

''With Bella and Michel,'' Samara nagged. She could never get through the barrier her mother put up. ''The Orchins don't count.''

They faced each other. ''Why not? I enjoy their company. Bella's my dearest friend. The way you talk, you make me out to be . . . I'm not sure what, but whatever it is, I don't like it.''

Samara felt frustrated. ''Whenever I bring up the subject of you dating, you stop me. I don't want you living alone.''

Lilli relaxed. She patted Samara's arm. ''So that's it. Samara, I have had the love of my life. I want that for you, too.''

Reference to her father always diverted Samara's attention. ''It was romantic, wasn't it, Maman?'' she asked rhetorically. She knew the story by heart.

Her parents had met at the Jardin d'Acclimitation, a children's park in the Bois de Boulogne, not far from avenue Foch. Her mother had taken David there to ride the miniature train. Afterward, they played ball. She tripped over a log, twisting her ankle. The handsome stranger who rescued her later became Samara's father. She often substituted the main characters for David and herself.

"True love at first sight," she said, sighing dreamily.

"Yes," Lilli replied wistfully, then brought the discussion back to the present. "Nathan phoned. Twice."

Samara recognized the ploy. Once again, her mother sidestepped the issue of her social life. Samara wouldn't give up. One of these days, she'd wear her mother down.

Samara reached into the cupboard for the dinner plates. "He's making me a surprise birthday party. Mimi told me."

"She shouldn't have," Lilli chided. "Now it's no surprise."

"Don't blame Mimi. She knows I wouldn't say anything to Nathan. She's counting on making me feel guilty, hoping I'll take pity on him. I won't."

Lilli set the bottle of Chardonnay on the table. "Nathan seems perfectly nice to me."

"He is perfectly nice. That's his trouble. Predictable, perfectly nice Nathan bores me. I want a man whose nose doesn't drip, who enjoys going to museums and discos, who doesn't look at me with cow eyes!" *He's not David. David doesn't have cow eyes. He has dreamy eyes.*

Samara told Lilli about Comtesse Levron. "She's so brave. It must be awful to lose a loved one. Was it awful for you to lose Papa?"

"It happened a long time ago. You can see I'm fine."

Samara hugged her tightly. "I'm so lucky. I couldn't imagine losing you."

Lilli smoothed her daughter's hair. "Nor I you. Now let's discuss your birthday. What would you like to do?"

"Let's go to Chartres. We haven't been away in ages. Not for nine years. You can read me the stories of the stained-glass windows."

Lilli gave her daughter an appraising look. "A few minutes ago you complained I'm in church too much. Now you ask to spend your birthday visiting one. You must admit this isn't like you."

Samara was determined to break her mother's routine,

before she married David. One vacation could lead to a second vacation, and then to a date! She forced herself to sound convincing. "I think it will be fun. There are other things to do in Chartres, too."

Lilli added a pinch of pepper to the stew. "I'd think a young lady going on nineteen could think of something more enjoyable, but if that's what you want, Chartres it is, including the hotel, the works. I shall read window after window, starting with the story of Joseph."

A delighted Samara twirled Lilli about the small kitchen, tipping the dress form over in the process, but as they sat down to eat, her gay mood again grew pensive. "Maman, why are you so devout?"

Lilli put down her fork. "That's a strange question coming from a Catholic."

"I don't see why it is. You're a saint."

"Mind your tongue. I'm no saint. We're all sinners. Myself included."

Samara chewed a piece of lamb. "Not you. I shall find you a man to marry."

Exasperated, Lilli slapped down her napkin.

"Did you love Papa so much?" Samara pressed, showing the same tenacity she showed as a child. She understood grand passion. The idea of a larger-than-life romance fed her fantasies. She and David would experience a love like the one shared by her parents.

"I loved your father," Lilli said, then switched the subject. "The lilacs are blooming. Tomorrow I'll buy an armful to cheer you up. I don't like to see you in this mood. Afterward we'll plan our trip."

"Mimi's invited me to sleep at her house after the cinema tonight. You'll come to Jules's to see me model the wedding dress tomorrow, won't you?" she asked as she refilled her dish.

"I wouldn't miss it for the world. Bella received a letter from David today."

Samara held her breath. *Please don't let him write he's fallen in love with an American.* "How is he?"

"Fine. He's working hard. I never told you this, but when you were six, you broke out in a terrible rash from peas. You were convinced you were dying. David offered to eat peas to prove you wrong. You refused. You told him you'd be busy in heaven. He must live to care for me.''

"What did David say?"

"He ordered me to let you sleep in my bed with me, and I had to make a snoring sound every few minutes."

"Why?" Samara gripped the table, hanging on to every wonderful word. She could listen to stories about David all day.

"The honking would remind you that you were alive. He sternly warned me not to fall asleep."

A flush of warmth filled Samara. She could see David doing that. "Then what happened?"

Lilli laughed. "I fell asleep. Bella and I had a good laugh over that today."

"With the awful experiences the Orchins suffered in the concentration camp, David's being a healer means even more."

A shuttered look came over Lilli's face. "Yes," she said quietly. "I expect one of these days he'll meet a woman, marry, settle down. Bella and Michel want grandchildren."

Samara's heart thumped. "Has he met someone special?"

"He dates, I'm sure."

Samara lost her appetite.

As was their custom after washing the dishes, they went into a spare bedroom once used by Samara and Mimi for their make-believe palace, the "thrones"—LeClaire discards—chipped gilt paint on faded red chairs. While "court" held session, anyone, including David, must first be granted permission to speak by the mischievous pair. They nodded or flicked their wrist. Up for yes. Down for no. The ploy drove their elders crazy—precisely the two madcaps' intention.

Samara sat on the couch that had replaced the thrones, cuddling next to Lilli. Focused on the small screen, she watched the newscaster announce Bjorn Borg the winner of the French Open, his third win. The station switched by satellite to New York City. Samara thought the anchor good-looking, but not as handsome as David.

"Ladies and gentlemen," he said. "Two days ago, I returned from a trip to Israel. I saw the carnage left by the latest PLO border dispute. The blast killed four, injuring schoolchildren, many under the age of ten. Israel vows retaliation. President Carter issued a statement decrying the loss of innocent lives. The government of French President Giscard d'Estaing issued a warning to terrorists everywhere to put down their arms. Next week the UN Security Council will take up the issue.''

The anchor paused, and a smile appeared on his face. ''I don't usually editorialize. Tonight is an exception.'' His smile broadened, and his eyes twinkled. ''It's with great personal pride that I announce President Carter today placed United States Federal Judge Murray Leightner's name in nomination for the seat vacated on the Supreme Court upon the death of Justice Simmons. Senator Max Gold, among others, enthusiastically endorses Judge Leightner's nomination. This is Avrim Leightner. Good night from New York.''

''Ohmigod!'' A scream tore from Lilli's lips.

Samara leapt up, her face etched in shock. Her mother's face was ashen. The words *heart attack* ricocheted in her mind.

''Maman, what's wrong?'' Petrified, Samara massaged Lilli's wrists. She frantically tried to recall David's first-aid advice.

Gently she lowered Lilli's head, bringing it between her legs. ''Stay like that,'' she ordered, dashing for a glass of water. She ran back. ''I'm going to help you to sit up. Please, what's wrong? Tell me.''

''No. Nothing,'' Lilli said, sipping the liquid. ''It passed. Probably indigestion.''

Tears spiked Samara's lashes. Her mother never got sick. Never! Perhaps a cold. Terror shot through her. The Levrons lost a child, but they had each other. Who would she have if something happened to her mother? Young and healthy herself, she had never faced the possibility of harm befalling her mother. Old people clutched their chests, not Maman. ''I'm calling the doctor.''

Lilli gripped her wrist. ''No. I'm all right now.''

Filled with apprehension, Samara didn't argue. Lilli's coloring, she saw thankfully, lost some of its pastiness.

''Promise me,'' she begged. ''Promise me if this happens again, you'll see the doctor.'' She kneeled down, becoming the anxious child, burrowing her head in Lilli's lap.

''You're all I have,'' she whispered brokenly in a little girl voice.

Lilli stroked Samara's long, satiny hair. ''I will if it happens again. Let's just sit here a moment longer.''

Fear engulfed Lilli. Dark demons strangled her. She needed

to talk with Bella and Michel. An hour later, she shooed a reluctant Samara out the door. She felt a flash of fear. Tonight she'd received a sign, an omen. Tears stung Lilli's eyes. The noises grew louder. She couldn't escape. She heard it all again as if it were yesterday . . .

Four-year-old Lilli sat patiently on the wooden bench next to *Untersturmführer* Karl Schmidt, under the austere portrait of Adolph Hitler. Karl resembled a clown. His red hair stuck out of his cap like mop strings. He had a big red bowl of a nose and closely set green eyes.

Lilli waited for her father, *Obergruppenführer* Hans Wurfel, to emerge from his office on the first floor of Gestapo headquarters on avenue Foch.

She longed to play outside on the grass, separating the inner *allée* from the main thoroughfare, and collect the fallen horse chestnuts. It was more fun than playing with Papa's shiny twin flashes that he removed from his lapels. Mostly she liked to smell the lilacs, but lilacs didn't bloom in August.

Lilli picked up her red crayon to draw a red horse. Papa's favorite color was red. Suddenly she heard her father shout, *"Schwein! Hund!"*

A man screamed. She jerked upward. The man screamed again. Lilli clamped her hands over her ears. It scared her to go to her father's office. She hated the hard bench, the sour smells, the awful noises. She buried her face in Karl's chest, waiting for the noises to stop.

There were things she didn't understand. She had asked Papa when Karl took her to ride the little train at the Jardin d'Acclimitation why a mother put on an angry face. Why did she pull her little girl away when all she wanted to do was play?

Her papa tickled her under the chin. He scooped her up high above his head, twirling her about. "You don't need them. They're no better than *Jüdin Schwein*. You've got me, *Liebling*."

She loved her papa. *Obergruppenführer* Hans Wurfel was so handsome with his silky golden hair, his blue eyes. Everyone said she resembled him. Her mama said Papa was a prince among men, that men rightfully obeyed him. Mama said Papa was the smartest man in the world. Mama said Papa was a master at interrogation, especially with Jews and resistance fighters. Lilli didn't understand the big words, but Mama was proud, so it must be good.

Papa used to keep a different picture on his office desk. She saw it once. The boy in the picture had big ears. The lady looked older than her mama and was not pretty at all. Mama loved flowers: begonias, roses, crocuses, daffodils. Lilacs were her favorite. Stella Des Pres. Her mama's name sounded like a movie star's name.

Every morning Papa allowed Lilli to pour twelve drops of cream from the Limoges pitcher into his cup of coffee, drop two cubes of sugar in, and stir. She held her breath until her father took his first sip, indicating his pleasure with her. She loved her papa even though he could be very strict. That's when she played the game of Quiet Mouse.

She finished the picture of the red horse just as her father opened his office door. She ran to him. He lifted her up.

"We'll go now, Papa."

"We'll go for a car ride another day. Let's go home." She bit her lip. She'd waited for nothing.

Papa told her to go to her bedroom and stay there. "No, darling, you've done nothing wrong," her mother said. "Papa loves you. Papa and I need to talk."

They didn't smile at dinner. Right afterward, her mama put her to bed. Her papa didn't tell her a story. They didn't sing their favorite song, "Prussens Glorie."

Night fell. The room lay in darkness. She heard the man's screams again. The monsters were back. They danced on the wall. She hid beneath the sheet.

The next morning her father kissed her hard. He squeezed her so tight she couldn't breathe. "I love you, *Liebling*. Come stand by the window and wave to me as I leave for work."

She scrambled out of bed. "Papa, aren't I putting twelve drops of cream into your coffee?"

He kissed her head. "Not today, *Liebling*."

Standing next to her mother, she waved good-bye. In the street, her papa lifted his head, waved his cap, blew her a kiss. "Papa's gone to Berlin," Mama said when he didn't come home for dinner.

That night her mother shook her awake. "Get up! We must leave at once!"

A dim light in the hallway cast shadows on the wall. Lilli

shrank. Monsters! She threw her arms around her mother's neck. "Tell Papa I want him."

"Shhh. Lilli, you must forget Papa. Don't mention his name."

Lilli pushed the heels of her hands into her eyes. Her mother yanked her pajamas off. "This is for winter," she protested as her arms went through the sleeves of her best woolen dress. *"Ich heiss."*

"Stockings," Stella muttered. "Stockings for my baby."

"No!" She didn't want to wear stockings and the winter coat her mother put on her next. She'd spied the suitcase packed with her clothes.

"Where are we going?" she demanded, always more at ease with her mother than her father. Her mother grabbed her with one hand, the suitcase with the other.

"My blue rabbit!" Lilli snatched it off the bed. Her mother half dragged her down the stairs.

Outside, she gasped. They were going to a party! She was in the middle of a carnival. Lights lit up the street. People sang. Kissed. Hugged. Cried. Church bells rang. Armored tanks, decorated with flowers, rolled through the streets. Tricolored flags appeared in windows. Wine bottles changed hands in toasts. Lilli craned her neck to take in the wondrous sight.

"Maman, what's happening? What are they singing?"

"The Marseillaise. They liberated Paris today. Remember, not a word about Papa." Her mother scooped her up in her arms. They ran.

Lilli's head bounced. Why couldn't she speak about Papa? She had no idea what the word *liberated* meant, only that it couldn't be good, not if Maman insisted she not mention Papa and she looked so sad.

They flew down the street, banging and shoving into crowds of people. In blurred images, Lilli caught sight of men in uniform, but not the color uniform papa wore. She heard snatches of a language she didn't understand.

"Remember, don't mention Papa," Stella panted when she put her down in front of an apartment house. Her mother lugged her up three flights of stairs. Dressed in hot clothes, sweat poured down her face, her neck, between her legs. Her mother paid no attention to her complaints.

"Remember, Lilli," she gulped, catching her breath. "I do the talking. Don't forget. Not a word about Papa."

Her mother removed an envelope from her purse. She dropped down in a quick crouch, pinning the note inside Lilli's coat.

"You've got to make a good impression. That's why I dressed you this way. It's important that people know I cared."

"Maman, I'm hot," Lilli wailed, tugging at the buttons of her coat. "I'm thirsty. Where's Papa?"

"Hush!"

A woman, her oily black hair shoved under a net, opened the door a crack. She stared at them. Recognition came swiftly. "Oh, it's you!" she shouted, waving a wine bottle. "Get away from here, you French whore, before I shave your head myself. And take your German bastard with you!"

Lilli recognized the mother of the little girl she'd tried to play with in the park.

"No, wait!" Her mother blocked the door. The woman cursed again.

"I've money." Lilli stared at the fistful of money. "See! Please, she's just a baby. She's innocent. Take her to Notre Dame des Champs, I beg you. I ask nothing for myself. Have mercy!" her mother begged.

"Collaborator!" The woman sucked in her cheeks and spit. Startled, Lilli let out a piercing yell.

Her mother wiped the spittle from her face. "Money. My little girl. Save my baby."

Without warning, Lilli felt herself shoved forward. She landed painfully on her knees.

"Maman," she whimpered, seeing the closed door. Where had her mother gone?

"Shut up! Your mama's run away, do you hear me? She doesn't want you any more than I do." The woman picked her up and threw her into a chair. Her head bounced against the back, jarring her teeth. Her feet didn't reach the floor.

"You move from there, you little German dreck, I'll slap your puny face! I'll rip your skin. I'll make you bleed to death! I'm going to bed. I'll deal with you in the morning!"

In shock, she swallowed her screams. Visions of her face being ripped petrified her. She would do as the woman asked. She'd be as quiet as when she waited outside her father's office. Paralyzed with fright, knowing if she closed her eyes the evil demons would jump off the wall and eat her, she jerked herself awake whenever her eyelids betrayed her. Whimpering, she bit down hard on her bottom lip, drawing blood.

She shook. Her parents didn't love her. They'd said they did, but they didn't. Her father didn't love her. He'd waved good-bye and never came back. Her mother told her not to speak about her papa and left. They didn't want her. They threw her away. She must be a very, very bad girl. She clutched her only friend, her little blue rabbit. Tears slid down her face onto its fur.

Disoriented, exhausted, she saw the monsters coming for her. "Maman," she sobbed silently. "Why don't you love me, Maman?"

She badly needed to use the bathroom. Holding it in hurt. She crossed her legs tightly. A moan of pain escaped her lips. She scrunched the rabbit tight against her face, holding her silence and her bladder as long as she could, but she was no match with nature. Urine soaked her underpants, seeped down her legs, sticking to the stockings. Unable to maintain her vigil, her head lolled down her chin.

She awoke to see light stream in the room. She waited to hear her mother singing in the kitchen, her papa calling to her to watch him shave. Where was Papa? Mama? This wasn't her house. Her furniture.

"Look what you did, you filthy animal!" the woman screamed, coming to where a terrified Lilli burrowed flat against the back of the chair, hoping to become invisible.

"Who's going to pay to clean the chair, you awful brat?"

"I want my mommy," she sobbed.

The woman hit her. "You're not worth any amount of money, you whore collaborator's scum!"

The little girl she had tried to befriend strolled into the room in her nightgown. With two fingers she pinched the bridge of her nose. "Phew. She stinks!"

She had never made a bowel movement in her pants, but it had happened. Her stomach had churned, and it had slipped out.

"Too bad I can't flush her down the toilet. Get up, dreck! We're leaving. Why your mother picked me, I'll never know."

Disgraced, humiliated, hauled from the chair by the woman yelling at her to keep up or be beaten, she ran in her wet, soiled pants. Her stained dress stuck to her bottom, and the stockings

matted her legs. When she stumbled, the woman slapped her
face. Quivering with fear, she redoubled her efforts. She fell
several times only to be yanked up by the arm. Blood oozed
from the cuts on her knees. As she ran, a clump of bowel
movement fell from her underpants onto the ground. Blocks
later, the woman slammed her against a large oaken door. She
slumped to the ground.

"Sit! Don't talk!"

Semiconscious, Lilli couldn't speak if she wanted to. Her
rigid body ached. Her knees bled. The woman repeatedly
banged the knocker until a nun answered.

"Sister, someone deposited this filthy child on my doorstep.
I don't know who she is or who her parents are," she lied. "I
did my Christian duty."

Sister Jean, of Les Soeurs de Sion, standing in the doorway
of Notre Dame des Champs, glanced down at the tiny heap of
human rejection dumped in her doorway. The child's lips were
parched, her eyes frantic, the little knuckles white around the
stuffed animal she clutched.

Without a word, Sister Jean crouched down. She stretched
out her hand. Oblivious to the stench, the soiled clothes, she
lifted Lilli tenderly in her arms and kissed her. She retreated a
step and resoundingly banged the heavy oaken door shut.

She held her a long time, rocking her in her arms until some
of her quaking subsided. Then she tended to her bruises, gave
her a soothing bath. Stella's letter, unpinned from inside Lilli's
coat, confirmed her suspicions. That night, and for the next
month, Lilli slept with Sister Jean's arms about her. Trauma-
tized, suffering deep psychological shock, she believed the
story of her background supplied by the good sister. She was
Lilli Bousseauc, last surviving member of a Basque family
tragically wiped out in the war. Her memories, her nightmares,
lay buried in a deep, dark place, where even she couldn't reach
them.

Until the day in New York when a French priest visited her
and handed her Stella's letter that he had found in Sister Jean's
desk after the nun died.

"She must have believed saving it was God's will," he told
Lilli.

Chapter Three

New York, 1979

Solange Gold darted between a Mercedes and a Volvo, a silver streak in Bali pumps. A cabby floored his brakes, narrowly avoiding hitting her. Tires and voice screeched in unison. Furious, he shouted, *"Puta!"*

"You only wish," she yelled back. He wasn't entirely wrong. This afternoon she intended playing whore to her heart's content. Solange flew across Madison Avenue, past St. Patrick's Cathedral, across Fifth, to Rockefeller Center.

"Avrim's back! Avrim's back!" Her heart beat time with her feet. Not a few men raised appreciative eyes, watching her skim over the pavement. Pretty girls were commonplace in New York, but hellbent-for-somewhere, drop-dead gorgeous girls with platinum-blond hair weren't.

Solange increased her speed. Avrim should be winding up his noon NBC telecast, exiting 30 Rock any moment. She didn't dare be late, not with the fun and games she'd planned. The anticipation was almost as good as the actual thing. Not quite, but damn near. Solange thrived on good times.

Lunch at the American Festival Cafe. Steamy sex at his apartment, time-out for Avrim's six P.M. broadcast, dining at the Four Seasons, back to his place for a repeat performance— this time with flutes of Blanc de Blancs by the bedside and, to cap the festivities, Xenon's. Studio 54 was getting to be a bore.

Solange whipped around a corner, slamming into a man's chest. "Move!"

He gaped in dismay as his new shirt flew out of its gold-embossed shopping bag. The white silk landed on the sidewalk. "Fuckin' bitch! Watch where the hell you're going! That shirt cost me fifty bucks."

"Up yours, mister," Solange trilled over her shoulder. "It's on sale for forty-five." She had recognized the distinctive Gold's wrapping. Gold's, her family's store, located on Fifth near Tiffany's, rivaled London's Harrod's. She knew how lucky she was. How many women in America owned a clothes closet five stories high?

Solange adored New York.

Give her Manhattan's skyline, Broadway's opening nights, posh restaurants, she was in heaven. She relished the knowledge that she could disco in trendy private clubs where burly bouncers barred the paparazzi. (Unless they were on the take!)

Life was terrific. Live and let live, she always said. Panhandlers didn't bother her any more than the homeless beggars drifting on the streets. As long as the vagrants stayed clear of her, didn't try any of that window-washing crap when she stopped for a light, expecting a handout. The Senator's gift for her eighteenth birthday—a diamond and sapphire ring—winked its approval. She'd be nineteen soon. My God, she was halfway to thirty-eight!

A policeman blew his whistle, abruptly halting her progress. Solange impatiently waited for the light to change, then she bolted. She made a colorful sight in an electric-blue LeClaire suit, worn with a Paris pearl Sonia Rykiel sweater. Labels ruled the world; to think otherwise was stupid. She clutched the Hermès purse she had grabbed from the counter at Gold's, telling the salesgirl to charge it to her account.

Had it really been a month since she'd seen Avrim? While he covered wars—or were they skirmishes?—she squeaked through her freshman year at NYU, gave two parties for the Senator, spent a glorious five days with a friend in Escondido, California, at the Golden Door.

Spying Avrim scanning the lunchtime crowd, Solange sprinted to her destination. He was tall, two inches over six feet, with powerful shoulders, an athletically trim physique. His hair was darker than it appeared on television. A rich nutmeg-brown, it had a tendency to curl. But it was his eyes that she loved the best. Talk about drowning in the deep blue sea . . .

"Avrim!" She flung herself at him, kissing his cheeks, his

lips, oblivious to the smiling people who recognized the handsome newsman. "Rogue, you grew a mustache! You look like a billboard advertisement, good enough to eat," she cried joyously. Her eyes roved over him, admiring the way he filled out his navy-blue pinstripe suit, his shoulders broad and commanding, stretching the light blue shirt he wore with a red silk Givenchy tie she'd given him. She nipped his ear, flicking the folds with her tongue. "Maybe we should skip lunch. I want to find out if the mustache tickles."

He patted her bottom, hugging her, letting her feel he was as anxious as she. "Shut up, you little reprobate. Do you want the world to know what a hot number you are?"

She wiggled closer, arching her neck. He'd once confessed White Linen made him horny. "You're wearing it, aren't you?"

"What else?" she teased, delighted to see him, his breath doing crazy things to her nerve endings. "I'm a creature of habit. You should know me by now. In case you forgot, I planned our whole day and evening, horizontal and vertical."

"That's what I like about you," he said with amused indulgence. "You're a take-charge woman." He tucked her hand in his, purposely bumping hips as they followed the blond hostess down the steps to their table.

The spring temperature was in the high seventies; the hostess led them to a table in the courtyard. Seated under a red umbrella, they feasted on each other with smiles and chuckles, grins and subtle hand messages, while ordering gin and tonics.

Avrim leaned forward, his gaze focused on her pouty lips as his thumb erotically teased her palm. Few women could add that elusive extra glamorous insouciance to clothes the way Solange could. It was as if the designers created with her in mind. With her unusual eye and hair coloring, she would stop traffic whether she wore a burlap bag or a ten-thousand-dollar gown. At five feet eight inches she was a knockout. "You get prettier every day, Solly. How the hell do you accomplish that trick?"

"Pampered bone structure and terrific genes," she replied, telling him the truth.

His dark eyes lifted in bland inquiry. "I like your outfit. Did you buy it at a flea market?"

Avrim's offbeat humor, she suspected, frequently masked

the horrors he saw on assignment. He was so self-confident, unafraid to take risks, a real man's man. And hers, she thought, enjoying his deep, seductive baritone.

Her eyes glowed. "Thank you, darling. As a matter of fact, I picked this little number up for a bargain price."

His glaze slid to the diamond-faced Rolex on her wrist. He doubted if she'd ever stepped foot in K Mart or J.C. Penney. "In other words, Solly, you raided the family joint."

She stuck out her tongue and scrunched up her nose. "For free a girl can't be choosy." Avrim was probably the only man in the world with whom she felt completely at ease. They knew each other as well as two people could—two people who still kept secrets.

"Look what I filched for you."

A slow, dazzling smile spread over her face. She whipped a red bikini out of her purse. Hooking her little finger into its band, she circled the air, dropping the skimpy underwear on the table as a centerpiece.

His mouth fell open. "Geez!" Avrim slapped his hand over the skimpy briefs. "Solly, what am I going to do with you?"

Her eyes glowed with mischief. She giggled. "Should I tell you or show you?"

"Both," he said. He threw back his head, roaring at her outrageousness. He loved her when she acted free, when she joked and teased; not when she lapsed into a serious discussion about her great father, the Senator, how important she was to his career.

Avrim thoughtfully circled the face of the timepiece. Even on his salary it would take years to afford her outfits and jewelry. He wished he knew what he wanted from her, from himself, where their relationship was heading, or if this was it. Not that his parents cared. He knew they'd just as soon he met a nice professional woman—preferably an attorney, associated with a power firm—marry, and present them with grandchildren. Although neither parent said it, he sensed they tolerated Solange for Max's sake.

Avrim gazed at her speculatively. "Solly, how long have we been together? Four, five years?"

Solange grinned. "Four and a half." Neither would ever forget the afternoon she'd rung his bell, announcing she was in the neighborhood and could she please use the bathroom. He couldn't know that she'd practiced for days, wandering past his apartment, almost ringing his doorbell on four different occasions.

She had interrupted Avrim in the middle of writing an article. He'd waved her inside, returned to his desk, but when she stepped out of his bathroom naked, her boyish curves molding to her shapely legs, her elegant breasts high and proud, her blue-green eyes holding his, her tongue peeking between her teeth, he knew she wasn't leaving his apartment until he'd had his taste of her.

"I was fifteen. You were twenty-five." She trailed a finger along his wrist. "You said, and I quote, 'Well now, aren't you a little young for this?' "

His voice grew husky. "And you said, 'It's either going to be you or someone else.' "

"It worked," she said, smiling into his eyes. "I used to lie on the couch when you were on TV. I'd watch your mouth and your hands." She shivered. "The things I imagined them doing to me."

They were lovers of long standing, knowing exactly how to turn each other on, with a look, a touch, a frenzy that left them always wanting more.

"It worked," he confirmed. There wasn't another Solange in the world. Furious and frightened after the first time, he'd sweated out waiting for her period. She refused to let him wear a condom. Feeling more like a child molester than a lover, he located a doctor willing to fit her for a diaphragm. He begged for out-of-town assignments, anxious to rid himself of his growing intoxication with her. She spelled trouble. Ruination. Solange was too young, too shallow, too egotistical, too self-centered. She'd bury his career. He'd be hauled in on rape charges. Bring shame to his family. Princeton would rip his picture from the yearbook. He leapt at every foreign assignment with a vengeance, then couldn't wait to return. It stunned him. She stunned him.

"You had an erection a yard long," Solange said, resting her chin on one hand, her elbow propped on the table. "I'm glad it was you, Avrim. I've never regretted giving you my virginity."

He opened his menu, but the words swam before his eyes. The truth was he didn't regret it, either, or any of the years with

Solange. It bothered him. He'd known her all his life. Their fathers were best friends. Each time he thought he'd uncovered the real Solange, another layer of her personality emerged: frail, fragile, yet tenacious, making him grateful he balanced his life by reporting stories that took him out of town. In work he understood the clearly defined issues. He'd built a well-respected reputation, earning the plum television anchor spot in the world's number-one market . . . on merit, not connections.

When he was away from Solange, he screwed other women, telling himself he was taking the cure. A cure that repeatedly failed. Even before his assignment ended, he would picture Solange naked in his arms. He hardened at the thought of her taking him into her hot body; he couldn't wait to get her into bed.

Avrim closed the menu. "Why aren't I the main man in your life instead of your father?"

She licked her lips. "You are, silly."

"Funny, I'd never guess," Avrim said, piqued.

"The Senator needs me, darling. You don't. It isn't the same thing."

Avrim broke a roll in two and told himself not to let it bother him. Solange ordered first, cautioning the waiter not to bring peas. "I'm allergic."

"I'll have the same." Avrim duplicated the poached salmon with a lemon chiffon sauce. "And a Molsen, please. Solly," he asked after the waiter left, "why do you persist in calling Max Senator as if he were some kind of deity? He's your father, for God's sake! Call him Dad, or Daddy or Pops or Papa, not Senator. He's not God or your boss or your husband," Avrim continued, the frustration plainly evident in his tone. "He's got Maggie."

Solange snapped a carrot stick in two. "Don't mention Maggie McPherson to me. The Senator's relationship with her is purely physical. I hate it when you get on your soapbox, Avrim. Just because you work with Maggie is no reason to fling mud in my face."

"I am not flinging mud in your face. I'm merely—"

She cut him off. "You're defending her. Who is Maggie? A well-dressed tart, that's who! She's a Florida hick who took elocution lessons and slept her way to New York. That's your precious Maggie! The Senator gets urges, just as I do!''

Avrim gripped the sides of the table. "In other words, Solly, what we have is defined as an urge—an itch—a way of letting off steam. Your real mission in life is caring for him, is that it?''

Her eyes snagged his. "Don't start this crap with me, Avrim! The Senator and I are a team. You forget he brought me up all by himself. He didn't farm me out to relatives after Mother died. When I didn't like living in a boarding school, he brought me home. A lot of single fathers wouldn't have bothered. I owe him allegiance, even if you think I don't. I'm damn well going to live my life as I please!''

Avrim wanted to say she always had, but held his counsel. If Senator Gold raised Solange to believe she could do no wrong, who was he to try to alter the great one's teachings? "All right, Solly, drop it.''

She didn't want to. She drummed her fingers on the tablecloth. "Avrim, you've implied something nasty about my love for the Senator, my concern for his health, my ability to entertain his political cronies. Your implication's ugly. I won't have it. It's Maggie's fault. She fills your head with garbage. She feeds you lies. I will not feel guilty for taking my rightful place by his side.''

A silence fell between them. There was no doubt that Solange was an excellent hostess, but whether she wanted to hear it or not, the situation smacked of abnormality. Avrim, shocked by her heated outburst, dropped the forbidden subject, saddened that Solange felt threatened by Maggie.

Maggie McPherson was a fine, intelligent woman, anxious to succeed in a tough, competitive world. Her interviewing style was rapidly turning the redheaded, green-eyed Irish beauty into a media celebrity. He genuinely liked and admired the anchor, who also hosted a weekly program, *Happenings.* With a steadily increasing Nielsen and Arbitron rating as evidence of Maggie's magnetic personality, she blossomed in the longer format, striking the right balance between professionalism and friendliness. Maggie drilled a guest with a velvet tongue, while eliciting unexpected detailed information.

Unfortunately Solange's blind spot for her father was equaled by Max's adoration of his only child. And why not?

She mingled with the country's most influential people, elegantly gowned and coiffed. Her social graces assisted her father. Avrim knew she managed his home and social gatherings with panache.

"Have you ever wished for a brother or sister?" Avrim asked, thinking she would have been better off if she were one of ten children.

"Why would I wish for that?" Solange asked, calming down. "The answer is no. Have you?"

"Yes," he replied. "Plenty of times. I wanted a brother to horse around with, you know, play baseball, borrow the family car, go hot-rodding, that sort of thing. I'd have borrowed his girlfriends, too," he teased.

Solange regarded him. "Suppose this imaginary brother were five years younger? Or stole your toys? Or demanded an unfair portion of your parents' time? Being an only child has decided advantages."

"Don't be a wiseass," he retorted. "In my dreams my brother was perfect."

Although he was teasing, her face wore an expression of absolute seriousness. "Life isn't perfect, Avrim. I deal with reality."

Reality meaning Maggie. Solange's antipathy toward her amounted to an obsession. Avrim's concern grew. "So, what have you been up to while I was gone?" he asked, trying to salvage the afternoon.

Mischief lit her eyes. "Congratulate me. I passed my freshman year. Needless to say, the family is in shock. Tell me more about you. How was Israel, darling?"

He shrugged. "It was okay. Except for the times people were getting killed," he said, cautiously cementing their fragile reconciliation. Tonight his father would question him. His parents remained active in the B'nai B'rith, gave to the U.J.A., attended Fifth Avenue's Temple Emanu-El, where he had celebrated his bar mitzvah.

A slight breeze lifted her silvery hair, and she tucked it back in an unconsciously graceful gesture. "Tell me more."

"There're crazies on both sides, but when you see a school bus overturned, killing four children, it makes you wish the leaders would face off in a room, draw swords, and hack away at one another. The PLO says it's in retaliation for an attack on one of their camps. Israel will send planes to retaliate. Then the slaughter starts again.''

Solange wasn't religious. She simply wanted to preserve her way of life, and she was concerned about her father's continuing stature in the Senate. "Will the war ever end?"

"Who knows why men kill each other? The Palestinian question should have been settled a long time ago.''

"Do you think it will be?"

"No," Avrim replied. "I think it'll get worse before it gets better. Palestinians also need a homeland.'' The sun felt good on his back, the peaceful blue sky a blessing. Avrim recognized others newsmen openly admiring Solange. He leaned forward. "Solly, how do you feel about your dad's running for the presidency? He told my dad he's going to announce in November.''

Her fork clattered onto the table. Her eyes opened wide. "Bite your tongue! Let's hope he changes his mind before then.''

"What have you got against his running?" Avrim asked.

"Who wants to be another Luci or Lynda Bird?" she replied heatedly. "Can you just see me ducking a slew of Secret Secret agents on my tail? It'll crimp my style, Avrim. If the Senator won, I'd be expected to tout some stupid cause. The press would hound me the way they did Jackie if I dare refurbish the White House. Who needs it?''

Solange wagged her fork, then put it down on her plate. "How can we have privacy if those hound dogs you associate with snoop at us? I hate the paparazzi. Why ask for trouble? The Senator's better off where he is. I bet Maggie's encouraging him. You can tell her I don't appreciate it one bit," she said harshly.

Avrim listened in amazement. Senator Gold and Maggie were rarely seen dating; when they were out together, people assumed it was business, since an interview always seemed to follow. Only Avrim's parents and Solange knew the true nature of their relationship. It often puzzled Avrim that after all these years Max and Maggie hadn't tied the knot.

"Solly, my love, you take the cake," Avrim said.

"Why? For telling the truth?"

"For missing it," he replied. "My sweet viper, you're the only woman I know whose priorities are screwed up. You'd rather have a free fuck than see your father in the White House. Max is a good man. The country could do far worse. As New York's senator, he's done a lot for the people.''

She scoffed. ''Those same people who love him now will crucify him if he runs.''

Although he didn't think Max's running as an Independent had much chance, he prodded her. ''When did you become a political maven? Max has a power base on the Appropriations and Judiciary committees. He'll challenge Ted Kennedy. Your father's got more support than you realize. He'll have financial support from your grandparents. They're prepared to throw the family resources behind him the way Joe Kennedy did for Jack.''

''And exactly where did it get him?'' she snapped back. ''Jack's dead. Bobby's dead. All because Joe Kennedy insisted his sons live his dream. Well, let me tell you, that selfish old man paid a fortune for heartbreak! I pity Ted Kennedy if he runs. Chappaquiddick should have taught him a lesson. He's a glutton for punishment.''

He stared at her. ''You are serious, aren't you?''

''I don't happen to have a spare father,'' she retorted. ''You're an only child, too. The difference is your dad's Supreme Court nomination keeps him off the firing line.''

Avrim's voice softened. ''Solly, don't be frightened.''

Undaunted, she elaborated. ''Okay, forget the Kennedys. Let's talk about the presidency. Vietnam ruined Johnson. Watergate almost impeached Nixon. The people kicked Ford out after one term. Now they laugh at Carter. Compare pictures of the presidents when they first take office and when they leave. Ford's having a ball playing statesman. The Senator's already a statesman, so why put him through this to get to where he already is?''

Her convoluted thesis intrigued him. ''Aren't you being unfair? Max wants to be president. He's devoted his career toward that end.''

She dismissed it, frowning. ''Avrim, the presidency's a dangerous, thankless job. It's a curse in disguise. A Jew would be crucified.''

The sun glinted in her hair, softening her, making her appear angelic, at odds with her emotional outburst. Raising Solange couldn't have been easy for Max. "Meaning you'll help your father reassess his priorities?"

There was no apology in her voice. "Naturally."

Avrim's mind spinned. While Solange developed her absolute opinions, he felt suddenly depressed, morbid, the mood he'd been counting on to provide a few hours of happiness shriveling. Solange needed to be in control the way flowers need air, water, sunlight. Jealous of Maggie, he assumed she counted on Max's not marrying out of respect for his religious parents. Or maybe, Avrim thought, Max might have already proposed, and Maggie might have refused him to avoid a hassle with the volatile Solange.

"So what do you think?" Solange asked, resting her hand on his wrist, smiling into his eyes.

Avrim blinked. "About what?"

"Xenon's, tonight," Solange repeated, her mouth making a moue at his lack of attention.

Avrim shook his head. "Sorry. I'm not ready to spend the evening rubbing bodies with people dressed in aluminum foil and pink hair. I'm attending a gathering of doctors at Columbia."

She pursed her lips, pouting. The afternoon wasn't going as planned. "Isn't Columbia a little off your beat?"

Avrim grew annoyed. "I'm on assignment. Armand Hammer's introducing a French-American medical team. They're working on research for bone marrow transplants. Do you want to come along?"

She couldn't think of anything she wanted to do less. "If you already know about it, why attend?"

"I'm working. We're doing a feature on a few of the doctors. It's good for my soul to know there are people trying to save lives, not destroy them. I know you think vitamin C is a cure for everything, but you're wrong. Come with me. You might find it interesting."

She grimaced. "No. Had I known you were going to be such a spoilsport, I wouldn't have dressed up."

He laughed at her, correctly reading her petulant smile and the teasing light in her eyes. Dropping his arm, he rubbed her leg under the table. "Yes, you would."

"You're right," she admitted ruefully. "You really are a

stinker for lousing up my plans. Have we time for a quickie? I brought a special brand of dessert.''

"Lower your voice," he hissed when the couple at the next table stopped talking. Solange never failed to shock him. He whispered, ''Will you put a cherry on top?'' She did something with her tongue that made him groan. He paid the bill in record time and hailed a cab to take them to his place at York and 62nd. ''No sense wasting time,'' he said, kissing her in the cab, his hand riding up her thigh, hers rubbing his erection.

She was wet, squishing in her tap pants by the time they entered his apartment. She whipped off her skirt, flinging it rodeo style to the far end of the bedroom. Avrim unzipped his trousers. She was hot for him, her desire fueled by their arguments. Naked before Avrim, she reached for him.

''Faster, damn you, get out of those clothes.''

Avrim hopped on one foot, willing his body to think of anything for a few seconds but Solange's ten magic fingers.

''Jesus, quit it, Solly, or I'll come in your hand.''

She laughed into his mouth, falling backward with him onto the bed, legs and arms entwined. She offered her body to his lips, his marauding hands, the tongue expertly hidden in her vagina.

''Oh, God, stop! Put it in,'' she whimpered, clutching his shoulders. ''Put it in, hurry.''

He braced himself on his elbows. ''What if I don't?'' he teased thickly.

She wiggled down the bed, taking him in her mouth, rolling her tongue in expert circles, sucking hard until he felt himself about to lose control. ''Jesus!'' he cried, pulling away suddenly.

He entered her with a single thrust. Hot flesh sleeked and strained toward hot flesh, desperate to climb the peak. He knew her body well, knew she cursed when passionate. Stroking her with his fingers, his swollen organ slid in and out of her. She writhed and moaned and cursed. They toppled over the edge in a violent orgasm, their spasms so strong that neither moved for a long time.

''I'm weak,'' he grunted. Finally he rolled off her, his arm flung over her narrow waist.

Solange propped up on her elbow. Next time they'd take it slower. Avrim was an after-sex talker. In the beginning, he had wanted her to tell him everything she felt, when it was best, where she liked to be touched. He had guided her into knowing what pleased him. They were two perfectly oiled, perfectly matched machines.

Avrim kissed her breast, brushing the nipple with his mustache. "Mmmm, that's nice," she said, reveling in the texture. She kissed the top of his head. "Your mustache is better than a dildo. I like doing it with you more than anyone."

She might as well have doused cold water on him. Solange didn't have a faithful bone in her body, neither did he. It was one thing to think about sex in the abstract, quite another for Solange to lie in his bed after he gave her pleasure, hearing her cavalierly comparing him to others.

"Get dressed. You're leaving."

Solange shifted her body and swung her legs over the side of the bed, stamping her feet on the carpet. She glided toward the bathroom in regal splendor. At the door she paused. "Avrim, you're a hypocrite. I saw your picture with Mona Lawson. You slobbered all over her, so don't tell me you play monogamous. It won't wash."

Avrim bemoaned the snapshot taken of him with the popular Israeli actress. "How do you do it?"

"What?" Solange asked, turning to give him another full gaze of what he'd be missing if he kept up this nonsense.

He glared at her, confusion on his brow, his fist whacking the air. His gaze fell to the downy triangle between her legs. He wanted more. "Make me into the bad one."

Solange's elegant nostrils flared. "You weren't listening. I complimented you."

"Do me a favor," he growled. "Save your shit compliments."

She shrugged her shoulders, lifting her long mane of silver hair to cover her breasts. She tipped her head in the direction of the bed. "You need a new mattress. It sags in the middle."

Abruptly he got up and crossed the room. "No wonder you don't want Max in the White House," Avrim stormed. "I can see where it might interfere with your professional duties. What the hell do you do, Solly? Make comparison studies for Kinsey?"

Solange pirouetted. She surprised him by throwing her arms around his neck, kissing him, wiggling her nakedness on his.

"Avrim, we're two of a kind. Why pretend otherwise? You should be very happy to know I prefer your cock to others."

Avrim yanked her hair. She sparked fires in his brain. "Why do you put me through this?"

"Are you going to change your mind about tonight?"

So, she was getting even for having her plans spoiled. "No. I told you I'm working. Change yours, Solly. Come with me. It's time you grew up."

Illness made her squirm. She rubbed her foot sensuously along his calf and rolled her hips. "Let's make up."

"You bitch," he snarled into her mouth. He carried her back to the bed. He lifted her legs around his waist. He rode her hard and furious, not kissing her. Solange took tiny bites of flesh with sharp teeth. Her fingers clawed his back. "Whore," he muttered, straining.

Remembering thc cabbie, shc laughed. She tightened her muscles, trapping him in her heat. "Darling, I'm your *puta*."

An hour later, Solange tripped down the sidewalk, humming merrily. One of these days she'd like to redecorate his apartment, make it into a showplace instead of a set from *The Front Page*. As rich as he was, Avrim had no regard for the trappings of wealth.

Comfort to him meant living in sloppy surroundings, the way he cherished his old slippers. His apartment overflowed with papers, magazines, books, and research materials. The furniture in the living room consisted of a tacky brown convertible sofa, a plaid recliner, and a green chair, beside an entertainment center and a wet bar. There were shelves of books, mainly history and political tracts, in the living room and spare bedroom that Avrim had converted into an office. He wrote on a computer atop a metal desk, surrounded by mounting piles of paper, the manuscript for his third book. His first two books on the politics of the Middle East had made the *Times* bestseller list.

The day hadn't been a total loss, Solange thought happily. Avrim was still hers.

Chapter Four

Solange's bedroom suite resembled a romantic confection of vanilla and champagne. Striding across the white Aubusson rug, she tossed her purse onto one of the white velvet poufs footing the king-size bed. A ceiling drapery created an intimate alcove effect. Opposite the cozy nest, Chinese Chippendale gilded pier mirrors balanced an intricately carved fireplace. Neither the objets d'art on its mantel nor the paintings by Renoir and Monet drew her interest. She preferred modern, yet for some inane reason her father refused to redecorate.

Snatching a pack of Camels and the TV remote control, from the Wedgwood dish on a round table covered by a shawl of champagne lace, she flopped down on a flower-strewn chaise lounge. Flipping the channels, an old Judy Garland picture caught her attention. A scene depicted the unhappy star forced to live at a boarding school. As Solange puffed, she empathized. Like poor Judy, she, too, had been forced to live in a boarding school.

She would never forgive granite-faced Frances Manfred, headmistress of Regents Academy. The bitch had reigned supreme over thirty prime Connecticut acres in New Canaan.

Parental love—as far as she could tell at the time—wasn't worth warm piss if she couldn't live home. At least there she could eat in Pepita Juarez's warm kitchen. Redolent with earthy spices and hip-jiggling Spanish music, she could listen for hours to Pepe's hilarious stories about her large family in Puerto Rico. Of the stream of servants hired to care for her after her mother died, she liked Pepe the best.

To pass time in school, she had eavesdropped on other girls' phone calls, pretending she was speaking to her mother. Mrs. Manfred caught her.

Pepe taught her to curse in Spanish. Mrs. Manfred was a prime *puta*. The *puta* had meted out three weekends of demerits. "It's for your own good."

Like hell!

After two weekends of despised detention, Solange swallowed her pride and borrowed a page from the Senator's diplomatic handbook. One mea culpa—if necessary, several.

She paused outside Mrs. Manfred's office, hands up in the prayer position. With the door partially open, Solange could hear her talking on the phone. Solange's eyes nearly bugged out. Her hands flew to her mouth.

Fat-ass Mrs. Manfred sat with her back to Solange, spouting dirty sex to the new nerd history teacher, Mr. Simpson. Solange diplomatically glued her ear to the wall, thanking God for her good fortune.

Solange hit hallelujah pay dirt. Fanny and Musty cooed like lovers. Illicit lovers! Solange chomped on her hand to keep from breaking in with a loud "Holy shit!"

Suddenly Fanny switched topics. Solange heard her whine *her* name. *Hers! Solange Gold!* Fanny called her impossible. A disgrace. Doomed to devour comic books and dreadful pulp magazines. She learned for a gospel fàct that Mrs. Manfred hated Democrats, blacks, Catholics, and Jews, including her senator father. Her rage turned to stupefied shock.

Fannie taught Solange a valuable lesson: Do unto others before they do any more unto you.

Solange placed an ad in the Sunday *New York Times*: The Search Committee of Regents Academy sought applicants for the position of headmistress. The inundated Search Committee (all letters came addressed to the School Board) received 172 applications—including one from Guam!—before tracing the hoax to Solange.

Mrs. Manfred summoned her father. Hauled before the court, Solange sat erect on the chair, not in her usual antagonistic slouch. Mrs. Manfred listed her shortcomings, academic and social. Solange's stomach knotted. Max puffed his cigar. Solange glanced at his set features, quaking.

Driven by panic, propelled by fear, she jumped to her feet, her shoulders trembling. In a shaky voice, she recounted Mrs.

Manfred's condemnation of the Golds, Jews who earned their money in the rag trade.

Solange's pretty face mottled. "Don't deny it! I heard you tell it to that man you're boffing—Mr. Simpson! God you're disgusting!" she screeched. "I know what a tongue job is. I asked Lou-Lou."

Mrs. Manfred howled. Her eyes bulged at the reference to the daughter of a distinguished alumna, a member of the board of trustees. Undaunted, Solange wagged her finger at her.

"I heard you beg Mr. Simpson to do it again!"

Mrs. Manfred screamed like a woman possessed. Her chest heaved. Her hands fluttered to her sides. Her thighs fell apart.

Max dragged Solange out of Mrs. Manfred's office. He stormed the staircase. He attacked her room. He emptied drawers. He dumped uniforms, lingerie, and shoes into Solange's steamer trunk. A petrified Solange barely salvaged her little blue rabbit.

With a vicious kick, the trunk rattled, bounced, blitzkrieged down flights of stairs. Teachers and students jumped out of harm's way. Max hustled Solange into the Lincoln. He slammed the door shut.

They sped off in a cloud of dust. Steel-belted radials shot streams of pebbles onto newly sodded grass. Genuinely frightened, Solange spent the first five miles of her freedom sobbing, apologizing for listening in on her classmates' phone calls, pretending she was speaking to her mother. (She omitted her crime of listening in on Mrs. Manfred.) Thanks to the look of utter woe on her father's face, hope lay on the horizon. When her grandmother, Tessie, who no longer cruised Bloomingdale's to keep abreast of unadvertised one-day specials, learned Solange was home for good, she balked.

"Solange's birthright demands the best schooling."

For reasons Solange failed to understand, her grandmother's remark incited her father. It was as if they were engaging in a clash of wills.

Max enrolled her in Manhattan's exclusive Mrs. Lincoln's Girls' School on the Upper East Side. He insisted she learn French. Why French? Solange wondered. She couldn't parse English, for God's sake! Avrim warned her that if she wanted to continue living at home, she'd better learn French.

"Speaking French will help your father," he said, unwittingly tapping the clue to Solange's subconscious motivation.

She loved it when Avrim popped in. He listened and laughed with merry, mischievous eyes. Tall and handsome, smelling of men's cologne, he dressed like a sloppy reporter from an old forties movie. Each time she saw him, he seemed more virile and handsome.

Solange felt strange, exciting stirrings.

As one birthday flowed into another, she developed a sensuous arrangement of curves and planes. Her breasts were small but high, her skin porcelain. Her unusual silvery hair, her expressive blue-green eyes, her lush lashes, and her generous rosebud mouth stopped old and young men in their tracks, fantasizing.

She reserved her fantasies for Avrim. What would it be like to be held in his strong arms, locked by his muscular thighs, fondled in the secret place between her legs? Her skin flushed. She tingled. Although she fantasized about sex, she remained clearly focused on her ultimate goal.

Power—the aphrodisiac fueling her politician father—fueled her. In Washington, D.C., and New York, she met people of legendary power—titans in government, industry, and the arts. Politics revolved around soirees, galas, and select dinner parties. The more she hovered on the edges of power, smelling it, tasting it, hearing it, the more she desired power.

Solange turned her back on adolescent concerns. Light-years ahead of her classmates in determination, she grilled Max. He bemusedly tolerated her nit-picking interrogation.

She tailored her educational curriculum to her own needs. She met with consultants from Gold's and Tiffany's, read books, devoured the social columns. Motivated, she listened and learned. Her father quietly dated Maggie. Solange doubled her efforts to make herself invaluable to Max.

Looking beautiful in a sunny yellow cotton dress with bell sleeves and a fitted bodice, her hair styled in a chignon, Solange joined Max for breakfast. The year was 1974. In Washington, the House Judiciary Committee had warned Nixon to turn over the Watergate tapes. In France, Pompidou died; Giscard d'Estaing became the new president.

"I'm ready to assume my role as your official hostess. You said yourself that we're a team. We don't need anybody." She told him she thought he should give a party honoring the French ambassador. Max put down the *Times,* eyed his pretty daughter, and granted permission.

Solange glided into the role of hostess as if she were born for it. The party's theme, *L'esprit de l'amité,* toasted the spirit of friendship. Solange created a royal eye-catching entrance, even to color-coordinating Cordon Rouge—the hue of the wine matching the red drapes in the living room. Garlands of fresh lilies of the valley and pink and red roses graced the tables. Sèvres vases, placed on sideboards, overflowed with lilacs.

Solange's menu included an appetizer salad of hot and cold foie gras, truffles on beds of radicchio, bowls of court bouillon filled with bay shrimp, supreme capon seasoned with fresh ginger, garnished with shreds of caramelized ginger, and truffled vegetable cushions. Dessert included chocolate mousse and croquant aux fraises.

Each Tiffany's place card Solange set proved the ideal choice to encourage stimulating conversation. Solange gracefully and charmingly anticipated the wishes of her father's guests. Resplendent in a black velvet embroidered LeClaire gown, she spoke with the French ambassador in his native language.

A society photographer captured Solange's radiant face as Henry Kissinger, Senator Javits, and Dina Merrill, the beautiful socialite actress and daughter of Mrs. Marjorie Merriweather Post Close Hutton Davies May, smiled at her, appearing to pay her homage. Solange glittered. The absence of Maggie McPherson made the evening all the sweeter.

Solange wisely avoided invoking the jealousies of wives and mistresses. While she couldn't hide her youth, she took care not to flaunt it. For these occasions she dressed conservatively, chose understated jewelry—a strand of matched pearls at her neck, tiny twinkling diamonds at her ears. By the following year, the sexually liberated Solange had enticed Avrim into bed. Young and beautiful and wild, she was a drug he couldn't resist. After the first time she slinked into his room naked, he showed her exactly what Mrs. Manfred meant by a tongue job.

Solange played and experimented with Avrim. She pumped him for tidbits of gossip relating to the national scene, convinced her credentials as a hostess would secure her place in the world populated by beautiful, powerful people.

A world she chose. A world in which she'd stand on her own two feet, not rely on the fickleness of men. She'd select a husband to complement her station in life. The good life in a good world. A world Avrim couldn't care less about. Too bad it couldn't be Avrim. *C'est la vie.*

Being smart, she played the angles. Adapt, achieve, accomplish, attain. A damn good philosophy to live by. Gold's was her nest egg. Max was hers. Avrim would stay hers, too. Life would be good, better than good, the best. She deserved it.

She frowned at the TV monitor. "Too bad you didn't ask my advice, Judy."

She clicked off the set, hopped off the chaise, went to her closet. Her fingers flew past a cache of couture: Halston, Trigère, LeClaire, Blass, Ellis, Armani, Lacroix, Ricci, Ungaro, Chanel. She didn't show partiality. Whoever suited her fancy.

She snatched a yellow-and-black bodysuit and wraparound skirt by Hyoko, a new young designer whose bold prints had caught her eye. Rumor had it Mick Jagger planned to make an appearance at Xenon's. She wanted him to notice her. Why not see if a rock star could hold a candle to Avrim? She tossed the bodysuit onto the bed, along with five gold chains, and bangle earrings. First a relaxing bubble bath, then a nap, she'd be ready for a night on the town. Anticipation pumped through her.

"Avrim, sweetie, you should have said yes for tonight." She shivered deliciously at the memory of his tongue bringing her to a shattering climax. She licked her lips.

"Don't you worry about a thing, Avrim, sweetie. Momma's never gonna lose you. Not even when I marry. We'll work out an arrangement. Momma loves you. Momma ain't never gonna let you go."

Picking up the bottle containing his favorite perfume, she sprayed her breasts. Spreading her legs, she sprayed her inner thighs. "Here's to you, honey."

Laughing, she lifted her arms, giving herself another spritz.

Chapter Five

Lilli circled the kitchen table that she had set with cups of currant tea for the Orchins. Wringing her hands, her mouth would open, then close.

Bella, a short, plump woman with graying hair, exchanged an anxious look with her husband, Michel. Captured by the Nazis in their native Munich, Bella and Michel met in Dachau. Michel's will to live burned through his then emaciated body; it renewed his determination to leave his seed on earth. Married within months of the war's end, they emigrated to Paris. Equally determined to remove the hated numbers from her arm, Bella saw a doctor who informed her it couldn't be done. Trudging home in a state of dejection, she prepared a solution of lye to remove the tattoo.

Michel found her in time to prevent a catastrophe. He rocked her in his arms, murmuring to her of her perfection, telling her the future was theirs. Together they'd make a miracle. A baby. A miracle to thank God for saving their lives.

The thought of a child born in freedom infused Bella with renewed purpose. When she couldn't become pregnant, she grew depressed, convinced the near starvation diet in the camp had left her unable to conceive. Then their miracle happened. She gave birth to a son, only to be plunged into inconsolable heartbreak when the infant died in two weeks. A few years passed, and another miracle happened. They named him David: beloved one, from the biblical David, King of Israel. For years she remained haunted by fears she would lose him. Looking at Lilli now, she recognized the same haunted fear in her eyes.

"Samara said you became ill while you were watching the news."

Lilli clamped her right hand over her left to still her shaking hands. "Yes, it took me by surprise. I reacted without thinking. Imagine, Avrim on television, talking about Max and Murray. What should I do?"

Michel spoke. "So that's it. Do nothing. There's no reason for her to connect your past with the newscast."

Lilli knew better. "Once Samara gets frightened she doesn't let go. She still sleeps with the blue rabbit I bought her to match mine, the one I left with Solange. Today Samara modeled for Comtesse Levron. You recall the Levrons' daughter died. It affected Samara far more than I realized. The girls were the same age. Samara wants me to remarry, not to be alone when she does. Life's closing in on me, Bella. God is punishing me."

Bella grabbed Lilli's hands, giving them a good shake. "Nonsense. I won't listen to gibberish. You sound as gloomy as Samara did earlier. Absolutely nothing's changed."

She and Michel knew Lilli's story. Found at the age of four, Sister Jean raised Lilli. When she was sixteen, Lilli came to live with them. Her whirlwind courtship, elopement, and marriage to an American, Max Gold, ended in bitter ashes when Lilli couldn't adapt to America or cope with his parents' hostility. Neither she nor Michel had condoned the union, but in their estimation, Max was a damned fool for splitting the girls—never once attempting to see Samara! Who could blame Lilli for taking back her name, not telling Samara about her father? He was as good as dead as far as they were concerned!

Lilli took a deep breath. "All right. First, I love you both. You've been more than friends, more than family. I've accepted that love without deserving it."

"What nonsense is this?" Michel asked.

"Please, just let me say this. You've never betrayed my trust, even though it forced you to go along with the story Samara believes. But it's time to tell you the whole truth of what actually happened. That's why I asked you here tonight."

She took a deep breath. "I deserted Max and Solange. He didn't set the conditions. I did. I'd still be with them if it weren't for Père de Vitale."

Bella's and Michel's faces mirrored their confusion.

"Who?"

"Sister Jean's priest. He visited me in the United States. I didn't know she had died. He found a letter from Stella Des Pres. My mother.''

Bella gasped. "Your mother, how wonderful!" Michel cried instinctively.

Lilli handed Bella a faded envelope. "Read this."

Bella did. She screamed. Michel tore the letter from her hand. "But this can't be!" His face reddened with rage. "Hans Wurfel! . . . The beast of Dachau . . . Your father?" As if burned, he dropped Stella's letter on the table.

"I didn't know. I've read that a terrible shock can trigger prolonged amnesia. Sister Jean gave me a new name, a new identity. I believed her."

"Why didn't you tell us when you found this out?" Bella demanded.

"Fear. Sister Jean had died. I couldn't stay in America. So I came home. Samara needed family. I couldn't deprive Samara of you and Michel and David."

"What did Max say when you told him?"

"I didn't tell him. Do you think I would have married him had I known? Max and his parents financially assisted Simon Wiesenthal." The Orchins knew of the famed Nazi hunter who tracked criminals who had escaped the Nuremberg war trials.

"Wiesenthal left a list of names with Max. Until Père de Vitale's visit, they were mere names to me. My mother's letter revealed my true identity. My father's name topped the list. She wanted me to remain proud of my father, as she was proud of him. In bits and snatches, I would recall snippets—scraps of information. I dreaded each clue of the puzzle. Max repeatedly asked what was wrong. How could I tell him I heard voices in my head? I couldn't learn English, and suddenly I understood German!"

"Good God!" Michel shouted.

"Music. Marching music floated through my head. In my mind's eye, I saw myself perched atop my father's shoulders, my mother standing proudly by his side. We watched the First *Sicherungsregiment* march around the Arc de Triomphe . . ." Lilli shuddered. "God help me. I loved it. Our chauffeur, Karl, drove us in Papa's Mercedes-Benz. Mama wore beautiful clothes, silks and woolens, not the fabrics made of wood fibers they called Mode Martiale, and jewels. My father bragged that we didn't have to ride bicycles—*velocabs*—or those make-do cars, the *gazogenes*. I'd feed my babies and see myself as a child measuring cream into my father's coffee cup. I waited for his kiss of approval.''

Lilli hung her head. ''He took us to a restaurant to celebrate my birthday. I wore my best Belgian lace-trimmed dress. My father hit the waiter for serving him ersatz coffee. Blood dripped down the man's face! My mother took me aside, telling me the man needed to be taught a lesson! A lesson, can you imagine that? I screamed the day I remembered that in the nursery. The twins howled. It was awful. Overnight my breast milk soured. The doctor didn't know why. I did. How could I, the bastard daughter of a heinous German murderer and a French collaborator, justify myself to Max, his parents, or myself?

''I made mistakes, too. Big ones. I wanted to do something nice to surprise Max and my in-laws. I found a priest to baptize the babies. He taught me the English words to announce my news. I picked Friday night Shabbes dinner. Max's parents were appalled. There was a big argument. Shouting. Pointing. Max rushed me out of there. The Nazis had murdered his mother's two brothers, his father's aunts, uncles. His parents assumed the girls would be Jewish. From then on, I insisted he go alone on Friday nights.''

''Lilli,'' Bella broke in bitterly, ''the priest should have destroyed the letter. What good did it do?''

Michel agreed. ''Your mother gave you to the church. She cut you off from hatred. Whatever your parents did, you weren't to blame. You should have trusted Max.''

Lilli shook her head. ''Politically, Max has achieved his dream. Can you see the American people voting for a Jewish man whose wife's father is a Gestapo killer? I don't know if my father's dead or alive.''

''No,'' Michel conceded.

Lilli shredded a napkin. ''I had to convince Max I no longer loved him, that our marriage was a terrible mistake.''

''Politics isn't as important as family. How could Max give up Samara?'' Bella asked. ''Didn't he try to contact you?''

''I left a note threatening to commit suicide if Max followed me.''

''Suicide! You! A staunch Catholic!'' Michel cried in astonishment.

"I had to impress Max that I was serious." She kneaded her hands. "The lie protected him and the girls from scandal. It freed Max to pursue his public career. It prevented his parents from suffering more anguish, from having to either accept me or choose a permanent break with their only son.

Lilli put an arm over her eyes, as if drawing up the curtain on the final scene. "Max stormed up the stairs to the nursery. We'd been arguing. Viciously. I'll never forget the look in his eyes. What I did to this wonderful, kind, generous man! He promised to stay home more, to give up politics, to help me learn English, to take a firm stand with his parents."

Lilli buried her face in her hands. "He said he loved me. Bella, every part of me yearned to throw myself in his arms, to let him know I loved him more than life itself."

"Oh, Lilli, Lilli, Lilli," Michel chanted. His eyes welled up with tears.

"Max warned me he'd stop me." Lilli crumpled into herself. "I told him we'd each take one of the girls. He screamed at me. He said our babies weren't oranges to be divided in two." She gulped. "He asked me what kind of a mother gives up a child?"

Bella threw an arm about Lilli. "Enough. You're torturing yourself."

Lilli stayed lost in the past, spilling out her story. "He yelled the French princess says it's over, so it's over. He said his parents were right, he should have married an American. Don't you see? I did what I had to do. I picked up Solange, cuddling my crying baby to my breast, kissing away my infant's tears.

"Max snatched her from me, put her back into her crib. I picked up Samara. She smiled. Samara was ready to play. Samara always responded to him with gurgles of delight. Max said he wasn't Solomon. He refused to help me destroy his life.

"Have you any idea how hard it is to choose one baby over another? My heart will bleed until the day I die. I undressed first one, then the other. My fingers trembled over their tiny naked bodies, for I knew that soon I would no longer see them side by side. I kissed their chubby legs and arms. I nuzzled their belly buttons. When I lifted Solange, she must have gotten the idea she was about to be bathed. She howled. I dressed her. She didn't stop. Max hovered over me, pleading.

"I . . . I nearly gave in then. But I saw my father in his

office at Gestapo headquarters. I heard screams. Thuds. Whacks. Beatings. I saw his name on Wiesenthal's list.

"I made Max hate me. He asked what I wanted him to tell his child, the one I'd choose to desert. I blurted out, tell her I'm dead."

"Ohmigod!" shrieked Bella. Michel covered his eyes.

Lilli's voice dulled. "Max spent the night in the nursery. He refused to speak to me. I waited for two days until he believed I might change my mind. On the third day, I left."

"But how did you make the final choice?" Michel asked, his voice low and sad with disbelief.

"Solange did it for me. A mother's instinct. Solange will always need more than I could give her."

"Avrim is old enough to recall you had twins. What did he think happened to Samara?" Bella asked.

"The Leightners lived in Washington, D.C., at the time. Murray worked for the Justice Department. Max and I saw Ceil and Murray only when they visited his parents in New York. Avrim only knows Solange, according to Murray. I saw Murray years ago."

"You did?" Michel asked, amazed.

"Max sent him. Max begged for the truth to come out. He felt the girls should know each other, despite everything. We could have figured something out. It scared me to death. I became ill, threw up. Murray saw a crazy woman, but he also saw a happy, normal little girl playing outside with David. He took that home to Max. I'm certain he repeated my suicide threat to Max. Max never bothered me again. I . . . I suppose Solange thinks I'm dead." Her shoulders sagged. "It may have all been in vain."

"Why do you say that?" Michel said.

"God punishes sinners. I sinned."

"Rubbish!" Bella declared. "I may not agree with what you did, but it took great courage."

Lilli gazed at them. "No. Seeing Avrim on television tonight was a sign. I believe in omens. I'm so sorry," she said as they sat in glum silence. "So very sorry for dragging you into this without knowing the truth."

"You foolish girl." Bella gathered Lilli to her bosom. A woman of vast compassion, she couldn't hate the girl who'd been a younger sister to her. "You broke your heart and Max's.

You looked around corners instead of enjoying life's wonderful moments.''

The thin thread on Lilli's emotions snapped. "It destroyed me. Daily I pray for my family, for Samara, for Solange, for Max, for God's forgiveness. But I believed then, as I believe now, that I did right for my family.''

Michel rested his head in his hands. "What a burden. You've been weighed down by a yoke of guilt. No one expected you to serve your parents' sentence."

"You're wrong, Michel. I'm the devil's spawn. My mother turned her back on her own people. She loved my father to the end. I'm like her. I hid the truth, took Samara. She belonged with her father, with Solange. I haven't helped Samara. I overprotected her by sending her to the *couvent*. Poor girl thinks I'm a saint. She wants to go to Chartres for her birthday. She doesn't. She thinks it would please me.''

Bella gripped her arms. "Stop this. Samara's fine. Jules predicts a fine future for her. Give her credit for resiliency. You brought her up the best you could. Stop blaming yourself for a decision you made years ago."

Lilli shuddered. "You won't tell Samara or David? It would kill Samara.''

"Of course not," Bella assured her, seeing the wildness in Lilli's eyes.

"Never. Promise Samara will always have you," she insisted.

Bella faced her squarely. "We promise, don't we, Michel?"

"How could we hurt her?" he asked. "She's our daughter, too. We love her. We'll never tell. Don't worry. And don't worry about God. I'm sure He forgives you."

Lilli was too drained, too tired to argue. She knew that it wasn't true. After the Orchins left, she carried their half-empty teacups to the sink. She washed and dried the dishes, then put out the light. She removed her clothes, washed, put on her nightgown. She slipped her weary body into her narrow metal bed. On the wall above the bed hung a picture of the Virgin Mary holding the infant Christ.

From the oak night table next to her bed she lifted her rosary from on top of her worn Bible. She fingered the smooth, familiar beads. As she did each night, she brought the crucifix to her forehead and made the sign of the cross.

"I believe in God the father Almighty . . ."

* * *

The following day, Paris wore its best face. A light wind carried the warmth of the sun. Tourists and residents walked with a spring to their step. The Eiffel Tower reigned in stark snootiness upon a sparkling city. On avenue Montaigne at the House of LeClaire, Jules's pampered guests sipped champagne and nibbled goose liver paté before taking their reserved seats.

Born in a little town in the mountains of Savoy, near the fashionable resort town of Aix-les-Bains, Jules was the only one of his mother's four sons to survive the war. Hitler's armies cut the others down in cold blood. Their deaths, coming in rapid succession, devastated the young man and his mother.

Anxious to do his part to avenge his brothers, he offered himself to the local leader of the French Resistance. The man worried that the demon-eyed Jules would get them all killed, and he told him so.

"Let me prove myself," Jules begged. "No job is too dangerous."

"What can you do?"

"A lot."

"Explosives?"

"Yes." He had never rigged a charge in his life, nor done anything more dangerous with his hands than make love to pretty women.

Jules took a half-hour course under the direction of a fellow Frenchman. The next day a plastique charge backfired, blowing his teacher's body to bits, promoting Jules to senior explosives technician. He discovered a talent for working with his hands; his fingers attached threads so fragile that no one dared venture near him as he combined the necessary elements.

He mustered out of the war determined to produce something more noble with his hands than death and destruction. His mother, Madame Helaine LeClaire, desolated by the loss of her other sons, applauded Jules's desire to be remembered for leaving a mark of beauty in the world. Now as the models walked the runway in her son's magnificent creations, the elderly woman with the still beautiful china skin sat at the edge of her chair, her granddaughter, Mimi, by her side.

Mimi clasped her hands tightly. Her eyes darted to the door. Where was Lilli? She herself had made a last-minute call, without telling Samara.

Samara's timing was off; she knew it. She pranced, swirled, shifted her shoulders, elongated her step, tossed her hair, swept down the runway, surreptitiously scanning the salon. With each costume change, she searched for her mother. She prayed Lilli would arrive.

In the *cabine,* she slipped the gown over her head. Jules adjusted the diamond tiara, checked to make certain the blush on her cheeks matched the pale pink underslip. Security guards handed Jules two black velvet boxes. Finally the helper attached the long lace train to hooks at her shoulders. Throughout the fuss, bleak ruminations plagued Samara. She was consumed by a sense of impending doom, a persistent feeling that her mother needed her. She put cold fingers on Jules's proffered arm and took her place beside him, awaiting the attendants to roll out the red carpet, for the music cue to announce them.

"I'm worried," Samara said.

"Nonsense. Lilli is probably seated in the back. Here we go."

They stepped onto the runway to be greeted by gasps and tumultuous applause.

Samara shimmered. Atop her glistening silvery hair and at her elegant neck, blazing flawless diamonds ranked a poor second to her radiance. The tightly fitted bodice accented the soft swell of her breasts. In satin shoes with tiny heels she glided gracefully down the red carpet, an ethereal blond madonna; her expression subdued, lips slightly trembling, chin held high, eyes fixed on a point straight ahead. With every gesture she was a demure eighteenth-century royal virgin bride, dazzling the kingly court as she went to greet her fate.

The applause increased. Her gaze darted to the back, to the one empty reserved seat. The tiny smile died on her lips. Lilli hadn't come.

At the conclusion the models rushed out to take well-deserved bows. Jules beamed, posing for a bedlam of fashion photographers. The guests moved to another room. Waiters circulated, offering more champagne and a selection of hors d'oeuvres. Samara rushed backstage. A helper unsnapped the long train. Ten minutes later, Jules and Mimi found her staring out the window.

"What is this? Come join the party," Jules urged, his face

flushed with excitement. "Comtesse Levron wants to introduce you to the comte."

Tears welled up in Samara's eyes. "Maman missed it. She didn't come. She promised."

"She'll come, silly girl. Mimi, bring wine. Samara, keep the wedding dress on a while longer. I'm sure there's a logical explanation. A customer detained her, or she stopped at the bank to make a deposit and the lines were long."

"This isn't the day Maman goes to the bank," Samara said hastily.

Jules watched the quick, frantic movements she made with her hands, the biting of her lip. "Didn't you say Madame Dier was due in for a perm? The woman's unholy, the way she talks and talks and wastes time."

"Mimi, what do you think?" she asked hopefully. Mimi agreed with Jules. She handed Samara a flute of champagne. She was rewarded with a weak smile that didn't reach Samara's eyes.

"I should have insisted Maman see a doctor. What if she fainted again? What if she can't reach me?" Her voice rose hysterically.

"Samara," Jules said, "I assure you there's nothing to worry about. You said yourself Lilli was fine when you left last night. Stop looking so frantic. Careful when you drink that not to drip on the gown. Mimi, bring a napkin and a few crackers. She needs food. When Lilli comes, we'll walk down the aisle so she can see you."

Flushed with success, finished giving advice, Jules rushed off to count the orders and mingle. Mimi stayed with Samara.

"Did it ever occur to you," Samara wailed fifteen minutes later, "that Maman may have suffered a heart attack?"

It had occurred to Mimi, but she said, "Samara, don't be dramatic. Papa's right. You'll see. Lilli will come soon. Why, I bet she'll arrive any minute."

"I should have stayed home with her last night. I should have insisted she see a doctor. If something has happened to her, I'll never forgive myself."

She heard the door behind her open. She swiveled around. Seeing Jules, her heart leapt with joy. He'd come to tell her Lilli had arrived.

"Jules, did Maman come? Is she waiting for—" The words

died in her throat. Jules seemed to have shrunk. His shoulders drooped. His eyes were red.

Her brain recorded the scene. Jules, accompanied by two men, walked toward her. She saw him motion to a maid to leave the room. She saw the maid scurry out, heard her broom clatter against a metal bucket.

She didn't recognize the heavyset man at Jules's right. She did know the arthritic, aged, ashen-faced man at his left. Père de Vitale, the family priest she'd known all her life. She could feel her pulse start to pound, and she automatically backed up. Her heel caught on her hem. She stumbled. Mimi, Jules, and the priest rushed to her side.

The heavyset man's rumpled suit reeked of stale cigars. "I'm Police Inspector Truan. You are Samara Bousseauc," he gently confirmed.

Police! Fear roared through her.

The inspector sighed. His daughter was this girl's age. Hating his sad task, he gazed at the exquisite young woman with the platinum-blond hair, wearing a wedding gown fit for a queen. The old priest had identified his parishioner's broken, bloodied body. A crowd of curious onlookers gathered to stare at the mangled corpse. She had been carrying a huge bouquet of lilacs. He was glad for the priest's presence. The girl would need him.

"Miss Bousseauc, there's been an accident."

Jules snatched the crystal stemware from her wildly shaking hand. Dry-mouthed, barely able to swallow, she formed the dreaded questions. "Maman? Is she badly hurt? Will she be all right?"

"I'm sorry," the police inspector said. "Your mother died instantly. She stepped off the curb. A witness said she wasn't watching the traffic."

A scream ripped from Samara's lips, drowning out the music of the four-piece combo.

"She isn't dead!" she yelled. "You're lying. Maman's alive. Go away!"

Père de Vitale's eyes were red. "Dear child. It's true. I administered last rites. She didn't suffer."

"Noooooo!" Samara ranted. "You're lying, too! You have to be." She clamped her hands over her ears. Jules reached up to take her hands away. "I refuse to listen," she snarled, scratching Jules like a caged animal. She threw off his hands. As she whirled away, she bumped her hip on the edge of a table.

Tears flowed down Mimi's face. "Don't, Sam. Please don't. They wouldn't lie, you know that."

Caught by the enormity of what she read in their ravaged faces and in their sad eyes, a deep shudder racked Samara's body.

"Maman . . ."

Her hands fluttered downward, catching the folds of the exquisite heirloom wedding gown her mother would never see. "Maman," she sobbed. "Don't leave me alone, Maman."

The room spun.

The world tilted.

Mercifully, she fainted.

Chapter Six

Avrim Leightner squeezed past a line of people, hunting for canapes without squiggles and strange colors, food he recognized. Cocktails and hors d'oeuvres were served in the fourth-floor Faculty Club of the Physicians and Surgeons Hospital on 168th Street, a short walk up from the Julius and Armand Hammer Health Sciences Building, the same building in which Dr. Hammer introduced the new French-American cancer research team to invited dignitaries and the press. In Avrim's humble opinion, Dr. Hammer embodied the true Renaissance man.

Judging by the Secret Service protecting Vice President Walter Mondale in deep conversation with Secretary of State Henry Kissinger, not everyone needed food as badly as he. Then again, not everyone spent a rigorous afternoon with Solange. After their second frenzied coupling, both settled down. For a while. He'd uncorked a bottle of wine, sipping champagne from her silken skin, lapping it from strategic places, barely making it in time to the editing room to view the file footage he'd requested.

Working with the tape editor, Mary Koster, he decided to lead with Margaret Thatcher becoming Europe's first woman Prime Minister. God help her husband! Strong women could kill a man. He should know.

He made another pledge to God: Give up Solange in return for his sanity. A simple exchange. He faithfully promised to attend shul on High Holy Days, fast for the entire day on Yom Kippur, actively seek the companionship of a sensible woman who didn't use sex as a punishment.

Avrim plucked a cocktail from a passing tray. He did a quick head count of the overcrowded room, noting the capacity sign: 144 people. He spotted his coanchor, Maggie McPherson, in a side room, perched on a stool at the bar. Her flaming red hair matched her red leather suit; she stood out like a flame. Spying him through the mirror, she swiveled, sending him a desperate signal. Apparently she wanted to be rescued from the man next to her. Avrim could guess why. Each time the man's face inched closer to hers, she arched backward.

Avrim let out a chuckle. The scenario was ripe to play a joke on Maggie. He'd first met her while he was on assignment in Florida. Maggie attended the University of Miami, majoring in law with a minor in communications. She had volunteered for a radio job no one wanted—the seven A.M. news, earning a big two dollars per hour and a lot of gratitude. After her initial broadcast, the station manager commended her on her good voice and assigned her the weather intro for the eight P.M. news anchor.

Eventually Maggie teamed up with Benny Ableson, a TV reporter, working for the same organization as she, assigned to cover the same stories. They saw the foolishness of covering the same beat, filing duplicate stories for two mediums, spending double on gasoline, when one car would usually do. Benny, a native of Detroit, was married with three children.

Benny's downfall and Maggie's big break into television resulted from Benny's penchant for the ladies, especially the cute ones with, as he put it, "nice buns."

Benny hunted "nice buns" like a jackrabbit. One day Benny was there; the next he wasn't. He'd split with a cheerleader from Florida State, a girl with buns nicer than anyone else's, including Benny's wife's. Ten minutes before airtime, Maggie felt honorbound to tell Benny's news director of his defection. The news director predictably exploded. "Fuckin' shithead! What the fuck am I supposed to do? He knows this fucking place operates on a fucking shoestring!"

Maggie didn't flinch. She'd heard worse words growing up with seven brothers. Lightning struck from the ashes of defeat. By the process of elimination—Maggie was there, Benny wasn't!—the apoplectic station manager hired Maggie on the spot.

"I assume you can speak if you're already on radio." So without an interview, without anyone viewing her on tape,

Maggie McPherson broke into television the same way she'd broken into radio. Through sheer happenstance. By week's end, she proved her worth. She wasn't a bimbo, she wasn't a flash-in-the-pan. Maggie delivered the local news, adding the national feed by the end of the month. She worked like a demon, winning praise and more airtime. She continued the morning radio show so the credits would add to her résumé. The law books gathered dust on the shelf.

She told Avrim at the time, "I'm still going to be a lawyer." The look of excitement in her eyes convinced Avrim that Maggie wouldn't be satisfied behind a book of torts. Maggie, like Avrim, thrived on action.

Avrim showed her how to work the tape recorder, timing her copy to end for a commercial break. He taught her to speed up her speech without sounding as if a train were about to roll over her. He explained the rudiments of the audio and switcher boards, graphics, microphones, key, back and full lights, camera angles, and how to use the camera as a friend. Maggie went him one better. With Max Factor pancake hiding her freckles, she made love to the camera. The lens emphasized her classic bone structure, her vibrant good looks, her pert profile, helping her to create a magical persona. Maggie found her life's work.

"Always check your facts," Avrim repeated incessantly. "A good reporter checks and double-checks his facts. If you're caught, it's your fault. You'll lose credibility."

Avrim didn't see Maggie as his career took off in New York, but he heard about her in the industry grapevine. Maggie copied Pauline Frederick and Nancy Dickerson, two women in broadcast news she admired. "I don't want to be a piece of fluff." She and Avrim bumped into each other at a National Public Radio Convention in Washington, D.C.

Her legal career on hold, Maggie strove to see how far she could rise in the field of communications. Wearing dual hats in radio and TV, she attended crossover conventions. Avrim caught up with her again when he, too, attended another radio convention to shoot the breeze with old cronies. Over drinks Maggie filled him in on her career.

"Fate," she reported, stepped into her life again. Julian "Cannonball" Adderly, the great jazz saxophone player, died. He was eulogized in Tallahassee, Florida. Maggie covered the

star-studded funeral. Afterward, Maggie phoned New York—
company headquarters—to see if they'd be interested in a tape
of the stars she interviewed. At first Maggie met with a "Don't
call us, we'll call you" response.

"You could tell the guy didn't care if I sent the tape. I
persisted, Avrim. I think he caved in as a last resort to get rid
of me."

Maggie spent two and a half years in Jacksonville, Florida,
gaining a statewide reputation as a solid, reliable reporter. She
spent another two years in New Haven, Connecticut.

Fate stepped in again when she summoned her courage and
asked her boss for a raise. He told her she already made top
dollar—twenty-two thousand dollars a year. Maggie left his
office, returning an hour later to say she needed a job. Could he
please write her a recommendation?

"I'll see what I can do." Luckily the station manager was
amused by her nerve. He phoned a friend in New York who
agreed to run her tape. Two weeks later Maggie landed a
network job, finding a home in the Big Apple, working her way
to coanchor with Avrim. Their friendship strengthened, although Avrim never told her about his affair with Solange.

Maggie's interview with Senator Max Gold changed her life.
He asked her to stay for follow-up questions, not telling her he
designed the questions to keep her there. Enthralled, Max
invited the red-haired beauty to lunch. Over espresso and eye
contact, Cupid's arrow pierced her heart. For Maggie it was
love at first sight. Max was the second man she'd been with in
her life. They made love on the couch in his office after their
third date.

Years later his secretary advised him to get rid of the couch.
"Never!" Maggie screeched, protecting *their* love nest like a
mother bird. "We either bronze it or donate it to the Smithsonian." It found its way to her apartment where they toasted it,
lying naked and exhausted from having made love twice in one
hour after a hard day's work.

Max gently but firmly insisted on not parading their affair.
"If we do, the press will have a field day. You'll become the
object of interviews instead of the interviewer. Although I'm
honored if men envy me, I think it's best we keep this out of the
limelight."

As far as Maggie knew, Max's wife had died years before.

Her Irish Catholic family disapproved of her liaison with Max. They didn't want her wasting her youth on an older man—a Jewish one at that. She told them unless they accepted her feelings, they'd never see her again. She meant it, they knew; besides, Maggie had never felt happier, never looked prettier. She wasn't a run-of-the-mill woman, so why should they expect her to live a run-of-the-mill life? Maggie wisely omitted the downside. Her family knew nothing of Solange's animosity toward her.

Avrim wondered where the affair between Max and Maggie would end. Solange hated Maggie. Lately relationships were paramount on his mind. Solange. It all came back to Solange, his hidden love. It was better Maggie didn't know, and Solange agreed, although she freely told him what she thought of his coanchor.

"Isn't Max a little out of your league in the age department?" Avrim had asked Maggie not long ago.

Maggie stared at Avrim as if he'd lost his mind.

"Age?" she asked incredulously. "Age? Where Max is concerned? I can't believe you, Avrim. Max is the youngest man I know. Any woman would be thrilled to be in my place."

"Where do you see your relationship going? If he runs for the presidency, he'll have less time for you."

"We'll always find time. What we do is none of the public's affair. We're single. If we're seen together, it'll be okay. Loving Max gives me the opportunity to be near a good man. We respect each other's right to our careers. I can't deny that his power adds to his attraction. I respect his intelligence, his social conscience. Have you ever seen a man more trim? More fit?"

Or more connected to Solange, Avrim thought.

He ambled over to Maggie. Instead of rescuing her, he remained rooted to the spot, absorbed by a thread of celery stuck between the two front teeth of the man seated on the bar stool next to her. It wiggled as he spoke. Should he or shouldn't he? With a straight face, Avrim reached behind Maggie for the plate of macadamia nuts, looked at her, and smiled broadly.

"Fancy meeting you here."

"Oh, Avrim," Maggie gushed. "You're late." She turned to say good-bye to the boring man, whose gaze seemed frozen on her cleavage. "Sorry to break this up. Avrim and I have important business to discuss."

Avrim applied steely pressure to her arm, preventing her from rising. "Don't be silly," he said smoothly. "It'll keep. I can see you're enjoying yourself." The man's eyes widened as he recognized Avrim. "Maggie," Avrim continued, his thigh doing a hatchet job on hers, "I've got to see someone. Catch you later." He bussed her cheek. "Stay as long as you like, honey. No rush."

He extended his hand to the man, taking a last wistful glance at the celery. "Nice," he murmured. Maggie choked. "Nice to meet you."

Avrim eased his way back to the selection of food. He picked up a plate, piling it with miniature bagels with cream cheese and lox, passed over the ham, choosing instead a mushroom wrapped in bacon, a few triangles of rye bread topped with roast beef, others with turkey. He added a couple of triangles of pumpernickel topped with salami, popped a black olive into his mouth, and had his hand poised over the potato salad when from the corner of his eye he noticed David Orchin watching him with an avid look of interest.

Avrim grinned and shifted his plate. "David Orchin. I never forget a face."

David admired the man's memory. "That food looks good. Are you trying a new cuisine, or is this soul food for you as it is for me?"

Avrim shifted the plate to his left hand, extending his right. "A landsman. A French landsman," he said, using the descriptive term borrowed by German immigrants, meaning "He is our kind of person."

David rocked back on his heels. He had lived among the ocher cliffs of Morningside Heights so long now he was beginning to get used to it. It almost seemed like home. Not that anything could take Paris's place in his heart, especially tonight when he was filled with an overwhelming wave of loneliness. "All Jews aren't in the Promised Land. How was it over there?"

They eased over to an empty table in the side room opposite the bar. Henry Kissinger's distinctive guttural voice could be heard answering a reporter's question.

Avrim popped a knish into his mouth, offering the plate to

David. "Nothing's changed. They used to give free samples in the food section of the department stores when I was a student. I saved a lot of money."

David glanced at the plate piled with food. It was obvious the anchor could pack it away.

Avrim found himself drawn to the young doctor with the perceptive eyes who didn't appear to be older than he. He studied him with a reporter's eye, waiting for the opportune time to request an interview. They were evenly matched in height and build. "You speak English quite well."

David munched a sandwich, wiped his hands on a napkin, started to reach for more food, then thought better of it. "I should. I studied English for ten years in school."

Avrim raised his eyes to David's. "You're one reason I'm here. How would you feel about an interview? I think you'd make an interesting guest."

David shook his head. "I'm afraid it's out of the question."

"Why?"

David shrugged. "Politics, medical ethics, whatever. You're better off speaking to the head of the department." He glanced around the room, noting the famous attendees. "Shouldn't you have a pad and pencil out or something? It's not every day we have such notables here."

Avrim followed his gaze. "Catch tomorrow night's broadcast. We taped Dr. Kissinger this morning. Let's get back to you a minute. Perhaps I might work this out to everyone's satisfaction."

"How?"

"In the first place, you're hardly a peon. To be chosen as part of this research team, you probably scored in the top percentile of your graduating class in med school. Suppose I arrange it with your department head, would you agree then?"

"I'd be honored," David replied, "provided you ask him, too."

"Maybe I can help the cause. People won't swallow dry statistics unless we coat the pill. Publicity never hurts. Television will give you a chance to reach millions of people."

David smiled. "When do you want to do this? My schedule's tight. I split my time between research and being on duty in the hospital."

"Why don't I phone you Friday? I'll get in touch with the

head of the department first. I should have a better idea by then.''

David shifted to a more comfortable position. ''What kind of questions will you ask me?''

''I'll ask you a few about yourself, then segue into more technical stuff.''

David's attention was caught by several men near Dr. Kissinger and the vice president. ''I suppose they're Secret Service.''

Avrim looked over his shoulder. ''Naturally. They're the guys who don't eat. They always look as if they're talking into their lapels.''

David chortled. ''I'm impressed.''

''You should be,'' Avrim quipped, straightfaced. Female viewers were going to fall in love with this unassuming doctor. He could pass for a movie star. ''The first thing I learned was how to spot faces in a crowd. I guess you know Dr. Hammer's father once lived in Paris.'' David nodded.

David snitched a black olive. ''Dr. Hammer's a generous man. One of these days, I'm going to Washington, D.C., to see his art collection at the National Gallery.''

Avrim wiped a ribbon of mustard from his lip. He wanted to know more about the cancer specialist, what made Dr. David Orchin tick. ''So what made you specialize in oncology? Why not another specialty?''

''The numbers are too high in cancer,'' David said simply. ''I thought I'd try.''

Avrim sensed more to his reason but didn't press. He wanted this man for a friend. ''Do you have time for a private life?''

''Not much. I usually just attend hospital functions.''

''Sounds restrictive.''

''It is.''

''Arrange some time off. I mean, if you want to get out of the womb of your profession, or do you prefer associating only with doctors?''

The question, although uttered innocently, caused David to do something he rarely did with strangers. He confessed his homesickness, admitted he was tired of the cloistered existence of being with medical personnel all the time. ''I really don't mean that the way it sounds.''

Avrim understood. ''How long have you been here?''

"Eight years."

A low whistle escaped Avrim's lips. "I don't think I'd like that. Don't you miss your family?"

David said he did. "They make regular trips, sometimes twice a year."

"Is there a particular girl in Paris?"

"On the record or off?"

Avrim grinned. "You're a fast learner. Strictly off, if you prefer."

"I do prefer." David's thoughts drifted to Samara. "There's a girl I've known for a long time. I'd like to see her." He shook his head no when Avrim asked whether she was married or engaged. An unfamiliar but strong pang of jealousy ripped through David as he visualized Samara in the arms of a man. "From what I hear, nothing's changed."

That wasn't true, David thought, keeping the rest to himself. Samara's pictures confirmed the fact his little cabbage had turned into a beautiful swan. Much as he wanted to write to her, he felt as if there was nothing to ask that his mother hadn't written. Samara was interested in fashion design. Jules Le-Claire was helping her achieve her dream.

David absentmindedly twirled a straw. "I practically brought up *mon petit chou*. My little cabbage," he translated. "I either called her that or pest. Both names fit."

Avrim sipped his drink. "Where were her parents?"

"Her father died when she was an infant. Her mother runs a beauty parlor. Samara plagued me after school instead of her mother. She treated me like her big brother or an uncle or a possession."

A blur of red crashed into Avrim's shoulder. "So here you are, you stinker!" Maggie cried, interrupting their conversation. She cuffed Avrim on the back of the head. "I ought to kill you, you louse." She giggled, then caught David staring. For a minute their eyes held; in typical Maggie fashion, she gave David a thoroughly frank, admiring appraisal.

He did the same.

"Introduce us," she demanded. "You look important, are you?"

Avrim warned, "Don't try getting the good doctor's life story. He's my assignment, and if you'd gotten here on time, you'd know who he is."

Maggie scooped Avrim's drink from his hand. "Don't trust this big lug. If you're smart, you'll give me the interview. This rat left me to drown at the bar. How could you?" she asked, nuzzling Avrim's cheek. Bubbles of laughter escaped her lips. "I'll get you for this, Leightner. Celery of all things!"

He patted her hand. "Don't mind her, David. Maggie's a woman of limited horizons. This novice doesn't appreciate my leaving her alone with the CEO of a five-hundred-million-dollar-a-year company, a man who, according to his company's latest prospectus, earns a cool six million plus perks. The fact he appreciates cleavage shouldn't detract from him. What do you think, Maggie?"

"You're kidding!" Maggie's eyes widened. "Six million and perks!"

"A peasant I'm not. See if I help you again."

"Excuse me," Maggie chirped, handing him back his drink. "I've got to find that dear man and remove the celery from between his teeth. Pleasure meeting you, David. Don't say I didn't warn you. If you're wise, you won't have anything to do with Avrim."

David admired her swaying hips.

"She's taken," Avrim said bluntly.

"So what else is new?" David shrugged, reaching over for a last olive. "The good ones usually are taken."

Avrim thought of Solange, how she infuriated him. Solange might play the field, but he'd be damned if he'd pimp for her, even with a man as nice as David Orchin.

His mood soured, Avrim stood up. "Duty calls. I've got to go back and write my intro for the eleven o'clock news." They exchanged cards. "I'll be in touch."

Chapter Seven

David signed the CAT scan order. "Get her to detox," he fumed, referring to the spaced-out sixteen-year-old mother who had dropped her month-old infant on its head, thinking he was a doll with a stash of coke hidden in its body. "This baby isn't going back to her if I have to hide him myself."

The nursing supervisor drew him aside. The staff respected Dr. Orchin. His kindly manner allayed children's fears. "David, your eyes are spiderwebs. Fred's on duty. Take a break."

He'd been on duty at Babies Hospital for thirty-two hours. Of all the hospitals comprising the Columbia-Presbyterian Medical complex, his work at Babies affected him the most, especially when it came to dealing with child abuse. Yawning, he gratefully squeezed her hand. "If you see Wendall, would you tell him I need to see him?"

The nurse sighed. Her raging crush on Wendall hadn't gotten her anywhere. "If you see him first, tell him I need him."

David first met Wendall Everett-Lawson when the bushy-haired redhead sat down at David's table in the hospital's cafeteria. Over a serious discourse about the sexual efficacy of women with mustaches, Wendall found a willing listener in David, who collapsed at his crazy sense of humor—or maybe the hysteria stemmed from exhaustion due to overwork.

Wendall, thirty-year-old scion of one of Connecticut's founding families, could, if he chose, live a life of luxury without ever raising a finger—or a scalpel.

"Mumsy's having a little gathering. Before she lets her sonny boy have a roommate, she insists on first looking you over," Wendall joked, forcing a reluctant David to take a day off.

The "home" overlooking Long Island Sound in Connecticut sat on nearly one hundred acres of prime property deeded to the family by King George III. "One of his more judicious decisions!" Wendall quipped.

The house contained thirty-eight rooms beneath a shingled roof with ten chimneys and enough mullioned windows to keep a staff of window cleaners busy nonstop. Many styles of furniture filled the house. None of the antecedents threw anything out as one generation passed the home to the next generation, adding more.

"Part of the fun is sitting on your husband's ancestors," Wendall's mother said to David.

Liking her on sight, David understood where Wendall got his sense of humor.

The grounds boasted a guest cottage, an Olympic-size swimming pool, a tennis court, and a nine-hole golf course; for the water lovers, a sixty-foot boat docked at a private pier. Born with four silver spoons in his mouth, one for each socially prominent grandparent, Wendall would one day inherit the Everett-Lawson fortune, forged in steel and railroads, expanded further by a successful foray into the microchip world of communications.

"Just think, I'm the only child. Such a burden." Wendall grinned, plucking two flutes of champagne from a passing waiter. David offered to be his brother.

"Come on, I'll introduce you to Mikhail Baryshnikov. He's around here somewhere, probably in another one of his heated discussions with Rudy Nureyev."

They were walking through an arbor of Norwegian maple trees, leading to a sweeping expanse of manicured lawn. David felt as if he were strolling through a canvas. His gaze wandered to the sailboats passing over the horizon in the Sound. "Why do you work? Why be a plastic surgeon?"

Wendall shrugged his shoulders. He dropped his bantering tone. "I despise it when a person is treated like shit, short-changed in receiving the best medical care, due to a lack of money. The best way I can spread some of my luck is by working with the poor."

The following week they became roommates.

Now Wendall hated to wake David. He lay sprawled facedown on the cot in a room reserved for pooped professionals. He resembled a choir boy with a five o'clock shadow. His feet, shod in white sneakers, hung over the end of the narrow mattress. The beeper lay on the floor within reaching distance. A single grimy window let in shafts of dull light. A sign, Kilroy Slept Here, tilted at a crazy angle above the bed on a mauve wall in need of paint. The phone in the room had an Out of Order sign taped to it, with a two-week-old repair request.

Wendall leaned down to tap David's shoulder; when that didn't work, he shook him. David groggily opened an eye.

"Go away," he mumbled. "I'm dreaming I'm sleeping for three uninterrupted days."

"Would that you could, dear man. Rise and shine, lover boy. A lady's desirous of your dulcet tones."

"Stuff it, pervert."

"'Tis true. From gay Paree, sweetheart. You been holding out on me, fella? No wonder you're too busy for our poor American hothouse flowers. Hey," he called as David flashed out of bed and raced down the hall, "ask her if she's got a friend."

In minutes David returned, his face drawn in a preoccupied frown. "I've got to fly home."

Wendall knew the seriousness of that statement. Doctors didn't take off on a whim.

"Has someone died?"

David tied his shoelaces. "Lilli."

"Lilli?"

"Lilli Bousseauc, Samara's mother. That was Mimi Le-Claire, Samara's best friend. Samara needs me."

David shoved the beeper in his pocket and stuffed his shirttails in his waistband.

"You've been holding out on me, haven't you? How important is this girl to you?"

"It's not like that. Lilli once worked in my mother's beauty shop. She lived with us before she married. Later her husband died, and she rented an apartment in our building when Samara was nine months old."

"So how come this is the first I hear of Samara?"

"I haven't seen her since she was eleven, since I came to Columbia."

Wendall did a fast count. "That makes her—"

"Nineteen on the twentieth," David said automatically.

Wendall raised a telling brow. Occasionally they squired a nurse or a doctor to a medical function. David rarely talked about his private life, his sexual exploits.

"I'll be back in a minute. I've got to phone in a prescription," Wendall said.

David splashed cold water on his face and neck, shocking himself awake to digest Mimi's news. Lilli dead! Killed instantly by a car while crossing boulevard Raspail against the light. She had been carrying an armful of lilacs. The police theorized the boughs could have blocked her vision. Jules paid for the funeral arranged by Comte Levron. A grief-stricken Samara insisted Lilli be buried in a cemetery in Saint Chēron. But why hadn't his parents contacted him?

"The undertaker did a good job," Mimi had said. "Thank goodness makeup covered Lilli's bruises, or we don't know what we'd have done with Samara. David, I'm frightened. I think you'd better come home. She needs you." He explained his grueling schedule, saying he'd phone immediately.

"Make the time, David," Mimi ordered angrily. "There's all ways to bleed, David. Samara's bleeding. After the funeral she let us near her, but now she's holed up in the apartment. Half the time she refuses to open the door. I phone, and when she does answer, she's curt. David, she's different. She assures me she's fine. If she's fine, I'm crazy. She's given up."

"Mimi, she's lost her mother, her only living relative. You know how close they were. Give her time."

"The change is too abrupt." Mimi's voice crackled with impatience. "One day she's crying in our arms, the next she's dry-eyed, aloof. She's brittle. I'm worried. She needs you!"

He explained that Samara's brave front helped her cope with the pain. Mimi shrilled into his ear. "Stop patronizing me! Do you think I'm stupid? How many grieving people act catatonic?"

"Not many." Recalling Mimi's penchant for drama, he asked, "Is she showing signs of catatonia? Is she in a stupor? Are her limbs immobile?"

"Yes." Mimi snarled in disgust. "She's in a stupor. Come home, dammit. You're her only family now! I know her better than anyone in the world, including you. I tell you something's going on. I wish to God you'd believe me. You're her last hope."

"What about my parents? They must be caring for her."

"You're dense. If they were, do you think I'd be calling? Your mother says she needs to be alone, which is news to me. I can't understand your mother's attitude."

Mimi sounded hysterical. She was wrong about his parents. His mother loved Samara as a daughter. She grew up in his house. Drawn to Samara, he knew he must go home, do what he could.

"All right. I'll cable you when to meet me."

David dried his face, checked the room to see if he'd taken his keys. Wendall caught up with him at the elevator.

"Don't worry about a thing, David," he said. "I'll explain you had an emergency." Wendall looked at him quizzically. "I guess what they say about still waters running deep applies to you."

David wasn't in the mood to play games. "Meaning?"

Wendall shrugged. "Meaning I'm surprised you never mentioned Samara."

"There's nothing to say. She's a kid. Do you talk about kids you befriend?"

Wendall clapped him on the back. "Can't say that I do. But I know one thing."

"What's that?"

"I sure as hell don't remember their birthdays."

David booked the morning flight out of Kennedy. Too keyed up to sleep, he read and chatted with a honeymoon couple on their way, as they said, "to the City of Lights."

He couldn't help grinning. They held hands—and more when they thought no one looked—throughout the flight. If one used the bathroom, the other watched the door; then it was back to lingering kisses, and fondling beneath a blanket. If the plane wasn't full, he would have given up his seat to afford them privacy.

At dinner they surfaced. He accepted a glass of wine from the steward, offered a toast to Kathleen and Harry Swenson. He learned they lived in Eagle, Wyoming, and were flying the Atlantic for the first time; that the bride, a pretty blonde with freckles marching like a band of honey across the bridge of her nose, was a seamstress; the groom, whose tawny brown hair stood at attention a full two inches atop his head, made furniture.

"Chairs." Kathleen beamed, saying he sold them through catalogues. "I watched his hands caress the wood and couldn't help falling in love with him." She turned beet-red.

To ease her embarrassment, David said, "I was born in Paris."

"Really!" she exclaimed, asking a barrage of questions. He marked the thirteenth arrondissement on their tourist map. "You'll be interested in the Musée des Sièges—Museum of Seating. It's part of the Mobilier National, which comes closest to the Smithsonian in Washington, D.C. It's a treasure house. Designers and craftsmen come to study, and you need special permission, but I know someone who works there. Give me the name of your hotel. If he knows you're on your honeymoon, he might bend the rules in the name of love for a fellow craftsman. See the Louvre and Versailles on two separate days. If you visit a chateau, my personal favorite is Azay-Le-Rideau." He marked the map at a place north of Paris. "Clignancourt has a famous *puce,* a flea market. Don't let the name mislead you." He reminded them it was open on Saturdays, Sundays, and Mondays. Visualing his memories, he felt himself growing excited. "Take a bus to Chartres. The cathedral dates from the twelfth and thirteenth centuries. It's the finest example of stained-glass windows in the world."

Kathleen leaned across her husband. "I brought a sketch pad with me to copy the designers. What do you think?" Thinking of peppery Jules, he marked a spot on avenue Montaigne, advising her to copy LeClaire.

"See as much as you can of the French countryside. We are a country of history, culture, couture, and churches."

"And romance." Kathleen sighed, gazing deeply into her husband's eyes. David felt like an envious voyeur, a man missing a joy, a love he'd never known. He envied their passion. He would like to experience a grand passion, to bring a bride home to Paris, to show her off to his parents, to share her excitement. He knew the difference between passion and *passionate*. He felt passionate—dedicated, not amorous— about his work; his family that included Samara, whose shattered world he hoped to mend. Romantic passion should be overwhelming: intense, transforming, spiritual. It didn't seem likely he would experience that sort of passion for years, if ever. He lived in a world of controlled chaos, amid a frenzy of life and death decisions made by overworked physicians.

His glance slid to the Swensons; his envy eased. He was happy for them. For Kathleen who fell in love with Harry's hands caressing wood. For Harry who had found a far more enjoyable way to use his hands. They'd found a passion that might very well limit how much they would see of Paris or the French countryside.

He drained his wineglass. The remainder of the flight passed quickly. The plane banked, and the seat belt light went on. He peered out the window of the Pan Am jet. Off in the distance he spotted the Eiffel Tower. Excitement coursed through him. He might not have come home with a bride, or in love, the circumstances were sad, but he was home! Wishing the couple well, he pocketed the card with the name of their hotel; within minutes of landing at Charles de Gaulle Airport, he gathered his carry-on luggage, slung his flight bag over his shoulder, and joined the throng of people inside the terminal. It was good to walk.

A voice called his name. "David?"

"Mimi?"

He glanced down at a short, plump young woman. Behind her glasses, serious brown eyes stared up at him. "It's me," she affirmed. David smiled with genuine pleasure. Her hand thrust forward. "I'm sorry I sounded so sharp on the phone."

"Forget it. Surely after all these years we can do better." He embraced her affectionately.

Mimi nearly swooned. Allowing herself to be charmed by his deep and easy tone, her heart did a little pitter-pat. She returned his warm greeting, feeling the solid musculature beneath her hand. He was tall and sexy, with a taut frame, hazel bedroom eyes, broad shoulders, casually dressed in jeans and a sweater. A bubble of pure joy expanded in her heart for Samara.

"You've filled out," she blurted.

"I think you stole my line." He chuckled and started walking. Tucking an arm under her elbow, he led her to a bank to exchange dollars for francs. "This garment bag is all I brought with me."

In the parking lot, she apologized for her tiny Renault. "You may become a pretzel."

"I'm so glad to hear people speaking French that it's worth bending myself out of shape." He asked her to repeat everything she knew about Lilli. "When she took ill the night before she died, what did the doctor say after examining her?"

"Lilli refused to see a doctor. She said she felt fine, otherwise Samara wouldn't have gone with me to the cinema, then sleep at my house."

"It's a judgment call," he agreed. "A lot of people run to doctors needlessly."

"Lilli promised to attend Papa's couture collection the next day. Samara wanted her to see her in the wedding dress."

He tried to picture Samara in a wedding gown. Mimi swerved, speeding ahead of the car in front. David tightened his seat belt.

"It was so sad, David. The lilac petals mixed with her blood. They were strewn over her face and suit. Samara buried her beneath a blanket of lilacs."

Mimi went on to say many men desired Samara; she didn't want Lilli living alone after she married. "She feels so guilty."

His head swung around. "Is Samara thinking of marrying?"

Mimi mentally crossed her fingers. She sighed in her best Sarah Bernhardt impersonation. "Many men want her, especially one." Nathan *did* want her! "I've said too much."

"I thought the idea of bringing me home was to help her!" David snapped.

Mimi flew past two cars on the Peripherique. David's palms started sweating, and he tried to concentrate on the view. St. Denis was more crowded than he'd remembered.

"I suppose it's okay for you to know of Comte Levron's interest. I mentioned his kindness on the phone. He's offered his chateau on the Cher near Chenonceau, or his Paris villa."

"What for?" David asked, vaguely irritated.

"For Samara to recuperate in, of course. Naturally he'd be there, too."

David demanded to know his age.

With great satisfaction, Mimi slid a glance at David's angry features. She missed her calling. She should have been an actress. If Samara wanted David, she'd do whatever she could—including lie or stretch the truth like a rubber band about to snap. "Don't worry. The comte is able to care for her in a grand manner. I can tell you when he saw her glide down the runway in her wedding gown, his eyes lit up."

David grunted. "Then why is Samara alone?"

Mimi switched the subject. "David, how long will you stay?"

Bristling, he drummed his fingers on the door. "As long as necessary."

His reaction encouraged Mimi. Recalling the wording on the card attached to the flowers sent by *both* Levrons, she continued her improvisation. "Papa's arranged for Samara to be photographed in *Elle*. Papa is considering *Marie-Claire*, too. The comte's thrilled. We were keeping it a surprise for Lilli."

Mimi leaned on the horn, blasting the eardrums of the driver in front so that he shot forward. She rode his tail. David rolled his neck in a useless effort to relieve a crick.

Mimi gunned the motor, zooming past two cars. David gritted his teeth. "Marvelous man, the comte. What did she say when you told her I was coming?" he asked when his mouth started working again.

Mimi sighed. They entered the outskirts of Paris, coming off the Peripherique. "Yield!" David shouted. Mimi screeched to a halt. Both jerked forward.

"I yielded. I yielded. See, you're okay. You might as well know," she said, moving the car and her story forward. "Samara doesn't want to see you."

Stunned, David jolted upward, banging his head on the low roof. He rubbed the throbbing pain. "What do you mean she doesn't want to see me? Slow down, dammit, or let me off at the nearest Métro! You're a freaking maniac."

Mimi giggled. "That's what Papa says. Relax, we're almost there. I guess I shouldn't have dragged you home."

With David muttering airplanes were safer, Mimi zipped in and out of streets, arriving none too soon for David on rue Chomel.

"Say hello to your parents. Kiss Samara for me. If Comte Levron phones and you answer the call, give him my best."

David was beginning to hate the man, sight unseen.

An air of sadness tempered his homecoming with his parents. They kissed and hugged and reaffirmed their little family unit in the *petit salon,* painted a soft shade of green.

Tightly woven plaids in long-wearing wool blends covered the chairs and sofa.

"It's awful." Bella dabbed her eyes. Michel held him in a fierce hug. His father's face was gray, his deepset brown eyes brimming. Both seemed to have aged overnight.

"I miss Lilli," Bella said. "I keep thinking she'll phone any minute, we'll have tea, chat, sew, go for a walk. But she's not coming back."

He put his arm around her, comforting her. "You have Samara, Mama." Parsley, sage, thyme, and dill grew in pots on the windowsill. "I see she's still planting herbs."

With an arm about each of his parents, David walked through the apartment, familiarizing himself with his home. Mahogany tables and chairs, standing lamps, shelves of books, classical records in a cabinet next to a Motorola record player, a Russian samovar, a Singer sewing machine. His anniversary gift to his parents last year, a twenty-five-inch color Sony television. The upright Steinway brought back fond memories of his father playing piano at family song fests; of Samara, at age four, standing on his lap, her heels digging into him, singing off-key at the top of her lungs, the party to honor his bar mitzvah. No one had the heart to tell her she couldn't carry a tune. In his bedroom, he looked longingly at his bed and feather pillows as a wave of weariness set in. On his knotched pine desk stood his first microscope, a pen and pencil set, a dictionary, and a formal picture of him framed in silver taken on his thirteenth birthday.

He picked up a miniature car, then put it down, and his hand came up to cover a yawn. "Why didn't you tell me?"

"David, we don't need you to accuse us of negligence."

His head swung up. "Mama, I'm not accusing you of anything." Her brusqueness surprised him. "It seems odd that Mimi called, not you."

"Mimi!" Vehemently she shook her head. "Mimi's an interfering child. She had no right to call you. Will you get in trouble for leaving New York?"

"No. What is it? What's wrong?" He touched her arm. Bella took a step back and sprang away. She opened an armoire, reached up to a shelf, and dragged down an extra blanket, smoothing it nervously over a comforter in the overly warm room.

"Mimi drives me crazy. The one time she dealt with death was when her spaniel died. She carried on for months. You'd have thought the dog was a person."

Stunned, his surprise held him at bay. His mother and father stood on one side of the room, he on the other. *Like we're choosing sides*, he thought. *For what? Why?*

"Lilli was a person," he said quietly. His mother's face closed.

"Son," his father pleaded. "Your mama isn't herself."

"I'm not trying to upset you. I merely want the facts before I see Samara. It's habit with me, I do that with all my patients. Mimi said that Lilli took ill while watching television. She told Samara she felt fine. The next day Lilli stepped off a curb and died."

"Coincidence!" Bella cried. "You're making it sound like she committed suicide! A car hit her!"

Her outburst stunned him.

"Mimi makes trouble," she ran on wildly. "Mimi should stay home, not drive us crazy. Samara wants to be left alone. We're honoring her wishes. She knows where we live."

"Who feeds her?" David pressed, his worry increasing.

"She feeds herself. No more questions!"

"Bella, *shah!*" Michel quieted his wife and turned to David. "Forgive Mama," he implored. "Lilli and your mother were like sisters. When Mama and I lost your brother, she acted the same way. Give her time."

A cold chill ran through David. They should be showing empathy for Samara, not worrying about themselves. He could never remember his mother acting so selfishly.

"Mama had you," he told his father. "Who does Samara have?"

He left the apartment before he could see Bella's ravaged face. "Michel, how are we going to keep our promise to Lilli? David thinks I'm a terrible person. I am. I can't face Samara. I'm afraid of what I might say."

They clung to each other. "Samara's not alone, Bella. She has David. David will care for her."

"And when he leaves?"

Chapter Eight

David's heart raced; he felt alarmed, at a loss to discern his parents' apprehension; their obvious reticence to discuss Samara. He rapped on her door and waited. He knocked louder, banging on it after five minutes, shouting in frustration, "Samara, it's me, David. Open the door."

Minutes passed. His anxiety mounted. Finally he heard the lock change position. The door opened. He fought to conceal his initial shock. He had expected her to be in mourning but he hadn't expected to see this drastic transformation. He'd thought, incorrectly, that Mimi was being her usual dramatic self.

Lifeless, her long platinum hair dull and disheveled, her normally expressive eyes blank, a barefoot Samara wearing a stained, frayed bathrobe stood before him, her face devoid of emotion. The waiflike creature blinked at him through lashes laden with tears.

Swiftly he searched her face, examining it, separating his personal feelings to deal with them later. Dead on her feet, lorn and lost, her shining beauty lay buried beneath the surface, beneath layers of human misery. The picture of her that his parents had brought to New York wasn't this Samara. In that one he'd seen a vibrant beauty with high, proud cheekbones, a sensuously shaped mouth, and eyes to capture the viewer's attention. She'd been snapped on a turn of her head, her hair whipping around her face like a corona, a hint of an impish smile on her face. In the car Mimi had said Samara was a vision on Jules's arm, gliding down the runway in the wedding dress, that the audience cheered. They'd cry if they could see her now. He wanted to cry, too, to take her pain, to give her back

85

her sunshine world. Mimi used good judgment in alerting him. How could his mother and father have read the situation so inaccurately?

"It's David," he repeated gently. "I've come to take care of you."

"David . . . hello."

Did she even know who he was? Fear ripped through him. He didn't need to be a doctor to know that Samara was suffering a deep psychic pain. "My sweet *petit chou,* I'm so sorry about your maman. Baby, I'm here, I'll take care of you."

The familiar endearments signaled the start of renewed grief. She began to sob, tiny heart-piercing hiccups of grief. Big fat teardrops slid down her face. With a cry he didn't know he was making, he opened his arms, gathering her close. He stroked silky thinness, skimmed delicate bones, gently massaged her spine. No one could understand all they'd been to each other, moving from a brother-sister relationship to . . . what? She needed care. Perhaps for a long time.

"*Mon petit chou,* I wish I could take away your pain."

She pulled away. "No one can, David."

He looked around him at the messy apartment, at the issues of *Le Figaro* scattered about the floor. The place needed dusting, vacuuming, airing. The Samara he remembered prided herself on neatness, on her person, in her home. He glanced into Lilli's bedroom. Boxes and papers were strewn on the bed. The bedspread was half off, trailing onto the floor.

He followed her into the kitchen. There were dead lilacs on the windowsill, dead white roses in a white vase on the table. David read Comte Levron's card. He pitched it and his flowers into the garbage pail.

Samara swayed past him. "Forgive my manners, David. Would you like tea before you go back to see your parents?" She pulled open a cabinet, then seemed to forget why she was there.

"Samara, Bella's made your favorite soup. Why don't we both go upstairs for a bowl? We'll eat, then we'll talk."

She stared past him, fixing on a point over his shoulder. "No thanks. Go to your parents."

"Samara, I didn't fly here to see them. I came to see you.

Mimi's half out of her mind with worry. Why are you shutting your best friend out? Why aren't you dressed? Why haven't you combed your hair? This isn't like you.''

"Why don't you mind your own business?'' Samara spoke in the same lifeless tone she'd used to say hello. "You've been gone eight years. People change.''

Exhausted and worried, David lost his objectivity. "So you do remember how long it has been. Good. Then you also remember I was the one you ran to when you were upset. Don't shut me out. You are my business, Samara. You've always been my business. I changed your diaper when you were nine months old. You sucked my finger when you teethed. You took your first steps with me there to watch you, to pick you up when you fell. You grew up as my shadow. You nagged me to take you to the cinema with my friends. You relied on me to tutor you with schoolwork. When you worried your breasts were flat, no boy would want you, you marched into my room. Do you remember what you did? What you said?''

Her silence incensed him.

She'd come into his house, interrupting him while he was studying. "Look at me!'' she wailed. "I'm a flat board.''

To get rid of her, he humored her. He instructed her to pirouette. Instead she yanked his palms, thrusting both onto her breasts like a smack. She rolled his hands on them. The nipples rose to hard buds. Although she'd been unaware of the effect she had on him, he had a wet dream that night. In the dream Samara wasn't a child. She looked, he realized now with a start, much like the beautiful girl he'd seen on the picture his parents had shown him.

"When you hurt, I hurt, Samara. After eight years of not seeing each other, the best you can do is to ask whether I want tea. What the hell kind of hello is that?''

Nothing. He might as well address the wall. He wanted to shake her, to rattle an expression, anything to get a reaction.

"Talk to me,'' he begged, scared by her stony silence.

She shrugged, granting him a minuscule concession. "It's the best I can do, David. As you can see,'' she said, tipping her stringy hair, "I'm not equipped to entertain. I've things on my mind.''

He wondered when she'd last eaten a decent meal. "I want to help you. So do my parents.''

Samara suddenly roared to life. Her high, shrill laugh ricocheted off the walls. She struck his chest with uncharacteristic strength. "Help! Oh, that's good! Is that your panacea? You wouldn't know where to begin to help! Help how? You haven't the faintest idea what I'm going through. Who am I?" she shouted.

"You're Samara. Who do you think you are?"

She laughed. Alarmed, appalled by the growing realization that she was on the verge of a nervous breakdown, he cupped her face between his broad palms. He spoke directly into her eyes. "You are Samara Bousseauc. Say it. I am Samara Bousseauc."

She twisted out of his grasp. She faulted him, renounced his parents for withholding the truth from her after her mother's death. "You're all in on it. You all know."

"Know what, for God's sake?"

She screamed. "Who I am, you idiot! Haven't you been listening? What a laugh. I planned my life! It included—" She stopped abruptly. She walked into the other room. "Go home."

David tore after her. "Stop it. You're making yourself ill."

"Maman's dead, and it didn't have to happen!"

"You can't blame yourself for Lilli's death."

"Not true, David. I should have been told."

More confused than ever, he asked, "Told what?"

But her outburst unleashed another wave of grief. Tears formed rivers down her face. Her nose ran. Without thinking, he took out his handkerchief and wiped her face. A great shudder started at the top of her head, working its way down her body in waves until there was nothing left of her outburst.

"That's the joke," she muttered. Her shoulders sagged. "Maman," she whimpered. "Poor, poor Maman. What she went through." Swaying, she lost her balance. David caught her before she fell. He carried her into her room, placing her gently on the bed. She flapped a protesting hand. Worn out from her tirade, her hand fell heavily to her side. Her eyelids fluttered and drooped.

David removed his shoes. His large frame indented the mattress, making a squeaking noise as he lay down next to her. He wrapped his arms around her. She weakly beat her hand on his back. "Doctor's orders," he murmured. He kissed her forehead. "Sleep. I'll take care of you. Haven't I always? You're not alone. Shhhh."

"David . . . David . . ." she wept. "I wanted—"

"Shhhh . . . Later, baby. Later, *mon petit chou.*"

In moments she slept.

Samara snuggled closer, arousing him in her innocence. He shifted, careful not to awaken her, but she kept curving her body to his shape. Cursing savagely under his breath, he gave himself the pleasure of pressing a kiss on her face, then broke into a cold sweat as she found a more comfortable place to rest her knee—directly on his burgeoning erection. As if that wasn't extreme torture, her knee expertly massaged him.

Samara kept finding him, with her hands, her breasts, her breath on his neck, her lips on his flesh. Exhausted himself, afraid to leave lest she awaken and need him, he tried concentrating on his patients. He reviewed protocols he had prescribed for his most seriously ill. But by trying to avoid the very part of her he most craved, she became the object of his wildly erotic dreams, once he finally fell asleep.

Sometime during the night she awoke.

"David."

"Mmmmm?"

She shook his arm. "David."

He blinked past the mist shrouding his consciousness, becoming aware of the sounds of weeping. Suddenly it hit him. He was in France. With Samara. In her bed. He'd fallen asleep holding her in his arms! As the remnants of sleep lifted, patches of Samara's confusing conversation seeped into his brain.

"David . . ."

She moaned, calling his name a second time. Sighing, he opened his arms. She seemed to have no memory of the night, thank God.

"Shh, *mon petit chou,* I'm here."

Like a child seeking solace, she sought him. Her face, in the moonlight, was all eyes. Tears poised on the tips of her lashes, and more glistened on her cheeks. "It's all right." With his thumb he gently wiped the corners of her eyes, giving her the time she needed. Grateful for it, she sighed his name against his neck, and slept. He remained awake, stroking her soft skin. With their breaths mingling, he cursed himself for his prurient, unprofessional thoughts.

Hours later, he slipped out of bed. He wrote Samara a note that he'd be back soon. He returned to his apartment to shower, change clothes.

"What's wrong with your bed?" Bella asked. "Did you sleep on Lilli's?"

David caught Bella's implied rebuke. They both knew the answer to that one. Forget being a grown man. The way his mother speared him, he might have been twelve with his first hard-on. "I slept in a chair."

"Lilli's chairs are for midgets, not a man your size."

He poured himself a *café noir,* pretending interest in its murky contents, nettled that at his age his mother could make him feel like a callow youth. He dipped his brioche in his cup, then immediately discarded the bun that he had absentmindedly dipped in his black coffee.

Michel stirred his *café crème.* "Bella. Enough."

"Samara's saying things I don't understand," David said. "She thinks you're withholding something from her about who she is. It doesn't make sense. Do you know what she's talking about?"

"That's absurd," Bella said. Michel coughed. "We know what you know, what everyone knows. She's Samara Bousseauc. She's suffered a shock. She'll be all right. Here, take her this food. Tell her we love her."

He didn't fare better when Samara awoke and spotted the tray with orange juice, eggs, roll, and milk. "I'm not hungry."

"Drink your juice."

She pushed his hand. "Drink it!" he ordered, his demeanor brooking no nonsense. "You need your strength." He waited while she drank. "Now eat."

She threw her head back on the pillow. "You eat it."

He speared egg onto the fork, cupped her chin. She snatched the fork. "I can feed myself. Did Bella or Michel say anything?"

She was back to that. "Yes. They said they love you. Eat the damn food."

They fought at forkfuls for fifteen minutes. He managed to force her to eat a bird-sized portion, but at least it was nourishment. By the time he returned from washing the dishes, she had fallen back to sleep. Bone weary, he pulled up a chair and sat. She awoke two hours later.

He threw a smile on his face. "Terrific. Just in time to join me for a walk." He flung open the window. The weather was tailor-made for tourists, with a robin's egg blue sky and wispy cirrus clouds.

She flung her hand to her eyes. "You go," she muttered. "I'm busy."

He tossed the blanket off the bed. Her thin nightgown left nothing to his imagination. "I can see that." She shot him a surly look. "Samara, get up, or I'll drag you out of that bed. I want you showered and dressed in twenty minutes."

"You've got some nerve."

He lifted her boldly from the bed, steered her into the bathroom, turned on the shower. "Get out!" she snarled.

"Get in," he ordered. He stared her down. Finally she tossed her head and said she would shower just to get rid of him.

Secretly delighted to get a rise out of her, he added, "Wash your hair. It's matted. Put on perfume. Make yourself pretty for me."

"Tyrant." She stepped beneath the shower, letting the jets pound water on her. Through her anger, she remembered awakening in his arms, his physical strength tempered with gentleness, his muscles sinewy beneath her fingers, his skin smooth and hot to her touch, and she remembered its salty taste. For years she had dreamed of their reunion. Now he was here, more ruggedly handsome than in her longings, lean and strong. She had inhaled the masculine fragrance of his cologne, steeled herself against kissing him the way she'd dreamed, even up to two weeks ago. All had changed. She knew how she sounded. Looked. She couldn't bring herself to care. She hadn't lost her mind as she knew he must be thinking. She'd lost far more. She'd lost her identity. Until she unraveled the mystery, she couldn't go forward.

David stripped the bed. He aired the room and changed the bed linens. He laid out a set of clothes for her to wear. "Get dressed," he ordered. "We're going out."

"I'm not going anywhere."

"All right. I'll dress you. I warn you, Samara. You're getting out of this place if I have to drag you out."

Anger put pink back into her cheeks. Although she wore no makeup, she looked good, he thought. He fought the purely male reaction of seeing her in hip-hugging blue jeans and a

pink sweater that showed her nipples when she lifted her arms
to tie a ribbon around her ponytail.

After two blocks of grumbling, she was ready to quit.

David wrapped an arm about her shoulders. "Humor me."

Reacquainting himself with the seventh arrondissement, they
walked the neighborhood streets. At the corner of rue de Sèvres
and boulevard Raspail, he led her inside the Hôtel Lutétia,
through the stately quarry-stone facade. Noticing Samara's
fatigue, and not wanting to go home too soon, they sat in deep
plush red armchairs beneath gracious chandeliers in one of the
reception lounges. Gazing at the charming art deco surroundings, he wondered how long it would take before she smiled
again.

She turned lunch at Les Deux Magots into an ordeal.

"You eat it!" She left her asparagus omelette untouched.
Paying the tariff that in France includes a fifteen percent tip, he
resumed their walk. From time to time she'd cry. When that
happened, he'd hold her until her grieving spell subsided. By
the end of the afternoon, he was as worn out as she.

"Are you sleeping there again?" Bella asked later.

"Let it alone, Mama," David snapped irritably. He passed a
tired hand over his eyes. Holding Samara, forcing himself to
remember his role as doctor, strained his patience. "I'm doing
what I think is best for her medically."

"Is she still asking strange questions?" Bella wanted to
know.

"She's over that," David said, leaving before he heard
Bella's sigh of relief or saw his father throw a comforting arm
about his wife's shoulders.

During the next few days David forced Samara into a
routine. He kept up running commentaries while pushing her to
take care of herself. She balked constantly, grumbled on the
elevator, and after walking one block, she was ready to return
to her apartment.

At night he would slump in a chair by her bed, his chin
dropping onto his chest, hoping she would fall asleep. That
didn't work. She seemed genuinely afraid to sleep alone at
night, confessing she hated the nightmares.

Drugged from lack of a solid night's rest in weeks, David
gave himself permission to let her fall asleep in his arms,
silently promising himself to return to his uncomfortable chair.

He never kept that promise. Samara needed him. She burrowed into the curves of his body, straining to get closer to the source of her only nighttime solace. Each night his erection mocked him.

As nights passed, Samara slept, and he became more tired. Bella criticized him for spending the nights with her. "How does it look? Ask Mimi to sleep there."

"Enough, Mama!" Michel warned.

Bella prepared meals, sending them with David along with her standard message. "Tell her we love her."

David needed to break the routine or go nuts himself. He borrowed his father's Peugeot and bundled a protesting Samara into the car. He sped through the Bois de Boulogne where he'd once taken an excited Samara to watch the French Open Tennis Match, then to eat at Le Vert Gallant. With the car windows open, the sun beating on his arm, they reached Versailles in time to share a salade nicoisse and a bottle of Chardonnay at a local brasserie before entering the palace grounds. They strolled along the statue-lined paths overlooking the spectacular verdant lawns. They sat on the stone steps leading to the Tapis Vert, the green carpet or royal avenue, that stretched between the two ponds dedicated to Apollo. In the past, Samara would have slowed to inspect the vases with their decorative patterns typical of Versailles: sunflowers, fleur-de-lis, cornucopias, laurel and oak leaves evocative of the royal virtues and bounty.

She walked without bothering to notice them or the Fountain of Apollo, the gilded statuary of Apollo, sitting on his chariot drawn by four fiery horses, emerging from the ocean.

David had hoped the distraction of the jetting fountains, the statues of children sculpted by Buirette, Le Hongre, Lerambert, and Mazeline, using the drawings set down by Le Brun for Louis XIV when the palace was enlarged in 1671, would hold her interest. He was wrong.

It hardly mattered what he did or planned for her. Whether he took her to Versailles or the Castle of Ussé, she remained impassive. He remembered when a seven-year-old Samara visited Sleeping Beauty's tiny tower room for the first time. An alert guard scolded her for trying to touch a priceless sixteenth-century inlaid mother-of-pearl and wood cabinet to count whether it really did contain forty-nine drawers as claimed. "If the drawers are secret, how do you know they're there?"

By week's end her eyes lost their haunted look. She washed, brushed her hair, and dressed without him forcing her to care for herself. Once or twice David caught her staring at him, as if measuring him as a man. When that happened, he felt the instant reaction in his loins that tormented him at night.

Just as he thought the worst was over, she awoke one morning crying hysterically, as if her heart had shattered anew. Breathing in the subtle perfume she'd begun to use again, he rocked her in his arms.

"It's no use," she sobbed. Her fingers curled on his bare chest. "I tried to figure it out. I've got to tell you or I'll go out of my mind."

She swung her legs over the side of the bed, beckoning him to follow. In Lilli's bedroom, she went to the armoire, rummaging on the top shelf to get a small metal box and a key. She raised the lid of the box, then handed him a paper.

"I want you to read this. I found it hidden inside another box."

The official birth certificate jumped off the page. He unfolded the document to read the inside information. Samara Gold, born June 20, 1960. Affixed on the lower left corner was the official gold seal of the State of New York, signed by the attending physician and the hospital administrator. He saw her tiny left and right footprints; her mother's thumbprints. The infant's sex, female, and weight, six pounds fifteen ounces, were noted, along with the family history. Mother: Lilli Bousseauc Gold. Father: Maximillian Gold.

The breath whooshed out of him. "It's genuine!" he cried, awestruck.

"Yes, I know. You met my father in the park. He brought you and Maman home after she hurt her ankle."

David drew a blank. He shook his head. "I don't remember him. I only saw him once. I must have been at school the other times he came for your mother."

Samara handed him a stack of letters. Twin spots of color stained her cheeks. He stared at the embossed return address: Murray Leightner, Attorney at Law. The address, New York. "Leightner!"

"What is it?" she demanded.

"Nothing," he amended, wishing to God he knew what the hell this meant. Judge Leightner's good friend, Senator Max Gold, had recently praised the nomination of the able jurist to the Supreme Court. If Senator Max Gold were her father, as he suspected, then Samara's family also owned Gold's! Until he had absolute confirming proof from Avrim, he decided not to speculate aloud. In her agitated state, it would serve no purpose to tell her anything. She needed to be emotionally strong to face what lay ahead of her. "Avrim Leightner is a TV anchor in New York."

"I know that."

He reluctantly explained that he knew him. Predictably, she pressed him for details. He said they met at Columbia at a medical gathering Avrim covered for TV. "Go on," she urged. "Read the letters. I want you to."

He bent to the task, amazed by the contents, stunned by the connection between Avrim Leightner's father and Lilli. He read each letter in sequential order, two letters per year, written almost on the identical dates and months. Brief letters, longer missives, letters exchanged to give and glean information. But not one word about Max Gold. Odd, to say the least.

He understood at last the reasons for Samara's erratic behavior, and why Mimi, without knowing the truth, was right to be concerned. He didn't know how Samara had handled the shocking revelations as well as she had. What part, if any, had his parents played in this monstrous charade?

"Now that I think about it, there were clues." Samara recounted how Lilli had blanched upon hearing Leightner's name on television. How she insisted on speaking to David's parents. How Bella agreed it was foolish for Lilli to see a doctor.

"There's more." Samara handed him several blue bank books stamped in gold lettering: Chase Manhattan Bank of New York. He needed to adjust his perception of Samara, to think of her as rich. Her bank account held a staggering three hundred fifty thousand dollars. She would never need to worry. But why hadn't Lilli withdrawn any of it for Samara?

Samara sniffed the books, as if she were drawing in their implicit wealth. She fanned her face with them. She looked regal, her chin high, the light in her eyes burning fiercely. "The dates in the bank books started shortly after Maman returned home to Paris. I've thought about why she never told me about my father."

It was a question uppermost in his mind, one he intended to ask of his parents.

"Maman married a monster." Samara accommodated her deduction to a livable solution. "He took advantage of a young, beautiful girl. He tired of us, threw us out when we needed him the most. The money was meant to buy her off. Maman was too honorable, too decent to be bought. She maintained her integrity."

David thought it a farfetched deduction.

"Why didn't she spend any of it for you, send you to design school?" he wondered aloud.

Samara sat down with a sigh, staring at her hands. She lifted uncertain eyes. "I don't know—that's part of the unknown."

A very big unknown. It was clear she needed more clues to unravel her past. Lilli had gone to extraordinary lengths to hide her true identity, including giving Samara a different surname. He didn't think it fair. He wondered what Lilli would have done had Samara applied for a passport, needed to show her birth certificate. The American passport in the box had expired. He liked to believe Lilli meant to reveal the truth one day. Whatever the truth, it lay sealed in Lilli's grave. In her fragile condition, Samara didn't need more grief. He wished he had the time to get her away from all of this, perhaps a few days in Nice, or in San Remo on the Italian Côte d'Azur.

"I think you need to go away for a few days. Then you ought to consider enrolling in the Chambre Syndicale's school. Jules can't teach you everything."

She stared at him as if he'd taken leave of his senses. Tightening the sash on the robe he'd given her, she returned the papers and bank books to the metal box. Locking it, she pocketed the key.

Wistfully she ran the tips of her fingers along the top of the metal bed Lilli had slept alone in all these years. She spoke in a low, pained voice. "I used to crawl into bed with Maman. She carried with her the scent of lilacs. I'd ask her to tell me stories of my father. How that must have hurt her, having to lie." She wiped her face. "She told me my father loved me. Look what he did to her."

Nothing in the room bespoke wealth. The room was Lilli. Spare. Secretive. Adorned only with religious icons.

Samara shuddered. "You advised me to go to school. I'll tell you what I'm going to do.'' She snapped the lock on the armoire, sealing it like a coffin. With her shoulders thrown back, she drew her spine into a straight, unforgiving line. "I'm not going to school. I'm going to do what any sensible heiress would do in my circumstances, David. I'm going to America to find my father and ruin the son of a bitch!"

He didn't want her to. Not yet. Not until he thought her ready to withstand more shocks. "How?" he asked, stalling.

"What do you mean, how?" she asked in a voice as smooth as silk, her blue-green eyes ice-cold, so cold, so remote that she shocked David.

"You're in no condition to make wise decisions. This isn't the time."

"Time," she scoffed, tossing her head defiantly. "I need answers, not time. I'm not getting them around here."

"All right," he said, trying to settle her. "But don't be surprised if you don't like what you find."

"Meaning?"

"Be sensible. Look about you. Lilli chose this Spartan life. The reasons you've given yourself may not be true. You're wealthy. You could have lived a life of luxury. If your father is the monster you claim him to be, why did he continue sending money? He had to have known she never withdrew any of it. Lilli didn't need to work. Ask yourself why she refused to use the money to make your lives easier. On the other hand, if your father is evil, you're no match for him. You're a child—"

"I am not!"

"Then prove it." He knew she wasn't a child, but a beautiful, desirable woman. "Keep an open mind. Maybe there's another side to this story."

"Are you saying I should throw my arms about him?"

"I'm saying nothing of the sort," he countered. "You need a plan, not a half-cocked emotional response."

She arched a dissenting eyebrow. "I refuse to wait. It's out of the question."

"What if you learn a more painful truth?" he asked.

"Anything's better than this. I'm going with you. Alone, if you refuse. Comte Levron will use his influence to get me an emergency passport."

"All right, but I hope you won't be sorry," he retorted, sick of hearing that man's name.

Chapter Nine

"Shit! I'm pregnant."

Solange didn't need a rabbit to keel over for confirmation. Sick to her stomach, she gripped the sides of the marble washbowl, wishing she could turn back the calendar. She ought to sue the manufacturers for making a defective diaphragm. If she had a crystal ball, she never would have run like a marathon racer to get Avrim into bed. She'd been puking all week.

Since August 13, of her thirteenth year, the day she first began her menses, she'd been as regular as clockwork. Thirteen was a lucky number, she bragged to her pals, many of whom suffered from horrid cramps, irregularity, or, thanks to exercise, threw their flow out of kilter. Not her. She normally breezed through the curse. One day heavy, two normal, two to taper out. Finis. No sweat. Her hormones were rejuvenated. She never felt depressed. Raring to go was more like it.

Until now. All she wanted to do was sleep. And never eat again as long as she lived. She retched for the third time in less than an hour, and her mouth tasted vile. Perspiration beaded her forehead. On top of her miseries, her father expected her to join him for breakfast.

She gagged at the prospect of smelling food, of passing lox and bagels. "Please God, deliver me," she groaned, cursing Avrim. There was no question that he was the father. Who else could it be? It suited her to let him think she slept around, but the truth was, except for him she'd been celibate for the past six months.

She rinsed out her mouth, brushed her teeth, and gargled with mouthwash. Oh, Lord! How would the world-traveling anchor like it if she told him he was about to become a daddy? Probably pass out cold! Just like she would unless she found a solution to this problem.

Which wasn't as easy as it sounded. She didn't dare go to an abortion clinic. The Republicans, reporters, and gossip columnists would have a field day. She wasn't stupid enough to go to a butcher who'd rip out her insides. Or worse—leave her to bleed to death. She sure as hell couldn't tell her father. After he killed Avrim, he'd kill her.

"How could you disappoint me like this, Solange?" he'd ask in his old-fashioned moralistic tone—after he got over the shock of learning she and Avrim had been intimate!

Maggie, the bitch, would gloat. "You got caught, and I didn't! Blah . . . blah . . . blah." Maggie would move in for the kill. "Why don't we make this a double wedding, Max darling?" *Not yet, sweetheart. Not by a long shot. Daddy's mine, not yours. I loaned him to you.*

Solange tipped her head back, gargling. She rinsed her mouth, spritzed with breath spray, then liberally sprayed the bathroom with air freshener.

Her grandparents expected her at next Friday night's dinner. How would they like her little bombshell? Their views on the need to propagate more Jews were well known in the family. *Tessie and Barney Gold, I've got a little surprise for you. Here's a hint. It's smaller than a bread box, about the size of a small roast, give or take a pound.*

Another wave of nausea hit her. She barely made it back to the toilet bowl. When she finished retching, she splashed more cold water on her face, repeating the routine: mouthwash rinse, then breath spray. Raising the window, she drew in deep breaths of air, praying for her stomach to settle.

Avrim, you louse, you did this to me. "Did it to you!" she imagined he'd retort. "Aren't you a little confused here? I offered to use a rubber. But, no. You swore on a stack of Bibles diaphragms are safe. Congratulations, baby. You lose at Russian roulette."

Or the scenario might differ, she thought, closing the window. Avrim might be ecstatic, relish impending papahood, buy out FAO Schwarz. She gave a quick thought to phoning him at his news desk, casually telling him. Always one to rely on instinct, she decided against it. Much as she loved Avrim, she did not want to marry him. Avrim, bless his fertile dick, preferred living a different life-style. Even if she wanted a baby, which she didn't, having it was out of the question. She had no intention of marrying any man who didn't know which country he'd be sleeping in, expecting her to wait at home like the good little woman. When she married, she intended to glide down the aisle on her father's arm, ravishingly beautiful in a Priscilla gown of white-beaded satin, looking pure as the driven snow. No tainted baggage, no little bastard flower child. She'd choose a prominent husband, a man who would stay put. A man who would escort her to opening night galas, parties, charity balls. They'd travel for pleasure: London, Gstaad, Acapulco, Cannes. With the Washington shuttle, she'd be able to continue her role as the Senator's official hostess.

She'd have it all, just as she planned.

But first she had to get rid of her problem.

How? Her brain shifted into overdrive.

She needed to find a reputable out-of-town doctor to perform the abortion. She also needed a reason for leaving home, one that would satisfy her father, not raise his suspicions. The answer came after she threw up again. Mapping out her plans like a military strategist, she went over it in her mind, looking for weak spots.

First she'd say she had a change of heart, she wanted to help him campaign.

How? he'd ask in his thorough manner. By visiting a college campus, she'd respond. Then she'd offer to take a straw poll. Unofficially. To get the real pulse of college kids her age.

"Where will you conduct this poll?" he'd ask.

Dartmouth! She'd go to Lou-Lou, her old friend from Regents Academy, now a senior and teaching assistant at Dartmouth. That's where she'd go. She knew for a fact that Lou-Lou had had an abortion. Therefore, she'd recommend her doctor. She'd return with the sad results of her imaginary poll, kill two birds with one stone. She had no intention of helping her father win the nomination. Solange gave herself a mental hug for brilliance. A knock on the door interrupted her self-congratulations.

Pepe came in. Hands on broad hips, she said, "Your father's on his second cup. You know he hates waiting."

"I'll be down later."

"What's wrong?" she asked, noticing Solange's pale face.

"Nothing. I'm sick."

She felt Solange's forehead. "You're cool. Where were you last night? What'd you eat?"

Solange batted her hand away, temporarily forgetting she needed Pepe as an ally. She stalked to the other side of the room. "I stayed home. I didn't eat."

"Better get some food in you."

"No," Solange moaned. "Food's the last thing I need. My tummy's upset."

"You have a bowel movement today? Yesterday?"

"Knock it off. Yes and yes."

"I'll fix a hot bowl of soup. The warmth will do you good."

"Pepe," she snapped, "it's eight o'clock in the morning, for God's sake. I don't want soup."

Pepe shrugged. "Suit yourself. What do you want me to tell your daddy?"

"Nothing." Solange sighed. "I'll be down in a few minutes. Tell him I had a late night, okay?"

"Is there something you want to tell me?" Solange avoided her eyes. Although Pepita knew most of her secrets, she didn't know about Avrim. If she did suspect, she knew better than to say anything.

Solange got rid of Pepe and locked her bedroom door. Caught by another wave of nausea, she waited until it passed. Stripping out of her pink baby doll nightgown, she stared at her slim reflection in the full-length beveled mirror. She pressed her palms against her flat stomach. No one could tell. Why should they? Her breasts were high. There was no doubt in her mind she was *enceinte,* as the French called pregnancy. Lovely word for a shitty, pukey condition. She couldn't begin to fathom why any woman in her right mind would go to a fertility clinic.

She applied her makeup carefully, added extra blusher to hide her pale complexion. She had a part to play. She adjusted the straps on her Emilio Pucci rasberry-sherbet teddy, decorated with French lace, ribboned edgings. Patting her stomach once more, she selected a bell-sleeved cotton gabardine that cost a mere five hundred dollars, three hundred dollars more than her undergarment. Stepping into Prada slingbacks, she walked back to her vanity table. Seated before the mirror, she twisted her thick hair into a sleek chignon, securing it with pearl-encrusted combs.

Her stomach lurched. With her hand covering her mouth, she dashed to her night table for a package of saltines that she'd put inside the drawer. Munching saltines helped take the edge off. She chewed, waited for five minutes to be certain she felt up to it, then, poised and collected, she left her bedroom.

Max breakfasted in the solarium. A pink-and-white linen tablecloth covered the wrought-iron table. Hedgerows of privet and a tall fence protected the glass-enclosed room from prying eyes.

"Good morning, Daddy." He looked in an exceptionally good mood. She supposed she had Maggie to thank for that.

Max smiled. He lifted the Sèvres cup, decorated with miniature roses. He took a sip of cappuccino.

"Sleepyhead. Pepe said you had a late night."

She silently gave thanks to the servant for covering for her. Her father lived by the infernal clock. "Some of the gang were in town," she said, kissing his cheek.

Max Gold returned his daughter's kiss. She smelled of lavender soap and perfume. "Where did you go?" He passed a basket of cut bagels in her direction.

"We hit the usual places. I stayed out too late. I'm tired."

His face showed his disapproval.

Solange toyed with her cup. She broke off a small piece of plain bagel. Her hand slipped to her belly. She refused to think of the life growing in her as a baby with arms and legs and tiny fingernails. She concentrated on her future.

"How is your campaign coming along?" she asked, sipping black coffee.

He bit into his bagel. "So far so good. We'll announce in November."

"Daddy, I'd like to help you with your campaign."

He put down the *Times*.

"That's a change for you. You've never shown any interest in campaigning."

She smiled and wished herself luck. "You've never run for the presidency. Your previous elections have been shoo-ins. Now you'll face hard campaigning. It's time I put the country first. You're the epitome of a successful, winning politician."

He looked dubious.

"Yes, you carry yourself erectly, you wear American tailored suits, your smile is genuine."

"I also wear Savile Row suits, slump, and frown."

"Not on the campaign trail."

He laughed. "What do you really want?"

"Not a blessed thing." *Or a blessed event!*

His eyes twinkled. "Deliver me," he teased, ready to give her anything she wanted.

"I'm serious. I've given this a good deal of thought. You believe deeply in the rights of the little people and you work hard to ensure your congressional district gets its fair share of the pie."

He sat back. "You didn't mention I voted for liberal tariff laws."

She wouldn't be sidetracked. "On the theory an open market promotes greater harmony in the world."

He raised his brows, his smile replaced by a thoughtful look. "You've been doing your homework."

Solange tipped her head. She swallowed hard, pushing down the bile in her throat. "Senator, you're an honorable man. You refuse to vote on any measure in which you have a financial or personal interest. To your credit you've never campaigned on Yom Kippur."

He grinned. "Suppose I make you my campaign manager. To what do I owe the honor of this bountiful praise?"

"You need my help," she declared, explaining her plan. "No fanfare, no press. I'll rap with college students and report back to you. I'll be gone for a week."

"Isn't this a bit of a turnaround for you, Solange? I thought you were cool to my candidacy."

"Whoever gave you that idea?" she asked prettily, guessing Maggie's pillow talk criticism prompted his statement.

She lifted her pretty shoulders. "All I've ever wanted is your safety," she said, for once telling the truth. "I accept the inevitable. You belong in the history books. I'm lucky to have you for a father. Are you leaving for Washington today?"

"Yes," he confirmed. "You're the best daughter a man could have, honey. All right. Which college will you go to?"

"Lou-Lou's invited me to Dartmouth."

"As long as you're home for your birthday party at Lutèce. Grandpa and Grandma are counting on it."

She threw her arms around his neck. He smelled of lemony after-shave lotion, a present from Maggie. She loathed the smell of lemons on a man. "I told you years ago not to worry. We're a team."

She made it upstairs to her bathroom in the nick of time. She flushed the toilet to hide the sounds of her puking. She rinsed her mouth, then dialed her old friend.

"Lou-Lou, it's Solange. I need a favor . . ."

Avrim needed a good news story. Solange was driving him crazy, he decided later that week. He was a grown man, letting a kid jerk his balls like some callow, panting youth. She splattered his creative juices, mucked up his thought processes, pulled his strings. If a man's penis didn't rule his brain, he didn't know what did. His personal life interfered with his work. Important work. He resented Solange.

His desk was piled with briefing books, papers, statistical data, and raw information he needed to wade through to prepare for tomorrow's show. He couldn't write a cohesive narrative to save his soul.

Solange had disappeared. Just like that! He didn't go to the disco with her; she punished him by not telling him where she was. He shouldn't let her bother him, but when he was in the United States, he wanted her. Frustrated, horny, he missed her, missed their sex games. He'd called her private number numerous times.

Distracted, he leaned back in his chair, doodling on a pad instead of helping to assemble tonight's eleven o'clock newscast. Swearing it would be the last time, he took a chance, dialed the direct line to the house, not Solange's private line.

"Is she ill?" he asked Pepe when she said Solange couldn't come to the phone.

"She's not here. She went to a college."

That surprised Avrim. Solange couldn't wait to get away from school. "What for?"

"To gather information for her father's campaign."

His hand came crashing down on his desk. Pepe elevated imparting information to cryptic highs. "I don't believe it! Solange hates the political scene."

"You heard me."

"Which college, Pepe?"

"I forgot."

He yelled into the phone. His tone switched to combative. "You live in her house. Pepe, quit playing games. Didn't she give you a number where to reach her? We both know she tells you everything. I'm a busy man. I must speak with her. On business."

Pepe's snort told him what she thought of the business. He didn't doubt she also knew they were having an affair.

"Solange'll be back for her birthday party."

"Back from where?" he asked again.

"Avrim, you're not listening. I'm not her social secretary. Call the senator in Washington. Ask him. Oh, yes, Solange said to tell you not to worry."

"Worry about what?" he asked.

Pepe cursed in Spanish. Not her usual friendly curses, but serious "fuck you" expletives that alerted him.

"I gotta go," Pepe said, "I'm washing the kitchen floor."

"The floor can wait," Avrim barked. "What did Solange mean, 'I shouldn't worry'?"

"Ask her. Good-bye."

Click.

Maggie picked that moment to poke her head in the doorway. "My, aren't you the busy one." She leaned across his desk, reaching for the mason jar.

"Leave the candy alone. You'll look fat on camera."

Maggie unwrapped a lime-flavored lollipop. She licked it, made a face, and dumped the candy into the ashtray. "I wish you'd buy Godiva. I'll settle for Perugina. You're tacky to serve this junk. It's bad enough that a man who commands your princely salary lives in digs the Salvation Army would reject."

"I'm not serving candy," he said sourly. Maggie's comment about his apartment waved a red flag. Solange had complained about it, too. "Maggie, I'm busy. I've no time for chitchat. I'm researching."

"I can see that you are." She moved the pad to examine his squiggle lines. "Are you interviewing Dalí?"

Maggie wore her new cha-cha outfit, a little black mini. Skintight, scooped low at the neckline, the dress revealed the creamy tops of her breasts. With Max in mind, she had purchased it at lunchtime in a 52nd Street boutique. She couldn't resist wearing it out of the store to show her secretary. The robin's egg blue Lagerfeld suit she'd wear on camera hung in her office closet. She shimmied into a chair, crossing a shapely leg.

Avrim let his eyes rove over her. Too bad, he thought glumly, he couldn't be in uncomplicated love with Maggie instead of complicated love with Solange. "Are you on the make or what? You look like a hooker."

She tented ten Manchurian red fingernails. "Darling, I knew you'd love me in this. It's the real me. See, I took your mind off work," she quipped. "I'm wearing this tonight to close an important deal. Women's lib means choice, or haven't you heard?"

He folded an eight-by-ten piece of paper. "Maggie, peddle your crap somewhere else."

She gave him a hard stare. For the past few days he'd acted edgy, jumpy. "You're being shitty rotten. I didn't come here to be insulted. I've got my own troubles. Might I remind you that you requested my help in choosing Solange's birthday present." His interest picked up, too fast, she thought, for a man so consumed with work that he resorted to making paper airplanes and doodling.

"I'm on my way to Tiffany's for Max." It galled her, but she couldn't deny his request. After they had made love she had told him for the first time that she wanted to be married, to go public with their love.

"We're free. I want a baby—your baby, Max, before I get too old." Her nesting instinct surprised her. "I'll quit my job and get tubby fat and read Dr. Spock and buy out FAO Schwartz."

"I'm old enough to be a grandfather," he protested.

Maggie, in love, was relentless. "Bullshit."

"I want it right between us," Max countered with patience. "Besides, sweetheart, you're too ambitious to twiddle your thumbs and weigh in every day."

What he prudently refrained from saying, but what she knew as fact, was his parents' opposition to interfaith marriage. Maggie recalled Barbara Walters asking that question of Max's mother. "I long for the day bigotry ends. Then it won't matter who marries whom," Tessie had said. Maggie's father saw the interview and agreed.

"It's best to stick to your own kind," her father said.

Contributing to her lousy frame of mind today was the knowledge that although Max knew no love was lost between Solange and herself, he asked her to choose a present for the child he loved like a blind fool.

"You have wonderful taste, darling."

It galled her to realize her future happiness depended on his family's approval.

"Make a decision, hot shot," she said to Avrim.

He sent a paper plane flying. She caught it, looped it into a graceful arc, sending it back. He smiled his easy lazy smile. "Shoot, pick up something real pretty, something flashy. I've known Solange all her life."

How well? Maggie wondered.

After she left, Avrim sank back into a blue funk. Solange maddened him even as he wanted her passion all the more. Everything about her stirred him; the hint of her smile, her educated lips, the enticing way she rubbed up against him. At the thought of cupping her buttocks, of her quivering around him as he buried himself inside her, he started to sweat. He shifted to ease the pressure from the rigid bulge in his pants. Damn her. If he could talk to her, he'd offer to make it up to her. He'd put on his best suit, take her dining at La Côte Basque, anything but a crappy disco. As long as the evening ended in bed so he could eat her for dessert.

Disgusted with his mental begging, he snatched up a briefing book. Not for the first time, he wished for a good news story to take his mind off her, not the dull crap coming in over today's wires.

Chapter Ten

Pan Am Captain Fred Hubley apologized to his passengers for the third time. "Unfortunately, folks, these nasty upper air currents aren't cooperating today. To show how sorry we are, drinks are on the house. The flight attendants will be around to take your order. Sit back, relax, and enjoy the rest of your trip. We're estimating arrival into Kennedy in approximately an hour and a half. Off to your left we're passing—"

"I wish he'd shut up," Samara said fiercely. "Do they always give out free liquor, or is it only when we're about to crash?" Groaning, she blocked out the remainder of the captain's folksy news. Pale-faced, she clutched the arms of her seat. Her head on the backrest, she squeezed her eyes shut. She wore a blue denim shirt, its yoke appliquéd with basket-woven satin ribbons and matching appliquéing down her pants's side seams.

"You okay?"

She sent David a withering look. "How can you ask that when we're about to die?"

He prayed for patience. "Read your magazine."

She caught the sharp edge of his tone. "You're so disgustingly unflappable!" she scolded, unwilling to admit to herself what a dashing figure he cut dressed casually in jeans and a light blue crewneck sweater. She'd seen the stewardesses cast admiring glances at him.

The plane took a hard jolt. Frightened, she whipped her head around to David, who remained engrossed in his reading.

"Don't you give a damn that we're going to splash to earth, that we're about to become bird fodder?"

"No, we're not," he said tiredly.

108

An attendant leaned over. "May I get you something?"

Samara ordered a gin and tonic.

David put down his magazine. "You shouldn't drink liquor. Order a Coke."

"You're not my keeper!" she sassed, snapping down her meal tray. When the drink came, she took a swallow, then she fell into a coughing fit.

He shoved a napkin at her. "Satisfied?"

She swiped it from his hand. "Okay, David, get the rest off your chest."

"Forget it." He gritted his teeth. She was remarkably pretty when angry: her eyes lit up like burning sapphires, she pouted her ruby-red mouth in a way that was sensuously attractive, yet for all her appeal he hated being her whipping post.

Samara tapped five pink frosted nails on her empty glass. "I'm ordering another gin and tonic."

David slammed the magazine shut. "Fine. Order a bottle. Drink the whole damn thing. Make a drunken ass of yourself. Who am I to stop you?"

"Your metaphor stinks. I hope you're satisfied!" she snarled, baiting him. "I have a perfect right to be angry. Your parents should have told me the truth. They knew my father was alive!"

He exploded. "What did you expect them to do? Storm into your house, snatch you from under your mother's nose, and tell you about your father? Use your head! Lilli was alive. Given the circumstances, you'd have done the same."

"Don't tell me what I would have done!" she exclaimed harshly. "Why didn't Bella tell me *after* Mama died? Why did I have to discover it the way I did? Why?"

"Lilli made them promise not to tell you he was alive."

"Which proves my original contention," she said stubbornly. "Max Gold discarded us. He robbed me of relatives. I grew up thinking Maman was my only family."

David shuddered. Inexorably the Bousseaucs, Golds, Leightners, and Orchins were intertwined, woven into the web of lies. "Lilli must share the blame."

"How dare you accuse Maman?"

"Don't feel as if you must avenge Lilli. Can you deny she perpetuated the lie? Samara," he argued desperately, "I'm thinking of you. After you speak with your father you may change your attitude. Wait until you know the facts. You need to get on with your life. Your behavior today was inexcusable. You were cruel to people who love you.''

Samara lashed out. ''Bella and Michel are your parents. Naturally you defend them.''

''Your father may not have robbed you of anything,'' David said for the umpteenth time. Samara was too incensed to deal with rationality. He questioned the wisdom of bringing her to his apartment, of placing Wendall in an awkward situation, but to have left her might have caused her more trouble.

He'd rather forget this confusing, miserable trip. She didn't know it, but he had fought bitterly with his parents. He wasn't proud of it. They'd suffered, too, especially his mother.

''You can't help Lilli now,'' he had maintained. ''What else should I know? Tell me. I'll choose the right time to tell her.'' He sensed that his father wanted to tell him something, but his mother had interrupted, saying they knew nothing more. No amount of cajoling on his part had worked.

He understood Samara's pain, sympathized with her plight. He'd done his best to absorb the brunt of her wrath, but it hurt him to see how she rejected his mother.

''Who will we have if she turns on us?'' Bella sobbed.

''You and she are our only family.''

''Give her time, Mama,'' he advised, caught between two loyalties. He preferred to forget the good-bye scene at the airport. Samara standing stiff, her face a cold, beautiful mask. She refused to kiss Bella good-bye. His mother, weeping on the arm of his father. His father leading his mother back to the car. David's heart ached for all of them. He picked up his magazine, hoping to get his mind off the subject.

Samara had a good idea why David was acting so abominably. He was saddled with her. Well, so what! She gripped the arms of the seat. There wasn't one person in the world who understood how alone and confused she felt.

By nature, she hated controversy. Morosely she wondered what would she have done in Bella's place. The liquor helped to calm her agitated state. As the hours passed, she mulled over David's comments. Could he be right? Had she been cruel? Was Bella at fault for keeping Maman's promise?

Suppose Mimi had asked her to keep a promise. She would. She had. She knew things about Mimi her parents didn't know, secrets she'd never tell. Reluctantly she came to the conclusion that if Mimi had asked her to keep a promise of the same magnitude the Orchins kept for her mother, she would. That's what David meant. She couldn't fault Bella for being her mother's dearest friend.

Sickened by her behavior, she choked back a sob. Tears trickled from her eyes. She hadn't meant to be hateful, she just couldn't help herself. Her head buzzed from the liquor. She needed to use the bathroom. She was loathe to maneuver the aisle in the bouncing plane. She wished she were back in Paris with Mimi. More than anything, she wished it were possible to turn back the clock so that none of this heartache had ever happened. But she couldn't, she thought miserably. Her mother, who wanted her and loved her, was dead. Her father, who didn't love her or want her, was alive.

Her lower lip trembled. She rested her cheek on her hand. "David, was I really cruel?"

"Cruel and rude," he said curtly. His eyes were serious. There was no trace of sympathy in his face.

She had stored up nuggets of anger; now they threatened to overpower her. "I didn't mean to be horrible to everyone." Her voice quavered. "I'll write them and apologize. I'll send Comte Levron a thank-you note for using his influence with the American consulate to get me an emergency passport."

Customs Inspector Pete O'Brien shut the young woman's suitcase. She sure was a pretty thing, he thought. Long legs. Great hair. Fabulous figure. Terrific tits. Not too shabby in the rear end department. He'd noticed that when she had bent over to pick up a magazine. Most people struck up conversations with him, particularly the young ones. They thought it distracted him from examining their luggage too closely. Not this one with the huge, sad eyes. She just stood there not uttering a word. Too bad.

His gaze flicked to her tall, grim-faced traveling companion. The inspector prided himself on his ability to read people. She and the boyfriend probably had a spat on the plane. Oh, well, he thought. They'd have fun making up in bed. He stamped her United States passport.

"Welcome home, miss."

"*Merci.*"

Despite her fatigue, despite her reason for coming to the United States, Samara's spirits lifted. Like a volcano's eruption, her fight with David released her stress. From the air, New York's breathtaking skyline had captured her attention, building her natural curiosity and excitement at being in the land of her birth.

"When I saw the Statue of Liberty from the plane, I realized it really does look like a larger replica of our statue at pont de Grenelle. Listen to all the Spanish," Samara said, poking David's arm and pointing toward excited groups of people greeting loved ones.

"America, the land of the melting pot. You'll hear Spanish where I live, too."

"Do you speak Spanish?" Samara asked.

"Yes. I'd prefer speaking to my patients without an interpreter." David hailed a cab to take them to the city.

They bounced over a series of potholes. "Just like the plane. It's hard to imagine that I was born here."

"I promise we'll take a Dayliner cruise up the Hudson. It's very much like the *bateaux-mouches* on the Seine."

"Where are we now?" she asked, her head swinging to see out both sides of the car windows.

"This is the Van Wyck Expressway. Soon we'll be on the Grand Central Parkway, then we go over the Triboro Bridge, onto the Harlem River Drive."

He explained that the huge complexes they passed were low-income city housing, and he told her there were five boroughs in New York. "Bigger arrondissements," he said at her confused expression.

"There's a world of things to see and do in the Big Apple. You'll love Chinatown, Soho, Little Italy, Greenwich Village, Lincoln Center, the Metropolitan Museum of Art."

"I'll never remember," she groaned, halting his recital. "Anyway," she reminded him with a positive force to her tone, "my first priority is attending to family business. Playing tourist will wait."

He hadn't forgotten. He only wished she would forget. On Haven Avenue, between 170 Street and 171 Street, the cabbie drew to a stop in front of the Towers. "Don't expect anything fancy," he said, leading her to the elevator. "It's two bedrooms, a small kitchen, a living room-dining room, and one bathroom.''

"I'm inconveniencing you and your roommate," she apologized.

"Don't be ridiculous," he said, glad to see her in better spirits. "Most of the time we're at the hospital."

She began to speak about her plans, reminding David that she wanted to meet Avrim Leightner as soon as possible. "If I barge in on Judge Leightner, I'll lose my advantage. When you invite Avrim, don't mention me."

David considered telling her his suspicions, but again decided to proceed with caution. He held the elevator door open for her, then punched the button for the eighth floor.

"David!" she protested, conscious of her appearance. "I can't have your roommate see me like this. "I look awful."

"Wendall's not home." He unlocked the second door on the right. "He teaches an anatomy class today. You'll have plenty of time to shower and change."

She took a good look at his home. It was nothing like she'd imagined. Light came from gooseneck brass lamps. Besides a blue couch, a tan recliner, a persimmon wing chair, and a green footstool, there was an ebony Kawaii.

"Wendall's?"

"He plays for relaxation."

"Is he any good?"

"Awful," he said, riffling through a stack of mail. "Whatever you do, don't be polite. Don't compliment him. He'll play encore after encore if you do."

She examined the titles of the books in a large bookcase. The shelves contained medical books, several dictionaries, a few Dick Bolt mysteries, and issues of the Americal Medical Association *Journal of Medicine*.

"The couch opens to a bed. I'll take it, and you can use my room."

"Oh, no!" she protested. "The couch is fine."

He gave her a no-nonsense look. "Doctor's orders."

She wandered into the dining-room area, fingering the scratched surface top of an oak table. She followed him into the bedroom that had a king-size bed, covered by a geometric bedspread. His desk was near the window.

"David, they're lovely," she bubbled, spotting the bouquet

of daisies in an earthenware vase on the night table. The unexpected sound of delight was so welcome to his ears that he came over to give her a gentle squeeze.

He grinned. "There's a surprise in the refrigerator for you when you're ready to eat." She hadn't touched food on the plane.

"What is it?" she asked.

He leaned against the doorjamb, smiling lazily. He was bone weary, yet watching her act like her old self was worth prolonging the time before he went to bed.

"It swims, buttonface, that's as much as you'll get from me." He rapped his knuckles on the door. "Welcome home, Samara. It's good to see you smiling. You ought to smile more. You could be downright pretty when the corners of your lips aren't pointing south."

"You sound American." She laughed, thrilled by his backhanded compliment.

"You're the American," he said, heading for the kitchen to prepare a light supper. In a few minutes, he checked on her. "Are you all right in there?"

"Yes," she called back. "I'm about to shower."

"Are you hungry?" he shouted.

"Famished. I'll be there in a minute."

He'd asked Wendall to buy lox, knowing Samara loved it. He wasn't going to serve it on toast in the manner it was served in France. He'd introduce her to New York bagels, cream cheese, tomato, onion.

Wendall's mother's kitchen rejects were stacked on the yellow Formica counter: a toaster oven, a blender, a popcorn maker, a waffle iron, and a coffeemaker.

He washed his hands, heated two bagels in the toaster oven, then set the round butcher-block table.

Wendall breezed in and clapped David's shoulder. "Hey, welcome home, buddy. You look like shit."

David sliced Bermuda onion. "Sell it to Hallmark. You're no beauty."

Wendall gazed around. "Where's Samara?"

"Primping. For you yet. Poor girl doesn't know how ugly you are. She's in the shower. What are you doing home so early—aren't you teaching?"

Wendall blanched. "Oh, no, I left Murphy—"

"Christ!"

Both men raced down the hall. They weren't in time. Samara's piercing screams rent the air.

"David," she screamed. "There's a dead person in here."

They barged into the bathroom. Samara, wide-eyed with fear, gulping for breath, hovered in a corner. She was also naked—a trembling, glorious, golden-skinned Venus.

She leapt into David's arms, clutching him, rubbing up against him, pressing her naked body so close he felt everything. She sobbed until he thought his heart would break with hers.

His quelling look stopped Wendall from staring.

"Jesus, I'm sorry, pal," Wendall said, snapping out of a stupor. He snatched the plastic skeleton that was hanging from a hook on the back wall of the shower. That was what had frightened her. "I forgot Murphy."

David nodded. He snatched a towel, sheltering her, soothing her, kissing her cheeks, her eyes.

Hysterical, she continued sobbing. She burrowed her head into David's neck. "Shhh, *mon petit chou*. It's plastic," he said, purposely dropping Murphy's name so she wouldn't think in human terms. "Wendall uses it in class. It's plastic, not real, I promise you." Samara was beyond hearing. She'd had enough. She vigorously shook her head.

"David," she whispered, lifting her tear-stained face. "Maman . . . Maman . . . when is she going to become a skeleton?"

"Hush, don't even think such a thing," David said hurriedly. He signaled to Wendall. Wendall raced for his medical bag.

David lifted Samara up under the knees, tucking her close to him, the towel useless as it slipped from her body. Gently he laid her down on the bed, then turned to look for a nightgown. Distraught, she gripped his hand. "Don't leave me," she pleaded. "Don't leave me."

He covered her with the sides of the blanket. "I won't, *mon petit chou*." He bent down, kissing her cheeks, brushing tendrils of hair away from her face. Wendall handed him the hypodermic needle with its vial of peace. He explained he was giving her something to let her sleep, then he quickly inserted the needle. She winced. So did he.

Wendall approached the bed. He tucked the blanket under her chin, shuddering. "I'm sorry, Samara. This is a rotten way for us to meet. Please forgive me. I promise not to bring Murphy home again. Get some sleep now. David, I'd better leave, I'm late."

Neither David nor Samara noticed when he closed the door behind him.

David sat next to Samara for a long time. Where would this end? Hours later an exhausted David left his vigil for his own bed. As sleep overtook him, he wondered how so many sensory impressions could assault the human mind at one time.

Sometime later he heard her whimpering. Groggy, David pulled himself out of bed, dragging his sleep-starved body into the bedroom to check on Samara.

"Dammit!" he muttered, catching his ankle on the bed frame. He fumbled in the dark.

Samara was wide awake, her eyes large saucers in the dark. "I didn't mean to wake you and Wendall," she murmured.

Yawning, David pushed the hair from his forehead. "Don't worry. Wendall's not home. Tomorrow's his day off. He's on a date. What's wrong, buttonface, can't you sleep?"

He wore only pajama bottoms, and in the dim light his chest was broad and magnificent. She lifted her gaze and saw the tender expression in his eyes. "It's just a little strange for me, that's all. David, about before . . ."

"Forget before," he said gruffly. "Do you want me to stay with you awhile?" She nodded. He pulled the blanket aside, slipping into bed next to her.

"Go to sleep, Sam. I've got an early call tomorrow."

She snuggled into the position they'd used for the past week, her derriere tucked into the curve of his body. David thanked God for exhaustion. It was a hell of an epitaph, being grateful his pent-up yearnings wouldn't torment him tonight. Sleep would come easily.

At nine A.M. the following morning, Wendall paused in the doorway to Samara's bedroom. He had spent the night contorting with a cute little redhead from Altoona, P.A., who had come to New York City to be a Broadway star. He had returned for his medical bag. So far all Marsha Dorothy—he called her Maisy Daisy—had landed were one-liners in off-Broadway plays. Comforting the sexy redhead was one of Wendall's best pleasures.

His brow raised at the intimate sight before him. David, clad in pajama bottoms, and Samara, the strap of her sheer peach gown slipping from her shoulder, slept wrapped around each other. Dead to the world, David's hand cupped her breast, and hers flopped over his side.

Wendall glanced at his watch, noting that David was late. He heard him mumble in his sleep, saw him move slightly away from Samara. Searching for him in her sleep, she snagged him back with her foot, throwing one leg over his. Like one, they fitted, snuggled, slept.

Wendall tiptoed down the hall to his bedroom, closing the door quietly behind him. He dialed the hospital, explaining that Dr. Orchin would need three more days to get his affairs in order. Pleased with the pun, Wendall dashed off a note to David, informing him of his lucky reprieve.

He had gotten the answer to a question that had plagued him last night when he saw David kiss Samara. Had they been brotherly kisses? The answer was a definite no. The hard-on he just saw popping out of the slit in David's pajamas was no piss hard-on.

He snapped off the bedroom light. A thought occurred to him as he tiptoed past the room with its sleeping occupants. At the rate those two were going, knowing David, who did everything by the book, he'd soon be out one roommate. Naturally he'd serve as his best man. Maybe his mother would offer to throw the bash at their home. What the hell! He was in a generous mood. He'd give them the furniture and play the piano at their wedding as wedding presents.

Grinning, he left the apartment.

Chapter Eleven

David awakened. When he saw his hand cupped on Samara's breast and felt hers on his throbbing penis, he muttered a low oath, eased off the bed so as not to awaken her, and headed for a cold shower. She couldn't know the hell she put him through. A beautiful, desirous woman with soft, velvet skin and lustrous hair, she made him ache to kiss her until she writhed in his arms and he buried himself in her sweet warmth. He loved her, yet wouldn't dare tell her. The timing stank.

Compared to her youth, his almost twenty-nine years made him an ancient lecher. Yet no one could have been more shocked than he to realize he wanted her in that way. Who'd have thought his *petit chou* would be the woman for him. She simultaneously made him happy and miserable. Miserably happy, he grunted as he splashed cold water on his face.

Wendall poked his head in the doorway. "How is she?"

"She had a nightmare, but she's okay now."

Wendall grinned. "Good. I think you're just *who* the doctor ordered." Whistling, Wendall sauntered into the kitchen to make coffee. David suddenly suspected Wendall had seen them in bed and approved.

Samara awoke blissfully refreshed, unaware of the turmoil she'd caused. She washed and dressed, putting on jeans and a green sweatshirt. She approached Wendall shyly, asking him if she might prepare his breakfast.

He rocked by on his heels. "Best offer I've had in days. David is a klutz."

"No, he's not," she protested, knowing the word Bella often used.

Wendall put the bacon and eggs on the countertop. "Without me to care for him—and now you—he'd starve."

David came into the room. His dark damp locks curled from showering. Dressed in comfortable old clothes, he draped an arm about Samara's shoulders. Her perfume teased his senses.

"I heard that, Wendall. Sam, the first thing you must know about carrot top is that he's a congenital liar. I not only boil water, on holidays I add potatoes." His teasing coaxed a smile from her lips. Unable to stop himself, he sampled a taste. "Good morning," he murmured.

Samara assumed that David acted extra nice to steady her nerves, knowing today she would meet Avrim. Still, having him take the initiative, kissing her, filled her with warmth.

She prepared bacon and eggs, watching like a mother hen as he and Wendall devoured the food. Over coffee she told Wendall her story.

"I wish you well, Samara. You're a brave lady. If I can help, you need only ask." He embraced her, sealing a friendship destined to last a lifetime.

Thinking of the appointment with Avrim, David sought to keep Samara occupied so she wouldn't worry. He explored the neighborhood with her, traversing the huge Columbia University Medical complex, from Ft. Washington Avenue to the stores on Broadway. He introduced her to the owner of the bodega where Wendall and he shopped. She also met Korean shopkeepers and the Puerto Rican couple who owned a variety store. She met the owners of the Jewish delicatessen, where they lunched on corned beef on rye sandwiches and half-sour pickles, washing it down with Dr. Brown's cream soda.

They stopped at the bank where he withdrew several hundred dollars in various denominations, plus assorted change. Seated at the kitchen table, he gave Samara a basic lesson in the monetary system. After some stumbling, she got the knack of it, proudly showing her talent to Wendall who returned to check up on her.

He rumpled her hair. "One good turn deserves another. I'll play the piano for you."

David threw up his hands, objecting. "You don't mind if I leave." Wendall told David to be his guest.

"You're a virtuoso." Samara giggled, watching his hands go up dramatically before crashing downward to attack the keys. The apartment shook with Wendall's discordant, rotten rendition of Chopsticks.

"I sing, too," he teased, beginning another earsplitting enthusiastic round. From the bedroom came the competing high volume sounds of David's radio.

"I hate breaking this up, but I'm due at Neuro in fifteen minutes." He shouted over his shoulder to David, "Sweetie, you can come out now. He lacks culture, Sam, it's disgusting." Rising, he kissed her cheek, squeezed her arm. "Good luck, honey. Avrim's gonna melt. He'll give you all the information you want."

"David, do I look okay?" Samara asked, her stomach hurling insults. The time drew near for Avrim's arrival.

"You're fine," he said, scanning her black dress, white lace collar, back pumps, and pearl earrings. "Quit worrying." What he yearned to say was don't put all your hopes and dreams on this meeting. He didn't want her hurt. He'd much rather tell her how gorgeous she'd looked in bed with her hair tousled on the pillow, her breath feathering his cheek.

The doorbell rang. She made the sign of the cross, tucked a stray hair behind her ear, flew to the couch, threw a pillow behind her back, trimmed her spine, and fastened a smile on her face. Sitting ramrod straight, she heard her heart beat a fast staccato. *This is it!* she told herself.

Avrim's friendly response to David's greeting relaxed her. "I want you to meet a very special lady," she heard him say.

Stopping short in the entrance, Avrim whirled on David. He raked Samara with a look of pure disgust.

"I suppose this is your French version of a practical joke. What part are you playing today in that getup, Solange—Little Miss Innocent?"

"See here!" David objected, snapping out of his surprise. Samara's jaw dropped open.

Avrim railed at the young woman on the couch. "Just don't give me any more of your fucking excuses, Solly, or ask Pepe to lie for you. Where the hell were you all week?"

"That's enough," David said. He'd made a terrible mistake.

"Smart try, Solly," Avrim railed. "David, she may have changed her hairstyle, but I know Solange as well as I know myself. Okay, Solly, you've had your fun. Before I leave I'd like to know when you two met, since you refused to come with me to Columbia. I'm a simple newsman. I like to tie up loose ends."

Samara's initial impression of the anchor whose mustache and white teeth added enormously to his good looks abruptly switched to fear. Reflexively she rose to get away from the madman. With the palm of his hand Avrim shoved her back onto the couch.

"Touch her again and I'll kill you!" David snarled, hauling Avrim backward. "Get out!"

Avrim, incensed at Solange's betrayal, worried sick after speaking with Pepe, remembered the last time he made love to Solange. Afterward she had delighted in tormenting him with her teasing, comparing him to other men.

David's clenched fist galvanized Samara into action. "Don't, David, don't. You'll hurt your hand. I'm sorry," she gulped, her only thought for the man who would never harm a fly. "Don't," she whispered brokenly.

Avrim froze, hearing the true French accent, far different from Solange's Americanized version. "What did you say?" he asked, letting his arms hang limply at his sides.

"I'm sorry," she repeated. Avrim gaped.

David crushed Samara to him, blocking her from Avrim. "Hush, baby, hush. It'll be all right. Avrim, get the hell out!"

He apologized. "I made a mistake. I'm sorry. I mistook you for Solange."

"Save your apology!" David cracked.

"Who are you?" he asked, refusing to budge.

"She's Samara Bousseauc Gold," David answered, rather than let her speak. "We made a mistake in thinking you could help us. Now leave. You've done enough damage."

Avrim reeled, dumbstruck. He'd never known, had never *heard* about Solange's twin. Not from his parents or Max. Certainly not from Solange. He was absolutely certain she had no idea. It was evident that neither girl knew of the other's existence. What a shock!

With Solange tying him in knots, the sisters' likenesses almost identical, he'd been fooled, but upon closer examination he noted subtle differences. Samara's widow's peak was less pronounced than Solange's, who rarely wore her hair back, preferring a softer line. Both shared the same unique hair color. He judged Samara's height equal to Solange's. Samara's eyes were bluer, the dimple in her chin less pronounced. He had a sudden urge to ask her to smile, wanting to see the comparison.

"You owe me an explanation. Why the subterfuge?" Avrim asked.

"We thought the element of surprise better for Samara."

He snorted. "Well, you two sure accomplished your goal." He had strolled in like a lamb to the slaughter.

He pushed his fingers through his hair and slipped off Solange's gift, a Gianfranco Ferre gray silk sport coat. He held up his palms in a gesture of peace.

"Christ, David, relax. You threw me for a loop. I came here expecting to interview you at your suggestion."

With the immediate threat to Samara past, David hesitated. Samara eased out of his embrace. "Wait a minute." She ran into the bedroom, returning with her birth certificate. "This proves who I am."

"I can see who you are," Avrim said. "What do you want of me?"

"I need to know about my father, about why your father wrote these. I want to know why you mistook me for someone else." Samara handed him the letters.

"Just a minute," Avrim snapped. "One thing at a time." He read the letters, first quickly, then slowly a second time, memorizing, categorizing, trying to make sense of seeing his and his mother's names! His father's letters written to Max's wife, a woman named Lilli, dating back over eighteen years!

"Make a pot of coffee," David advised Samara. "We're going to need it."

"Don't either of you con me," Avrim said brusquely. "If this is some kind of plastic surgery blackmail, it won't work."

David gritted his teeth. "It's nothing like that. You knew I flew home on an emergency. I brought Samara back with me after her mother died. She didn't know her father existed until she came across the letters."

"Before I answer anything, I want to hear her tell her story," Avrim stated flatly.

She recounted her story, adding that the letters proved her parents had never divorced. "Who is Solange?"

With David and Samara waiting for his answer, Avrim wished for the wisdom of Solomon; failing that, he wished he could be anywhere but in this sunny kitchen, knowing he was about to set off a powder keg. God alone knew where it would end. "You'll get no further information until I'm satisfied. Why didn't you go to my father with these? He wrote them."

"It was an error," Samara admitted. "Please, tell me about Max Gold. And Solange."

He couldn't stall any longer. "I know it's hard for you to believe your father is a good man. I've known him all my life. For your sake, I advise you to reserve judgment. Surely your mother must share some blame for concealing the truth." He looked at her kindly. "Your father is Senator Max Gold."

Samara gasped. David groaned. "Dammit, I figured as much," he muttered.

Samara whirled on David. "You knew," she accused. "Why did you hide it?"

"I needed proof. It was suspicion, not fact."

Samara's mouth tightened. "Have I a large family?" He said yes. "Grandparents?"

"Alive and well. They own Gold's Department Store in Manhattan on Fifth Avenue, not far from Rockefeller Center where I work."

"David, Jules does business with Gold's!"

He had time for one abstract thought. He should have told her everything he knew or surmised. She needed truth more than protection.

"I know. Go on," David said to Avrim, reassuringly patting Samara's hand. "Where does the senator live? When he's not in Washington, I mean?"

She gave him a hard look. "You should have told me," she said. She wrote down the Riverside Drive address. She stood up and said to Avrim, "I can't stop you from leaving here and warning him. I wish you wouldn't. He's had all these years to know about me. Let me have something?" she asked, a winsome smile lighting her incredible eyes.

It was difficult for Avrim to think of her as Samara, not Solange, yet as she spoke, the differences in pitch and style became apparent. Samara was softer. She unconsciously sought David's approval. Avrim didn't know the connection between the two, but it was evident they cared deeply for each other, that David had withheld information in the hope of sparing her pain if it weren't true. He sensed that beneath Samara's desire to find her father, a frightened young woman relied on him, as if it were the most natural thing in the world. He wondered if they were lovers.

Max shouldn't have cheated his daughters. He blamed his father for being a party to it. "All right. I won't tell him. But you should know your coming here presents problems you couldn't anticipate. Samara, your father is expected to throw his hat in the ring."

David, looking grim, moved to her side, wrapped an arm about her shoulders. From the expression on his face, Avrim knew that David wished he'd kept quiet.

David's worst fears had materialized. Samara was out of her league. He didn't doubt that Murray had written those letters to protect his friend.

Uncertain, Samara asked, "Ring? I don't understand."

"Your father is going to run for president of the United States. If he wins, he'll be the first Jewish president."

A shock wave went through her. "My God! I'm part Jewish." As Avrim's momentous declaration sank in, her anger flared anew, but not at the religious surprise. "He wants to be president!" she stormed, incensed at his arrogance. "Where did he think he was going to hide me?" Recovering from her initial surprise, Samara asked, "You mistook me for a girl named Solange. Who is she?"

Avrim sighed. "Please brace yourself for a shock."

"Jesus Christ!" David exploded, fully as surprised as Samara. He'd never followed Max Gold's family life, only his political stand on the issues. "Hasn't she had enough?"

"It's all right, David. What could be worse than learning what I already have?"

Avrim saw her lower lip tremble and her hand shake. He knew with sudden clarity that for the rest of his life he'd remember her reaction.

"You have a twin sister," he said gently, looking first at her, then at David.

She went numb. Her mind refused to absorb it. "A sister," she whispered at the daunting knowledge. "I have a twin sister."

"Good God!" David cried. He hadn't expected that!

"That's why I mistook you at first. There are slight differences, but to people who don't know you well, who haven't seen you together, you'd look almost identical."

Samara leapt from her chair. Reaction and cold fury set in at the exact moment. She pounded the table, then paced the floor. ''It can't be true!'' she shouted, becoming hysterical, shaking her head, as if the denial would take away the pain of rejection. Her father had kept a child from her mother, a twin sister from her!

Keening, her whole body trembled at the awful cruelty, the tremendous waste, the unaccountable loss of years she could have spent growing up with her twin.

''Does Solange know of me?''

''No,'' Avrim said, thinking of Solange's selfish attitude toward her father, her hatred to Maggie. ''I wish she did.''

Samara wanted to cry, but the tears wouldn't come.

Why? The question screamed in her head. Why had Maman never told her? Why had her father kept silent? Why had her grandparents never contacted her? Why? . . . Why? . . . Why? . . . Why hadn't she been wanted, too?

She shuddered. ''He didn't want us,'' she stated, clarifying the contemptible truth. ''He kept Solange, threw Maman and me out. He never came to see me. Not once. Not a postcard, nothing. I wasn't worth the price of a phone call or a stamp.''

Gently Avrim tried to deflect the blame. With one remaining parent, with her sister Solange, it would be to Samara's advantage to reserve judgment.

''Samara, there must have been a reason your mother went along with this. You must accept the fact that your parents agreed on a course of action, even though you don't yet understand the reasons. I know Solange wanted a mother. She lost out on a mother's love, just as you lost out on a father's love.''

''Madness.'' Samara wept, deaf to the kernel of truth. Her body shook. Bile filled her mouth. She felt nauseated, as if she were swaying on the deck of a ship in turbulent waters. Her knees buckled.

Seething with fury at her parents, David carried her to the sofa, bringing her close to his chest. He murmured words of comfort in French, stroking her knotted spine with one hand, the other hand cupping her head. Max and Lilli had made a terrible mess. Since he couldn't resurrect Lilli, his one over-riding emotion was a violent urge to break Max Gold's neck! David's stormy gaze met Avrim's.

"I wouldn't suggest it," Avrim counseled, correctly reading his thoughts. "At least not until we learn the whole truth."

Earlier Avrim had wished for a good story. Of all people in the business, he would be the one to break the story, report Max's hidden past, perhaps ruin his chances to run for the presidency. Solange despised the press. Once he went on the airwaves with these revelations, she would lump him in with the rest of the paparazzi.

For the first time he resented his job.

Chapter Twelve

Samara sat alone in the back of the taxicab, heading for her father's house. She was amazed at how calm she felt now that the violent hammering of her heart had subsided and she resolved to take matters into her own hands. She had pleaded a headache, telling David and Avrim she needed a walk to clear her head. Putting money in her purse, she thanked Avrim for coming. She told David she'd see him later.

Determined to meet Solange before another day passed, she left the men discussing the daunting ramifications posed by the revelation of her existence. *Remarkable,* she thought, silently repeating the portentous words: *daunting ramifications.* Avrim admitted she posed a high-priority political liability for her father.

Despite Avrim's desire to prepare Solange, she reasoned that if she had been able to live through the shock, so would her sister. In her heart she knew Solange would welcome her. They had come from the same egg!

All during her childhood, she fantasized a perfect companion, a soul mate. Mimi would always be her dearest friend. Twins, however, share a uniqueness, a special bond. They would rediscover theirs. If she had to await the proper setting, the opportune moment, she'd die of nerves. Without knowing the full truth, she couldn't go forward with her life, fulfill her destiny. She refused to live the life of a fractured person.

She envied Mimi's large family. Jules often spoke of his deceased brothers. David's parents kept their relatives alive for him through a rich background of family knowledge, despite their deaths in the Holocaust. Her entire world, thanks to her father's rottenness, had consisted of Maman and herself.

The discovery of the letters formed the bridge to her future. She must learn the truth. When she married David, she wanted to build a healthy family with him. Healthy families have generational pasts. They know their relatives' names, their medical histories. They interact. They establish clear boundaries with each member contributing. Why had her father abandoned her and Maman? Why had he emotionally cut them out of his life?

She smiled sadly to herself as her mother's face came into her mind. She missed her desperately. If only she were alive, she would let her know she forgave her for keeping her secret. Samara stared out the window, forcing her mind to safer channels.

"Where are we?" she asked the driver.

He glanced in the rearview mirror. "You're not from this country. Where are you from?"

She was tempted to tell him she was born on Long Island. "Paris."

"Lucky you. You're pretty enough to be a model."

She blushed.

"I drive this heap to help pay my college tuition. We're on Riverside Drive. That's the Hudson River. Over there is Grant's tomb where Ulysses Simpson Grant and his wife are buried. Grant was a Civil War general and the eighteenth president of the United States."

Her father wanted to be president! "Have you heard of Senator Gold?"

"Sure. Why do you want to know?"

"I'm an exchange student. He's my assignment. What is he like?"

The cabbie stopped for a red light. "We don't exactly travel in the same circles. If you mean do people like him, they like him enough to keep him in the Senate."

She leaned forward. "Do you mind my asking if you approve of him?"

"I don't mind saying I do. He's for the people."

She wondered what he would say if he knew the truth about his respected Senator Gold. "Good luck. This is his house," he said, interrupting her thoughts.

She tipped him generously.

She let her gaze sweep upward to the top of the four-story

house. Beneath its pointed roof, and between the blue painted dormers, a limestone bas-relief depicted a lion. Climbing ivy covered the exterior. French doors on the second and fourth floors led to terraces, surrounded by wrought-iron railings. Had Maman stood on those terraces? she wondered.

Taking a deep calming breath, she marched up to the house before a fresh attack of nerves shot her in the opposite direction. She rang the bell.

A tall, red-haired woman opened the door. Samara recognized her as Maggie McPherson, Avrim's coanchor, having seen her on television the previous night. Makeup had hidden her freckles. "Your father's in a snit, Solange," she said. "You're late."

Samara caught the woman's unfriendly tone, briefly wondered what business she had there, and then everything in her went still as her attention riveted on an elegantly attired man in a blue pin-striped suit, coming to stand near Maggie. *This man was her father!* He had a rugged complexion, dark brown hair sprinkled with gray at the sides, gray eyes, arched dark brows, a well-shaped mouth, and a determined jaw.

He looked annoyed with her.

"Dammit, Solange. I appreciate your help, but the least you could do is arrive home at a decent hour. We'll be late. Have you forgotten your birthday party tonight? Your grandparents will be at Lutèce by five o'clock. Come in and change your clothes."

Samara didn't move. An irrational laugh bubbled in her chest. He had mistaken her for Solange! She had received Solange's reprimand.

"Well?" Max demanded. "What's gotten into you? Aren't you going to say hello to Maggie?"

Samara swallowed hard. After envisioning this scene countless times, she never dreamed he'd greet her with a scolding. She relished his error.

"I'm not Solange. And tomorrow, not today, is our birthday."

His whole body went rigid.

"I'm Samara," she affirmed. Then said to the woman by his side, "Hello, Maggie."

Avrim had said her father personified savoir faire. *Not so,* she thought dispassionately. With breathtaking speed, she had rendered him speechless. His face registered shock and incredulity, and then to her utter surprise, his eyes brimmed and overflowed.

"Samara," he cried in disbelief. Used to suffering his grief in private, Max was unaware that he was in the throes of a violent emotional anxiety attack. His lower jaw dropped open. His hands shook. From the corner of his eye, he saw Maggie reach out to help him, but he waved her off, grabbing the railing for support.

Weak from the joyous knowledge, he barely brought his next words past the lump in his throat. "It's true. It's true. It really is you. God has answered my prayers."

His reaction stunned her. God answered *his* prayers. Tears! From him? From the man who had discarded her! Or were they crocodile tears for the benefit of the television anchor who inadvertently witnessed the return of the living skeleton in Max's closet?

"Max!" Maggie shrieked, staring at him, as if he were a stranger. "Max, what's going on?"

Max had eyes only for his daughter. Questions tumbled from his mouth. "When did you arrive? Where are you staying?"

"Yesterday. I'm staying with a friend."

"You're actually here," Max said, his face breaking into a smile. "Samara, I've dreamed of this day. I never stopped hoping Lilli would let you come to me."

Protective rage for her dead mother welled inside Samara. "How dare you lay blame for your absence on Maman! Were you so poor you couldn't write a card? Or call?"

"There's much I have to explain. Lilli, how is she? You can't know how happy I am that she's finally changed her mind. I've wanted this for years."

Samara recoiled. "I don't know what you're talking about. Maman died ten days ago. You're a widower. You can stop acting."

Max gasped. As if hit by a body blow, he sagged against the door. From his throat came an unrecognizable sound. "How?" he cried. Both he and Samara ignored an ashen-faced Maggie, her pallor matching Max's.

Samara sketched the essential facts. "Maman was struck by a car. I buried her in Saint Chēron, near Chartres."

"Why there? Why not Paris?"

"Maman loved Chartres. We were planning a trip there for my birthday." The words blurred as the tears rolled slowly down her cheeks. "I wanted to bury her close by."

Shuddering, Max covered his face with his hands, taking a few moments to recover his composure. He reached out to cup Samara's cheek. His sadness, his genuine sorrow, kept her from slapping away his hand. For the first time in almost two decades he touched his daughter, and both knew it to be momentous.

"We were married in the nave at Chartres." He wiped his eyes. He remembered the young wife he had brought home to love forever. But that hadn't happened. His wife had run away from him. She had stolen his child, set down inhumane restrictions. At Murray and Ceil's urging, he had sought understanding from a psychiatrist.

The physician lacked a family history to help unravel Lilli's problems. He conjectured her sheltered religious background, being a war orphan, her extreme difficulty in adjusting to America, and, more specifically, acceptance of her Catholicism by Max's Jewish parents presented obstacles she couldn't emotionally overcome. "We take suicide threats seriously. Perhaps she needs to see France again, to familiarize herself with the world. Give her time. Maybe, if you don't press her, she'll change her mind and return."

Max accepted Lilli's conditions, hoping she would change her mind. She never did, although he had tried unsuccessfully more than once to make that happen with Murray Leightner's help. He hid his personal anguish, showing one face to the public and another to his mirror. He cried in private, sobbing and clutching a baby blanket of Samara's until there were no more tears left. He toughed it out for the sake of Solange and his sanity.

Max sighed. How ironic. He was living a Greek tragedy. An airplane ticket to Paris lay in his desk drawer. He'd planned to see Lilli himself, speculating that after all these years, she'd see he wasn't a threat to her. He wanted her to know his political plans, beg her to see reason, bring the girls together. Besides, he deserved a life. He loved Maggie, wanted to be free to tell her the truth, to ask her to marry him. She wanted children. Even at his age the thought of starting a family appealed to him. The church would grant Lilli an annulment. He'd made inquiries. By November when he would announce his campaign to run for the presidency, the story would have died down, providing they presented a united front to the press. Politically, his opponents would see the wisdom of not attacking his private life, especially since he'd been scandal free. No candidate wanted to chance alienating either the Jews or the Catholics or both.

While Max thanked God for Samara's safety and at the same time experienced a new turmoil, her emotions skidded, flying off into uncharted directions. Devoid of sanctuary, her consoling hatred went haywire, muddling her primary objective: to learn what caused her family to unravel, a family that now included a twin. She had steeled herself to meet a suave, controlled politician. At best he would treat her untimely intrusion into his life in a cold or cordial manner. Instead he invoked God's prayers and devoured her with his eyes, as if he were afraid she'd vanish.

"There's so much we have to say to each other. You, Solange, and I."

"You're eighteen and a half years too late," she said tightly, unwilling to ease his conscience. "I came to meet my sister. I have only one question. Why did you throw Maman and me out?"

Max cast a worried glance at Maggie. "Please come inside, Samara. Solange will be home soon. We'll talk. Maggie, I know you have to get back to the studio. I'll call you later and explain."

Maggie felt as if he'd stabbed her in the heart. "I'm staying." Her tone matched the ice in her eyes. "Apart from the fact that you've lied to me, too, all these years, Senator Gold, this is a breaking news story."

"Maggie," he implored. "I wish you wouldn't. If not for my sake, then for Samara's. She doesn't merit being put under a microscope."

Maggie snorted. "You've run out of options. You've heard the saying 'What goes around comes around.' The public deserves to know your ability at deception before they cast a vote for the presidency."

Solange sat in the back of a cab, retracing the same route her sister had taken earlier. Instead of looking out the window at the familiar sights, she took out her gold compact from her Judith Leiber purse, both presents from Avrim. She examined her creamy skin, her long lashes, and her bright eyes. She looked the same.

Lou-Lou's doctor performed the abortion, accepting in advance his fifteen-hundred-dollar fee. She couldn't stand him or the series of questions he tossed over his shoulder as he washed his hands.

"Who is the baby's father? Does he agree with this abortion? He has a right to know, young lady. You didn't do this by yourself."

For the "occasion" she purchased a black wig, filled in a false medical history on the form his nurse handed her. Apparently her answers satisfied the doctor. The next thing she knew she was on a table being suctioned.

"Honey," he teased, washing his hands again. "We both know you're a natural blond. You didn't need to wear that hideous wig or lie to me. I did this as a onetime, special favor for Lou-Lou. I know your real name, not the phony one on the chart. I'm no quack. Had anything happened, I would have contacted your father. If you get caught again, use another doctor. Your dad wields a lot of power. I'm happy with my life the way it is. I don't need hassling from the medical board. For the record, I'm advising you to abstain from intercourse for six weeks. The nurse has your instructions. She'll tell you when you may leave. Have a nice day."

On the way down the elevator, Solange considered the doctor's advice. Six weeks abstinence. That ought to go over big with Avrim. By then they'd be clawing at each other. He'd accuse her of sleeping around. She knew she shouldn't tease him, but she couldn't help herself. Sex with Avrim after she riled him up was the absolute best sex in the world. She loved it when he took her with violence. God, what a turn-on! Three weeks, she decided. Three weeks at the most.

"Lou-Lou," Solange remarked that night as she relaxed on the spare bed in her friend's room. "This sounds nutty, but I half expected after the suctioning for the doctor to say, 'You may spit out now if you wish,' like my dentist does. What do you think of him?"

"Charles is rather wonderful," Lou-Lou replied, which brought Solange's keen examination to her savior, the only good result of her stay at Regents Academy. Lou-Lou, the academician, rarely gushed over topics more modern than ancient Greek mythology. Lou-Lou's fabulous waterfall brown hair lay straight down her back. Her eyes shimmered with tears, which she quickly brushed away.

Solange's eyes widened. "Don't tell me Charles fathered your baby?"

Lou-Lou took her lower lip between her teeth and stared down at the rug, before bringing her eyes upward. "Charles and I love each other madly. Unfortunately he's married and has four children."

"Unfortunately for you, you mean," she snorted. That louse dared to counsel her! "What if he knocks you up again?"

Lou-Lou winced. "He won't. He tied my tubes. His wife is a bitch. She'll never divorce him. I don't want to get married."

Like hell you don't.

As a favor to Solange—who decided it would be smart after all to poll the students—Lou-Lou asked her students if any of them would vote for Senator Gold for president. Most believed the United States could be governed better by anyone other than Jimmy Carter, who barely received fifty percent of the total vote when he ran. A minority of the thirty students queried said they would consider voting for Senator Gold for president, providing his stand on the issues coincided with theirs. Carter had carried the South for the Democrats in 1976, but he lost Virginia. His thin plurality had depended on his huge margin among the blacks, rather than the southern whites. To win the presidency, Max must carry the South.

Solange gave Lou-Lou her evaluation. "My father's liberal, people-oriented, northern background might work against him in the South. He has always championed the minorities, and he's smear free. On the other hand," she added gloomily, "he looks terrific on television."

"How do you feel about hitting the campaign trail?"

Solange made a face. "How would you feel about a steady diet of rubber chicken and Holiday Inns?"

Lou-Lou chuckled. "Point taken. Do you intend to marry Avrim one day?"

Solange turned thoughtful. "No. I love him, but he and I don't see eye to eye. One thing, though, I'll never give up Avrim. He'll always be mine."

All in all, Solange concluded as the cab neared her home, her sojourn to Hanover, New Hampshire, had resulted in a personal victory on two counts. She wasn't going to be a mommy, and neither Charles nor Lou-Lou would say anything. Knowledge is power. The man's a shit with a medical degree. Lou-Lou ruined her life. No amount of makeup hid the puffiness under her eyes. Still, her friend's secret guaranteed her privacy. Silver linings. You find them in the most unexpected places. Now she wanted nothing more than to sneak into the house and rest for an hour before dressing to go to Lutèce . . . and pretending to be thrilled.

She paid the driver, then glanced up. Her luck! A welcoming committee at the front door. Her father and Maggie, who for once looked like hell as if she'd been run over by a steamroller. Solange's gaze swept past her to the third person.

"Here's Solange," she heard her father say. Her high heels clicked up the path, bringing her closer to the trio.

Samara whirled around.

Astounded, Solange gaped at her mirror image. "What the fuck is going on here? Who are you?"

Max made the introductions. Samara's first impulse was to touch, to reach out, to grab her sister's hand, to hide behind a locked door, and to talk and talk and talk. For hours, days, months, however long it took to fill in the blanks. She understood her sister's shock. They were absolute strangers, look-alikes introduced by a father familiar to one, unknown to the other. Inherently cautious and reserved, Samara vacillated between a desire to throw her arms about Solange and kiss her, or respond with a "How do you do."

To say Solange was dumbfounded would be an understatement. The surprises she liked came wrapped in expensive paper, fit in the palm of her hand, and could be worn on her finger. When she judged herself in a mirror, she saw with satisfaction a stunning, uniquely beautiful girl with a full pretty mouth, a delicate neck, and slim shoulders, whose face was dominated by slightly almond-shaped blue-green eyes, long curly lashes, and incandescent hair. The best thing about her was her originality, her very oneness. With a well-defined instinct for preservation, she knew Samara's sudden reappearance spelled a shift in the status quo. "I never dreamed you existed," Solange stammered.

"Nor I, you." Samara sadly told her of Lilli's death. Solange gasped. With narrowing accusing eyes, she swung her gaze to Max. "You owe me an explanation."

"To us both," Samara agreed, reveling in the new, heady kindred spirit she felt for her sister.

"Samara," Solange asked, testing the name on her lips, "where do you live?"

"Paris," Samara replied, giving vent to happy tears.

"Will you be staying in America?"

"I wasn't sure at first, but now I think I will stay. You're my only family, Solange. We've found each other at last. Isn't it wonderful?"

Not by a long shot! Solange didn't relish a clone. She hid her true feelings by returning Samara's embrace.

The present and the future were all that mattered to Solange. She had no intention of squandering time or energy mourning a mother who had rejected her. What was wrong with her, for God's sake! How could her mother not want her? If it weren't for that woman, *she* never would have attended those lousy boarding schools. She still remembered the nights she whispered in the dark to a make-believe mother. In fact, now that the shock was wearing off, she was damn mad. If her mother stupidly left her to live in France, she deserved her fate. Curiosity aside—and she would demand answers!—she would let no one, least of all Samara, intrude on her turf.

"Come inside," Max said.

Samara, intensely curious about the house, followed the others through an Italian marble foyer into the library. She admired the masculine mix of antiques and leather. One wall of the large room housed a fireplace, embellished with a mantel that displayed a picture of Max shaking hands with President Carter, another of a sparkling Solange dressed in a peacock-blue, pearl-trimmed gown with matching silk georgette shawl. The furniture facing the fireplace consisted of a comfortable cinnamon leather and nailhead-trimmed sofa, a matching chair, and an ottoman. Max's walnut desk shone with the warm glow of rich patina. Hanging behind his desk were plaques honoring years of public service.

"Did I ever live here?" Samara asked.

"For the first nine months of your life. I have pictures of you and Solange."

He felt the fusillade of three pairs of sharply probing eyes. What could he say to Maggie? "By the way I forgot to tell you I was still married." To his daughters? "Your mother threatened suicide. She hated America, refused to learn English, couldn't make the interfaith adjustment. She resented my being in politics." He could see how that would go over. With Lilli dead, unable to defend herself, he didn't dare risk the truth. Even if Solange would forgive him, Samara would not.

The explanations—plausible excuses at best—would have to wait. He first needed to check with Murray to question him about the contents of the letters, to learn what Samara knew. Hindsight told him that he should have requested to read Murray's letters before he mailed them.

Solange and Samara sat. "What's she doing here?" Solange pointed to Maggie. To think she had frittered and worried about Maggie. If nothing else, she had the satisfaction of seeing the look of dawning misery on Maggie's Irish puss. Maggie was dead meat. She'd been shacking up with a married man without knowing it.

"Why don't I start the interview, Senator Gold." It wasn't a question.

"This isn't an interview, Maggie. I admit I owe you an explanation, but this isn't the time."

Maggie sizzled. "On the contrary, Senator, you owe the country answers regarding your hidden past. Breaking news never makes an appointment. Either you give me the interview, or I phone in the story with what I have so far."

Max went to a sideboard, poured a Scotch, and knocked it back in one gulp. "All right, Maggie."

"When did you and your wife part?"

"Before the girls reached their first birthday." Her brows shot up. "You never divorced?" she prodded, her anger obvious to all. Max shook his head. "Never filed for divorce?"

Samara gripped the edge of her chair.

"No," Max said quietly, keenly aware of the effect on Maggie and the girls.

Maggie's hand trembled. "Your choice or hers?"

Max's heart doubled pumped. Maggie's scent drifted past his nose. Last night she had lain in his arms; he had dabbed perfume on her breasts, her stomach, her thighs, before sinking himself into her warmth. "It was a mutual decision."

Maggie persisted. "Why?"

He shoved his hands deep in his pockets. "I doubt if the public needs to learn old news. They'll vote on the issues."

"Wrong," she scoffed. "Personally I want my leader to be a man whose moral code isn't in doubt."

Solange hooted.

"So do I." Max said. He knew how deeply he'd hurt Maggie. For a brief moment his gaze locked with hers. She blinked back the tears.

"All right. Next question. Why have you hidden your other child?"

"I didn't hide her."

"Sorry. I'll rephrase the question. Why did you keep her a secret?"

Max's patience unraveled. "I haven't hidden her or kept her a secret. I'm delighted she's here."

"So delighted you've never spoken of her?"

"Maggie," Max beseeched, "I'll issue a press release after I speak with my children. Not before."

She scribbled. "The senator refused to answer."

"Really, Maggie, that's enough!" Solange cried. "Where do you come off interfering with family business? You and the rest of the news sharks can wait. Wouldn't you prefer privacy, Samara?" From her twin's vindictive undertones, Samara assumed Maggie's involvement with Max was more than professional, and thinking of Lilli's pristine existence, she resented the years Lilli had spent alone.

Maggie ignored Solange's verbal jab. "Samara, the press will want to interview you, find out where you've been living. They'll ask questions about your mother."

"Maman is dead," Samara replied. "She was a very private, religious woman. Can't we leave it at that?"

"Don't you care about the damage you'll cause if you put this on TV tonight?" Solange asked, her energy revitalized. Smelling her advantage, she rose and glided to her father. She tucked her hand into his. If she played her cards right, eliminating Maggie would be like shooting a sitting duck.

"Samara's only just come back to us," she purred. "We're dying to talk with her, to welcome her into our home. How could you be so crass?"

"Crass!" Maggie seethed. "This isn't one of your little

dinner parties where you control the guest list. This is the real world! What you don't know about it and politics can fill all those books on the shelves, so butt out.''

Secretly delighted, Solange audibly sucked in her breath, feigning insult. ''If father is too polite to ask you to leave, I'm not.''

Max eased away from Solange. He sent Maggie a pointed look, then said more sharply than he intended, ''I'd appreciate it if we all calmed down.''

Without asking permission, Maggie picked up the phone, dialing Avrim's direct line to his news desk. In moments she told him she was detained at Max's. She ask him to cover for her.

''Does this have anything to do with a girl named Samara?''

''Yes.''

''Damn. Maggie, I met her today. It was a total shock for both of us. You remember meeting David Orchin at Columbia. He brought her back from Paris. They go way back together. He's extremely concerned about her. She's had a very rough time compounded by the shock of learning she has a father and a twin sister. Christ! I can imagine Solange's reaction. Maggie, my father wrote letters to Max's wife. Let's not hurt innocent people. Another day isn't going to matter.''

Without replying, Maggie hung up.

The darkening sky washed patterns of mauves and blues and grays through the panes of beveled glass. A strong, steady rain had begun falling. Its sounds dripped discordant notes on the windowsill.

Solange said,''In view of the circumstances, I think it would be wise to call Lutèce. Tell our guests I've got a twenty-four-hour virus and had hoped to be well enough to attend. Invite everyone to have a wonderful time on us.''

''Good thinking.'' Max rubbed a hand across his forehead, his mind accepting the wisdom of Solange's suggestion. ''Girls,'' he said, pridefully aware he had included Samara, ''I'd appreciate a few minutes alone with Maggie. Call the restaurant, Solange. I'll join you girls in a little while.''

Samara was only too happy to leave the emotion-charged room so that she could be alone with her sister.

Solange paused at the door for one final dart. ''All I can say is the Senator's a lucky man to find out who his true friends are, and who's been using him to get ahead.''

The moment the twins left, Maggie denounced Max. ''You married bastard. You fucking liar! You shit! Oh, you took me in all right! I should have listened to my father. He doesn't trust politicians. 'We can't marry because of the campaign,' you said. When I think how I told you that I wanted a baby. Your baby! How you must have been laughing! You'd still be lying if your secret child hadn't arrived on your doorstep. Couldn't you have trusted me? Are you such a politically arrogant animal that you would allow your blind ambition to invade our bed?'' She wept openly, as if she were delivering her own eulogy.

''Maggie, I love you,'' Max pleaded, trying to find a way to convince her, to take the hatred from her voice. ''I wish I had been free to marry you. Don't you think I, too, dreamed of a new beginning for me, a family with you? I couldn't tell you.'' His hand snaked out to seize her arm.

''Go to hell, you lying bastard! You trust me to select a present for your precious Solange, but not with something as important as this. Love, you bastard, means trust!'' She quivered with indignation, putting distance between them. She dug into her purse for a tissue. ''Don't you dare try to manipulate me. You with your convenient amnesia! We both know AP and UPI will move this on the wires. You're hot news, Senator Gold. You'll make both television and print news.''

''Maggie, please.''

''You're too late.''

''Yes, love means trust. It also means protecting your children. Whether you accept this or not, Maggie, I do love you. You've been the only other woman in my life, and yes, I lied to you. I lied by omission. I sinned. I had no option. I still don't. I'm pleading with you not to go public with this for Samara's sake. Samara's young. She's hurt. Bitter. She just buried her mother. Surely you can appreciate what she must be going through. I wish I were free to tell you why I had to remain silent all these years. I'm not. All I can say is that my wife wasn't emotionally strong. A long time ago I lost her and Samara. It broke my heart, but I survived. I beg you, give me time to bring my family back together. Solange lost a mother, too.''

Maggie beat his hand away from her. ''Spoken like a politician. The right syrupy soap opera touch. Suppose you tell me what kind of people contrive to tell children one of their parents is dead?''

His lips thinned. A muscle jerked along his jaw. ''The worst kind. All right!'' he hissed, losing his temper under the strain. ''Whatever else you think of me, Maggie, know this. I'm willing to do anything—give up anything—if it will ensure Samara's happiness.''

''The presidency, too?'' Maggie asked, almost willing to take him on faith, to forgive him.

''If necessary.'' He tried to take her in his arms.

Maggie stiffened. She had seen the flicker of doubt in Max's eye, lured by the prize: the White House.

''Go to hell, Max,'' she blazed. ''For Samara's sake— because I fully sympathize with her, not you, not Solange—I'll sit on this story for twenty-four hours. Then you can expect a full media blitz. The works. I'll rake you over the coals if another reporter goes on the air with this story first. Call it payment for services rendered.''

He dragged his hand through his hair. ''If you insist on going on TV with this because I've hurt you deeply, or because the reporter in you must be satisfied, then say this: Senator Gold wishes to announce his great pleasure in having his daughter Samara home in her native country, America. Until the recent death of her mother, she resided in Paris. The senator appeals to his constituents for a few days of privacy, to give him and his family a much-welcomed reconciliation. He reminds everyone this is a difficult time in his daughters' lives.''

Maggie shrugged off her first twinge of uncertainty, conscious of the way her senses heightened, knowing she had the power to help destroy him. Supported by Max's love, she had known cocky, self-confident happiness. Whenever they were together, he had treated her like a princess. *Idiot,* she told herself, *idiot for being Max's mistress!*

''You're good, Max,'' she said, hiding behind her wall of anger. ''I hope the next woman you dupe won't take as long as I did to catch on to your technique.''

''Stop it, Maggie. I won't grovel. Not even for you. You

couldn't begin to know what I've lived through, so shut up. Take your wounded pride and leave me alone. If you want to ruin me, then do it. I can't stop you. We've both learned something—neither one of us is a paragon of virtue. You think I'm a lying bastard, and I think you're heartless for not trusting me when I can't help myself. Have I ever asked anything of you? Ever?''

Images of them through the years ricocheted through her mind. Carefree countryside picnics. Making love on a carpet of grass. Trysts in Canada. A weekend in a cabin in the Catskills. Max, virile and handsome, lugging in firewood that he had chopped. Cruising the sun-drenched lime-green Caribbean aboard a luxurious private yacht. New Year's celebrations with the Leightners. Always racing toward each other. She had been so in love. She hadn't listened to her family. Max had been her idol.

Pushed by demons, Maggie lashed out. ''One last question. For me, not the press. Had your wife reappeared on the scene, would you have taken her back?''

Max briefly closed his eyes. He thought of his parents, the awful days following Lilli's disappearance.

''Good riddance to bad rubbish,'' his mother had said. ''Let the bitch go. Thank God we have Solange.''

Retribution, Max thought. Everyone, including Maggie, had a thirst for retribution. ''Your question is moot. Lilli never had any intention of returning.''

Maggie seethed. ''What an opportunistic ass you are. So why didn't you tell me? Wasn't the time ever right? Are you such a fucking coward, Max, that you couldn't trust me? Is it because you thought I'd blackmail you?'' She slapped her forehead. ''Of course! How stupid of me! You thought I'd hop from bed to television with a scoop! Well, far be it from me to prove you wrong!''

The electrically charged air eddied around them.

His eyes narrowed. ''Don't cheapen yourself, Maggie.''

Coldly furious, she snapped, ''You can stop hiding behind the Fifth Amendment.'' Grabbing her purse, she swept out the door. ''So long, Max.''

Pain settled on his features. Lines cragged his forehead and bracketed his mouth. He advanced toward Maggie, then halted, watching her go out of his life. She was so beautiful, with her milk-white skin, her slender neck, her thick lashes tipped with dark mascara. He stood at the window for several long moments, his jaw clenched. In his pocket was a jewelry box, delivered from Cartier. He had planned to present her with an emerald pendant to match the color of her eyes.

Max knew again what living hell meant. His heart thundered in his chest. He fell into the nearest chair, burying his face in his hands. He had loved Lilli with every fiber of his being, but that love hadn't been enough to make her want to stay with him. When Lilli took hope from him, years of desolation passed. Then one bleak November day Maggie McPherson had breezed into his office, a young, gorgeous, intelligent woman. She fired a series of questions at him. He sat gawking at her, trying desperately to make his answers sound sensible. A business luncheon followed, then another, until he ran out of excuses to disguise his growing need for her.

Twice in his lifetime love had come to him when he least expected it. Maggie taught him to love again. Today he repaid her with the cruelest of lessons.

He destroyed her trust.

Chapter Thirteen

Samara stepped into a gilded cage lined with cerulean-blue quilting. "You own an *ascenseur*!"

Solange dismissed the extravagance. "There are four floors. My room's on the third. I usually use the stairs. It's good exercise." She didn't add that after an abortion the elevator was a godsend.

Samara peered at a small drawing on one wall. "Goodness! Is this a Matisse?"

Solange shrugged. "Yes. This place is a goddamn art gallery and museum. If you like Impressionist paintings, we've got a slew. If it's old, we've got it. For reasons beyond my understanding, our father prefers wandering around in another century. The dining-room furniture is Regency, with bull's-eye mirrors, a neoclassical chandelier, and Chinese urns on pedestals. It makes no sense. You can't imagine how often I've pleaded with him to let me redecorate. Eclectic is the kindest thing you can say about this place."

Samara thought it sounded wonderful.

The elevator stopped.

Samara dragged her feet behind Solange. She didn't know where to look first—at the Chinese silk wallpaper, the delicately painted Sheraton chairs, the green-and-gold velvet Louis XIV settee, centered by a Louis XV *table à écrire*, the Lalique and Sèvres vases filled with scented roses, or the Impressionist paintings.

In the doorway to Solange's bedroom, Samara stifled a gasp. Astonished by its opulence, she let her gaze sweep the light and airy suite, noting the gleaming woods, the Régence desk, the alcove for the king-size bed, the Renoir and Monet, and the superb pier glass.

Samara wondered what had gone wrong between her parents. The splendor raised feelings of unbearable sadness. Her mother must have suffered greatly. Why else would she flee her husband, child, and a lavish home on a tree-lined drive with its impressive frontage on the Hudson River? Why would she settle for life in a drab apartment? Why would she deny herself personal happiness?

Solange banged the bedroom door shut and lit a cigarette with one hand while she dialed Lutèce with the other, then asked to speak with her grandmother. She made her excuses without once mentioning Samara. All motion, she kicked off her shoes, yanked Samara's arm, and pulled her to the mirror. "Look at us. We're bookends. When you speak, it's as if I'm speaking with a French accent."

Their dual images dazzled them, and they examined themselves critically. In short order they stared, measured heights back-to-back, and launched into a breathless tumble of comparison. Samara announced her eyes were bluer. Solange countered that her widow's peak was more pronounced. Samara divulged she'd had measles at the age of four. Both girls had had their tonsils removed at age seven. Both giggled when they learned they shared an allergy to peas. Both loved to sing. Neither could carry a tune. Neither cared. They tolerated school, deplored spelling. Both had started their menses at thirteen. Each wanted to know who was older.

"I squeaked through my first year of NYU." Samara gave her a blank look. "NYU, New York University. I refused to go to an out-of-town university."

"I never went to university."

"Why not?" Solange asked, envying her.

"No money." Then Samara brightened. "Now that's all changed. And thanks to Jules LeClaire, I'm learning couture. One day I'll be famous. Jules's daughter, Mimi, is my best friend. What are you going to do with your life?"

"I'm going to give parties."

"That's what you want to do?" Samara asked, her tone dubious. "Give parties?"

"Damn right," Solange replied, puffing smoke. "Parties should be statement-making events. Some people freeze. Don't let anyone kid you—choreographing a gala, a charity function, or an intimate dinner is as much an art form as painting or designing. The canvas changes. You work with diverse personalities. The trick is to keep the style the hostess wants, yet make a statement. The color scheme of the linens, flowers, music, and food contribute to the visual effect. I gave my first party for the Senator when I was fifteen. Worked like a charm.''

Samara considered that bit of news. ''I imagine you'll give your fill of parties if he wins the presidency.''

''No.'' Solange slowly shook her head. She let a rueful smile touch her lips. ''You saw Maggie. All she thinks of is her career. She'll go on TV with this. Dad's probably downstairs planning his strategy. You may have ruined his chance. Don't you see the problem? A daughter, literally dropping out of the sky. I admire you, Samara. I wouldn't have the courage to face a parent who rejected me. Be prepared. Despite the act he'll put on later, he wishes you'd disappear. Let's face it, he's planned his entire career to run for the presidency.''

Samara scowled. ''How do you feel about my being here? I thought you loved him. You don't sound very loyal.''

''Oh, I do love him,'' Solange quickly demurred. ''He's wonderful to me, but I'm not blind to his ambition or his ego. Incidentally, why do you wear a cross? Did a friend give it to you?''

Samara fingered the crucifix. ''I'm Catholic.''

Solange burst into laughter. ''You're what?''

Samara scowled. ''Catholic.''

''That's rich. That should thrill Tessie and Barney. Our grandparents have a thing about religion. When did you convert?''

Samara looked stunned. ''I didn't. Maman was Catholic. So are you.''

''Ridiculous! I was bas mitzvahed!''

''Doesn't Jewish law say a child is the religion of the mother?''

''Bullshit! She may have been *your* mother. She sure as hell wasn't mine! My *mothers* were a series of servants, most of whom spoke Spanish!''

Samara bristled. ''Don't you dare condemn Maman! While you lived in luxury surrounded by antiques and priceless works of art dripping from every wall, I lived in an apartment on a treeless street in a working-class neighborhood! We worked. Hard. I didn't attend fashion school. I modeled. How do you think I felt learning I have a Jewish father? A senator who wants to be president!''

''What have you got against Jews?''

Samara nearly blurted out that she loved a Jew. ''Nothing. Our best friends are Jewish.''

Solange rolled her eyes. '''Some of my best friends are Jewish,''' she mimicked. Samara's chin jutted forward. Her eyes narrowed, sending a warning signal through Solange.

''Okay,'' she said. ''My mistake. Let's both calm down. If we go at each other's throats we'll never get anywhere.''

Samara refused. ''No. I prefer to discuss this. You intimated our grandparents are prejudiced.''

With the cigarette clamped between her lips, Solange threw up her hands. ''Christ, Samara! Stuff it. If they hate Catholics, why do they love me? As you said, we have the same Catholic mother. In a few minutes,'' she added, artfully concealing her motives, ''our father's going to join us. We'd better have a list of questions ready.''

''I have one. Why did he desert Maman and me and keep you?''

''Reverse that and you have my question. Until today I believed my orphaned mother perished in a fire. Naturally you didn't exist. The accident happened while they were out of the country. Papa couldn't bring her body home for the burial. How about you? What excuse did she give you?''

Samara's throat constricted. ''My orphaned father drowned at sea.''

Solange snorted. ''How disgustingly unoriginal. By eliminating their bodies, they eliminated the charade of us visiting graves. They conveniently wiped themselves out.''

Samara shook her head, her face reflecting her dismay.

''How did you find out?'' Solange asked. Her manner guarded and cautious, Samara told her about the letters.

''It's logical. Murray is Dad's best friend, his personal attorney. Naturally he'd honor his lawyer's oath of confidentiality. It proves our parents made a pact to conceal the truth from us.''

Contemplating the perfidy implied in Solange's accusation,

despair brought tears to Samara's eyes. "*C'est impossible*. Maman never—"

"*C'est* very possible," Solange snorted. She stubbed out her cigarette and lit another. "Lilli must have asked about me in her letters."

"I have no idea what Maman wrote to Mr. Leightner. He only mentioned his wife and Avrim."

"On her deathbed, before she died, did she realize her error?" Solange prodded. "Did she leave a message for me?"

A pain, a physical ache, gripped Samara as she struggled to understand her mother's reason for saving the incriminating letters. Surely there had to be a higher reason. But what? In a burst of understanding, it came to her. Samara hugged her sister, who, caught unguarded, stood with her hands at her sides, the cigarette dangling from her lips.

"Don't you see, Solange? Maman wanted us to meet, to love each other. Her spirit guided me to you. That's why she kept the letters. She's here. I can feel her presence in this room. Can't you?"

Solange couldn't feel a thing. She didn't believe in religious mumbo jumbo. "No, I can't. She did a shitty thing to me—to us."

Unwilling to brand Maman, yet sharing her sister's loss, bonded by birth, Samara offered a pledge. "I want us to be friends, true sisters."

Solange sidestepped the pledge with a question. "Why did you contact Avrim? Why not Murray?"

"David knows Avrim. Oh, dear! May I use your phone?" Solange nodded. "David needs to know where I am."

"Who's David?"

"David Orchin. He flew to Paris for me. I live with him."

Solange choked on smoke, smarting her eyes. She viewed her twin in a new light. Despite the loosening of moral restraints, she had avoided testing her father's old-fashioned mores, especially with marvelous Maggie lurking in the wings. As long as she continued to live at home, Max would feel obliged to live there, too, if only to keep an eye on her. Which suited her fine. "You're living with a man."

Samara dialed the number. "Two men," she replied distractedly.

"Two men? Who is the other one?"

"Wendall Everett-Lawson. He and David practice medicine at Columbia-Presbyterian Medical Center."

Solange let out a low whistle. "Wendall's society. I know his cousin Mavis." Personally she abhorred doctors, her opinion reaffirmed by the sleaze-ball physician Lou-Lou adored. Doctors were money-hungry grubbers who shielded their mistakes behind medical degrees. She avoided them by taking vitamin C daily. If she felt ill, she doubled up on her vitamins. The single reason for marrying a doctor was for his social value. Hostesses loved having a few token physicians at their parties.

Because it was imperative that she learn all Avrim knew about her sister and David, she decided to see him later. She'd use her period as an excuse to avoid sex. Or maybe she'd let him hold her while they did everything short of insertion.

Samara frowned. "There's no answer."

"Are you engaged to David?"

"No."

"Is he in love with you?"

"Oh, no!" Samara protested.

Solange peered at her beautifully manicured, pampered hands, her brain whirling. From the way Samara blushed, she'd swear the twit was a virgin. "Then what's the connection? Are you in love with him?"

"We're friends. We lived in the same apartment house. I've known him all my life." Tinged with unmistakable yearning, her soft voice floated into Solange's sharp ears.

Solange's eyes were as sharp as her ears, and deep inside her searching, impatient nature, she squirreled away the information for future use. *Friends, my foot! Samara, you're transparent gauze. You can't wait for David to claim your precious commodity.*

Solange tamped out her cigarette and climbed onto the bed. Leaning back on the white, lace-edged pillows, she patted the space next to her for Samara. She gently imprisoned Samara's hands in hers. "You'll phone later. Tell me about David."

Samara described him as a combination Adonis and Pied Piper: handsome, brilliant, caring. "Children love him as he loves them. He'll make a fabulous father."

Solange's brain clicked into action. Why would David Orchin—supposedly a mere friend—fly to Paris to bring

Samara to the United States? Why? Putting herself in his place, she came up with a chilling scenario.

Besides requiring the latest in medical equipment, he would need to be showcased in an attractively furnished office at a good address, plus a staff. He would need a fully furnished home and late model car. Her cash register mind tallied—money, money, money.

She pegged her twin as naive, but she just bet her bottom dollar David was one smart, goal-oriented cookie. He didn't win a scholarship for stupidity. After Lilli's death, his parents must have advised their darling sonny boy to make his move. And that, she decided, prompted him to return to Paris for Samara.

Christ! Here she thought Maggie her only problem. She'd just bet her lovesick twin promised to set David up in a grand Parisian office. He'd be so grateful he'd marry her!

"Go on," she said dulcetly.

"Maman and David's mother Bella were like sisters," Samara said, informing her of Lilli's beauty salon.

"Sonofabitch!" Solange exploded, flying off the bed, charging around the room. All facsimile of polite facade fragmented. "My mother abandoned me to be a beautician! That's quite a trade-off! I was excess baggage! You think I enjoyed life dumped in those fucking boarding schools?"

Samara jumped off the bed. She grabbed Solange by the arms, giving her a good shake. The pleasant interlude of peace shattered. "Don't talk against Maman. How do you think I felt when I found the letters? I knew Maman. You didn't! If she gave you up—gave this life up!—there had to be a good reason. Do you think we lived like this? I assure you our apartment is modest. There's an overhead pull chain in the toilet. There's barely enough hot water for one bath, let alone two. When the outside weather gets hot, the *ascenseur* in the building often breaks down. Then we hike up five floors with our daily food purchases. Before Maman died, I saved to buy her a sewing machine. So how do you think I felt learning my father is a rich senator, whose family owns Gold's, and who wants to be president of the United States?"

Max tapped on the door. In shirt sleeves, his top shirt buttons open, his hair messed, he glanced at Solange, then at Samara, giving her a tentative smile of unconcealed longing. He couldn't have picked a worse time.

Samara froze. She felt each drop of her blood rush pell-mell through her veins and arteries. With each step he advanced, she retreated one. Bumping into a chair, she maneuvered around it, barricading herself. Max grimly noted his daughter's rejection.

"This was our bedroom," he said, searching for a way to start the conversation. "Lilli loved attending the auctions at Sotheby's or Christie's. We bought pieces she liked. We were happy in the beginning. Happier still when we learned of her pregnancy. After you were born, we'd bring you girls into our bed to watch you play. I gave you your first bath, Samara."

She clamped her lips together.

"After . . . after Lilli left, I couldn't bear to sleep in here. I kept hoping . . . Solange, I'm sorry I couldn't tell you about your mother and Samara."

"Why didn't you?"

Max rubbed a thumb at his temple. "It's rare for me to be at a loss for words, but I'll tell you what I can."

"What do you mean?" Samara snapped, her neck and shoulders tight with tension. "*Can* isn't good enough. Talking about auctions and playing with babies isn't good enough. We demand to hear the truth. All of it."

Max gave a ragged sigh. "The truth isn't easy, particularly if it hurts people you love. I still don't understand it. There aren't adequate words to describe how delighted I am you're here now, Samara." His soft gray eyes encompassed first one daughter, then the other. "I loved Lilli. The first time I saw her, she literally took my breath away. I wouldn't leave France without her." His shoulders sagged. Tears misted his eyes. "In a different way, I never stopped loving her. When I look at you, Solange, I see Lilli. Both you beautiful girls inherited her magnificent eyes, her extraordinary hair coloring."

He fell silent, as if he'd forgotten his audience, as if his dreams of a Camelot world still lay before him on a golden beam.

"Which one of us is older?" Samara blurted.

Max blinked. "You, by five minutes."

Solange and Samara exchanged looks.

"What went wrong?" Solange clipped.

He rubbed his neck. "I wish I knew. We were both busy.

Your mother devoted herself to the two of you. She insisted on caring for you herself.''

"Apparently she changed her mind." Solange snorted.

Samara resented her implication, but the facts were irrefutable, so how could she be angry with Solange? They shared identical feelings—for and against the opposite parent.

Max continued. "Avrim's parents thought it might be postpartum depression, but you girls were nine months old. I discounted it. I thought if she learned English, she'd adjust. She was homesick for Paris. Between my business and my political career, I couldn't get away. She could only take one of you. Two would have been too hard. She . . . she decided to stay . . .'' His voice broke.

Solange wasted no sympathy for her mother, whom she considered a weak, stupid woman. If Samara's fortuitous arrival eliminated Maggie, however, it once again proved her theory—only a fool disregarded a golden opportunity. "Does Maggie know this?"

Max's eloquent shrug spoke volumes to Solange's receptive ears. Her father's gaze was on Samara. Apparently he couldn't get his fill of looking at her twin.

Samara stewed, then exploded. "How neat! You claim Maman went to France on a visit, took one baby, then decided to remain. What gaps you leave out! You expect me to believe she'd leave an infant? Forever? You really expect me to believe she preferred living in our cramped apartment?''

"That's not exactly what I'm trying to say."

"Spare me your lies," Samara scoffed. "I can see by your evasiveness you're incapable of telling the truth. You picture yourself as a loving husband. The injured party. You expect me to believe you couldn't perceive your young wife's needs? You gave her two babies in her first year of marriage. One would tax most women, let alone two. Maman needed you. What did you do to solve her unhappiness? You advised her to learn English while you concentrated on business and politics. How dare you make it sound as if this loving, kind soul set harsh conditions, ones you meekly accepted?''

Livid, quelling the crack of doubt he raised despite her tirade, she snatched Solange's hand, her action forcing her twin to present a united front.

"Maman is dead. I'll speak for her. *Alors!* Perhaps there's another truth. You tired of her. You realized your error in marrying a foreigner. A liability. A young woman whose sheltered background couldn't help you rise to the top of your political ambitions. Isn't that closer to the truth?''

Max passed a hand over his face. ''No,'' he said raggedly.

Samara shook with anger. ''You expect me to believe you're glad to see me! You knew where I lived. Airplanes fly to France. Overseas phones work. No! The truth is that you forced Maman to agree to your monstrous lie. You threatened to steal both her babies if she refused. You sent money to keep her quiet. Money she couldn't bring herself to spend because of what it represented. Isn't that the truth?''

''No, it's not!''

A whiskey voice, booming from the doorway, brought all eyes swiveling to its source. ''Stop castigating your father. You're absolutely wrong, child. If that were true, he'd have wanted Lilli to take Solange, too. Samara, come here, let me look at you. It's time I made peace with my other granddaughter.''

Samara got her first look at her grandmother, Tessie Bergen Gold. A tiny tornado, the honey-haired, tiger-eyed woman marched forward on two-inch heels, a four-star general, panache in a red Valentino uniform, her insignia of office a double strand of flawless matching pearls, three-karat dazzling diamond drops in her earlobes.

''Your grandfather's at the restaurant playing host,'' Tessie said. Barney Gold had fully recovered from a mild heart attack the previous year.

''Mama, go downstairs,'' Max ordered. ''You'll ruin everything. Samara's back—don't send her away.''

Tessie's chin lifted imperiously. ''I certainly can't do worse than you, Max. You're making a mess of it. I eavesdropped. It's time the girls hear the truth—all of it. They're old enough to judge, to forgive. Life isn't a neat package. Come here, Samara.''

Rendered speechless by the imperious cyclone, she remained rooted to the spot.

''Well, where are your manners? Aren't you going to greet your grandmother?'' Tessie demanded. Dumbstruck, Samara's legs moved as ordered. Tessie squashed her in a halo of L'Air du Temps. She gave Samara a smacking kiss on each cheek, then held her at arm's length.

Young and old inspected each other, peering up and down, compensating for the differences in their heights. Moist eyes betrayed Tessie's brusque manner.

"Max, bring me a chair. I refuse to talk on these stilts. Ferragamo's teeter-totters weren't designed for comfort."

"You're interrupting us," he growled, dragging over the chair.

Solange and Samara adopted identical poses. Hands on hips, teeth clenched, eyes narrowed. Both fearful. With good cause. Tessie was a tiger.

The daunting Tessie began. "A lot of hurt has been done to a lot of people. When I'm through, you all may despise me. I sincerely hope not. Samara, I'm truly saddened by Lilli's death. Girls, I owe you an apology. First, we wanted Max to marry in his religion. Second, I didn't speak French, so I ignored her. I'm sorry on both counts."

"I wish to hell you'd go away!" Max glared at her. "This is my responsibility."

"Why did you tell me my mother died?" Solange demanded of her. Samara rallied to her side.

Max broke in. "Mama, I'll do this. Girls, please sit down."

They sat, and as they listened in growing shock, he told them it was Lilli's decision to leave, that he'd kept the house exactly as she left it, hoping she'd return.

"I don't believe you," Samara said.

"She left a letter."

"Mama!" Max implored.

"Show it to them."

A tense silence fell on the room.

He sighed, then nodded. In minutes he returned. "I never wanted either of you to see this, but Grandma's right. It explains why I agreed to your mother's wishes. At the time we thought the lie was kinder. Solange, your mother loved you, too, although I know it's hard for you to accept."

Samara and Solange hunched next to each other, their faces drawn in concentration. Solange cursed beneath her breath. Samara recognized Lilli's handwriting. *Suicide!* She gasped, made herself read on. A few words were blurred. Teardrops. Dried teardrops? Maman's tears?

"Impossible! All this proves is Maman's unhappiness," Samara conceded. "She was young. Distraught. Did you take her to a doctor?" Max nodded. "Well?" she demanded.

"He advised me to let her go."

"How do I know that you both aren't trying to make me—us—believe this terrible thing in order to present a united family picture to the press? You want to be president."

Tessie showed all her seventy-four years. "Yes, he does, and we want it for him, too. You're wrong, though, Samara. I took a terrible risk mentioning the letter. Would I jeopardize Max's and Solange's happiness? There's been enough pain. I'm praying you'll see the wisdom in going forward. You girls belong together."

Samara's blood chilled. Seeds of truth pushed beyond the barriers of doubt. Her mother's violent reaction to Avrim's newscast. Her refusal to see a doctor. Her insistence she spend the night at Mimi's. Her daily prayers. But if that were true, David's parents knew about Solange!

"What do you say, girls?" Tessie asked, opening her arms. "Will you forgive me? Samara, let me show you a grandmother's love. Murray tells me you're talented. Lilli wrote of her pride in your talent. Gold's needs new blood. One day it will be yours, as well as Solange's. Barney and I will amend our wills to ensure you inherit your half of our estate. We provided for your father years ago. I'd like to think your mother would approve."

Samara wasn't proof against her grandmother's plea. It took courage for Tessie to admit she wronged her mother. Max's ravaged face spoke of years of pain. He'd suffered. Maman lied. She'd turned her back on Solange and prevented Samara from knowing her father. Yet she knew that her mother wouldn't commit suicide. Her side of the story lay buried in the grave. With all her heart Samara wanted to believe her mother's spirit had led her to Solange. If she denied what her lonely, aching heart beseeched, she alone would bear the guilt for keeping the family apart. God forgives. She could do no less.

She gazed into her grandmother's luminous brown eyes and took a hesitant step forward. Clasped to her grandmother's bosom, she felt Max place an arm about her shoulders. As her grandmother's tears mingled with hers, she didn't see Max place his other arm about Solange's shoulders, bringing her twin grudgingly into the family circle.

Telling the others she'd join them downstairs in a few minutes, Solange waited until she was alone. Then she snatched a Limoges dish and hurled it with all her might at the fireplace.

The shock of reality hit her in the face. In one day her world had turned upside down. She needed a drag of marijuana or a stiff shot of bourbon. A jealousy unlike any she'd ever experienced ignited into hatred, building in intensity from a spark to a raging flame. Her bitch mother abandoned her— chose Samara! The sight of her sister reducing her father to ordinariness turned her stomach. Not only that. The house was a shrine to her mother!

Solange felt a surge of disgust. Before her eyes the father she had idolized lost his luster, his aura of power with his stupid tears and supplication. For whom?

A woman with abominable taste! A weak woman who couldn't adapt to America! A quitter! A beautician!

How quickly her grandmother spoke of her and Grandpa changing their wills! They all had another guess coming if they thought she'd take this lying down. Samara. David. Max. Tessie. Her grandfather, Barney, and anyone else who tried to get in her way. What her mother had started, she vowed to finish. Consumed with white-hot rage, she refused to allow her rightful inheritance to slip through her fingers. The quid pro quo decided long ago would remain.

She'd see to it.

Chapter Fourteen

Max introduced Samara to Pepe and to Vittorio Guzman, the family chauffeur of a dozen years. In his middle forties, the onetime prize fighter was well built. Medium height, with strong chiseled features, thick black hair, dancing dark eyes, his mouth hung open. "Vittorio tells me what I do right and what I do wrong. When he's not gaping, that is."

She tried to ease his discomfort. "I don't blame you for being surprised."

Pepe frantically fanned her chest. She uttered a string of *madre de Dioses*. "Sit down before you fall down. I was just as surprised as you," Solange noted dryly.

"Isn't this nice," Tessie declared, smiling at everyone. "For once both those gabbers are speechless."

Max invited Samara to move back into the house. "I'd love to see both my daughters living here. We have rooms going to waste," he said wistfully. "Tomorrow is your birthday."

Solange tucked her arm through Samara's, giving it a gentle squeeze. Her head throbbed, and if she didn't get off her feet soon, she'd collapse. "Daddy, Samara needs time to adjust to us. She wouldn't feel comfortable here. Not yet, anyway. Sis, I've got an appointment I can't break tomorrow. Come for lunch the next day. We'll celebrate. We'll gab, make all sorts of wonderful plans. Isn't that better? I know you want to rush home to tell David your good news."

Solange purred this last to please her father, a father who owed her! Samara wasn't the only twin whose life had been ripped apart.

Tessie issued an order. "Bring your doctor friends next Friday night. Grandpa wants to meet them. I'll invite the

157

Leightners. We'll continue the celebration on Shabbes.'' Max seconded the invitation, saying he hadn't seen David since he was a little boy. ''I want to thank him for bringing you here safely.''

Samara accepted. She sat in the rear of the Lincoln, her fingertips idly skirting the soft leather seat. She wanted to remember every detail of the remarkable reunion. She'd spoken to Wendall. David would be home late, eleven-thirty at the earliest, he'd said, adding he himself would be away for the next couple of days.

She felt a wave of undiluted pleasure. Today marked a turning point, a new beginning. She'd taken matters into her own hands. She would do so again. Tonight. If she waited for David to make the first move, she'd be ancient. Twenty-one at least.

She'd seen desire in his eyes, felt the bulge in his pants the night they'd slept together after her nightmare. She'd felt his hand cupping her breast, bit down on her lip to keep from moaning aloud. A little smile curved her lips. *David, my sweet darling man, there's no way you're going to avoid me tonight.*

Another thought dawned on her, one that carried with it a sense of renewed commitment. She ran the risk of David assuming she'd move in with her family. ''Vittorio, could we please stop at a market if it isn't too much trouble?'' Vittorio swung the car around a corner, heading toward Broadway and 80th Street.

''We'll go to Zabar's. It has everything.''

Entering the famous store, Samara sniffed the plenitude of mouth-watering aromas. ''This is wonderful,'' she exclaimed.

Vittorio pushed the cart. He was enjoying himself immensely. He didn't care what she said, as long as she kept speaking to him in her lilting French accent.

From among the loaves of bread displayed in an attractively woven straw basket, she quickly selected a crispy baguette. Forgetting whether David preferred soft or firm Brie, she bought wedges of both kinds, plus a good Camembert. ''The art of making great cheese is in the aging,'' she informed Vittorio with a smile. ''David loves cheese,'' she said, explaining about David being her friend.

Three bouquets of roses and apricot tulips went into the cart, along with a plastic-coated pink tablecloth, pink dinner napkins, two plastic champagne flutes, and vanilla-scented candles.

"And you love flowers," he said, correctly surmising she was in love with the French doctor. He only hoped he loved her, too. If not, he was prepared to dislike him.

"Atmosphere," she quipped, studying wine labels before deciding on Chardonnay.

She declined help at the cash register. She meticulously counted the sum of money owed, the tip of her tongue showing her concentration.

This time she opted to sit beside Vittorio. The flowers lay across her lap. "May I?" she asked, her fingers at the stereo console.

"Miss Samara, this is more your car than mine. Of course you may."

More yours than mine. His statement made it clearer to her than all the antiques and beautiful furnishings in her father's house, clearer than the money deposited in her name in the bank, that from now on the world would associate her with wealth, power, and social status. Her foot tapped to the soft rock beat of the Doobie Brothers singing "What a Fool Believes."

Vittorio appreciated her company. Solange limited her conversation to her destination and when to pick her up. Promptly. Samara's gentle aura, paired with the natural exuberance of youth, made for an intoxicating mix of gamine and gentlewoman. He couldn't help wondering what Solange thought of her twin.

Back at the apartment, Vittorio declined her invitation to come in for coffee, saying her father needed him. She whipped into action.

She set the kitchen table with the pink tablecloth and napkins. She filled the earthenware vase in David's room with the tulips, their salmon-rose centers glowing to apricot at the edges. Using empty orange juice bottles for a centerpiece and as vases, she put more flowers in the living room and bedroom. She flew to the stereo and switched to a station playing romantic songs.

She arranged the cheeses and crackers on a platter, rinsed the plastic flutes, and popped the cork on the wine bottle to let the wine breathe. "So it's not Tour d'Argent."

She sat at David's desk, scribbled a note, and taped it on the bedroom door. She wanted David to see her at her glamorous best. She showered, washed and dried her hair, and brushed it until it shone, recalling a scene in a book where the author extravagantly described the heroine's hair as a bounteous mantilla.

Squeezing a ribbon of toothpaste on her brush, she scrubbed her teeth and rinsed her mouth. With shaking fingers she applied her makeup. Her hands trembled as she slipped the translucent pale blue nightgown over her head. She stared at her reflection in the mirror. The gown fit like a satin glove. *I might as well be naked,* she thought. Her nipples puckered, pushing out the material. Dear God, she wondered if all virgins were nervous. *It's David,* she reminded herself. She'd slept with him, but they hadn't made love! In her fantasies they'd made love countless times. In fact, he had explained the facts of life to her when she was eight years old. Mimi put her up to it. She'd barged into his room demanding to know if he did *It.*

When he realized what *It* meant, he told her to get out of his room and let him study. "I'm tired of being the only dummy in class. The nuns won't tell me, and neither will my mother." He closed the door. In clinical terms he described the basics, then warned her he'd beat her to a pulp if she tried *It.*

She could be eight years old again, except then she hadn't been nervous. She'd saved herself for David. She'd never engaged in heavy petting. Her thoughts skittered, swinging back and forth like a pendulum. Suppose David liked women with more flesh on their bodies? Larger breasts? Wider hips? She countered with her overriding argument. *It's now or never. If you don't, you'll have yourself to blame. You love him. Love makes it right.*

She lay down on the bed, then jumped up. A brown-and-black geometric bedspread and matching sheets weren't romantic. It seemed too harsh, too angular. She scrambled to the linen closet. She found two sets: Mickey Mouse chasing Pluto, and plain blue. Wendall was a Mickey Mouse freak. She chose the other, stripped the old linens, and remade the bed with the blue. She put two vanilla-scented candles on the dresser, two on David's desk, and set them in dishes to prevent a fire. When she finished, she surveyed the small, plain bedroom.

The bed had no headboard. The brown shag carpet had seen

better days. The picture on the beige walls was undistinguished; the surface of the desk was scratched. She wished it were a beautiful bedroom with flowered wallpaper, overlooking the Seine, or a bedroom like Solange's with a canopy bed, a fireplace, magnificent paintings. She'd done all she could to make the place look better.

What if David resented her for putting him in a humiliating position? She would embarrass him and degrade herself. Suppose all he felt for her was pity? Suppose he didn't want to be stuck with her? David was a man of the world. Why would he want a virgin whose sole experiences with sex took place in her mind? What if he'd gotten hard in bed from a reflex action? Men did. It was in their hormones.

She bolstered her confidence by convincing herself again that she had to try or be sorry for the rest of her life. Concentrating on the aphrodisiac named David, she could almost feel him touching her, being in her, exploding in her. Her imagination fed her, inflaming the fever her mind created. She lay down on the bed. Although she hadn't expected to, she fell asleep in moments.

Thanks to Samara, David's day went from bad to worse. Awash with animosity, he bypassed the elevator. Angst thrust him down two flights of stairs. His white doctor's coat flapping in his wake, he thwacked open the double doors. His nurse and ten second- and third-year medical students struggled to match his long, loping strides. Where the hell was Samara? he wondered. It wouldn't surprise him if she gave him a bleeding ulcer. How dare she disappear on him for so long. Didn't she know by now he worried about her?

Steely-eyed, he charged down the corridor, slapping his clipboard against his thigh, pretending each thump landed on Samara's butt. Without bothering to detour around a machine spewing water from its sides, enabling a worker to mop the floor, David sloshed straight ahead, fuming.

Wasn't it enough he worried about Emmett Brown, who wasn't responding to treatment for leukemia? He didn't need Samara to compound his life, to interfere with his mind during surgery. Three times he'd sent a nurse to check his office for messages. When had he ever done a thing like that before?

Never! Had Samara the decency to call by the time he started rounds? No! In ten more minutes, he'd phone the police!

He banged into a food cart. "What the hell is that doing there?" he snarled, his arm throbbing.

He deserved a row of Good Conduct medals for crawling into bed with her and not touching her. Where the hell were her brains? The next time she had a nightmare, he'd wake her up. Toss her out of bed! Throw cold water on her face. What did she think he was made of? And how dare she vanish? She didn't know New York. She drove him fuckin' insane.

He fired a question at a student, glowering at him when he failed to diagnose a Wilm's tumor. "I suggest you pay attention!"

"What the shit's wrong with Orchin today?" hissed a second-year student. "He's got a burr up his ass."

David whirled about, knocking the man's clipboard flying. Like a shot it zoomed to the far wall, clanked off it, boomeranged in a perfect trajectory, and crashed onto the startled owner's shoe. No one dared comment on the incredible feat that defied the laws of physics.

David poked the presumptuous student's chest. His eyes speared him. "I heard you, mister! The name is *Doctor* Orchin. In answer to your question, nothing is wrong with me today! Since you have so much time for unnecessary comments, suppose you put your mouth to good use. Tell us what you'd prescribe for this next patient."

David's reputation among the students, who unofficially ranked the staff, placed him at the top. If possible, most would opt to remain on his service. They'd never heard him tear into a student. Until now, he'd been unfailingly polite and patient. Their hero worship trampled and tattered, the group hid its disappointment.

"Kind" Dr. Orchin had metamorphosed into "Killer" Orchin.

The fifteen-year-old girl suffered from Hodgkin's disease. The student stammered an acceptable answer.

Relentless, David pursued him. "The pathologist took a biopsy of the lymph node tissues. What was he looking for?"

A third-year student jumped in. "Reed-Sternberg cells, the abnormal cells associated with Hodgkin's."

"Very good," David said to the woman, grateful he didn't

have to waste his time discussing diseases, duplicate symptoms, and diagnoses.

David turned toward the chastised student. The man's ears were bright pink. His right eyelid twitched. In a minute he'd have to shove the jerk's head between his legs to stop his hyperventilation. Feeling absolutely no remorse, David wanted to ram his fist down the man's throat.

Grow up! he wanted to shout at him. *All you have to worry about is passing school. What about me? You try being responsible for an ungrateful brat! You don't know what trouble is. You sleep next to a sorceress. I dare you to walk around with a perpetual cement shaft.*

David's nurse imperceptibly tugged his sleeve. His head swung around. Their gazes locked. Her eyes narrowed in warning. He struggled to calm the fierce pounding in his chest. With difficulty he reined his temper, taking immense satisfaction in promising himself to save *all* of it for Samara: *she* deserved it, *she* was the root of his problems.

David slapped a pathologist's report in the student's hand. Only a moron could miss the precise summary and his own protocol attached to the bottom of the paper.

"The patient's undergone lymphangiograms and a computed tomography. What do you suggest?"

Pink Ears blinked. He coughed. "I'd recommend radiation and chemotherapy."

"Correct. Excellent. You'll make a fine doctor," David said mechanically. The praise restored a measure of Pink Ears's pride. The man's eyelid ceased twitching. His breathing normalized. David's nurse smiled. His students breathed a cautious sigh.

Wendall came up behind David. Digging his fingers into David's upper arm, he propelled him to the other side of the hall. "Little uptight are we, sweetie?"

"Fuck you," David snapped, venting his rotten mood on his equal. "Besides, I'm handling it."

"So I noticed. I don't suppose you care that you're entertaining the rest of us. We heard the tongue lashing you gave your hapless student clear down to the nurses' station, where, I might add, you lost a hell of a lot of Brownie points."

"Tough shit!" David barked.

"Listen, pal, your pain stabs at my heart. Therefore I'll

alleviate your misery. I dropped by the apartment. *You,* my precious, forgot to activate the answering machine. Samara phoned as I was leaving. We chatted.''

He saw the leap of interest in David's eyes. "She called from her father's. She's met him, her sister, her grandmother, and Maggie McPherson. The chauffeur will drive her home. Lest you're ready to do battle with her, she said to tell you she needed to do this alone. I agree.''

An enormous surge of relief flooded through David. Just as swiftly he grappled with a countersurge of jealousy. She hadn't needed him! He took a belligerent step forward. "What right do you have to agree? She should have phoned me here. I'm no mind reader, dammit! She's driving me nuts!''

Wendall's cheerful advice floated across the hall to the group of eavesdroppers. "Certainly a Freudian slip. Nuts, that is. Orchin, you're a pitiful specimen. You're incapable of making a coherent decision *sans moi.* For the good of the staff, your patients, and our currently strained living conditions, heed my advice. Tell Samara you're sappy in love with her. Pop the question before you pop.'' At David's glowering expression, he whispered, "I've had the honor of observing you in extremis—if you get my meaning. You're champing at the bit.''

David reared back. "Shit!'' he yelled.

Fighting to choke a smile, Wendall tutted. "Let's not repeat ourselves. You do your part, I'll do mine. For the next three nights I'll bunk with Maisy Daisy. Not to be crude, but we'll all make out. If Samara's stupid enough to have you, I'll serve as your best man. To show you I'm a sport, if you beg nicely, I'll consent to play the piano at your wedding.''

David sputtered. His eyes glazed. His fists balled. "Are you crazy?'' he bellowed, oblivious to the fascinated audience. "I'm not in love with Samara. She's a kid. Do you realize her most precious possession is a mangy blue rabbit she's slept with since she was a baby? How can you say I'm in love with her, you dumb idiot? I diapered her.''

"Just think,'' Wendall said. "You're ahead of the game. You already know how to remove her panties. If you play your cards right, she can sleep with a broken-down grouch of a doctor. Stupid me, I thought you French invented *toujours amour.* Shows you what I know.'' He strolled away, laughing.

David's nurse and his students observed their mentor's face turn red. Returning to them, he wore an embarrassed scowl. They wore broad, sympathetic smiles. His face flaming, his ears pink, he gave them a sheepish grin.

Hours later, David escaped to his office where he holed up to try to find some peace. Glumly eyeing the digital clock on the wall opposite his desk, David slumped in his chair, mulling over his situation. He held a paper cup containing Scotch. He brought the smooth liquid to his lips.

Fortification versus fornication. Chivas Regal called it a tie. He knew better. Cowardice hailed him the victor. He splashed a liberal amount of whiskey into the plastic foam cup. He took a swig. If he dared go home before Samara was asleep, he knew where it would end. Right where his horny erection longed to be. Inside her wet warmth, sucking her sweet lips, putting his brand in her, on her forever and ever and ever . . .

Easy for Wendall—the horse's ass—to snort advice. Who was he to tell him to deflower a young woman in mourning? Samara's life was about to change for the exciting better. For the foreseeable future he'd remain a poor doctor, spending years in the hospital, dividing his time between puttering in a lab and seeing his patients. His cubicle office—scratched gunmetal gray filing cabinet, clock, hard oak chair, and desk—defied comfort. He had nothing to offer Samara—who wasn't the little girl he tried to make himself believe she was.

"An honorable Frenchman resists temptation when entrusted with the care and well-being of a young lady in transition, however enticing."

His eyes focused on the clock. Midnight. The witching hour. She could be watching television.

He fumbled in the bottom drawer to his desk, retrieving another bottle of Scotch, a grateful father's gift. His child's cancer miraculously disappeared a year ago. Spontaneous remission. God's way of letting man know He called the shots. It sure as shit wasn't the doctor.

"To transition," he grumbled, then changed his mind. Transition was a term used in the labor process. He knew how babies were made! Dispensing with the toast, he attacked the liquid. If he was very lucky, the fiery heat would strike his gut and kill him. Or numb his brain.

Reaching for the gooseneck lamp on his desk, he pressed a

button, illuminating the surface with a thin band of white light. "Samara," he muttered, sharpening every pencil in sight, "you are keeping me from needed sleep. In fact, you gorgeous brat, you are keeping me from everything."

Points down, he dumped the pencils into a tin holder. Then he picked up his cup and drank more Scotch. His shoulders lifted and sagged like a deflated balloon. Wallowing in self-pity, he took his frustration out on her. "Samara, I made an idiot of myself today. With Wendall's help. My students laughed at me."

Tomorrow he'd issue her an ultimatum. Move out. He'd done enough. He propped his feet up on the desk and lifted the plastic cup in a toast.

"To Wendall, the lousiest piano player I know. May your fingers rot off one by one."

He missed his mouth. The contents of the cup spilled onto his pants. He blotted the spreading stain.

"Now look what you made me do, Samara!" He grabbed a handful of tissues. "You're determined to make my life hell, aren't you?" His feet hit the floor. He belonged in the hospital, just as Samara belonged to her prestigious family and the fancy socialite world awaiting her.

When he could think of nothing else to blame her for, he went outside into the night. The night air hit him with a sobering blast. He peered up at a huge crane, its bucket hovering above the street. In the morning the jackhammers and the building would start up again. Columbia marching forward.

He walked up to Broadway, purposely taking the wrong route, delaying the time he'd return home. He bypassed a drunk sleeping on a subway grate. He heard the steady stream of a man relieving himself in a narrow space between two buildings. The driver of a Cadillac with New Jersey license plates pulled up to the corner, made a drug buy, then sped off. Someone tossed an empty soda can into the street. Most of the storefronts were boarded. Trucks and cars double-parked beneath signs warning motorists not to. An ambulance wailed by, its siren blasting. A policeman he knew said hello to him while his partner frisked a man, confiscated a switch blade and a snub-nosed pistol. Despite the early-morning hour, a woman wheeling a baby carriage paused to watch.

"Washington Heights. Perfect place to bring a bride,"

David muttered, yet even as he did, he knew countless honest hardworking men and women who lived there whose sole ambition was to make a better life for themselves and their families.

Inside the Towers, the elevator hummed to his floor. He turned the key in the lock, greeted by the strains of romantic music. He walked into the kitchen, saw the laden table, the wine, the flowered centerpiece. In the living room he saw the roses in juice bottles. He read the note she'd taped to the door.

Darling. Darling. Wake me. We'll celebrate our good fortune.

A sigh rivered through him. Do all men know when the inevitable stares them in the face? He'd tried to do the right thing. He loved her, but he also knew that beneath her talents as a model and emerging designer beat the heart of a romantic innocent who'd lived a sheltered life influenced by the church, Lilli, and Jules. He couldn't compete with the opportunities about to come her way. He had no right to hold her back. She deserved the best her family could offer her. She needed to be free to travel in her father's rarified social circle, free to meet, mingle, choose.

The note beckoned him. He hesitated momentarily, then walked into the room. He gazed at the outline of her figure, her hair flowing like silvery strands across the pillow. Beautiful witch, he thought, wanting her with every fiber of his being. He spotted the candles on the dresser and desk.

Samara slept on her side, one arm flung over her hip. Moonlight streamed through the window, highlighting long eyelashes, porcelain skin. His gaze lowered to the rise and fall of her breasts. A tiny moan escaped her lips. He kneeled at the side of the bed, catching the tiny explosions of breath.

He kissed her bare shoulder, sighed, and rose. In the bathroom, he showered, brushed his teeth, then came back to take up his vigil; but first he lit the four candles, adding the scent of vanilla and fanning warm pinpoints of light to the otherwise dark room.

He sat on the bed and looked down at her lovely face. She must have sensed him watching her. Her lashes fluttered open. "Am I dreaming?"

His expression softened. "I know I am," he said in a voice of rough velvet. A smile illuminated her face.

He lifted the blanket, slipped into bed, cradled her in his arms. He caressed her tenderly and began to kiss her eyes, cheeks, neck, light feathery kisses to stir her body awake. "Mmmm. You smell so good I could find you in the dark."

Her arms encircled him. "I've dreamed of this. Of me and you. Of us in love."

He raised his head, watching the myriad emotions on her face. "And are we both in love?" he asked, already so hopelessly in love with her that he felt his full heart would burst.

Her blue eyes were knowing and wise. Her fingers traced the outline of his lips. "Very much, my darling. David, of all the men in the world, I only want you to make love to me, for this to happen with you."

Samara offered herself to him, to the loving hands that covered her body, to the reverent mouth that tasted her wine. Oh, how incredibly naive she'd been. Now she grasped the knowledge that love meant much more than the physical act they were about to share, understanding from the adoration in his eyes the full import of devotion for the first time. Love carried a special privacy. A marvelous closeness. A unity of spirit. Love meant being cherished and cherishing. Love meant belonging to one man out of all the millions of men in the world.

David . . .

His hand found the curve of her hip. Reverently, so as not to alarm her, he kissed her bare skin as he removed her gown. She was slender, with long graceful legs, formed to perfection. Her skin glowed with the health of youth. He couldn't resist the touch and scent of her. He buried his face in her fragrant hair, kissed the column of her graceful neck, traced the outline of her lips. Dipping his head, he kissed first one breast, then the other. "My sweet temptress, how wise you are."

Samara whispered in a voice so soft he could barely make out the words. "David, you're very experienced. I'm afraid I'll disappoint you. I don't know what to do."

He stifled a shout of denial. The poignancy of her admission tore a groan from his lips. He brought her to him in fierce tenderness. In a gentle yet solemn voice he assured her she was perfect. "Just let yourself feel," he instructed. His lips touched her quivering eyelids, her trembling lips, parting them with his tongue to kiss her deeply, fully. The kiss exploded with all the years of pent-up hunger each had for the other. He kissed her long, lingeringly, lavishly. Craving him, she met him with unrestrained fervor, innocently driving the kiss to a heated pitch. Dizzy with desire, she instinctively gave herself up to his wondrous ministrations, thrilling him with her murmurs of delight.

His hand roamed her soft flesh, sliding down her rib cage, detouring to massage her abdomen, then continue its fondling quest. She threaded her fingers through his hair as his mouth teased her nipples and his fingers finessed and stroked the nub of sensory flesh. Samara felt herself taken on a journey of frenzied sensations, straining toward an unknown destination, needing desperately to reach the summit.

Clutching his lean, hard-muscled back, she opened to him. His hands and mouth learned her body, discovering the unique and wonderful taste of her skin. All the nerves in her body sprang to life. She moaned, greedily wanting more.

Aching for her, he brushed the hair away from her temple. He rubbed his cheek on hers, murmuring endearments in their native French. He crushed her against the hardness of his body, molding her to him. Beneath his powerful chest she felt his wildly beating heart. He took her hand and wrapped it around him. He was warm and hard and velvet smooth, feeding her own excitement.

Her world tilted and compressed, its boundaries confined to the nest of blue sheets, the mingling aromas of vanilla, roses, and musk. David moved on top of her, then she gasped at the invasion of her tight passage.

Deep, smoky eyes captured hers. Dipping his head, he pressed a kiss on her breasts, on her heart.

"It's all right, love," he said to soothe her, his voice tinged with regret that he'd hurt her. He bent over her, holding her still in his arms until the brief pain subsided. She smiled, her eyes bright with unshed tears, the pain forever behind her. By slow, careful degrees he settled fully into her welcoming warmth.

Her hands crept up his chest. She circled his neck with her arms. She savored his body heat. Holding nothing back, she wrapped her legs around him, consuming him to the very core of her. Propelled by passion, she scaled higher and higher, swirling in a storm of erotic stimulation.

Fighting his own rampant desire, he willed his fevered body to wait until she neared her climax. She held on tight to David, to her destiny. When her muscles tensed, he covered her mouth with his, sharing her cry of discovery, taking her soaring to the top with him.

Samara stretched languorously, her left arm draped over David. They slept entwined in each other's arms, their lips touching, their hands seeking even in sleep. How strange and miraculous life was, she thought, too overwhelmed by her emotions to speak. She'd crossed an invisible line; she'd become a woman in the truest sense. She was David's, totally and completely, and he was her man. Forever and ever and ever. He'd been so careful with her, so loving and tender. She'd been needlessly afraid, then she never wanted to end it. She'd never felt so good in her life.

In the rosy afterglow of David's caresses she knew that nothing in the world—not her dreams, her discussions with Mimi, the movies she'd seen—had prepared her for the glorious union, for the fabulous gift of sharing with a man she loved and who loved her.

David lay quietly, contemplating the depth of his feelings for Samara. If he could he'd barricade the door, put up a Keep Out sign to the world. Sighing, he recognized the impossibility of his wish; rather than dwell on the dream of an immediate marriage, he asked her to tell him about her family.

She described the brownstone house she lived in for the first nine months of her life. With obvious awe in her voice she described the furniture, the antiques, the Impressionist paintings, the plush, private elevator. In more subdued tones, she said she met Maggie, then related her first impressions of her father, Solange, and of Tessie, who demanded their presence at Shabbes dinner this Friday. "Wendall, too."

"Do you forgive your father and grandmother?"

She admitted it was difficult, confessing her feelings were raw. "I hurt for Maman. Solange is bitter toward her for taking me. But I know in my heart she'll get over that. We're very much alike in many ways. She's invited me to lunch day after tomorrow. Did I tell you she wants to open a business?"

"Doing what?"

"She wants to organize parties for socially prominent people."

"And will her important twin attend if her important twin invites her?"

"Yes," she said merrily. "Solange is as thrilled as I am that we've found each other. Max cried. It was so sad. Tessie said that Gold's will be mine, too. Can you imagine?" She chattered on. "The senator's not the monster I thought. I can't hate him."

David traced a fingertip over her temple, guiding it down the length of her nose, around the rim of her mouth, over her chin. Samara gave her heart, her generosity, in unqualified terms. She spoke from a reservoir of love. He listened to her reaffirm her empathy for Solange, explaining her spiritual feelings.

"At least I lived home. Solange attended boarding school. She didn't go to school in New York until she was eleven."

"Stop making her sound deprived. She wasn't."

"I can't help but feel sorry for her. She could never have what we have. Maman's letters guided me to her. That's why Maman saved them."

He doubted that, but if she defined Lilli's poor judgment as God's holy ordinance, who was he to refute her?

"I wish I knew why Maman threatened to commit suicide."

David's arms tightened around her. "Maybe it's best you don't know."

She pressed her face into his neck. Tears stung her eyes. "Promise you'll never let that happen to us."

"Baby, I promise. I'll never let you down."

Contented, she snuggled next to him. She lay in the circle of his arms, amid strewn rose petals, each petal earned with a kiss. She felt so protected, so adored. So safe and sure of her future. David, her precious, wonderful, magnificent lover. She felt sorry for every other woman in the world.

In her darkest hour, he'd left his patients, his research, to come to her rescue, never once making her feel she intruded on his valuable time, his essential work. He alone coaxed her back to health. She never thought it would be possible to feel happy again. Not truly. Not deep down inside her soul where it counted. Yet she was happy. Thanks to David's love of her. He healed her spirit, saved her. Now more than ever, she knew he wanted her with him always.

The hospital overworked him. He ate his meals on the run. He lived from one crisis to the next. She would care for him as he'd cared for her, share his concerns. She fantasized their perfect life. Destined to be world-renowned doctor marries destined to be world-famous couturier. They would live in a grand and beautiful house, with lilac bushes lining the front walk. They might even have their own *ascenseur*! They'd definitely have two sons.

As she opened her mouth to speak, David rolled over, giving her the kind of scorching kiss that sent her temperature soaring, her hands seeking, her body straining to be one with his. Afterward she flopped over on her back. She mentally tried out variations of her future name. Dr. and Mrs. David Orchin. Mrs. David Orchin. Mrs. Mother of Dr. David Orchin's two sons. Madame Orchin.

"David, when will we marry?"

His hand stilled. "I need to finish my obligation to the hospital first. You want to get started with your career."

"What does my career have to do with it? Why can't we have it all?"

"We will. You're young. Time is on your side. Look at this place. A whole new world is about to open for you, Samara. Take advantage of it. I'm not going anywhere. We can still be together."

She gave him a glum look, then smiled to herself. How typical of David to put his concerns for her before his own. Like this silly notion. A few more nights like tonight would make him change his mind. She kissed his chin.

"Do you think Maman knows what we did?"

"God, I hope not. I'd hate to have her see me naked."

"Let's call Bella and Michel," Samara said. "I'm ashamed of the way I acted at the airport. I don't blame them for keeping a promise to Maman. I want them to know I've been reunited with the family, that Solange and I will be true sisters, that Maman's letters led me to Solange."

The phone call was filled with a happy exchange of information. Bella found a woman willing to run Lilli's beauty shop. Samara gave her permission. Bella promised to phone Mimi and Jules, tell them to expect a letter.

"I forgot the most amazing news!" Samara exclaimed. "My father is going to run for president of the United States!"

In France, Bella hung up the phone. Samara and David sounded so happy. She told Michel she suspected they were lovers. Michel said he wasn't surprised.

"Michel, we can't keep Lilli's secret. Not now. Max must know the truth. If he doesn't, if it comes out, imagine what it will do to the girls, to him. The French and the American press will swarm here like vultures when he announces for the presidency. A presidential candidate's life is an open book. Every scrap of information will be dug up and printed. Think of the scandal. Think of David, too. Think of our grandchildren."

Michel handed her the phone.

Chapter Fifteen

Bella's shocker sent Max into an emotional tailspin. Bile clogging his throat, cold sweat dotting his brow, his voice shook as he asked her why she hadn't told him.

Bella's answer, that she feared for Lilli's actions if she had broken her solemn promise, left him numbly agreeing.

"Did Murray know?"

"Of course not. He would have told you."

"Did you tell Samara tonight?" He prayed she hadn't, but with everything else he was learning, he couldn't be sure.

"I promise you. She and David know nothing."

Relieved, he said, "Thank God. I'd like to keep her from ever finding out. Why complicate her grief?"

"Lilli was a loving, wonderful woman. A complex woman," Bella said.

Max saw that now. Bella and Michel Orchin had always known Lilli better than he had. They understood the dark voice of her misguided conscience without passing judgment.

"She had many good years with Samara, Max. Remember that when you think of Lilli."

He sat with his head in his hands long after he'd said good-bye to Bella. Every single syllable, every single word imprinted on his stunned brain. They made a collective mockery of his life.

Only a reason as momentous as their children falling in love could break Bella's silence. "Isn't it wonderful?" she'd said. "Samara and David." Their children linked the families, safeguarded the future.

Max couldn't deal with Bella's joy right now. Despair filled him. Regardless of her noble intentions, Lilli had made a grievous error. What a life she condemned herself to.

A life of martyrdom so he could win political favor!

After she left him, he'd turned his energies toward bringing up Solange and building his successful career. How could Lilli sacrifice so much for him? How could she think that by doing it she'd help him attain his ultimate goal—the presidency?

Poor Lilli. His darling Lilli. She had committed suicide long before a car killed her. To live with such guilt! And what of him? How could he have been so gullible as to let the psychiatrist talk him into accepting her lie, then build on his despair as the foundation of his future?

With a heavy sigh, he left the room. He had failed Lilli. Failed his daughters. Failed himself.

Failed Maggie.

It was raining hard when he walked outside without protection. He ambled along at a snail's pace in the pelting rain as others rushed by. Max, quite literally, was a man on the edge—a man riddled with enormous guilt. A man on a hellish private mission, a tragic figure seeking to understand how his judgment could have been so terribly wrong. Blocks, perhaps miles, later, a policeman stopped him.

"Jesus! I know you," the cop shouted over the driving wind. "Senator Gold, go home, sir."

Max blinked. Shivering, he felt the penetrating wetness in the marrow of his bones. "Thanks, officer. I'll get a cab."

The policeman hailed a taxi. In his preoccupied state, Max gave Maggie's address on East 57th Street. By the time he arrived on her doorstep, he was sneezing.

Her eyes sizzled with anger as she opened the door a crack. Then she got a good look at him, and her heart beat with fear. The venom died on her lips. Whatever happened between yesterday and today had sent him out in the streets as a candidate for pneumonia. "You're drenched."

"I must have given the wrong address for the right reasons. Maggie, may I come in and talk? Please."

She stepped aside. His shoes squeaked as he walked toward the living room. "Not there. Wait in the bathroom. Take off those wet clothes."

"It's not necessary," he said.

"Yes," she said pointedly. "It is."

She went into her bedroom, returning with his bathrobe and slippers. He kept a change of clothes and sleepwear in her apartment. "I'll make tea."

He joined her in minutes, his hair towel-dried and combed back. She set a mug of tea at his place. He sat, making no effort to hide his weeping.

She had never seen him cry, or in such a state of misery. Yesterday she had planned to ruin him, even when Avrim begged her to wait. All the while she was taking her anger and frustration out on Avrim, she knew she would never strike the first blow at Max. Hating herself for it, she recognized that her heart got in the way of her judgment. She was furious that someone had hurt him.

Taking his chin in one hand, she prodded the liquid to his mouth with the other hand. "Drink this tea, then tell me what's wrong."

Max shuddered. Pictures came to him in overpowering detail. Bella's call. Lilli . . .

"Oh, God!" The cry ripped from the depths of his being. Maggie caught the mug before it fell.

"Max, please," she cried. "Tell me what's wrong."

His sigh drained him. He found her face. Maggie's cat eyes. Maggie's hurt. His hands covered hers. "You didn't believe I loved you, Maggie. Lilli didn't believe I loved her enough. Oh, God, the mistakes." He rested his head in his hands and wept.

"I thought I was strong," he said, suppressing his bleak frustration to speak more calmly. "No more lies, Maggie. I'm going to tell you the truth. You deserve it."

Maggie's fears accelerated. How much more could she take? The raw pain of recent betrayal struck anew in her chest. "I was wrong. You don't owe me anything."

He deeply regretted the hurt he'd caused. He tipped his head back, his gaze rested on her imploring eyes. Determined to try to make amends, he said gravely, "Ah, Maggie, my Maggie. I've lost you. Until I received Bella Orchin's phone call, I never knew the real reason my wife left me and Solange. I lied to protect my children. I had to . . ."

In a ragged voice filled with despair and desperation, and often anger, Max related his story. He recounted his fury following Lilli's fleeing their home with Samara. He spoke of desolation, utter confusion. He told of Lilli's suicide threat, of his mother confronting Samara and Solange with the knowledge of the note. "The girls read it."

In a gentler voice, he told of his love for the young Lilli who had captured his heart with a look, that he had extended his trip to Paris to court her. He relived his marriage ceremony, the permission Lilli needed to be married at Chartres. He recounted his parents' profound disappointment, their treatment of Lilli.

Max confessed that he had beseeched, finally begged a reluctant Murray to write to Lilli so he could maintain contact with Samara, with the terms he had set. He told Maggie that after failing twice to arrange a meeting with Lilli, he sent Murray to Paris. "She became ill. She threatened suicide again."

Throughout the often choppy recital, Maggie remained silent. He reported his relief that Murray had seen Samara, a happy, normal little girl. In the strictest sense, his recitation served as a catharsis. He shared the most shocking part of Bella's phone call, telling him the name of Lilli's father. Stella's letter triggered Lilli's memory. It contained her parents' names and her father's role as an officer in the Third Reich. Lilli's subsequent actions, his years of misery. By then tears streamed down Maggie's cheeks, too.

"It wouldn't have mattered," Max sobbed brokenly. "I would have protected her. We could have made a life. We had our babies. Bella said that Lilli died certain she was a spawn of the devil. She didn't think she deserved happiness. She was a child, for God's sake! At the age of four she was brought to the orphanage. The cruelest thing I ever did was to take Lilli away from France, away from her church, the Orchins. I stole her away from her safe world."

"Why didn't Sister Jean destroy the letter?" Maggie asked.

"Who knows? Lilli was the bravest person I know."

Maggie dried her tears. She blew noisily into a tissue. "What will you do about running?" she asked, stroking his hand.

A long sigh came from deep within him. "Today I reflected on my priorities, on the meaning of life. I have unfinished business. I'm not going to announce for the presidency. I may have stopped loving Lilli as a husband loves a wife a long time ago, but I owe it to her not to have lived her years of sacrifice for us in vain. Bella broke her promise to Lilli for the girls' sake. She knows as well as I do what the press does to a presidential candidate. At best my running would have been an uphill battle. Carter's going to run again. It's one thing for the press and the public to accept a man separated from his wife—it's another if the wife is the daughter of a brutal Nazi. Whatever I say won't be believed. I can only guess at the reverberations. The country, the Jews, don't need to be ripped asunder by another moral issue. The Watergate mess is fresh in our minds. Nixon's family is still suffering from it. I won't put mine through this. You yourself know reporters would go to France, find the orphanage, identify Lilli's true parentage.''

"Oh, Max. You've wanted this so badly. Your whole career . . .''

"I'm disappointed, but I'm content with my decision. It's my turn now to protect my daughters. My term as senator is up soon. I'm going to retire from politics. The less public a figure I am, the safer for the twins. I'll resume my law practice.''

"You would have made a wonderful president. Finish your tea. Then come to bed. You're exhausted.''

He moved the refilled mug out of the way. His gaze roved her expressive face. She was intelligence and grace, and he loved her. "I don't need tea or sleep, Maggie. I need you.''

They lay together with the truth their blanket of absolution. Maggie exorcised his pain with her body. They made love sweetly, lovingly, then after they rested he turned to her and cradled her in his arms as if to certify she wasn't a dream, but his flesh and blood and marvelous Maggie.

While they slept, the torrential rain reversed its cycle. By morning the city was renewed, and so were they. Dawn played its rosy fingers at the windows. In the street below, a horn honked, a siren blared. The city awakened with a blast. Max shifted his weight, propping himself up on his side.

Maggie asked, "Will you tell your parents and the Leightners the truth?''

"No. There's no need. I'll blame my withdrawal on the reality of politics and my latest evaluation of the national scene. Incumbent presidents with one hundred billion dollars to distribute back to local governments are hard to beat.''

"Why did you tell me? Especially after yesterday. You know I'm a reporter, what I said I'd do.''

He threaded her fingers with his. "I love you. I trust you. I believe in your inherent goodness. I want to marry you. I'm selfish. I want to have a family with you.'' He cocked his head. ''Unless you think I'm too old.''

She pressed his hand over her womb. ''I've never thought that.''

''Maggie, darling, no more secrets. I promise. Marry me,'' he implored. ''I love you, Maggie.''

She caressed his mouth, tracing its outline with her fingertip. It was a hopeless request. After all this time, she couldn't accept. ''Darling, please try to understand. I'm happy you've been reunited with Samara. I'll always keep the trust you've placed in me. I'll never tell Avrim.''

''But you won't marry me,'' he said bitterly.

''I thought once I could. After yesterday, I'm not ready to take on Solange. She hates me.''

''Once she gets used to the idea, she'll be happy for us. I know she will.''

Maggie knew better. ''Max, look about you.''

He did.

Boxes and crates of books lined the floor. Her clothes closet was empty. More books and piles of papers topped her desk. Suitcases, stuffed with clothes, sat open across the arms of chairs.

''Are you going on a trip?''

''I'm leaving. I've taken a job with our affiliate in San Francisco. You know they've been courting me. I signed the papers. A real estate agent has lined up a few places for me to see. I'm flying there this weekend to choose. I want a house, Max. I need to feel permanent.''

He could feel the heat of her body and couldn't imagine losing her. ''When do you start?''

''The first of the month.''

''What about *Happenings*? New York is the number-one market.''

''When I agreed yesterday, my decision seemed like a good idea.'' She said it without rancor. Both knew the lie and Solange's hatred of her had been the final straw, prompting her to find a new life. ''I'll do *Happenings* from San Francisco. They're counting on me to bring up the ratings.''

''What's the length of the contract?'' Max asked, trying to adjust to Maggie living so far away.

''One year,'' she said softly.

"Will you let me visit you?"

"I would die if you didn't."

With tender solemnity, already missing her, he gathered her in his arms, kissing her. "Then I guess I'll rack up frequent flyer miles. I'm not giving you up, Maggie. I refuse. Absolutely. You have to marry me. I love you. One day you and I will have a son. I'm sure of it. What do you have to say about that?"

The future seemed bright again. Maggie snuggled against him. "I'd say your plans require an active participation by the two people directly involved in this most important project. If I were you, I'd start buying your tickets."

Chapter Sixteen

David gave Samara a new paisley bathrobe for her birthday. Showered, powdered, and perfumed with First, her favorite scent from Van Cleef and Arpels, she carefully opened the gift box, set aside the bow, and meticulously refolded the flowered wrapping paper. She grinned sheepishly at David, who was shaking his head.

"I can't help it, it's habit."

David came up behind her. He lifted her hair away from her neck, then helped himself to a kiss behind her ear. "That's my spot. God, you smell good. I meant it when I told you that I could pick you out in the dark." He winked. "I could pick you out by taste, too."

She smiled into his deepset, dark eyes, her lips curving impishly. "See that you do," she teased, going into the kitchen to prepare breakfast. Feeling like a bride, she fixed him a mouth-watering breakfast of orange juice, eggs Benedict, bacon, and coffee.

Inspired by love, she sat in the kitchen after he left with the sun streaming over her shoulder. She dreamily sketched the fall collection she intended to send to Jules for his approval.

David strolled in at four P.M. with a bottle of champagne and strawberries. He took her by the hand and led her to bed, where he said he intended to eat dessert.

She became daring, adventuresome, arousing David with her newfound feminine power. They bathed together, splashing water over the sides of the tub, laughing hysterically at the mess they were making. "Will it always be like this?" she asked. "Like a perpetual honeymoon?"

He squirted water on her breasts. "Baby, if this keeps

up—no pun intended—my students will have to carry me on rounds.''

She pouted. ''I'm not a baby. Or haven't you noticed that I'm old enough to be a mother?''

Getting out of the tub, David sucked droplets of water from her navel. ''I noticed,'' he said, his voice heavy and thick, his expression so heated that her heart seemed to melt.

There were moments when Samara's happiness mingled with rushes of guilt. Her mother was dead. How dare she have the temerity to be happy? Then her sad eyes would find David's, and the cold feeling would pass. It was as if God had given her a special dispensation.

The bathroom quickly took on the trappings of a couple. Samara hung her pink toothbrush next to his green one. Their towels occupied the same rack. In the medicine cabinet, she wedged her deodorant near his roll-on. Johnson and Johnson baby powder cozied up to First bath powder on a tray atop the toilet tank. Samara appropriated most of the closet space with her clothes, double-hanging David's. For good measure she spritzed her side with perfume. ''Hey, cut that out!'' he cried.

She noticed he didn't argue when her flimsy lingerie occupied the same dresser drawer.

He confided his worry about Emmett, who reminded him a lot of his childhood friend Norman who had died of leukemia. She cradled David in her arms, feeling more and more like a wife, sharing her husband's bed, his loving, his worries.

The following day Vittorio drove Samara to her father's house to lunch with Solange. ''Will you be moving back with us?'' Solange asked, tucking her arm through Samara's.

''I don't think so.'' Samara blushed. She paced her steps. She was sore in places she didn't know a person could get sore.

''My experienced twin!'' Solange gushed, wide-eyed. ''We must tell each other all our secrets.''

''Does it show?'' Samara asked.

Solange hugged her. ''Only to me. Does he have a pet name for you?''

Samara felt her cheeks redden. ''He calls me baby or *mon petit chou*. My little cabbage.''

Solange made a moue with her mouth. ''It sounds better in French. I'm not too certain about baby either.''

''Why not?'' Samara asked.

"I've got a theory that men who call women baby are never serious about the relationship. They're usually after something. I'm sure that's not true in your case," she said guilelessly.

She led her into the sun room where the table was set with cobb salads and iced tea. "I thought you'd enjoy the garden for a backdrop."

Tessie joined them unexpectedly. She brought a chocolate mousse birthday cake and told them their presents would be given to them at the party. She approved of Samara's cinch-waisted pistachio-green dress, her multicolored leather sandals. Despite the fact that she looked forward to being alone with Solange, Samara quickly fell under the spell of Tessie's mesmerizing stories. In her need to establish roots, she listened avidly to tales of her grandmother's childhood, then how she met and married Barney.

Tessie Bergen Gold had been born to Russian immigrant parents in a Manhattan hospital—not home with a midwife attending her mother as was the case with many immigrants. A bonafide doctor brought the squalling infant into the world, setting her apart from the other babies born on her crowded block on Manhattan's Lower East Side. From her first fussy breath, she exhibited drive, tenacity, brains. Years later she refused to allow a matchmaker to arrange her marriage.

With dispatch she discarded suitors, selecting for her husband a man of equal ambition. Miraculously Tessie and Barney fell in love at first sight. Tessie didn't intimidate him. They laughed from relief, admitting they had wondered where they'd find a mate to equal their restless needs. Impatient with formal schooling, Barney took to the streets, learning quickly not to repeat the mistakes he saw other men make. Barney was a visionary, a master salesman. His tall, dark-haired good looks set Tessie's heart beating. She loved her sexy, aggressive mate who possessed a drive equal to hers.

The young couple opened the first Gold's, a small women's apparel store on Houston Street. Through word of mouth it rapidly became known for superior service, excellent merchandise, and for providing extra touches to light up the mundane lives of its working-class customers, women who didn't own such luxuries as comfy slippers and the buttery carmel terry-cloth robes Tessie supplied. The women continued shopping while waiting for alterations to be hastily completed by seamstresses pedaling Singer sewing machines in the back room. Unbeknown to the customers, the mirrors Tessie had installed flattered the fuller female figure, making the viewer appear as curvaceous as her uptown pedigree sister. Loyal customers spread the word. Business boomed.

The Golds moved to a brownstone on Eastern Parkway. The wide boulevard streamed past the Brooklyn Museum, Brooklyn Botanical Gardens, Brooklyn Library, and ended at the Grand Army Plaza, where an arch replicated the Arc de Triomphe. It was a rich cultural neighborhood. Two doors down from their home was the Brooklyn Democratic Party headquarters. On the next block, the Brooklyn Jewish Center sponsored lectures by notables such as Helen Keller and Eleanor Roosevelt. Franklin Delano Roosevelt passed their brownstone in his touring car.

Tessie and Barney wisely stayed out of the stock market. When the Depression hit, they invested in real estate at cheap prices, including several summer homes on Sackett Lake in the Catskill Mountains near Monticello. Barney bragged that he owned a compound, like Joe Kennedy's in Hyannisport.

World War II elevated the Golds to the ranks of millionaires. Taking a page from Joe Kennedy, Max diversified, buying garment factories and contracting with the government to produce uniforms for the armed services. In more serious moments, he and Tessie talked of their ultimate dream: making Max president.

"Barney and I gambled, leaving lower Manhattan. We hocked everything to hire the best and the brightest." A smile lit Tessie's eyes. "Those years were the best. We tried innovative marketing techniques. We were successful. Today," she said with a snort, "we have malls and buying groups. Federated. Allied. Associated. We never imagined that Neiman-Marcus and Bergdorf Goodman would become subsidiaries of Carter Hawley Hale. Eben Jordan would turn over in his grave if he knew the store he founded in 1851 is an Allied Store."

Samara smiled shyly. "So is Bon Marché. And Amfac Inc. owns mushrooms, papaya, cheese, and Joseph Magnin."

Tessie's little fist slammed the table. "The Aussies bought Buffim's in California five years ago. That's never going to happen to Gold's! We're a family concern and we'll remain a family concern."

Clearly having a fine time, Tessie brought up one of her fondest memories. "I remember the day in 1976 when Queen Elizabeth and Prince Phillip came to New York. The queen visited Bloomie's and Gold's. It didn't hurt your father's political image one bit, let me tell you!"

Max arrived on Tessie's triumphant note, kissed Samara's cheek, then Solange's. Casually dressed in gray slacks, white shirt, and blue blazer, he seemed unusually relaxed. "Happy birthday, girls." Smiling broadly, Max presented them with gifts. He had stopped at Tiffany's, duplicating the gift Maggie had chosen for Solange. "We'll celebrate more at Shabbes. The wait will be worth it."

Samara gasped as she raised the lid on the blue Tiffany box and saw the delicate gold mesh bracelet.

"But you didn't have to buy me anything."

"Don't deprive your father of pleasure," Tessie said. "He has eighteen years to make up for."

"Thank you, Daddy," Solange said, kissing her father's cheek.

The conversation swung back to Tessie's recounting of how Barney enticed people into the store. "With daring window themes. He shocked them in! Worked like a charm," she said gleefully. "Then we got big and hired people."

Samara pumped her for details, her interest and enthusiasm in merchandising keeping Tessie talking. During a lull, Samara contributed a few names from Michael Emory's book *Windows*.

"Solange, what do you think of your sister?" Tessie beamed.

She smiled dulcetly. "We're lucky she's with us."

"My sentiments exactly," Max chimed in.

Samara found it easy to talk with her effusive grandmother. She responded affirmatively to her question asking whether she could produce a dress or ensemble from start to finish. "Can you drape? Prepare things for fittings? Have you had experience in working with piece-goods men? Do you know what a wholesale collection is? No, of course not. Samara, haute couture is a vanity operation."

"True, but the ready-to-wear line earns the basic bread and butter. If you wish dessert, franchise. A top fashion designer label attracts people to the cash register. The youth are the big spenders. With the constantly changing fads, they control most sales, regardless of who ultimately pays. Designers receive four to ten percent of gross sales, plus a minimum guarantee. Manufacturers advertise, too. Jules claims the short contract allows him to maintain control over his name. But . . .''

"What?" Tessie prompted.

Samara grew conscious of monopolizing the conversation, yet the subject was dear to her heart. "Times change too swiftly. I read in *Stores,*" she said, referring to the magazine of the National Retail Merchants Association, "that Macy's did an estimated $575 million in sales last year. The figures tied with Hudson's Detroit."

Clearly surprised, Tessie asked, "You read *Stores* in Paris?"

Samara nodded. "Jules subscribes to many American trade magazines. He keeps abreast of the market. Don't forget, Jules sells worldwide. Market trends and volume sales are important to him."

"I see," Tessie said, privately thinking Lilli should have spent Max's money to send Samara to Esmond Guerre-Lavigne School of Fashion Design in Paris. Samara kept abreast of the market, too. She reminded her of herself at that age: talented, eager to learn, unafraid to try. "Who are Jules's suppliers?"

Samara thought a minute. "Wherever he gets the best buy and workmanship. Italy and Turkey for leather. Philippines for embroidery. Japan for silks. Calais for lace."

"Who is his printmaker?" Tessie assessed her granddaughter, not Jules.

"Again, it depends. Etro, of course, but there are others."

Tessie sipped tea. "How would you go about promoting a line?"

A blush rose in Samara's face. Tessie neatly maneuvered her into center stage. She weighed her words carefully. "Advertise store-wide themes. Coordinate all the departments, including food. Invite dignitaries. Plan a television road show to promote Gold's name." Tessie asked her to explain.

Samara gestured with open hands. "Cassini brought his traveling fashion show to department stores and TV. Designer trunk shows are commonplace today, but why not take it a step further? Why not promote the Gold's label with a television trunk show? Gold's will benefit by direct and catalogue sales."

Tessie pursed her lips. "Wouldn't a designer rather promote his or her name, rather than a store name?"

Samara dreamed of presenting her collection to a national audience. "Many would; however, linkage is a great way to get ahead. If you license new, talented designers, or tie in with a Hollywood star or a sports personality as a draw, it benefits everyone. You create an exclusive Gold's line. By financing the collection, Gold's negotiates more favorable terms."

Tessie put down her teacup. "I sensed before that you take after me. Today I'm certain of it. You speak with a business sense rare in a woman of nineteen. I doubt even if you know what a gift you possess. Grandpa and I want to help. The jewel in the family crown will be the San Francisco store. It's yours if you prove yourself. I'll train you, bring you into the business."

Samara's jaw dropped open. Flabbergasted, she felt excitement course through her. "Grandma, I'm a fledgling designer. I have no experience in merchandising or business."

"Did I have any experience when I started?" Tessie replied. "Trust me. Experience comes from life. You're intelligent. You'll learn from experts, besides myself. You know fashion. You know style. Your ideas are sound. And you're my granddaughter! You can't lose with a winning combination!" she ended triumphantly.

Max leaned forward, agreeing. "Think about it. Don't say anything now. There's plenty of time."

Samara turned to Solange. "What do you think?"

Solange looked cool and lovely in a pink Givenchy sheath with large black buttons down the front. Silver loops hung from her ears. Behind her calm exterior she was alert, watching and assessing, with adrenaline pumping.

"Samara, it's your decision." She lifted her dainty shoulders in a shrug. "It sounds marvelous, but what if you don't like merchandising? Won't you waste valuable time starting your career as a designer? Aren't you wiser to let Jules complete your training? Paris is the fashion capital of the world. Can you afford to leave it for a gamble?"

Tessie strongly objected. "Samara, you can't afford to go backward. Your priorities must change. You're a Gold. So-lange, she's entitled by birthright, as you are, to all we can do for her. Aside from Jules, who's in Paris for her?" She brought David's name into the discussion without actually mentioning him.

Rendered speechless, Samara could name only a handful of designers who after years of struggle found backing money to franchise. But this! Tessie opened new vistas, a chance to learn from experts, to know that one day if she proved herself worthy, she could look forward to heading a prestigious store. This revelation was beyond her wildest dreams.

In a kind of dreamy haze, she saw herself in the corporate plum role, conducting staff meetings, interacting with department heads, offering sage advice. Jules would fly in from Paris to present his collection. And hers! Who is this young phenomenon? How does she do it all? the press would ask. Best of all, she saw herself walking through the gleaming corridors hand in hand with a beaming, proud David . . .

"With all due respect, Grandma," Solange said, "I still say it's a gamble. It's unfair to Samara."

Samara crashed back to reality. Solange was right. She'd been thinking like a kid instead of like an adult. She could mess up everything, disappoint them, destroy the good feeling that existed now. Then in her mind she heard her grandmother's enthusiastic endorsement. Why not try? She'd disappoint them even more if she didn't. She could prove herself. She could succeed if she worked very hard. She was used to hard work. She'd organize her time down to the last minute. On the weekends and at night she'd design and then send the collection to Jules. She'd spend her days at Gold's. *Please, God, help me to make David practice medicine in San Francisco.*

"You heard Samara talk," Tessie said, unmindful of the roller-coaster turmoil in her granddaughter's chest. "She's good. With her attitude, her knowledge, we'd jump at the chance to hire her for our manager's training program, even if she were a stranger. The fact she's family is a godsend. Besides me, she'll be trained by a team of very smart people, including the current president of Gold's in New York.

"Harry Shieffer," she said, naming him, "wants to retire in three years. We're prepared to make him an offer he can't refuse. He helps train Samara in the New York store, he oversees her first year in California, and we add a large sum of money to his retirement package. Several key managers have approached us about going to Gold's West. If for some reason Samara finds she doesn't like it, we promote one of the managers from New York to head Gold's West. No one loses."

Solange went on the offensive. "Except Samara's career as a designer. How could you make those plans without first asking her?"

"Solange, sweetheart, I am asking her. Now. Besides, Grandpa and I always make contingency plans. I merely want her to know she'll have all the help she needs. It's more than Grandpa and I got when we started."

Samara unclasped her hands. Her heart skittered and leapt in her breast. She gulped water to quench her dry throat. Family consideration and the outpouring of love of this magnitude were foreign to her. Her twin's argument with Tessie was on *her* behalf.

Her voice trembled. "Grandma, I'm overwhelmed. Solange, I can't thank you enough for caring. Truly. My instinct tells me to grasp the chance, but I'd like a few days to think it over."

Solange picked up her knife. She gave her a knowing look. "To talk to David?"

Samara blushed. "Yes."

"San Francisco is a beautiful city," David said carefully that night. "It's good for your career. You ought to accept."

Samara brought him a glass of wine. She had changed into a nightgown and her paisley robe. "*We* ought to accept. Darling, whatever I do I do with you."

He couldn't compete with the forces already in motion. "My commitment to the hospital ends in five years."

She gathered her dishes, putting them in the sink. Determined to find a solution, it took her a minute, but when she applied her brand of math, she grew more enthused.

"Okay. Gold's West is still under construction. It won't open for another year and a half. Builders are notoriously late on completion dates. That's three years or less of us flying back and forth, depending on whether I like the business."

"Baby, you know I can't pick up and travel on a steady basis. What do I do with my patients?"

"You're right. I don't mind doing most of it. Darling, we could still have a wonderful life."

And get married long before then, she vowed silently. In her ever-expanding perfect world, she saw herself as a doting wife, a loving mother, a successful designer, and head of Gold's West!

* * *

In his office, David transcribed his notes on Emmett Brown's chart. Wendall opened the door. He pulled a can of soda from his pocket, popped the lid, took a long drink, and sat.

"I hear the boy's worse. Can't you find a matching donor?"

David let out a discouraging sigh. "We're trying. One day we'll have donor banks. In the meantime, his white count is one hundred twenty thousand. His platelet count's dropping dangerously. There are immature leukemic cells in his peripheral blood. If his parents brought him in earlier, he might have had a better chance. He's only six years old."

"You're crazy about that boy, aren't you?" Wendall asked sympathetically.

"Yes," David admitted. "He reminds me of someone I knew. I lost a close friend when I was his age. Kids ought to have a chance to grow up. I've never understood how a woman can elect to have an abortion unless there are damn good extenuating circumstances."

Wendall agreed. "Emmett's folks belong to a religious sect, one that opposes medical treatment, don't they?"

David frowned. "Yes. Fear prompted them to change their minds. I wish we were further along in our studies of feline leukemia."

"So what else is new?" Wendall asked, thinking that David looked tired, as if he needed sleep.

Wendall's supposition was true. After making love to Samara, David had remained awake, thinking of how hard it was for him to advise Samara. He mentioned it to Wendall.

"Christ, you're an idiot. I can't believe you're not dragging her by the hair to the wedding chapel. You're practically pushing her out the door, you're so magnanimous. Get married. Sort out the particulars later."

"I don't expect you to understand," David scolded impatiently. "You were born to wealth. Any day you want you could move to a penthouse apartment. Samara's never had money or family. If I tie her down, I'll make it harder for her."

"How would you be tying her down?"

"Samara wants a family. The fact is, so do I. I may be strong enough to resist the idea now. If we married, one of us would get carried away. Next thing you know we'd be parents, flying back and forth between coasts."

"Others do it. Why not you? Assuming it happens."

"A child needs two parents. I want to watch my child grow. I want to be there for the teething, the toilet training, the first tooth, the first word. Everything. I don't want to miss one phase, one day. I grew up listening to people of my parents' generation speak about children of the Holocaust. Those who made it were farmed out to whoever would take them. We hear about the success stories, the children who made it to Israel, to a kibbutz. Many other lives were permanently devastated."

David became preoccupied with the folder containing Emmett's chart. "If a child is able to grow up with two parents who love him, who see him daily, who nurture him physically and emotionally, isn't that better than a bi-coastal arrangement?"

"Sure it is," Wendall conceded. "In Utopia, David. Don't forget there's a high divorce rate. People adapt."

"We see the results of that on kids, too. Samara's fathers were mine and Jules. That's not going to happen to our child. I love her. I'll love our children. Do you think for one minute either of us wouldn't sacrifice for the other? I know how she thinks. She's got it in her pretty little head that an instant family will replace the one she's never had. Her desire to marry now is part of the grieving process. She'd work with a papoose on her back. Can you see us having a baby here? I can't.

"Look, Wendall, the bottom line is this. You and I do what we want. We'd resent anyone who wouldn't let us practice medicine. I've given this a lot of thought. Samara deserves her chance. She's only nineteen. It can't hurt to wait a few years. We'll marry and have children, but when we do, her career will be on track, and she won't be alone."

Wendall rose. His red hair flopping over his forehead, he braced his palms on the desk. "Your good intentions suck. Despite your lofty arguments, you forget one fact in your smart equation."

"What's that?"

"The realities of life, pal. Too many things can happen in the interim. Suppose she meets a man out there." He grinned. "Or, if she stays here, I might make a play for her. She adores my piano playing. That's a start."

He closed the door before the pencil David threw could hit him.

Chapter Seventeen

Flanked by Wendall and David, Samara greeted Barney Gold in the entryway of his spacious apartment on Central Park South and Seventh Avenue.

The grandfather enveloped his nervous granddaughter in a bear hug, breaking the awkward formality. Shorter than Max, he had white hair, dark twinkling eyes, and a broad smile. Max elbowed his way in.

"My turn," he said, kissing her. "Samara, you look lovely. The bracelet couldn't be worn by a more beautiful owner. Thank you for wearing it tonight. It's good to see you again, David. Thanks for taking care of her, for bringing her to us."

The men sized each other up. It pleased David that Max treated the touchy subject of Samara living in his apartment with the grace of a politician. "My pleasure."

The Leightners and Tessie joined them. Strands of gray dusted Murray's thinning blond hair. His bright blue eyes crinkled. "Don't hog her," he joked. "Samara, welcome home."

"What about me?" Ceil Leightner dyed her caramel-colored hair to match her eyes. Chic in a red Chanel suit and diamond stud earrings, she put her arms around Samara. "I'm so glad to see you. Avrim will be here after his telecast."

The twins embraced. "Solange, I'd like you to meet David Orchin and Wendall Everett-Lawson. Guys, guess who this is?"

"We can't," they chorused.

Solange's ruby lips curved into a soft smile. In a white Dior, her hair spilling softly about her shoulders, a stunning Solange lifted her eyes to David. She gently squeezed his hand, sizing him up in the space of seconds. Tall, with dark hair, direct intelligent brown eyes, and a row of even white teeth set in a ruggedly handsome face, he wore his blended blue herringbone suit with the élan of a man aspiring to wealth. He carried his broad shoulders and lean frame with an air of bemused sophistication. The lift of his mouth held a touch of arrogance. A calculating charmer, she thought, confirming her previously decided opinion.

"Samara's told me so much about you. I feel as if I know you already." She noted the love for him blazing in Samara's eyes.

"What have you heard about *me*?" Wendall asked, drawing her attention to him.

"Mavis says you're terrible." Solange laughed easily. "Come on, Wendall, you look like you could use a drink."

They followed Tessie and Max through the travertine marble entryway into the living room. Walls of windows framed the corner apartment, facing Central Park South and Seventh Avenue. The modern sofa and occasional chairs were upholstered in shades of cream with citron and plum accents. The free-form glass-topped coffee table sat on a black marble base. Indirect lighting lent flowing space to the uncluttered area. A Jackson Pollack abstract hung on the wall.

"Now you see what I like," Solange said to Samara. "I helped Grandma decorate."

Barney served flutes of Dom Perignon champagne. "To the family. I hope this is the first of many family gatherings." Then he slipped in the news that he'd deposited thirty thousand dollars into each girl's bank account. As Samara gasped, Solange's eyes focused on David.

"I added ten thousand," Max said. "Happy birthday."

Forty thousand dollars! More money than Lilli or she earned in a year. Samara squeezed David's hand. "I don't know what to say," she stammered. "Thank you."

Barney questioned David about his specialty. Seated on the couch, his arm lightly riding Samara's shoulder, she tugged his hand when Barney turned his attention to Wendall. "Let's step out on the terrace."

From their view from the eighteenth floor, the traffic far below snaked past in a rumbling hum. Above, an ethereal sky burned with a misty orange glow in the night sky. David wrapped a protective arm about Samara. With his face close to hers, he pointed out the lights of Tavern on the Green in Central Park.

"There's a hansom cab making its way into one of the park's entrances. I wish I had time to take you on a ride."

She lifted her face to kiss him softly on the lips. "You will. One day, we'll do it all. Doesn't the park look like a green sea of tranquillity?"

"Mmmm," he agreed, breathing in her intoxicating scent. "Don't go there alone at night."

"David, what should I do about the money? It's a fortune."

As he contemplated her classically beautiful features and the shoulder-length moonlight cloud of hair, he felt her being pulled away from him. "It's not a fortune to your family, Samara. Money like this is a lot to us, not to them."

Samara never stopped to consider that Solange accepted the check as if it were her due. "Then you think it's okay to accept it?"

"Yes. You're a Gold. You're family."

Tessie announced dinner. With everyone seated in the dining room around the black lacquered, glass-topped table above which a chandelier cast rainbows of color, she began the ritual service. Her discerning eye had told her the minute she saw Samara with David that they in were in love. The blaze from their eyes could light the candle. Good, she thought. She would marry a nice Jewish doctor. Everything would work out for the best. Gold's would be in good hands. She lit the Sabbath candles.

"Amen. Good Shabbes." She removed the lace covering from her head.

"*Yom tov*," Barney, unfolding his linen dinner napkin, responded in Hebrew. "I've heard good things, Samara. About your work with Jules, your talents as a designer. I spoke with Jules today. He says to tell you this is better than having your picture in *Elle*. Mimi sends her love, too. Did you design your outfit?" She nodded. "You're good," he said, admiring the ambrosia wool crepe chiffon dress, classically adorned by a silk crepe chiffon scarf. "Grandma told me about your merchandising ideas. Not bad. I'd like to see your sketches. When you're ready, we'll arrange a showing. I know a few people in New York."

"Barney knows everybody," Tessie said. "It'll be fun for us to launch the next generation of talented Golds. Samara, would you like a private tour of the store after it closes? Solange, you come, too."

Solange lifted her flute of wine. She'd heard the afterthought put into Tessie's invitation. "I wouldn't miss it," she said dryly, covertly concentrating on David, who looked the way a virile sexual animal on the make ought to look.

A maid served chicken and matzo ball soup. Avrim arrived in time for the main course. After greeting everyone, he slipped into the chair beside Solange. "Penny for your thoughts," he murmured. He discretely handed Solange the gift Maggie had picked out for him to give her.

"They're worth a hell of a lot more." Solange dropped her napkin then peeked inside the box. It contained a pair of enamel-accented, 14K gold and diamond tiger earrings. She smiled at the apt symbolism. Her fingers moved surreptitiously up his inner thigh. "Thank you, darling."

Leaning down to help her, he covered her hand, moving it inward. "Name your price," he whispered. "I've missed you."

Platters of roast chicken, wild rice, string beans with almonds, and condiments disappeared as the conversation progressed. Much of it focused on Samara. When they'd finished dessert, Max clinked his glass and stood.

"Attention everyone!" Tessie ordered. "Our future president wants the floor."

Max's gaze lingered on his dazzling daughters, then swept past to encompass all present. "A toast to family, friends, old and new. Samara, dear child, my heart is full. I'm so happy that you're here. If I said more, I'd cry, so I won't. Family, the secret of true happiness."

A chorus of "Here, here" followed.

Max sipped his wine and cleared his throat. "I'm glad you agree. I hope you'll understand an irrevocable decision I've made, one I made upon advice and counsel," he lied. "After speaking with my staff and advisers, they concur it's best that I do not announce for the presidency in November." He paused to let that sink in.

Barney scowled and muttered something beneath his breath.

He gripped the table. Tessie uttered a cry. Her face appeared to drain of blood.

"Mom, Dad, please," Max said. "Assume that Jimmy Carter will be the Democratic Party standard bearer. Over the past few days I've reassessed not only mine, but other Democratic hopefuls' chances. I've also spoken with powerfully placed politicians and pollsters. I've concluded that an Independent will lose to an incumbent president who chooses to run. Why waste my time? I'd rather enjoy my family."

Solange secretly whooped with joy. She tipped her hat to Samara. Without her having to lift a finger, Samara killed the presidency. Solange wouldn't be dogged by the Secret Service. She also eliminated Maggie.

Barney guessed the reason for his son's dramatic decision.

"It's going to be the damn suicide note and Samara's sudden appearance. Mark my words. I know Max," he'd grumbled that morning to Tessie.

He compared Samara and Solange. Two outwardly ravishing beauties. A plastic surgeon couldn't improve on nature. Although his granddaughters were blessed by God with flawless complexions, high cheekbones, riveting eyes, and models' figures, Barney also knew that lasting beauty only grows from a nurturing soul. God help him, he thought disloyally. He'd never felt completely at ease with Solange, not like Tessie. He loved Solange, but he wasn't blind. He supposed it was his fault for not trying harder. From the moment of her birth Solange needed . . . more.

Lilli had been right. A mother knows her child, but why couldn't she have left the less demanding twin? As a baby Samara had been a pleasure to be around. Max indulged Solange's slightest wish. He'd probably felt a lot of guilt. Tessie said he was wrong to find fault with their darling granddaughter. She said that two generations removed made him blind to today's youth. Bullshit.

Barney's sharp eyes studied Samara. When she thought no one was looking, she slid adoring glances at that fellow by her side as if the sun shone directly atop his head.

From the moment Samara stepped into his home, a tall, exquisite creature surrounded by an air of innocence, she'd captured his attention.

Barney's gaze swung to Solange, then back to Samara before

coming to rest on Solange. A shiver of fear rivered through him. *That's the difference!* he realized, answering the question gnawing on his mind. The twins weren't mirror images. Solange looked at the world with cunning eyes. She demanded the cachet of exclusivity. He should have insisted that Max divorce Lilli, remarry, and give Solange a normal life.

Max cleared his throat, clinked his glass, and got everyone's immediate attention. He took a deep breath and sought Tessie's eyes. "There's a second announcement. In the past we've been separated as a family. I do not choose to live alone the rest of my life. I'm lonely. Samara, Solange, one day you'll marry. When those happy events come about I'll be the proudest father who ever walked down the aisle. You'll have the biggest and best weddings money can buy. I plan on being a doting grandfather. I'm going to make a nuisance of myself, so be warned."

Samara squeezed David's hand.

"For the past five years," Max informed his rapt audience, "I've loved Maggie McPherson. Mama, Vittorio and you gossip, therefore, you and Dad shouldn't be surprised. Frankly you should have been paying Vittorio's salary, not me. Solange, you've known, too, as have the Leightners. Maggie signed a contract to do her show from San Francisco. As often as possible, I'll fly there to be with her. If she'll have me, we'll marry when my term of office is up. Sooner if possible. I'm returning to private practice. This is what I want. Girls, unless you object, I'd like to release a statement to the press. I'll tell them your mother and I were separated. Out of respect for her religious teachings, we decided not to divorce, which is true. In these modern times, people will accept the fact that you lived with your mother, Samara. They'll want to meet you. I hope you'll stand by my side. And Solange, of course. Since I no longer will be running for public office, I hope that ends it. A united front should help quell any gossip. Avrim, I'd appreciate your cooperation for the sake of my family."

Max sat, then waited for the double-barreled announcement to settle. Ceil recovered first. She raised her wineglass. Murray followed. "Max, I applaud you. To yours and your daughters' happiness."

Tessie swallowed her disappointment for Barney's sake. Barney stared at his hands, thinking that God played a mean hand of poker. David and Wendall each gave Max high marks for handling a difficult situation with grace. Avrim never thought Max had a shot at winning the presidency. But, by God, he thought delightedly, Max and Maggie! Avrim joined his parents in raising his glass in Max's honor. To be polite, Samara raised hers. Max's solution to her arrival honored her mother's memory, yet it irked her to hear him announce his intention to marry so soon. With a start, she realized he hadn't seen her mother—his wife!—in nearly two decades. As to his not running, she didn't care one way or the other. But what, she wondered, could Solange be thinking?

With narrowing, thoughtful eyes, Solange studied David, whose finger curled over Samara's. A tense, exciting spiral of expectation coiled inside her. A small, indolent smile curved her lips. She turned to Avrim. The grin she gave him when she lifted her eyes contained supreme confidence.

No one noticed she was the only one who hadn't raised her glass to Max.

Engrossed in thought, David stared out the car window as the Lincoln sped through the night. After Max's stunning announcement, the conversation gradually drifted to the elder Golds' plans for Samara. It was going to be difficult, David thought. Even with Max renouncing the presidency, she'd be caught up in a social whirl. As soon as his commitment to Columbia ended, he planned to drag her down the aisle. Morosely he shifted his thoughts to Emmett.

From his side of the car, Wendall whistled. Sitting between them, Samara bubbled. She poked Wendall. "What do you think of my sister? Isn't she the most breathtakingly beautiful young woman you've ever seen? Tell the truth."

Wendall roared. "Coming from her identical twin, that's chutzpah. All right, I agree. She's beautiful. A knockout. Just like you."

Samara leaned back, sighing happily. "Thank you, kind sir." She tapped David's knee. "Darling, what about you?"

David blinked. "I'm sorry, sweetheart, what did you say?"

"Solange. Darling, what's your impression of my sister?"

He had felt Solange's heated appraisal, boldly assessing him. He hadn't liked it. "She seems older than you do."

Samara swatted him. "How dare you! I'm older by five minutes."

"Sorry, baby," he teased, dropping a kiss on her temple.

"Oooh, you!" she protested.

She waved a cheerful good-bye to Vittorio and to Wendall who was spending the night with Maisy Daisy. Her eyes alive with mischief, Samara marched into the bedroom and stripped to change quickly into a lacy black bra, black garter belt, and black seamed stockings. She bent a suggestive knee, rode one arm slinking up the door frame, perched her other hand on her hip, and licked her red lips.

"Come to bed, you old goat," she said in her huskiest voice. "Let this baby show you what she can do."

David's heavy-lidded gaze inched down her body. "My very own ambrosia," he murmured, drawing her away from the wall to breathe her signature scent. In the muted light, her hair glistened against her bare shoulders. He lifted her in his arms and gently lowered her to the bed. He sucked her silky triangle with deliberate aching slowness, creating tidal waves of anticipation. He kept it up until she writhed in his arms.

He lifted his head. "Now, baby, about your invitation . . ."

Chapter Eighteen

On separate coasts Avrim and Maggie reported Senator Gold's retirement from public life as straight news. The rest of the media had a field day. When the story left the front pages, it remained fodder for the covers of supermarket tabloids. Dubbed the platinum Gold twins by an enterprising reporter, the name stuck. Solange grumbled to Avrim that she would have been better off if Max had run and won the presidency. "The Secret Service could have slammed the door in those nosy reporters' faces!"

Max asked Solange to sign three legal documents. "These are joint ownership documents, Solange, for three properties I had put in your name. Now that Samara is with us, it's only fair for her to share equally in everything, including the bank accounts."

Seething with the injustice of having to sign or else appear to be selfish, Solange announced she didn't want to go back to college. "I'm taking a semester off."

"You'll do nothing of the sort," Max said bluntly. "Interrupting your studies is unwise."

"Samara's not going to school."

"She's different." Max put the legal documents into a manila folder. "She didn't have your opportunities."

Solange's lip curled. "Is that why Grandma and Grandpa offered her Gold's West?"

"No. They offered because she's talented. She's smart, which is what you won't be if you drop out of school." Kissing her, he left. Solange smashed her coffee cup against the wall.

In the weeks that followed, Samara's enthusiasm and her ability to learn confirmed Tessie's prediction, giving the elder

Golds a new lease on life. Their young granddaughter's presence assuaged their disappointment over Max's announcement. She became an avid reader of Kurt Barnard, publisher of *Barnard's Retail Marketing Reports*. She discussed retailing trends and projections with Harry Shieffer, the president of Gold's.

"Retailing is in her genes," he reported to Tessie and Barney.

In a lovely surprise that had everyone in the family except Solange beaming, Tessie and Barney invited the entire Gold's staff, vendors, and guests to an after-hours party. Tuxedoed waiters glided through aisles serving Louis Roederer champagne and assorted canapés. Surrounded by art deco treasures, Gold's shone with gleaming wood and brass. Samara strolled through intimate boutiques, their walls covered with richly extravagant brocades. Merchandise was displayed in étagères and trunks and draped on banquettes in uniquely bold and dicey presentations. Tessie admitted she adapted the idea for the ultra-posh fashion departments from the 28 shop in Marshall Field's of Chicago.

Tessie announced plans for a four-week store-wide promotion: Fête de France. Employees wore lapel pins depicting the flags of France and the United States. "We'll show Bloomingdale's a thing or two," the grande dame of retailing said loftily.

"Gold's is better and nicer than Bloomingdale's," Samara said loyally. Rolling her eyes, Solange, wearing a loosely belted Donna Karan, examined a silk hand-painted blouse.

Barney introduced Samara to a man with clear blue eyes and a fascinating smile. "Charlie Mandel is president of Mandel Merchandising Corporation. He's the best trend spotter in the business. If he tells us buy, we buy. With ten thousand clothing lines available in this city, who can sit through all those showings?"

In a bright blue fedora that matched his eyes, Charlie accepted the compliment. "You might sketch it in Paris and make it in Singapore, but you have to come right here to good old New York to sell it."

"In the old days," Tessie commented, "all I did was walk down Canal Street. Now it's a science!" She bussed Charlie's cheek, then led Samara to a courtly Japanese businessman.

"Darling, say hello to a true marketing genius, James Kwo." Samara had heard of the man with factories in China, backing in Japan, and headquarters in New York, who helped revolutionize the fashion industry by mass marketing.

Looking beautiful in a blue-and-white-striped silk-pleated skirt and matching top, Samara extended her hand in greeting.

"New York is where the contacts are," he said simply. "Wait until Mardi Gras season." At her confusion, he added, "Spring and fall are Seventh Avenue's hoopla times. Everyone's showing."

Excited, flushed with news, Samara repeated the exhilarating account of her experience later that night to David. "I brought home a platter of food for you, darling." She kissed him soundly. "I love life. I love you! I love Solange! I'm the luckiest girl in the world."

A preoccupied David ate, then returned to the hospital to check on his patients. At one A.M. he returned, wishing again that he could find a cure for Emmett.

The following day Samara lunched with Tessie and Gold's advertising director, Flavio Santori. He spoke of Gold's exclusive representation of bed linens by a fabulously talented new European female designer. After Samara heard the prices, she frowned but remained silent.

"What's wrong, darling?" Tessie scribbled on a piece of paper and folded it. "Are we charging too much?"

"No. The markup isn't enough for exclusive rights. It doesn't take into account Gold's envied image."

Tessie unfolded the paper. She'd written: *Too cheap.* A delighted grandmother conferred with her granddaughter, then told Flavio how much to raise the prices. The supply sold out.

Two weeks later, *Elle* sent a photographer to New York. Samara would appear on the Christmas cover, and on three pages modeling Jules's clothes. An article, written by her good friend Mimi, quoted Jules LeClaire touting Samara Bousseauc Gold as the brightest young fashion designer to come along in years.

Party invitations flowed in the mail. A busy David encouraged her to attend without him. Samara confided to Solange that the only thing that could make her life better would be David's ring on her finger. The money in her bank account sat untouched. Samara couldn't bring herself to spend any of it, saving it instead for when she and David bought their first house.

Whenever she could, she went to the Metropolitan Museum of Art. At the Met, she studied costuming, often telling Jules over the phone about a particularly intriguing bit of workmanship or embroidery.

"Learn everything," he kept saying.

"What's wrong?" Solange asked, noticing Samara's preoccupation one day. In David's apartment, Samara served shrimp salad for lunch. The castoff collection of furniture in the apartment confirmed Solange's opinion. Wendall, she knew from his cousin Mavis, didn't give a hoot. David's encouraging Samara to learn the business from Tessie meant, she decided, that he counted on her to deliver Gold's, too. Marriage meant children. Grandchildren would further dissolve what was rightfully hers.

Samara confessed her impatience. That morning she had put the finishing touches on her fall collection to send to Jules, giving her time to think about David.

"We make love. Later we talk about our day. There's a little boy he's especially worried about. Last night I told him Tessie wants me to accompany her to San Francisco to see the site for Gold's West. Confidentially, I hope it takes longer than planned to be built. I'm happy in New York. How can I leave him? I love him so much."

Solange sipped her coffee. "Samara, you're trying too hard."

"In what way?" she asked, grateful to be able to talk with her sister.

Solange shrugged. "I'm not trying to hurt your feelings, sis, but you throw yourself at David. If I notice you hanging all over him like a kid, others do, too. It's got to make him feel uncomfortable. He's not a teenager, he's a grown man."

"Do I really do that?" Samara asked, dismayed.

Solange covered her hand with hers. "You said yourself he calls you baby."

Samara bit her lip. "But that's as a term of endearment."

"Then I'm sure you're right," Solange said gently. "Are you interested in Gold's or are you reluctant to hurt Grandma and Grandpa?"

Samara ran her finger around the edge of her empty coffee

cup. "I appreciate everything they're doing for me. No, I'm grateful for the chance."

"I still say Jules is your best bet. But, of course, he's in Paris. Gold's West is in San Francisco. David's here, and you love him. All right, go for it. Forget what I said. With your talents, you'll make it work. By the way, let me have a spare key, if you don't mind. If you happen to be late for one of our appointments, I'd prefer not hanging around outside in this neighborhood."

Samara gave her the key, thinking it a good idea. That night she curled into a tight ball on her side of the bed. David was so exhausted he fell asleep the minute his head hit the pillow.

"How's it going?" Solange asked a few days later.

Samara shrugged her shoulders. "Fine, I guess. David's busy. I'm sure he thinks he knows what's best for me."

Wrong, honey, Solange thought. *He knows what's best for him. And what's best for him is making you deliver the goods!*

A week later, David rushed to the hospital in the middle of the night. Emmett died, and David took his death very hard. Samara invited Solange and Avrim over to lift David's spirits. She phoned Avrim's new desk, informing him she would also invite Solange.

"I'll be at Gold's. Why don't I pick you up when I'm through? We'll ride back to the apartment together."

She phoned Solange, made plans to see her at eight, saying that David had a rough night. "I made him promise to nap. He should be awake by the time I arrive at seven-thirty."

Much later, she realized she'd forgotten to tell Solange that Avrim would be joining them. Deciding to pleasantly surprise her, she went about her business.

Timing is everything, Solange thought, using her key to let herself into David's apartment. She smelled of Arpel's First, Samara's scent. Peeking into the bedroom, David's even breathing assured her he was asleep. With time to spare, she inspected the love nest dump. If it were hers, she'd burn the Salvation Army furniture, ditch the carpeting, fumigate. Better yet, she wouldn't be caught dead living here. She glanced out the window at the maze of hospital buildings and the littered streets. No wonder David dangled his little meal ticket to get all she could if she wanted him as the prize.

She studied her twin's designs, the swatches of materials, tacked up on the board near the window. *She's good,* she thought, peering at a sketch of a long coyote coat. Next to it another series of drawings completed the ensemble: turtleneck sweater, suede skirt, knee-high boots.

She flipped through a recent issue of *W.* In it, Jules LeClaire took credit for discovering Samara. He called her a true designer, not an adapter or a copyist. The article reported that Gold's would launch Samara's ready-to-wear line via a television trunk show. There was a picture of Samara modeling a gold lamé gown. The caption read "Gold and Platinum."

A twinge of regret hardened into determination. It wouldn't do to get mushy at this late date where her twin was concerned. Under other circumstances, they could have capitalized on being the platinum Gold twins, but these weren't ordinary circumstances. A girl's gotta do what she's gotta do to protect her future. She checked her Rolex. Time to get the show on the road.

She pushed her mane of hair back from her face. Having rehearsed the scene in her mind, she felt confident.

She went to her sister's worktable, picked up a pair of scissors and snipped the neckline of her dress, then returned the scissors to the exact spot where she'd found it. Starting at the cut, she ripped Giorgio Armani's silk tulip-shaped dress from neckline to hem. She shimmied out of her lingerie, then ripped that, too. Silently she removed her René Mancini pumps, making sure to leave one turned over on its side, the other closer to the bedroom door. She had no sympathy for David or Samara for putting her in this situation. In fact she was royally pissed that she had to break a perfectly good string of Mikimoto pearls. On tiptoe she entered the bedroom, strategically placing the evidence on the floor in the darkened room.

David slept, breathing the perfume from Samara's pillow. Samara, the romantic goose, had confessed she sprayed First on it to leave a lingering scent of herself there for David. Nauseating, but sweet.

Time to go to work.

Solange slipped between the sheets, thanking God for shades that turned day into night! She touched his arm. When he didn't awaken, she lightly skimmed its contours, getting the feel and texture of her prey. Her hand wandered down his smooth hip muscle to his solid thigh. He felt good. Damn good. She brought her hand over his chest. Beneath it, his heart rose and fell in a steady strong beat. She grinned. Before long that beat would bop. She kissed his shoulder, tasting his slightly salty skin. Bracing herself, she kissed his neck. Solange inclined toward him, until their bodies were perfectly aligned. She rubbed her tummy against his back, her hand finding his semitumescent penis. David turned over. ''I like that,'' he said drowsily.

Solange lapped the pulse point at the base of his neck. David's body became her palette. She drew exciting wet circles at his nipples. In his drugged sleep, David smelled Samara's familiar scent. He could feel her warm breath on his chest. He had been dreaming of Emmett, his pale face, his last earthly breath. Of the tears his parents shed, the pitiful piercing screams his mother made when she realized her son had died.

David reached for Samara. Their lips met on a pleasurable moan. With sleep slowly ebbing, his tongue traced lazy patterns on her lips. Darting out to meet his, hers played a dance. ''Mmmmm, I like that, too,'' he murmured. ''Don't stop.''

She cupped his face. Chuckling intimately, she sent her tongue on a deep search. Here was strength coming to life, she thought. He thrust his hips forward, grinding against hers. *Ah, yes,* she thought, proud of herself for making David rise to the occasion.

Solange imagined herself a lynx, licking, lubricating David's thighs, lapping his penis. Growing aroused, she went on her own erotic quest, touching David. Giving her best performance, her talented talons yielded deep groans of pleasure.

Had Samara ever gone down on him, or did they go right to the missionary position? With a little chuckle, she decided to chance it. She buried her face in his musky scent, sending her sister from her mind.

Scooting down beneath the sheet, she covered him with her soft, enticing, experienced mouth. She moved her head from side to side. Her tongue circled and sucked. Her mouth expanded as David's penis roared to life. His groans turned her on. Sixty-nine. Oooh, she pictured them intimately joined, mouth to mouth.

Doing it in the dark heightened the danger, the lure. Remembering her goal, she put her heart, soul, and talent into every lick, every draining, fucking suck. She eased him deeper into her mouth. David's groans became hotter. She stopped. Nothing would be worth it if he spurted into her mouth. Besides, this was warm-up time.

Solange put his hand between her legs. His finger found her creamy center. David was no slouch. The good doctor used his knowledge of anatomy, knowing exactly how to tease a clitoris. She closed her eyes, letting the rhythm of her body sing to his tune. Her breath came in shorter pants.

David kicked the unwanted sheet aside. He threw her legs over his shoulders to lean down. His mouth found her taut nipples, then went lower. Bending his head, his lips parted her vagina. Solange offered the delicacy of herself to his ravaging mouth. Jesus! Oh, sweet Jesus! Samara wasn't dumb. What a man! Who'd have thought David's tongue was such a fascinating instrument! Her toes curled. She shivered.

She came in a blinding, shattering orgasm.

David drew her up to kiss her. *God! she thought. The man's dynamite.* She tasted herself in his mouth. She mated with it, matching his explosive kisses, loving his wild frenzy, his racy roughness. Clutching his hair, she kneaded her fingers on his scalp.

He gulped for breath. He gasped for breath. Last night's death vigil vanished. Life soared through his veins. "How did you know I needed you today? God, Samara, I can't get enough of you."

Solange kissed his mouth shut. Their teeth clashed. She didn't want to hear Samara's name. Plastering her whole body against his, she cupped his scrotum, massaging it in a technique she'd learned that drove men insane.

He pulled away. "My God, Samara. Stop. I'll come."

Above her, David sought desperate release. He thrust forward, burying his pulsing shaft inside her. Samara erased his heartache. His heart bursting with love for her, he filled her with his thick, hard, full-throttled sex. Breath rushed from his lungs. Sweating, he bared his teeth, threw back his head, reaching for relief.

In the throes of ecstasy, triggered by the direct line of shivering nerve endings centered in her vagina, Solange flung an arm over her face. She wanted to scream. To curse. Oh, God, she needed to curse. Sanity returned only long enough for her to shove her fist into her mouth to stifle her screams. She came, ripped asunder by the most powerful orgasm she'd ever experienced. A second later, he emptied into the mouth of her womb with a mighty cry.

"You're the best!" he shouted.

The light clicked on, spotlighting the actors on the bed. Samara and Avrim choked on the sight, the smells of David and Solange, their naked, sweating, sex-satiated bodies forever imprinted into their brains. They had let themselves into the apartment. Hearing noises, Samara, carrying a bundle of lilacs, rushed in, worried that David might be ill. The flowers slid to the floor.

David, semen dripping from his still rigid penis, swung his head in confused, angry objection. How dare they insult Samara? He threw the sheet over her, protecting her from prying, unwelcome eyes. "Get out!" he snarled.

Solange scooted from the bed. She dragged the sheet with her, tripping over its hem. Shit! She hadn't expected Avrim.

"David raped me!" She cowered against the wall. "Samara, Avrim, for God's sake, do something!"

David blanched. "Ohmigod!" he cried.

Samara stared at him, at that wet part of him that betrayed her. He snatched a pillow to cover himself. In the dark, smelling of Samara's perfume, awakened and aroused, he hadn't dreamed, hadn't questioned. Recognition sank in.

"Bitch!" he shouted. "You tricked me."

"He's lying. Don't listen to him!" she screeched. The sheet slipped, revealing her breasts, the skin rosy pink from David's avid passion.

"Samara, you invited me here. You know you did." Gesturing wildly, she yelled, "David ripped my clothes. He dragged me in here. Look! Look on the floor. He broke my pearls. It proves I'm telling the truth. I begged him not to do it. He said ever since he met me all he's thought about is fucking the twin who didn't act like a baby. Samara, I warned you about him. I was right. He said he's sick of being saddled with you. He sleeps with you because you throw yourself at him. He wishes to hell you'd get out of his life!''

"No!" David roared. "No! You're lying!"

Solange shook with indignation. She cried in earnest, the wounded, abused victim. There was ample evidence of David's passion on her breasts, stomach, thighs. She peeked through her sodden lashes at Avrim and Samara.

"How could you waste your time on him? Avrim, do something, dammit!''

His eyes took in the sickening scene. He felt the blood drain from his veins. Solange had betrayed him in the worst possible way.

"You manipulating bitch! You goddamn actress!" he snarled. "Control! You've got to be in control, don't you? In school with Mrs. Manfred. With Maggie. With your father. Now this! You deserve an Oscar for your performance.''

He had to leave before he strangled her. He wrapped an arm around Samara's shoulders. "Let's go," he said, softening his voice for the shell-shocked girl. "Pack her things, David. Wendall can bring them to my house until she decides what she wants to do.''

Samara let out a strangled sob. It jolted her from her trancelike state. Avrim had known Solange as long as David had known her. He said she was acting. If that was true, she'd been a doubly naive fool. A gullible idiot.

She'd lived in a fantasy world of her creation, dreaming of her perfect life—a life centered around David. Mimi warned that her obsession could lead to heartbreak. She had only herself to blame. She saw it clearly now. From the beginning, she had thrown herself at him, insisted on coming to America with him when he tried to tell her to stay in Paris. Then she remained in his home, rather than move in with her father. She was the one who lured him into that very bed.

David never asked her to marry him. He shied away from a commitment when she'd brought up the subject. He used the excuse their careers would keep them on separate coasts. He encouraged her move to San Francisco!

Misery formed a tight hard knot, choking the air from her lungs. The perfect world that never was, could never be. In the space of time it took to see her life disintegrate, to face David's betrayal, Samara also faced the cold, irrefutable facts. One: his life didn't include her. It never did; she was too blindly in love to see it. She merely assumed and thus contributed to her own downfall. Two: her mother was dead. Neither divine intervention nor her mother's letters led her to Solange. The worst form of bad luck did. Three: it was high time she grew up.

She lifted her chin and threw back her shoulders. "I'm taking my rabbit and my sketches. David, you're free of me. Absolutely and forever. As for my clothes—throw them out. I want nothing you've touched. Nothing to remind me of you."

Distraught, he pleaded with her. "Samara, please. I don't want to be free. I never said those things. I'm sorry. I love you."

Her eyes blazed. She sent him a slow, scorching, scornful, scathing look. " 'I can find you in the dark. No one smells the way you do. Tastes the way you do.' Those were your exact words. Those and calling me baby. Good-bye, David."

Samara stumbled outside. The obscene images in her brain were so unbearable that she shook. She swayed dizzily as Avrim took her elbow, guiding her across the street. What a fool she'd been. Pain seared through her. Trembling uncontrollably, she didn't realize that the agonized passionate cry causing people to stare came from her.

"Samara, don't do this to yourself," Avrim said. "Solange isn't worth it."

Samara raised tear-filled eyes. "Don't you see, Avrim? The problem is I thought David was worth it."

Samara sat without speaking in the cab Avrim hailed. Not knowing how to help her and dealing with his private hell, Avrim gave his address to the driver. He felt terrible in the face of her agony, the brave front she mustered for his benefit. He paid the driver and ushered her into his apartment.

In the kitchen he pulled out a bottle of Canadian Club whiskey and two glasses. He poured a liberal amount in each glass. She held hers in both hands for so long that Avrim had to tilt it to her lips. Then she drank. The liquor burned fire in her chest, but she drained every drop, wishing in vain it would numb her brain.

"Solange is ill," Avrim said, telling her she'd been that way since childhood. "She's warped by jealousy. The signs were there: her need to control, her hatred of Maggie, Max's announcement he loves Maggie and wants to marry her.

Solange complained that Max made her sign properties over to you. Then you were offered Gold's West. Solange wasn't raped. Samara, believe me, she tricked David to get even with you to rid herself of the threat she thinks you pose.''

It didn't matter. All Samara kept hearing were David's words. *I could find you in the dark.*

''Avrim, it's too late,'' she said sadly.

''What will you do?'' he asked. The sheen of tears tracked her cheeks.

What would she do? She couldn't remain at Avrim's. Nor would she stay in New York where David lived or return to Paris where his parents lived.

''What about Gold's West?'' Avrim asked. ''There's still that in your future.''

''That's another pipe dream, Avrim. I'm through with New York. That eliminates my training. So you see, Solange got what she wanted. So did David. I don't know what the future holds, but whatever it is I'll do it alone.''

''Samara, Maggie's been hurt by Solange, too. Phone her,'' he urged. ''I don't blame you for leaving New York. Just don't cut San Francisco from your future. At least go there for a while. You need time to decide what to do.''

She heaved a sigh. There was no enthusiasm in her voice when she told him to make the call.

Briefly Avrim related the events. On her end, Maggie cursed. ''Solange is a bad seed. I pity David. I pity Samara.'' *You and Max, too,* she mouthed silently. ''Put Samara on the phone.''

''Thank you,'' Samara said a short time later, mustering her dignity. ''If you're sure it won't be too much trouble?''

''You'll be doing me a favor. I hate hearing the echo of my own voice bouncing off the walls.''

An hour and a half later, Avrim put Samara on a flight to San Francisco.

Chapter Nineteen

David's colleagues were so upset about the drastic change in him that they congregated in small groups, discussing ways to help him. David smiled mechanically at his patients, but never at his students. Often they found him slumped in his office chair, staring into space. He pushed himself, spending hours in the lab after everyone had gone. His coffee consumption went up; his weight went down. He wore a permanent haunted look. No one doubted his unhappiness. Short-tempered, driven, he no longer spoke pridefully of Samara, the pretty young woman who had captured his heart.

As if they contained a contaminating disease, he trashed the mattress and box spring. Even after purchasing new bedding, he couldn't find comfort in a room filled with Samara's memories. His closet and dresser drawers contained her clothes, her scent. Often he dragged himself to the sofa for a few restless hours of sleep. Attempts by Wendall to draw him out of his shell proved fruitless.

David phoned Avrim's secretary to learn that he'd taken a job in England heading the London news desk. David turned his anger on Wendall, lashing out at him for not telling him how to reach Samara. His letters to her waited for an address. "Where is she?" he demanded.

In the beginning, Wendall didn't know.

"You're a liar!" David charged. "She couldn't just disappear. You want her for yourself!"

In desperation David phoned his parents in Paris, shocking and dismaying them. He tried Mimi next. She hung up on him—after she cursed him for breaking Samara's heart!

Now, kicking his office door shut, he yanked open the filing cabinet so fast it began to tip. Cursing, he banged it upright. He sat down at his desk to read the file on a new patient.

"Hello."

His head shot up. His eyes lit with a smile . . . then fury replaced hope. She was the last person on earth he wanted to see. "Get the hell out of my sight."

Solange lifted her chin. "Gladly. After you give me the name of a doctor. I need an abortion."

He threw down his pen. "I told you to get out. I meant it."

"Listen," she snapped, her wrath matching his. "My life hasn't exactly been a bed of roses lately. It's your child. Help me to get rid of it."

He buried his face in his hands. His shoulders shook, "Oh, God. Will there never be an end to this nightmare?"

"Don't be so dramatic," she said. "I'm the one who's puking, not you. This is your baby. I don't want it."

He moved like lightning. Clamping his hand on her wrist, he dragged her out the door, down the corridor, past the gaping nurses, into the elevator. Solange open her mouth to protest. "Shut up," he warned. Seeing the black menace in his eyes, the hard set to his features, Solange bit back the retort on her lips. "Get out!" He pushed her out the exit to the maternity floor.

"Now just a goddamm minute!" she yelled, hearing the wail of newborn babies. "What the hell are you trying to do?"

"I told you to shut up! Open that mouth of yours, and I'll shove a fist down it." He grabbed her upper arm, propelling her to a small room off the nursery. "There's the sink. Wash your hands, then put this on." He shoved a white coat at her. Afraid, she did as he ordered. "Tie the mask." He opened the door to the nursery. "Sit down," he hissed.

"I will not!"

"Sit, you bitch!"

"Why? What are you going to do?"

"I told you to sit!"

She sat. Towering over her, his eyes as dark as night, his features set in anger, he placed a newborn infant in her arms. The tiny bundle of perfection smelled of baby powder and innocence. She hiccuped. Clear blue eyes looked up at Solange, and she yawned.

"Careful with her head," David cautioned.

The baby hiccuped again. Gas brought on a smile.

"Pretty, isn't she?" he asked. Wisps of blond hair poked out from beneath her little pink knitted cap.

Solange squirmed. "David, take her. She isn't mine."

"She's lucky. Now, you lying bitch, I'm going outside. Hold her, and while you do, think about someone killing her." He strode from the room to wait outside the glass-enclosed area.

Solange had never held a newborn infant before. As a child she'd broken her dolls, pulling off their arms and heads. Mesmerized, she studied the infant girl, absorbed by miniature eyelashes, tiny pink fingernails, a sweet rosebud mouth. She started to coo, then caught herself. *No!* she thought. *I will not feel maternal.* Frantic, her panic transmitted to a watchful David.

"All right. I'll take her," he said gruffly. He returned the infant to her bassinet.

"Get out of that mask and gown and follow me." She scrambled to do his bidding, catching up to him as he strode down the hall, this time taking the steps to his floor.

In the office he slammed the door shut. "I don't know what game you're playing now. Frankly I don't care. You're a lying piece of shit. For all I know, you're not pregnant."

Solange shuddered. Her life was a bitch. At home her father spoke to her only if absolutely necessary. Vittorio grunted. Pepe moped. Tessie and Barney blamed her for Samara's running away. Avrim refused to speak to her. She'd gone to his house the day after Samara left. He'd blasted the door closed in her face. Her scheme had backfired royally. She'd thought she couldn't become pregnant again so soon. Stupid. She'd never felt so ill in her life, not even the first time.

"All right. I'll find someone else. I'm not having a baby."

Nathan and Emmett flashed through David's brain. A lifetime ago, Samara boasted they'd have sons: David I and David II. Like a damn fool, he'd insisted they wait to marry.

"Have you had a pregnancy test?" She said no. He picked up the phone, then spoke to a doctor. "One way or the other you must be examined. Come with me."

Solange swept her hand in the air. "Does this mean you'll help me?"

"We are not having a conversation. So shut up. The less I have to say to slime, the better. Now walk."

The doctor confirmed Solange's pregnancy.

"Have the baby," David said when they returned to his office. "There are good families who will give it love."

"Are you nuts?" She hooted. She slapped her Chanel purse on his desk. "The last thing I want is yours or anyone's baby. I hate being pregnant. The last time—"

He whirled her around, his hatred palpable. He squeezed her shoulders. "You've been pregnant before! Whose child? Damn you, whose baby did you kill?"

She pushed up her elbows, braking his hold. "Avrim's! I aborted Avrim's child. I never told him. This one's yours. It galls me to admit it, but it's the truth. Avrim hasn't spoken to me since Samara left."

David banged his fist on the desk, sending papers flying. "I forbid you to mention Samara's name. Do you hear?" He plowed his hands through his hair, creating a disheveled mess. When he looked up, tears welled in his eyes. His punishment stood before him.

"Leave your phone number," he said dully. "I'll get in touch with you."

"Then you'll help me?" she asked.

"I need time to think."

"It better not be long," Solange warned.

The lights burned far into the night in David's apartment. He told Wendall he'd made a big mistake dragging Solange into the maternity ward. For all he knew, she could be one of those women who were frightened at the thought of labor. Or she might be so vain about her body she didn't want to lose her shape. Or she might be scared the baby wouldn't be normal. She would be saddled with a less than perfect child.

"So what will you do?" Wendall asked.

"I'll sign a paper, take the child. No conditions. She could be given a pain blocker, float through labor. As to her figure, women bounce back with exercise. I'll hire the bitch an exercise coach."

David spent the night in a cold sweat. The mere thought of speaking to Solange made him ill. Wendall handed him a Scotch whiskey to help psych him up before phoning Solange the next night. "Come to the office tomorrow to discuss your options."

"There's nothing to discuss. As far as I'm concerned, there's only one solution. Abortion," she said flatly. "It's no big deal."

"Wait! Hear me out. You have other options." He raced through his list of offers, repeating them again, stressing she would be free. "Don't kill the baby."

"You're amazing!" she yelled. "Your solution stinks. I refuse to face the social stigma of giving birth to an illegitimate baby. Forget it! Frankly I didn't enjoy your strong-arm tactics yesterday or the way you tried to humiliate me. I came to you for one reason. Make no mistake, David. If it wasn't yours, I'd have nothing to do with you. But this baby's yours, dammit! If you won't help me find a doctor, I'll find one. I'm getting rid of it. So thanks for nothing."

"She hung up, Wendall. She's going through with the abortion."

"How can you stop her?"

David passed a tired hand over his face. He shuddered. "Offer to marry her, promise to divorce her right after the baby's born, take the child."

"Are you crazy?" Wendall yelled. "After what she's done! She's destroyed your life and Samara's. And besides, it's the 1980s—why even think of marriage?"

"In the best of all worlds, a child grows up in a two-parent household, loved and nurtured by each parent. This mess is the worst of all possible worlds, but killing a baby isn't the answer. It merely makes it worse for me. So you see, as far as I'm concerned, the 1980s has nothing to do with this. Abortion does. My parents saw thousands of people murdered in the Holocaust. They ingrained upon me to cherish the sanctity of life. It's why I practice medicine. Whenever I see a child die, I die a little too, despite the fact that I know doctors shouldn't get emotionally involved. It's the way I am. I can't change, nor do I want to. Solange is serious. Here is a healthy woman with no medical reason to seek an abortion. She's had one before."

Wendall slumped into a chair. "Good God! Whose?"

"Avrim's. He doesn't know."

"David," Wendall pleaded. "You can't even be certain this is your child."

David looked bleak. "It is. She's already done her damage to me and Samara. We hate each other enough for her not to have come to me otherwise." His hand shook as he lifted the receiver from the cradle.

"Oh, it's you," Solange snapped.

"Have the baby," he said dully. "I'll marry you, take care of you through your pregnancy. Nine months to save a life. Can you honestly destroy a second child? We'll divorce when the baby's born. It will be legitimate. I'll sign a paper to take the child. Healthy or sick. You'll never have to see it again. You'll be free. Free, Solange."

There was a long pause. "I'll think about it," she said tartly. "Call me tomorrow. By six P.M., not eleven. You disturbed my beauty sleep."

David Orchin married Solange Gold in a five-minute ceremony at City Hall. No family or friends were present. The groom did not kiss the bride. His hands were clenched at his sides. He barely looked at her. He did not give her a ring. He returned to his office and drank himself into a stupor. Wendall took him home. Solange went shopping.

At Tiffany's, she lowered her eyelids, shyly confessing to the clerk that her husband simply couldn't wait. She tripped out of the store flashing a five-karat diamond engagement ring to set off her diamond wedding band.

Solange hadn't agreed to David's terms. In his misery, he offered to sign a paper. He hadn't asked her to sign one, too. Under no circumstances would she grant him a divorce, not until and unless she was good and ready. With Avrim out of the picture, being David's wife gave her certain social advantages. More importantly, the baby would ensure that Samara stayed out of her hair. She would entertain, be part of society. She wouldn't have to go back to school.

Tessie and Barney would come around. After all, she carried their first great-grandchild. Max would adore a grandchild.

Wendall found another apartment. Solange trashed Samara's clothes. She dumped Samara's perfume down the toilet. In one day she removed all traces of her twin, including Samara's hairs she found on David's hairbrush.

Solange's scent permeated the apartment.

She harangued David, saying she couldn't possibly go through a healthy pregnancy living in a dump. A few weeks later, Solange got her first wish. When Max learned of her pregnancy, he bought the newlyweds a renovated town house on the Upper East Side, not far from Sutton Place.

All in all, she decided, this wasn't a bad deal . . .

As Solange decorated her new home and David fought for his sanity in New York by immersing himself in work, Samara faced her lacerated life by turning the locus of her grief inward. Maggie brought Samara to her Victorian house on Steiner Street in San Francisco. The multitiered picture postcard "pink lady" was built by the balloon frame method, its bay window billowing outward, festooned with flowery brackets, like a sailboat regatta. Facing a park, the gingerbread-trimmed row house sat on a tiny lot. Samara took no notice of the many architectural details that drew professional photographers to snap pictures of the famous landmark street with its backdrop of a newer landmark, the Transamerica Pyramid, and the downtown skyline.

She put her sketches and her blue rabbit in the bedroom Maggie assigned her. Avrim had phoned again after putting Samara on the plane, telling Maggie Samara left New York with the clothes on her back. "We're about the same size," Maggie said. She opened the closet. "Feel free to borrow."

Seated at the butcher-block kitchen table, Samara wrapped her hands around a hot mug of tea. "Please don't worry about me, Maggie. I need a few days to get myself together."

Judging from Samara's woeful appearance, Maggie doubted it. "Don't rush things. Take your time to get your bearings."

"I understand about sorrow." An old hand at it, Samara lectured on the subject of grief. "When Maman died, I thought I couldn't go on. Some days will be worse than others. The important thing is to keep busy. I'll learn to drive. I'll work, be independent. I'll never rely on anyone but myself . . ." A sob ended her brave speech.

Maggie told a frantic Max on the phone after she'd put Samara to bed that she thought her heart would shatter. Max had said Samara adored David. Her eyes rarely left his face the night they'd dined at Tessie's. Maggie made a silent vow to herself to do whatever it took to help her.

In the days that followed, Samara fought to forget, but it was impossible. At night she thrashed about the maple bed. Consumed by nightmares, she gnashed her teeth in sleep. She would awake fatigued with a pain in her jaw from grinding her teeth, a tightness about her mouth. Purple shadows deepened under her eyes. She constantly relived the horrible scene with David and Solange. Despite his denial, his voice tormented her: *I can find you in the dark.*

With Maggie gone all day, and being uprooted from familiar people, from work, Samara felt more isolated than she ever had in her whole life. A lonely wanderer, hidden behind dark glasses, she sluggishly dragged herself up and down the steep neighborhood streets. Rarely did she initiate a conversation with Maggie. Maggie's efforts to draw her out failed. Since neither she nor Max knew her well, Max phoned Mimi. Distraught, Mimi advised giving Samara the time and space she needed.

"What else can we do?" Max said sadly.

A month passed. Then one morning Samara awoke. Fueled by anger, energy replaced lethargy. She entered a new phase. She asked Maggie if she could clean and cook. Understanding the need to work out her rage, Maggie gave permission. Armed with a mop, broom, vacuum, and other cleaning implements, Samara went on the attack. She polished wood, scrubbed bathrooms, kitchen floors, windows, with demonic zeal. Freshly laundered and ironed Priscilla curtains hung over sparkling glass windows. The living and dining-room chandeliers glistened. She repolished mellow woods to a glowing patina. She had chipped fingernails and chapped hands. After showering, she meticulously wiped the tile to prevent streaks.

And she baked. She slammed dough to make rolls, punching the centers with her fists. She cooked breakfasts and dinners and sumptuous desserts for Maggie, but picked at her own bird-size portion or skipped meals entirely. Her weight dropped. Her clothes hung loosely on a frame grown thinner, alarming Maggie who reported to Max.

After three weeks, Maggie called a halt. "Enough! My house can't take more cleaning. I'm getting fat while you're getting to be a scarecrow. That's it, Samara. Time to kick ass. If you don't, Solange wins. Do you want her to kill your spirit, too?" Samara winced. "Avrim loved her. You don't see him quitting. That's why he started over in London. Don't let Solange win. I'll help you in any way I can. Think about what you'd like to do. It's time you get on with your life."

Samara promised to enroll in driving school first thing in the morning. She promised to look for a job.

She didn't. The following morning she dangled her legs over the side of the bed, then listlessly fell back onto the mattress. Maggie found her burrowed beneath the blanket, her eyelids damp with tears. At wit's end, she phoned Max. The news of David's marriage to Solange had her gasping.

"Dear God, Max. You've got to tell Samara in person. I don't know what this will do to her."

As feared, the news devastated Samara, for somewhere lurking in her subconscious, she had been praying for a happy solution. Solange's pregnancy, her marriage to David, struck an irrevocable blow. Max handed her a letter from David. Grim-faced, she tore it up. "Tell him never to bother me again," she said in a choked voice.

Two days later, she kissed Max good-bye before he returned to New York. She pulled on a pair of jeans and a pullover, and hid her hair with a scarf. Devoid of makeup, she took a cab to the Golden Gate Park. Seated on a bench outside the Japanese Tea Garden, unlike others there to enjoy the serenely beautiful landscaped bridges, the miniature waterfalls, the statuary, the pagodas, Samara sought to divine the terrible crime she must have committed to deserve Solange's treachery. Her twin despised her. David betrayed her. The Orchins would get the grandchild they'd always wanted. So be it. She was through wallowing in grief.

According to Maggie, San Francisco combined the cosmopolitan chic of Paris and the energy of New York. She would remain here, make her mark as a designer. Haute couture was impractical, a money-losing proposition, meant for experimentation, inspiration, and promotion, dependent on licenses and ready-to-wear for support. It required an initial investment of far more money than was in her bank balance. If she designed loungewear and sleepwear, she could still apply her creative talents. Those creations required less fabrication—mainly cottons, silks, silk charmeuses, poly satins. Pastels for spring and summer, deeper shades for fall and winter. With her money she'd purchase a house and work from there for a start. That night she ate a complete meal. She outlined her plans to Maggie.

"What about Gold's West? Tessie still wants to train you for management."

Samara lifted mutinous blue eyes. "As long as Solange stands to inherit a share of the store, I refuse to have a thing to do with it. I told Avrim it was a pipe dream."

The next day Samara signed up for driving lessons. With fits and starts, she learned not to strip the gears. After passing her driving test on her first attempt, she bought her first automobile: a five-year-old blue Chevrolet. She scoured area stores, checking the latest fashions in her chosen field. On Union Square, the city's smart downtown shopping district, Gold's West's steel-and-glass edifice rose proudly into the sky. From what she'd heard, the builder would have it completed on schedule. She passed the site with a pang of longing.

She avoided driving on Divisidero Street and other streets that seemed to catapult off the edge of the earth. One day, thinking about Mimi's gutsy driving, she screwed up her courage and leapt off Divisidero.

"I did it!" she shouted happily, safely reaching the base of the hill. The leap symbolized the way she'd face her future: unafraid and independent.

Purpose and pride propelled her. Summer slipped into fall. She found her ideal house in Sausalito, across the bay from San Francisco. Along the picturesque narrow streets, silversmiths, potters, artists, and other craftsmen sold tourists their wares. Houses marched up hilly terrains to cosset inhabitants in havens jutting bravely outward from perches that afforded spectacular panoramas of the entire Bay Area.

"I can move right in," she bubbled, ladling out chicken soup with homemade dumplings. She had an enormous appetite. "I've always dreamed of a house with a porch and a view. I'll line the porch with herbs and flowers. Did I mention honeysuckle grows on a trellis?"

"Twice." Maggie smiled.

"It's a great place to sketch. The house itself has three bedrooms, skylights in two. There's oak-strip bleached floors in the living room, a fireplace, windows overlooking the sea. Wait until you see the kitchen. It's a dream. The cabinets are light ivory oak, too. The refrigerator is set behind custom-fitted paneling. There's plenty of counter space, even an island with a sink. I'll convert a bedroom into a studio and take it as a tax deduction. So what do you think?''

Maggie caught her infectious spirit, delighted with the enthused Samara. "Go for it.''

Samara did go for it. First she dragged Maggie to see the house. "Wait until I fix it up.''

Plunging into her task, she painted the living-room walls slate-blue, the fireplace mantel, built-in bookcases, woodwork and trim, white. Dressed in paint-splattered overalls, she spread dropcloths on the porch and tackled the day's project. She refinished a Dutch hutch to go in her dining room. She painted secondhand wicker rockers white. During inclement weather, she stenciled a floral design around both bathrooms' paned windows.

For durability, she chose tightly woven fabrics on the furniture: floral on the sofa, blue-and-white stripes for the oversize armchairs opposite the hearth. Rising early, she looked forward to the day that began by watching the sunrise. She planted pots of rosemary, chives, dill, basil, marigolds, and tubs of roses, setting them near the railings.

In the evenings, she either watched the fiery sunset dip below the horizon or the fog-shrouded Golden Gate Bridge. With no work to occupy her mind, her thoughts inevitably drifted to David. She didn't kid herself. The healing process took time. How long she couldn't guess.

Maggie and Max, who visited often, attended her first dinner party. Her father arrived tan and fit, enormously grateful to see a smile on her face. In tan slacks and black sweater, he bounded up the porch steps. He carried a squirming puppy in his arms.

"This is your housewarming present. It's a guard dog,'' he said, kissing her. He handed her the leash.

The moon-eyed mutt, a brown-and-white fur ball of infinite blends, thumped its tail. Delirious with joy, it bathed Samara's face with its pink tongue. Laughing hysterically, fighting whirling paws, Samara fell instantly in love. "I guess I own a dog.'' She took a quick look to determine its sex. "Hello, Fredrica.'' Max beamed.

Samara led him through a tour of the house. He particularly like the Navajo Indian art prints above the fireplace. Set between facing chairs, she'd placed a nineteenth-century seaman's trunk, with a decoupage on its lid, using it to hold her magazines.

"You've done a great job, Samara. I'm proud of you." They grinned at each other, mutually pleased by their growing friendship. She knew Max begged Maggie to set a wedding date. Gun-shy from Solange, she said to Samara, "God will determine the date. If I become pregnant, I marry Max immediately; if not, I'll wait until I've got the guts to be that tramp's stepmother."

In her chintz-upholstered bedroom, with its high window seat facing the bay, Max caught her hand and asked her to wait a moment. His eyes filled with soft compassion. "Samara, shouldn't we talk about Solange?"

Her good mood shattered. Her eyes ached with the sudden strain of holding back tears. "David and Solange are married, expecting a child. There's no more to say. Leave it be. Please," she implored, her cheeks taking on a pink blush.

Max could have kicked himself for ruining the festive occasion. He vowed never to speak of David and Solange again unless Samara brought up the subject. With a sigh he realized neither of his daughters was fine. Solange chafed at her pregnancy. From what Pepe confided, she made life difficult for David.

"Grandma and Grandpa wish you'd change your mind about Gold's West. They want to keep the management in the family."

Her lips thinned. "Not as long as Solange could ever have a claim on the store. Please don't ask me again." Working helped numb the pain. With Fred by her side, weather permitting, she sketched seven styles for the popular-priced line, including pajama, slit shirt, long and short gowns, seven ultrafeminine styles. One afternoon, the shrill ring of the phone brought her running inside. Hearing Mimi tell her the purpose of her overseas phone call brought a series of yells of disbelief. "You're coming here!" she cried, jumping in place. Fred, catching her excitement, did her dance of the tail.

Three days later, the two friends crashed into each other's arms, kissing, crying, jabbering in French. Samara calmed down first. She held Mimi at arm's length. "You look marvelous!" Several dress sizes smaller, Mimi looked svelte in a softly clinging jersey.

Mimi grinned. She pointed to her eyes. "Contacts. I told you I'd do it one day."

Mimi loved the house. With the dog on the bed between them, the two friends gabbed into the wee hours of the morning. "You were right, Mimi. I made David into an Adonis. What a stupid child I was. That's all in the past. I'm making a new life now." Samara yawned at the conclusion of her story.

Mimi squeezed her hand. "Sam, I'm here for a reason. Papa and I want you to form a partnership with us. Loungewear and sleepwear is a natural extension of Papa's work. If you agree, we'll use your name. His is licensed to a German firm that produces his perfumes, eyeglasses, and pocketbooks."

Samara was speechless. Everyone in fashion knew Jules LeClaire. He didn't need her. He'd made the offer to help, knowing how difficult it was for a new business to succeed. Despite dying to jump at the chance, she prided herself on not taking advantage of people, especially Jules, whom she adored.

"It wouldn't be fair to gamble with Jules's money."

"Don't be a pessimist. Papa wants you to prove you're as good as he says you are. The best part is that I come along with the package."

Samara, her mouth agape, stared at Mimi. "Mimi, it means a move to America."

Her eyes crinkled with a smile. "Shoot me. I'm a sucker for McDonald's."

"Why are you really doing this?" Samara persisted. "McDonald's is on the Champs-Élysées. France is home. You have a good job."

Mimi grew serious. "My job can be handled by others. When you left, it was the end of an era. We can begin a new one. I love Papa, but this is a chance for me to help build something, an opportunity to step out of his shadow. Sam, you'd be doing me a favor." Her voice caught with emotion. Samara swallowed hard to keep from crying. "Besides, Papa and Mama are thrilled not to have me drive him home. Mama says it will add years to Papa's life."

Samara's lower lip trembled. Mimi didn't fool her for a minute, and neither did Jules. "Won't you miss your parents?"

"I'll see them often," Mimi said. "Please say yes. It'll be like old times."

Samara ducked her head to hide her tears. *Nothing could ever be like old times.* Old times lay buried with dreams destroyed by Solange. Dear, dear Mimi.

"Say yes," Mimi implored.

The prospect of building a company with her dearest friend, of not being so alone, was more than Samara could deny. "Okay, partner. Let's do it." They hugged and kissed, bouncing Fred up and down on the bed.

"You've got to meet Maggie," Samara said the following day. "I don't know what I would have done without her."

Mimi and Maggie hit it off. In many ways, they were similar. Both were no-nonsense loyalists where Samara was concerned. Over candlelight, Montrachet wine, poached salmon, shirred baked potatoes, asparagus, and endive salad, the three cemented a friendship that would last the rest of their lives.

"It's great," Maggie said, rejoicing. "Calm down and tell me what's involved."

Samara took a deep breath. "Fabrication, a good silhouette, a fashion-forward line to attract buyers from upscale department stores and specialty stores. Advertising, a sales force, trunk shows. Buyers shop apparel marts in Dallas and Los Angeles. New York doesn't have one," Samara said. "Mimi's in charge of sales."

Aware that David was the reason Samara was reluctant to go to New York, Mimi added, "I'm opening a New York showroom and hiring a salesperson."

Maggie understood. "Who'll do the manufacturing, Sam?"

"There's a Mr. Tua in the Philippines. Eve Stillman and Josie Natori's people say he's good," she said, quoting two of the biggest names in lingerie. "First we need to sell enough orders to ensure him a cutting ticket."

"What's that?" Maggie asked.

"Fifty dozen or six hundred pieces minimum," Samara explained. "Everything goes by twelves per style. It doesn't pay a manufacturer to gear up for production otherwise. Fabrication in loungewear and sleepwear is less involved than in couture. Shipping, advertising, and fashion shows add more money. Stores will expect an incentive to buy, co-op advertising, five percent back on the net, on time delivery. That's a must. It can get sticky if stores advertise and the merchandise is late. They've got the right to cancel the order."

She described the overall role of the designer, then explained the jobs of sample hands, sketch artists, and stylists. She impressed Maggie, but not Mimi, who knew Samara had cut her teeth on fashion, had a sharp business head on her shoulders.

Samara added, ''I'll need to spend at least three weeks overseas, making certain the samples are made according to specification and to check the quality.''

''I smell success,'' Maggie said.

A glowing Samara replied, ''From your lips to God's ears.''

Chapter Twenty

In hard labor, Solange tightened up for another contraction. God, how she hated David. Marriage was a boring jail sentence. They slept in separate bedrooms, and never made love. They never went anywhere together. She'd spent a fortune decorating the house in the newest modern style. Did he compliment her? Not once. The man focused on one thing—the baby. He threw away her cigarettes and her liquor. He assigned Pepe to be her guard. He'd threatened to leave her if she didn't take care of herself. Her father was no better. He agreed with David's rotten laws. She'd gotten fat eating David's diet, drinking David's prescribed milk, sleeping David's prescribed hours, taking David's prescribed long walks.

She detested pregnancy. Throughout it, she had flatly refused to read one book or article David brought home describing the joys of pregnancy, the stages of fetal development. (Only a man would think that up!) Fuck fetal development! She was going to pop.

Her water had broken hours before. Or was it yesterday? Her ankles were swollen, her face puffy. She developed a rash on her thighs. For nine horrid months, David and his demon inside her controlled her life. "Now what are you doing?"

"I'm cranking up the foot of the bed. Don't bear down."

"I will if I want to." She hated him, his orders, the machines they hooked her to, the cell this prison dubbed a labor room. A nurse in a starched white uniform, gray hair, and stupid smile sailed into the room. "What are you here for?"

"To prep you, Mrs. Orchin." She lifted the sheet.

"Get out!" Solange hissed.

David sent a look of apology to the nurse. She sent him a sympathetic smile. "Solange, she's doing her job."

Solange caught the exchange. "All right. Get it over with. Don't drip that brown stuff on my legs."

"You might have been cordial," David said when the woman beat a hasty retreat.

"Shit!" Solange snarled, bearing down for another pain. Sweat poured out of her. David sponged her face. "Cordial. Cordial describes you, David," she gasped. "Polite. Cordial. Boring. You're a policeman. I hate you. This should be happening to you, not me."

He gritted his teeth. "You're making it harder on yourself."

She groaned, cursing him with every breath in her body. "How much longer?"

"Soon," he said. He read the graph coming out of the fetal monitor. He stepped outside the room and spoke quickly to a nurse. In minutes Solange's obstetrician, Dr. Grant, entered the room, examined the strip of paper coming from the machine. He and David exchanged worried looks.

"Solange, this won't take a minute." He took a pair of sterile gloves from a box and slid them on. When he pulled down the sheet, she made a futile attempt to clamp her thighs together. He drew her legs apart.

"I know it's no fun." He probed gently. He pulled off the gloves, motioned for David to step into the hall.

David returned in a few minutes. "Solange, listen to me. I know labor is rough. We're going to take the baby."

Her eyes went wide with fright. *Take* the baby. As in *cut her!* "Go away." She wouldn't let them mar her precious skin. She'd never be able to wear a bikini. She'd lose her muscle tone. Was he crazy? She whimpered, "No."

"I wish we didn't have to. We do. Your blood pressure is too high. There's the possibility of trauma to the baby. The head isn't crowning. You both could be in danger. Please understand why we have to do a cesarean section."

She twisted her head. "Nooooo! I don't want to be disfigured."

That was her reason! She didn't want a scar her lovers could see. A reason to kill a life! *Bitch.* He hated her with every breath in his body. He'd spent months of misery, witnessing her self-pity, indulging her demands while keeping a tight rein on his emotions. But now when a life hung in the balance, her disregard for the baby—her child!—made him ill.

"Solange, we have to save *your* child's life. *Yours.*"

Her face drew into a grimace. Another pain tore at her. She bit down on her lip, scarcely listening to him spout a bunch of crap she didn't want to hear and barely understood. Dilation. Toxic anemia. Amniotic fluid.

"Solange, I don't want you to hemorrhage. There are problems with the baby. You've only dilated five centimeters. A fully dilated cervix is ten. The baby's working too hard. I don't want the baby to die."

"I don't care." She moaned, then screamed with another pain. "You're going to take it anyway, aren't you?"

David nodded. "Yes. We have to."

"I'll never forgive you. Never."

"Add it to the list," he muttered beneath his breath. "I'll see you in a few minutes. I'm going to scrub."

A nurse accompanied her as orderlies took her down a long corridor. She covered her eyes, loathing the view of the crummy ceiling tiles. "I hate this place." The nurse told her it would be over soon. "Not soon enough."

"Here we are," the nurse said. "Best room in the house. The labor and delivery suite."

Solange groaned. *Suite!* What a misnomer. The nurse was nuts. A suite was in a five-star hotel, not some theater starring her as the main attraction. She closed her eyes, shielding them from the glare of light. She didn't want to be there. She wanted to be in control of her life. Home. Home with Pepe, back to the days when her tummy was flat and she had fun! How could her foolish friend Lou-Lou envy her pregnancy?

Medical personnel, uglier than the ones on all the television doctor programs, clothed in loose-fitting putrid hospital green, milled around in readiness. Every once in a while one of the masked bandits leaned over to say something snappy about motherhood. Bunch of shits!

She groaned. "Get them the fuck away, David!"

Above the white sheet draping her, David commanded, "We'll take care of you. It helps not to fight it."

"Won't be long, little Mama," chorused the OB and the anesthesiologist.

"What's that?" she asked, clutching David's wrist. Gleaming instruments lined a table next to her.

"A Mayo stand," he replied.

An alarm jangled in her head. The doctor would use them to cut her. She tried to twist off the table.

"I want out."

"Let's get started," a voice behind a mask said. Someone switched on a radio. She couldn't believe it. These butchers worked in tune to a damn concert. She was dying to the accompaniment of a lousy timpani!

David came to her side. She read the tension and worry in his eyes. No, she saw fright. David frightened? Could it be part of his fear was for her, too? The life she carried bound them forever.

The baby lurched, commanding her attention. He lurched again, but this time not as strong. She thought she heard him whimper, cry. Was that possible? she wondered. Could babies cry in the womb? For the first time she was sorry she hadn't attended a class or read the books David had brought home.

The anesthesiologist administered an epidural. Solange floated out of her body, leaving the sharp pain behind. She didn't hear the cacophony of noise or see the green-shrouded faces.

Caring hands lifted the six-pound seven-ounce infant into the world. His father hovered over his twenty-one-inch, blood-streaked bundle, checking to see that the nurse suctioned him properly. When the baby let out a healthy squall, David's face broke out in a smile. Tears filled his eyes. A quick check stanched the tears and brought a wide grin. David assured the rapt audience that the baby had his toes and fingers and requisite plumbing.

"Naturally," Solange muttered, but no one heard. Her job over, she slept.

She awoke in her private room. The yellow walls were painted with figures of clowns and teddy bears. The curtains, drawn apart to let in the sun, were interwoven strands of pink and blue.

"Tacky," she muttered, thinking a decorator could do wonders with this dump.

Opposite the bed was a chipped mirror. A former tenant's greeting cards were wedged in the frame. She caught a glimpse of herself. She looked as if she'd been in a war. Besides a shower, her hair needed washing. She lay back on the pillows, planning. Commensurate with her new status, she'd get a new hairdo, something light and fluffy. Carefree, that's the look she wanted. She touched her face. Yes, she could do with a facial at Elizabeth Arden's. She'd begin a strict exercise regime. She'd hold David to his offer to have an exercise trainer come to the house. He'd be a hunk or she'd get a different trainer to help her trim down to her former weight.

Pepe would just have to learn to prepare nutritious meals. Christ! There were enough cookbooks in her kitchen at home to choke a horse. She'd bought them primarily as a decorating touch. When she was thinner, she'd buy a whole new wardrobe, finally start her own company.

She found a pencil and paper in the drawer of the metal cabinet near the bed, jotting down eggshell embossed Tiffany business cards. Proud of herself, full of exciting plans, she smiled. There was a tap at the door. Half expecting David, she was mildly disappointed to see an aide. She brought in a huge basket of roses. Solange snatched the card.

Hello, Mommy. We love you and the baby. Good days ahead. It was signed by her father and grandparents.

She plucked a flower, twirling it slowly beneath her nose, breathing in the fragrant aroma. Already the baby was making a difference. The card proved it. The family wasn't going to risk being deprived of a grandchild. Amazing what a baby could do. From now on, everything was going to be fine. She was Mrs. Dr. Orchin, mistress of her fate.

The satisfied smile disappeared. She glowered. Oh, yes. She almost forgot. She intended to be as famous as Samara, thanks to that bitch Maggie interviewing her on television. You'd think designing nightgowns was an accomplishment. Wait until she strutted her stuff. Her parties for the rich and famous ensured her success. She'd become more famous. Moreover, she'd have fun. Her husband would be by her side. If he wanted to see her son, he'd better toe the mark. She was sick and tired of making excuses for her absent husband to her hostesses. Life was definitely about to improve. She would see to it. The room filled with the sound of her laughter. Her hand flew across the list. Birth announcements. She'd send her dear twin the very first one—from the happy parents!

* * *

In the nursery, David marveled at the newborn life he held in his arms. He had seen a lot of babies in his time, he wasn't prejudiced, but no baby was as beautiful as Asher. He was no scrawny pruneface. No, sir. His son was pink and warm—with hair! Lots of dark hair. Like his father! Later he would return with his camera and take pictures to send to his parents.

Fatherhood. Hot damn, it had a nice sound. That's him. Papa David. Old man David. Pops. Father. Daddy. Something happened to a man when he held his son. He grinned. Tenderly he gently stroked his infant's cheek. Soft. Softer than cotton. Worth tasting. He kissed his baby and smiled when the baby responded by snuggling contentedly. That meant his kid was smart. Damn right. He'd grabbed on to his daddy's finger. That wasn't reflexive either. That took brains.

It occurred to him that his son might wish to hear his father's voice. He mentally practiced several momentous speeches before settling on one befitting the occasion. He cleared his throat.

"I love you, son. You won your fight to be born, Asher," he crooned. He brought the boy to his chest, gently placing his face near the baby's head. "We're a team. Us. You and I. I'll make a good life for you. I'll never let anything bad happen to you, I promise." He held him at arm's length to see how his speech was received, then sat in blissful peace, content to be with his son, who wisely decided to go back to sleep.

It gave David time to mull over his speech. In a matter of minutes, the promises he'd made crashed around his head. How, he thought wildly, am I going to manage? An infant needs a mother. He wanted him breastfed. Where was he going to find a wet nurse? He couldn't swear for anyone in this drug-rampant society. He worked crazy hours. Help—good, competent help—was hard to find. In this neighborhood, that would be nearly impossible.

Rocking his precious bundle, he choked up. His eyes stung. His helpless son didn't know his father couldn't stand his mother, that his mother had tricked him, that's why he was conceived. The baby deserved better. Maybe he should return to France. Solange wouldn't care. She didn't give a damn if she never saw the baby again.

Calm down, get a grip on yourself, he told himself sternly, but it was too late for the tear had dripped on Asher's cheek. The baby blinked. Afraid he'd transfer his anxiety to his newborn, he hurriedly kissed the tear from Asher's tiny cheek. Asher moved his head, as if searching for his father's lips. David obliged. He kissed the rosebud mouth. Nothing in the world smelled as good as a clean, powdered baby. He sniffed to his heart's content. A fierce sense of pride surged through him. They'd make it, by God! They had to.

Wendall slipped into the nursery. "They told me you had a boy. I came as soon as I could. Congratulations. How does it feel to be a father?"

David proudly showed off his son. "You can hold him if you're careful to watch his head."

Wendall grinned. "Didn't take you long to get obnoxious, did it?"

"I mean it. He looks like me, don't you think?"

Wendall rolled up his eyes. "Sap. Actually I think he talks like you and has your walk."

David chuckled.

"Doctors," the charge nurse said teasingly, "this baby will be spoiled rotten. I don't approve of physicians breaking the rules. Besides, Asher needs his nappy changed."

"I'll be back," David warned. "I don't pay attention to rules. Not when it's my kid." The charge nurse laughed.

He and Wendall made their way to the cafeteria. "What are you two going to name him?" Wendall asked when they brought their coffee cups to the table.

"Not us," David retorted, his jaw flexed in anger. "Me. Solange didn't want any part of that. I've told you about her mood swings. I had hoped after she spent a fortune decorating the house that she'd be ready to talk about names. When I brought it up, she told me she didn't care what I named him. It's Asher. It means happiness in Hebrew. With us for parents I figured the baby needs all the help he can get."

"What will you do?" Wendall asked, propping his elbow on the table, resting his chin in his hand.

The conversation ceased as doctors and nurses came by to congratulate David and joke that now he could get a good night's sleep. His eyes were bloodshot.

"Solange needs to regain her strength," he said when they

left. ''I imagine she wants to be free of me and the baby as soon as possible. She agreed to a divorce before we married.''

How sad, Wendall thought. The two people in the world who should be the baby's parents weren't talking to each other.

He knew David wanted to hear about Samara. ''Samara's in the Philippines, David. Maggie says the business is writing more orders than they expected, especially with the European market. Sam's hired an assistant designer and a staff.''

David did his best to not look as if his heart were being ripped apart. One moment and his entire future gone from his life. Filled with guilt, the love he felt for Samara was all he had left. ''I've thought about contacting Mimi.''

''Why don't you?'' Wendall suggested.

David took the heels of his hands and rubbed his eyes. ''I'm not sure. I guess there's really nothing I can do. I tried and failed.''

''What are you going to do after the divorce?'' Wendall asked.

''Pray for a happy ending to this nightmare. I have Asher's welfare to consider. He needs me. Whatever it takes, I'll be there for him. He didn't ask to be born.''

Wendall wanted to cry for his friend. David had changed. The joy had gone out of his life. God willing, his son would give him back a reason for living.

Book
Two

Chapter Twenty-one

1984

As dense fog hampered her vision, Samara crept along the highway in her trusty Chevy on her way to Maggie's. Maggie still hadn't become pregnant. "It's not for lack of trying," she moped to Samara.

"Get married," Samara urged. "You'll be more relaxed. The doctor said there's no reason you can't conceive."

Maggie had given Samara's lingerie company thousands of dollars of free publicity on her nationally syndicated show, *Happenings*. Devoting an entire segment to Samara's line, both women closed the show modeling identical slinky liquid gold, palazzo polysatin charmeuse pants and softly draped blouses. A believer in trunk shows, Samara toured the country's major malls and department stores, bringing her collection to the people. Despite Mimi's pleas, she adamantly refused to go to New York, leaving that to Mimi.

Gold's West carried Samara's complete line, which would soon include perfume. Luminaries from the worlds of fashion, theater, and the press attended the gala party, set in the marble atrium. A glamorous Samara, lovely in an ice pink evening suit, its long-sleeved peplum jacket embroidered with silver and seed pearls, arrived on the arm of her partner, Jules LeClaire. Only when reporters asked her why the other platinum Gold twin wasn't present did her smile become tight. She brushed aside their questions.

Maggie flung open the door on the first ring. Samara stepped back to admire her yellow pantsuit, wide faux jeweled belt, funky earrings, multicolored sandals.

"You look terrific," they both said at the same time.

"It's my sixties statement," Maggie joked. "But when I need to, I know where to borrow a Chanel."

Samara rolled up her eyes. On her salary, Maggie could afford a closet of designer clothes. "Here's a pair of black silk chiffon pajamas. I wish you'd marry my father so I can call you Mommy."

Maggie tore open the box. "Not until I'm *enceinte*. I refuse to be Solange's relative one second early." Holding the pajamas up in front of her, she looked at her reflection in the hallway mirror. "This ought to do the trick," she quipped. "Thanks. Come in the kitchen. I'm making salad." She turned down the radio. "When's Mimi due back from Dallas?"

Samara bit into a piece of celery that she took from the snack tray. "Next week. She quit going with the dentist."

Maggie set the oven timer for the dinner rolls, then popped a vegetable dish into the micro. "I thought she likes Gus."

"She claims Gus has regrettable knees. I can't keep up with her."

"At least she enjoys an active social life. It's time you did," Maggie said. On the anniversary of the second year away from New York, Samara slept with a man she'd dated twice, accompanying him to his hotel room after fortifying herself with liquor. She did it as an act of defiance, a ritual. No amount of wine, flowers, or soft music could wash away the bitterness. She'd cheapened herself. From then on when she needed an escort to attend a social obligation, she tapped the generosity of a gay friend, a fellow designer.

"Don't start that again," Samara said now to Maggie. "I like my uncomplicated life." Both had seen the recent *Time* magazine article written about David. It hadn't taken a detective to know Solange sent the magazine, clipped to the right page. Seeing David's picture with Solange gazing at him in adoration, their son on his lap, had made Samara's heart sink. Her mouth dried up so that she could hardly swallow. It had taken her five minutes before she could look at David's face without shaking. Even after all these years, she still loved him. Gray speckled his hair. Lines fanned away from his eyes. He'd peered into the camera's lens, a handsome portrait of confidence. He discussed his research. It centered on trying to find a method to separate red and white blood cells from their stem cells. Storing the stem cells would avoid the necessity of taking the stem cells from bone marrow, thus making the whole procedure of transplantation easier.

The second picture showed David holding Asher. The boy was a miniature David, bright-eyed and dark-haired. He grinned impishly at his father. Solange's private and business lives thrived. She'd gotten it all. Here was a portrait of a happy family, despite Wendall's repeated attempts to say otherwise, the last time being his recent visit to his family's computer chip firm in the Silicon Valley. She told him bluntly she wasn't interested.

Samara brought her wineglass to her lips. "How come the dining-room table is set for three? Who else is coming?"

"Peter Watanabe." Samara asked half seriously if she was cheating on her father. "Peter's a friend. Be nice to him. He's coming from Los Angeles to meet you."

Samara aimed her celery stick. "Maggie, the last time you tried a trick like this I told you never to do it again. Had I known I wouldn't have come."

"That's why I didn't tell you." Maggie reached around her for a towel on the rack. "Samara, you're so pigheaded stubborn, I could shoot you. You won't go to New York, although you should for business, if nothing else. All you do is work and go home to a dog. It's unhealthy to keep men at bay."

The doorbell's ring prevented a blast from Samara. The sound of male laughter sallied forth from the entryway in response to something Maggie said.

Maggie led her guest into the kitchen, made the introductions, and behind Peter's back signaled Samara to smile.

Samara regarded the man with the toothpaste ad smile, whose hair, eyes, and brows were a glittering blue-black as if someone had dipped into a pot of midnight paint to fill in the canvas.

Several inches taller than Samara, he had the firm grip of a man with an eye on a new prize: Samara. Unaware of the sign language swirling about him, Peter Watanabe said, "You're prettier than the tape my scout sent me after you were on Maggie's show. I agree with him. You've got star quality. Would you like to be in the movies?"

"Peter's a movie director," Maggie drolled.

"There's no chance of my ever becoming an actress."
Samara disengaged her hand.

They dined on rare roast beef with horseradish sauce, red
potatoes sprinkled with parsley, and string beans almondine.

Seated across from him, Samara was as annoyed with herself
as she was with Peter, who didn't even try to hide his obvious
interest in her. She caught Maggie's eye and frowned. Maggie
excused herself to bring in the coffee.

"This is nice," Peter said.

Thinking he meant Maggie's house, she agreed.

"I didn't mean the table and chairs or the sideboard or the
fancy light fixture. I meant being with you."

"Thank you," she said tightly, wishing Maggie would hurry
back. She knew exactly why she was gone so long, and she
didn't appreciate it.

"Oscar Wilde said that when a person disappears, he can be
found in San Francisco."

Samara's gaze slid down to her wristwatch. "I didn't know
that," she muttered.

"Mark Twain called San Francisco the eternal springtime."

"Fascinating," she said sharply. She could feel her cheeks
grow warm. She wondered when it would be polite for her to
leave.

"I thought you'd be interested," he said blandly.

She stared into his fathomless black eyes.

"Gilroy," he said pleasantly, leaning back in his chair, a
smile twitching his lips, "is the garlic capital of the world. Did
you know that?"

The comment was so unexpected that she burst out laughing.
"Is your wife in Los Angeles?" she asked him, hoping he'd
answer she was. She wished he would cease his disturbing
ability to drink, undress her with his eyes, and tease her all at
the same time.

"That's better." He grinned. "You're even prettier when
you relax." If there was one thing Peter Watanabe admired, it
was a beautiful woman who believed very sincerely that she
knew her own mind. "In answer to your question, I'm not
married. Now. My trip to the altar lasted two years." He let his
gaze linger on her lips before bringing it to her eyes. Beneath
his intense scrutiny, she fumbled nervously with her napkin
and dropped it. "Are you married?" he asked.

"No," she said warily. She bent down to get her napkin.

"Engaged?" he asked when she came up.

"No."

"Going steady?"

She placed both palms on the table. "Mr. Watanabe. I assume you came here to eat dinner, not to interrogate me. My private life is private. If Maggie gave you the impression I'm available, she's wrong."

"Maggie gave me no impression." He spoke earnestly. "I saw *Happenings* and asked to meet you. I've been away in England and Yugoslavia, filming movies. I'm making up for lost time. Besides, it's all your fault."

"My fault?" she asked innocently. "What have I done?"

"You've made the mistake of being so beautiful I can't keep my eyes off you. I dream of you at night."

"I apologize for my parents' error. I suggest you imagine me old and wrinkled."

He chuckled. "You'll be beautiful, trust me. I know bone structure. It's my business. And legs. I'm a leg man. You'd be amazed at how many actresses clump around on ugly piano stumps. Your legs are perfect. I looked."

She cast about for a safe topic. "How do you know Gilroy is the garlic capital?"

"I grew up in San Francisco. Gilroy isn't far away. Where do you live?"

She should have seen it coming. "Sausalito."

"I love Sausalito. Boats. Artists. Stacked hills. I'm there often. I'm sure we'll meet again."

"By way of Yugoslavia and England?"

He laughed. "Touché."

"Exactly. We're both busy people."

"Not that busy." Samara saw the teasing gleam in his eyes, and she laughed at this impossible man. Maggie took her seat at the table, obviously pleased that her matchmaking hadn't resulted in blows.

Samara decided Peter was a harmless flirt who fit his line to suit the occasion. "You're not angry with me, are you?" Maggie asked after he left three hours later. "Peter's a good guy. Don't be fooled by his crazy manner. He was hurt badly by a wife who wanted to use him to get ahead."

"Then why did he offer me a job as an actress?"

"It's his way of making sure you weren't interested, Samara." Maggie squeezed her arm affectionately. "What do you think of dating him?"

Samara hooted. "Not much, thank you. Anyway, I'm safe. He doesn't live around the corner."

Samara hadn't reckoned on Peter Watanabe.

For the next twenty-one days he bombarded her with greeting cards, never once phoning. She received Thanksgiving, Christmas, Easter, birthday, high school and college graduation cards, and messages to wish her a speedy recovery. Her collection included congratulatory wedding, sweet sixteen, and bas mitzvah cards. All sizes and shapes.

She was dying to see him.

He phoned the evening of the twenty-fourth day. They made plans to see a movie that weekend. On Saturday night he brought a pumpkin. "Early Halloween," he said. He cracked a slow smile, surveying her persimmon skirt and sweater. Her hair swung loose about her shoulders. Gold loops dangled from her ears.

"God, you're gorgeous," he said.

She smiled impishly, then went to the hall closet for her gold wool fingertip-length coat. "Did you know that William Saroyan said that even the ugly are beautiful in San Francisco?"

"I did." He hustled her into his red Porsche, coming around to the driver's side. "You'll have to try harder. I warn you, it won't be easy to outwit me."

At the movie he bought her a large buttered popcorn, threw his arm about her shoulder, then watched her instead of the 1949 production of the *Son of Dracula*.

"Feel free to hang on to me," he whispered, but she was laughing so hard at the campy picture that serious movie buffs seated nearby told her to be quiet.

"He cheated," she groused when they came outside. "That was Dracula himself, not the son of Dracula."

"Very perceptive." He tucked her hand in his. At the Japanese Center, they browsed through art galleries and antique stores. In a boutique, she bought hand-printed silk-screen scarves for Mimi, Maggie, and Tessie. In a Japanese restaurant, they sat around a large cooking table, fascinated by the chef's ability to de-vein shrimp, wielding a knife so sharp it was a miracle he didn't harm himself.

Samara expected Peter to kiss her good night. She wanted him to as a test to see if she was over David. Instead, he pecked her lightly on the cheek, explained he had an early meeting, patted Fred's head, and left. Peter's manners were those of a perfect gentleman. Too perfect.

He flew out to see her twice during the following month. She told Maggie and Mimi that she was beginning to wonder whether there was something wrong with her. He seemed content to be her buddy.

"How is it that you're able to get away this often?" They were parked at the top of Potrero Hill, which offered the best view in San Francisco. "Isn't there post production you need to do? Looping? Voice-overs?" His long, telling look left little doubt that she was the reason he came to San Francisco. "Peter, I'm not the serious type. I hope you're dating others, too."

From there they drove to Ghiradelli Square to buy chocolate. Strolling outside, Peter stopped in midstride to stroke her cheek. With the aroma of chocolate mingling with the pungent air, he drew her closer so that the scent of her perfume filled his breath. He held her in a gentle vise.

"It's time you stopped being so afraid, don't you think?"

A startled Samara couldn't move. Now he chose to kiss her, with tourists swarming around them.

"This is nice," he murmured, confirming her suspicions. "Put your hands around my neck." She complied, threading her fingers in his silky hair. He nuzzled her ear. "I couldn't have written the scene better myself. Don't worry. The tourists think we're the main attraction. We'll probably end up in someone's scrapbook. Stop laughing, this is serious."

His hands framed her face. Lowering his head, his lips claimed hers in a kiss. Samara's eyelids drifted shut.

Minutes later, he placed her hand above his heart. She felt its rapid pace through his Irish cable sweater. He slipped his other hand down her spine. "I think it's time we make love, don't you?" At a loss for words, her heart beating erratically, she nodded. A tremor worked its way down her spine. *Please,* she prayed. *Let it work this time. Let me be over David.*

In her bedroom's chiaroscuro light, he slowly undressed her, kissing every curve in her body before claiming her lips. Samara pushed David's face out of her mind, furious that even now she couldn't stop thinking of him, of his lips at her breast as Peter's were now. She squeezed her eyes shut.

"Peter, it's been so long."

His chuckle sounded more like a groan. "We'll pretend it's the first time for both of us."

"Turn out the light," she whispered.

"Not a chance."

His lovemaking was wicked and sensual, teasing and erotic, a pulsing, passionate performance, until she felt she would burst. Only then did he bury himself inside her, giving them both what they wanted.

"I love you." He sighed, falling asleep as the words tumbled from his lips.

Samara stifled her own ragged sigh, sorry he had said he loved her. Her body had reacted without her heart. Out of her control, her heart beat for David. She wished it were otherwise. She liked Peter enormously.

Wide awake, she lay for minutes wondering what to do. Was it wrong to settle? To give Peter her body, take his love, let him believe a lie that she loved him? He deserved more.

She stared out at the stars through her bedroom window. Careful not to disturb him, she eased off the bed, covering him with the blanket to ward off a chill. Bundling up in a warm coat and a spare pair of sneakers and socks she kept in the hall closet, she stepped outside onto the porch to the railing. In the distance a four-masted ship's lights winked its passage to the sea. Others might think the sounds of fog horns lonely, but not her. Their lowing sounds were those of old friends. Daybreak slipped in on pink streaks of dawn.

"Couldn't you sleep?" A fully dressed Peter wrapped his arms about her.

"Peter, you startled me. I'm sorry if I woke you. Go back to sleep for a few hours."

"Samara, we need to talk."

She turned in his arms, putting on a bright smile. "I'll make coffee."

"No coffee. Talk," he said quietly. He cupped her cheek in his palm so she couldn't turn away from the intense light in his eyes. "Last night I told you I loved you. Your response was a ragged sigh you tried and failed to hide. Was my performance so disappointing? Or is it that you believe a Japanese-American is good for a fuck, a fling, nothing more?''

''How could you think such a thing about me?'' she countered. ''Peter, you were wonderful. It's me, not you.''

He released her. ''Who is he?'' he asked flatly.

She stared up at him and saw the grim expression on his face. Her eyes filled with an apology. ''His name is David Orchin.''

Peter ran a hand through his hair. ''I see. At least you're more straightforward than my ex-wife. Where is David? How long have you known him?''

''He lives in New York. I've known him all my life,'' she admitted. ''I flew to America with him.''

''And?'' he prompted, his eyes taking on a wary expression while a muscle jerked along his jaw.

She told him of the part David played in her life in Paris, that he'd nursed her to health after her mother died. ''He brought me to America. I lived with him. We had an affair. He's married to my twin sister.'' In brief terms, she told him the circumstances that brought her to California.

''Oh, shit!'' Peter cursed, slapping his fist into his palm. ''It's worse than I thought. He's still in your life. You're still in love with him. He's still in love with you.''

The breeze lifted her hair, and she tossed it out of the way. ''No, you're wrong.'' She placed a hand on his arm. ''I haven't seen him in years.''

''Damn you, Samara!'' Peter exploded. ''My competition's your freakin' brother-in-law! Someone you've loved your entire life. A living ghost! Why haven't you told me?''

She smarted under his blistering attack. ''Why should I? David's part of my past. I didn't press you about your marriage, your divorce. We have no exclusive rights to each other. I've encouraged you to see other women. I didn't plan to make love with you last night. You started it. I'm not sorry we made love, Peter,'' she said, softening what to her sounded callous and unfeeling. ''I'm sorry if you think I used you.''

''You did use me and you know it!''

She pressed her lips to his, trying in the only way she knew how to assuage his pain.

He caught her to him, kissing her so completely that when he released her they were both shaking. He gripped her shoulders.

"Christ! You're trembling even as you try to convince me that you don't love this David. You've got to see him again—"

"*What?*" She whirled out of his reach. "That's an insane suggestion. Didn't you hear me? He's married to my sister. They have a son."

Peter grabbed her hands. "So what? This has nothing to do with their marriage. I'm concerned about your feelings. *Yours!* You and he go back forever. In your heart, you haven't ended your affair with him. Can't you see you're not a free agent? You never will be until you find out whether you still love him. Do you think I'd suggest this if I didn't think it important? It's got nothing to do with your sister. This is between you and him and us. If there is an us," he ended bitterly.

"I never go to New York, Peter."

"It's not hard to guess why."

Her cheeks burned. In that moment she saw herself through his eyes, a captive chained to her past. She wanted to prove to him that he was wrong—that she knew what was best for her.

She stalled. "I'll think about it."

He snorted. "And in the meantime? What about us?"

"Have patience with me, please," she beseeched. "That's all I ask."

"Sorry. I can't buy that. You're stalling. I love you. I want to marry you, but don't ask me to play second fiddle to a memory. I've been burned once. If I don't get in too deeply, I'll recover with a minimum of scar tissue. One of these days you're going to have to deal with your past, face your feelings honestly. If you can find the courage to do that."

Peter left after that. Samara knew he was right. She had to come to terms with the past. Knowing it and doing something about it were two very different things.

She had no intention of going to New York.

Chapter Twenty-two

On Samara's twenty-fifth birthday in 1985, Tessie and Barney handed her a legal document. "Don't say no. Barney and I insist. Darling girl, we're getting older. Do this for us. Solange will never be part of Gold's West. It's yours. She'll inherit a share of Gold's New York."

Astounded, Samara conferred first with Jules and Mimi, refusing to do anything to impinge on their company. They saw no problem if she moved her showroom and office to GW's executive floor, where she could oversee the talented design staff. With everyone in agreement, Samara accepted, discovering she thrived on the demanding challenge of running a store as much if not more than designing.

"She's so much like me. Decisive!" Tessie bragged a year later. "The company report proves it." Barney agreed. Business was better than ever.

Her office reflected her taste. Peach with accents of muted earth tones, plants for greenery. Mounted on the walls were snapshots of a haughty Fredrica. Her favorite, framed in silver, sat on her desk. Taken the day the dog flunked obedience school, it captured Fred's *so there!* snooty expression. Samara smiled. She ran the business; the dog ran her. Even exchange!

She okayed the color ads for next month's *Examiner* and *Chronicle,* then hurried to finish the weekly bulletin she sent to her forty-five department heads. The phone rang just as she dropped her notes in the box of her secretary, Noki.

From Kennedy Airport in New York, a harried Mimi shouted over the drone of airplanes taxiing and landing at the busy terminus. "I'm in an outside booth," she yelled. "I've got bad news, Samara."

When Mimi finished, Samara asked, "You're certain customs won't release the shipment?"

Mimi's voice rose to near hysteria. "Not a chance, Sam. The shipment contains our entire holiday season, including the gowns for next month's Christmas fashion show you're doing with my dad. We spent a fortune publicizing the show, alerting the industry Papa will be in San Francisco. The stores committed advertising dollars, tied in to the launching of our new perfume line. My salespeople outdid themselves selling the holiday co-op advertising. How will it look if we fall flat on our faces?"

"Mimi, calm down."

"I can't," she wailed. "Don't you understand the gravity? We're facing a potential disaster. Mr. Tua's people shipped the wrong code numbers. It's not like they're new at this."

Samara could feel her palms begin to sweat. Imported merchandise was assigned numbers and checked by customs against the *Harmonized Tariff Schedule of the United States.* Each category of merchandise carried a different identifying number. That morning her assistant designer, Karen Mason, reported women clamored for the line. A week into November, the stores should have received the holiday shipment. *Stores have the right to cancel orders if a delivery date is missed.*

"Will customs release a partial if we get started on the paperwork?" she asked.

"No way. I'm dealing with a prick," Mimi said in disgust. "He absolutely refuses to let me have the shipment. Sam, I'm climbing a ladder of broken steps. The cartons are scheduled for redistribution, routed to the various stores. It's as bad as it gets. On top of that, some jerk left the shipment out all night in a torrential rainstorm. The netting used to hold it down isn't waterproof. Customs told me we've got water damage. Buyers are phoning me demanding to know what's going on. I'm tempted to rip out my phone!"

Samara could feel her legs drain. "How much water damage?"

"Who knows!" Mimi shouted. "I'm not allowed to examine anything. Customs examined it and taped the cartons with special tape."

"We pay good money to our customs broker," Samara said, furious with the hard-nosed government bureaucrat. "Tell customs to let Jack Miller do his job."

"Customs refused. Miller's hands are tied. He checks against the information sent by the manufacturer, which is incorrect. The agent assigned to Best Freight Forwarders treats me as if I'm a criminal."

"Because of a paper error? That's ridiculous!"

"Sam!" Mimi snarled. "We're being accused of bringing in unlisted merchandise. He says we're overvalued."

"What?" Samara cried, incensed at the injustice of it. Commercial invoices include the total gross weight, fabric and fiber content, product code, style number, and value of each individual piece. "They've got the master airway bill and the commercial invoice."

"Tell that to the man at Best who stamped the order: Released Pending Investigation. In a week the shipment goes into General Order."

"What's that?"

"General Order means they move the freight to another bonded warehouse. Guess who pays the storage fee? Can you believe this? How can I solve a problem no one lets me solve? You know what happens when I'm excited. I rattle in French."

Samara shook her head in disbelief. "I'll telex the Philippines and straighten this out with Mr. Tua. The error originated at his manufacturing plant. I'll ask him to send new invoices. Once I learn the extent of the water damage, we'll have him cut what we need to replace the damaged gowns."

"Please!" Mimi blasted. Samara shot the receiver away from her ear. "I'm no idiot. I've already tried that. Save your breath. There's no one at Tua's plant. It's closed."

"That can't be!"

"Oh, yes it can be! Tua's mother died. He shut the place. When I phoned, I got a recorded message. The plant reopens in two weeks. God knows where his mother died. Mr. Tua doesn't trust his people. Usually one of his family is on the premises. I'm not through with the horror story. Brace yourself, Sam. We've also got missing labels on some of the gowns. That alone is enough for customs to refuse entry. So while we stew and lose money—not to mention our reputation and goodwill!—our labels are safely locked inside Tua's warehouse.''

"Dear God!" Samara absorbed the enormity of their dilemma. Based on orders written throughout the country, with every reason to assume a healthy cash flow, they had invested huge sums of money for the holiday season. Stores pay after receipt of the merchandise. The success of the cycle depends on the sum of its parts. With water-damaged goods, missing labels, customs's refusal to release a partial consignment, being accused of overvaluing the shipment, they faced a potential monumental disaster—including possible lawsuits! No wonder Mimi sounded on the brink of despair.

"Samara, you've got to come to New York to solve this mess. I've tried calling your dad. He's out of town on a case. I can't stay. I've scheduled out-of-town meetings that can't be changed. I'm leaving in one hour. Get your butt to New York."

Samara sucked in her breath. What Mimi suggested struck terror in her heart. "I'll see what I can do by phone."

"No!" Mimi shouted, correctly deducing Samara's trepidation. "We have an emergency. I know David's the reason you avoid New York. Look what happened with Peter. You won't go forward, you won't go backward. You're stuck. Sam, you're a coward."

"I am not," she protested.

"Hah! I remember when the perfume chemist from Grasse flew to New York for you to choose the scents for the new line. You dumped that on me, too. You didn't care if I chose skunk!"

"I agreed to meet him in Chicago," Samara argued.

"Thanks for proving my point," Mimi shouted. "Your crappy excuses worked as long as they didn't bankrupt my future. When you wanted to accept your grandparents' offer, I encouraged you. You've got GW to fall back on. Papa's got his business in Paris. I have nothing else. I've spent years running around the country. For us! Why should I suffer? You let Peter slide through your fingers. You refuse to see David, hear his side. The poor man deserves it. It's long past time you two settle what's between you. Either you come here, or I quit. I mean it. If I can't rely on you, it's the end of our friendship and our partnership. I'll go it alone."

Samara didn't take Mimi's threat lightly. A lifetime of

friendship hung in the balance, more valuable to her than their business. She'd lost David. She couldn't afford to lose her dearest friend, too.

"Let me have the airway bill number, Mimi. The night flight will get me there in the morning. I'll book a suite at the Plaza. Leave any messages there."

The decision made, Samara flew into action. It occurred to her that every momentous act in her life followed closely on the heels of a disaster. Maman's death caused her to move to the United States to find her father. Solange's trickery and David's betrayal caused her to flee. True, she could go to New York and avoid seeing him. It was time to stop running, time to be completely healed, not act as Mimi said, like a coward.

She phoned Tessie in Palm Beach, Florida, where her grandparents wintered, asking for the name of a manufacturer near Kennedy who stocked lingerie fabrics. "Mr. Tua's people usually place the polysatin charmeuse gowns on top. It's possible they're the only water-damaged ones."

Tessie supplied the name of Sammy Friedman on Farmer's Boulevard, across the road from Kennedy cargo. "You should see David," she added, pooh-poohing Samara's thanks.

"Grandma, do you realize what you're saying?" *What everyone was saying!*

"Yes," came the firm reply. "I love Solange. That will never change, but I'm no longer blind to her faults. If you see David, you'll be able to decide about your feelings, about seeing other men. I want your happiness."

She stared in the mirror opposite her desk. Apparently she'd been able to kid herself, not anyone else. She hadn't been able to erase David from her mind. It was entirely possible that if she saw him now, she'd discover she wasn't still in love with him. Then she'd finally be free.

Before her resolve weakened, she dialed David's office, only to be told he was due back the next day. She left a message with the date and time. Unless she heard otherwise, she would assume he accepted her invitation to join her for dinner at the Plaza. On the long flight to New York she forced herself to concentrate on the movie, the book she'd brought along to read, and how she'd approach customs.

Entering the Kennedy cargo area the next day in tapered jeans, cactus-green turtleneck sweater, and long black trenchcoat, Samara caused a stir among the workers. Several men stopped to watch her progress, whistling when she passed.

The area buzzed with activity. Bonded trucks ferried shipments to container stations. Giant forklifts crisscrossed the tarmac in a lumbering ballet, ferrying pallets piled with merchandise to waiting airplanes or freight-forwarding warehouses. Men loaded cleared cargo onto waiting trucks.

Samara concentrated on her immediate crisis rather than on David. She glanced at the Pan Am airway identification 026, the eight-digit number assigned to her shipment. She strode swiftly past ABC Freight, Emery Worldwide, Randy International, and S.J. Stiles, before locating Best's hangar. A sign prominently restricted the building to authorized personnel.

Samara walked past the chain-link fence into the hangar. Blasting boom boxes assaulted her ears. A group of men paused to whistle at her. A few waved. A sharp finger tapped her shoulder. "Can't you read?"

Swinging around, she came face-to-face with a brown-haired Neanderthal, whose forbidding black eyes gave her a hostile once-over. Samara read his official badge. She'd found Customs Agent O'Malley.

Reminding herself that this man could make her or break her, she coerced a smile to her lips. "I'm so glad to see you, Mr. O'Malley. I need help with a problem."

"This is Friday," he said abruptly. "On Fridays I don't take on extra problems. If it's about a shipment, contact your broker." He jerked his thumb toward the group of men. "If one of these Romeos broke your heart, see him later. *Outside the restricted area.* That about covers any business we might have. You can leave the way you came in."

"Please," she said, determined to hold her temper, not to give the chauvinistic jerk a piece of her mind. "My name is Samara Bousseauc. You're holding my nightgowns."

"That's a new one." His lips twitched.

She saw the flicker of amusement in his eyes. Needing no more encouragement than that small crack in his tough facade, she prayed her inadvertent slip might be the clue to humanizing the big oaf. "You've been dealing with a Miss Mimi Le-Claire."

His smile switched to a scowl. "I repeat. Go through channels." He started moving toward the exit.

She stood her ground. Somewhere in this cavernous place, hidden among thousands of cartons, her shipment gathered dust while she and her partners stood to lose a fortune.

"How do you expect us to go through channels?" she asked defensively. "You won't allow our broker to check the merchandise."

The agent abruptly halted. "I checked it myself. Your stuff doesn't agree with TSUS."

"TSUS?"

As though she were a dolt, he snorted, "Tariff Schedule of the United States. TSUS. We get the correct paperwork, or nothing moves. I remember your case clearly, thanks to that woman who's made a pest of herself. You've got five cartons of gowns minus labels. The invoices are wrong. You're overvalued, which is an offense. You're lucky I don't throw the book at you. In simple terms, Miss Bousseauc, I think you're trying to pull a fast one. The government doesn't look kindly at people who try to ship more value into the country than they're willing to pay for."

She'd worry about his accusation later. Right now she needed information. "How much water damage?"

He shook a cigarette out of a package, lit it and drew deeply, rudely puffing smoke so that it hit her face. "Give it up, lady. I don't know how much damage. That's your problem."

Samara coughed. "I'll arrange for the missing labels to be sewn on the gowns. If we're overvalued, we didn't do it deliberately. Anything over the order we placed you can keep."

His eyes darkened. "That's what I call a bribe."

"We both know that between the Philippines and the store delivery, theft often occurs. If people try to slip contraband into the country, why hold me responsible?"

"So now you're lecturing me on my business," he said sarcastically.

She refused to be put on the defensive. "You don't care about people. As long as your paperwork checks, no one bothers you. Well, let me tell you something. Don't throw your weight around me. No one is going to ruin me or my partners. If necessary, I'll go to the newspapers. I'll cry foul. When I'm through, you'll wish you never saw me."

Glaring at her, he stepped so close she saw his nostril hairs quiver. "Are you threatening United States Customs?"

She glared back at him. No wonder Mimi grew wild in his presence. Between apprehension over seeing David and trying to reason with this rigid excuse for a man, she herself was well on her way to swallowing a bottle of Librax. "Of course I'm not threatening customs. I'm simply saying that your badge doesn't give you the right to play God. My tax dollars help pay your salary. I demand my money's worth—"

"See here!" he interrupted.

"No," she said. "You see here. I'm not the enemy. Instead of helping me, as a good public servant should, you gave me a macho speech about Romeos."

He took her arm. His fingers bit into her flesh. She wrenched free. He slapped the clipboard with his hand. "Lady, you're wasting my time."

It reassured her that he hadn't thrown her out bodily.

"Look, I'm sorry I blew. My manufacturer's mother died. The plant is closed for a few days."

"Have him send me the paperwork on company letterhead. It's regulations."

"By then it's too late. The stores are breathing down my neck for their holiday deliveries. They've spent good money for advertising. Come on, please bend a little. Let me check the cartons. How can I reorder unless I know the extent of the water damage?"

Her impassioned speech got nowhere.

"Impossible. In the first place it's highly irregular. You're not authorized to be here."

Samara at twenty-six wasn't the sweet innocent she had been at nineteen. She bluffed. "All right. You leave me no choice but to ask my father, Senator Gold, to intervene."

That got his attention. She pressed her advantage. "I'll contact my friends, Avrim Leightner and Maggie McPherson, the television anchors. They've got the best investigative reporting staffs in the business. It should make a great nationwide story. Rigid government official more interested in paperwork than helping honest hardworking citizens who pay his salary."

He glowered at her. She could smell the anger emanating from him. Good God! Had she overplayed her hand? She knew she didn't have a prayer of making good her threat. With luck the agent wasn't aware that her father had left office years ago, that Avrim worked in London, that Maggie anchored from San Francisco.

"Okay." He marched her to the rear of the hangar and pointed. "There's your order. I'm going to do you a highly extraordinary favor. Under *my* supervision, you have exactly thirty-five minutes to examine your shipment for water damage."

"Thirty-five minutes!" she yelled.

"The clock's ticking. Don't push your luck." Four sturdy men offered their help. They ripped off the tape, saving valuable minutes for her feverish inspection. Twelve cartons were damaged.

Sweat beaded her brow. As the last few precious minutes eroded, out of the corner of her eye she glimpsed a row of cartons wedged between two rows. Holes! Whipping out her camera, she snapped pictures in rapid succession.

"Hey, what do you think you're doing?" the agent demanded.

With David on her mind, she didn't have time to gloat. "I believe it's called gathering evidence for insurance purposes—and for the press. There are holes punched into the sides of those cartons. If I can see them, I'm surprised you didn't."

From the deepening red flush creeping up his neck, it was obvious that he hadn't sealed the cartons himself as he claimed, but had assigned another person to do it, raising doubt as to where the tampering had taken place.

"That won't be necessary."

"Mistakes are easily made, Mr. O'Malley." She took the diplomatic approach. "Will you allow me to ship the cartons in need of labels to a bonded warehouse on Farmer's Boulevard? Here's the company's name. We'll let the insurance people work out my loss due to thievery. I'll gladly redo the paperwork."

The agent sourly filled out the necessary forms.

"I'll see you Monday morning. Thanks for your help," she tossed over her shoulder.

Dashing across Farmer's Boulevard, she met with Sammy Friedman. If she brought him a pattern on Monday, he'd replace the damaged gowns and sew in the missing labels. She promised to bring the pattern Monday morning. By meticulously reopening the seams on a gown she had brought with her for that purpose, she would cut a new pattern for Mr. Friedman.

En route to the Plaza in a taxi, Maggie's final words of advice came back to her. "Do what feels right when you see David. You don't owe your shit sister a thing."

The cab drew up in front of the Central Park South entrance. At the desk she signed the register. "Is there a message for me?" The clerk handed her a piece of paper. Her hand shook. Dismayed, she crumpled Mimi's message wishing her good luck. It was six o'clock. By the time David arrived in two hours—providing he did arrive—she'd be too rattled to even say hello.

Chapter Twenty-three

1986

David moved his office from Babies Hospital to the Dana W. Atchley Pavilion on Ft. Washington Avenue when Asher was three. In a Plexiglas frame on his desk he kept a recent picture of his almost six-year-old imp seated atop a tricycle. Mickey Mouse adhesive bandages marched up Asher's skinned legs. His mischievous smile reached out to grab his father. The first time he visited his office he thought it was "neat." Solange dismissed it as a professional waste. "You could be earning a lot more money at a good address."

With Samara refusing to speak to him, he let the years pass rather than fight Solange and take Asher from his mother. Her love for Asher amazed him, and it benefited his son. He had fully expected her to reject her newborn infant; when she didn't, he settled for an empty void. Samara's message today brought back a rush of feeling. Tessie and Barney's faith in her ability to run Gold's West affirmed her capabilities. It also sparked Solange's jealousy. She had been the one to tell him about Samara's affair with Peter Watanabe.

"I'm surprised Wendall didn't tell you. The man's a film director. While you think of doing it with other women, imagine Samara spreading her legs for a Jap!"

"Why should I have told you?" Wendall retorted at the time. "So you'd stew the way you're stewing now?"

David railed, "Everything to you is black or white. What can I offer her? Have you forgotten I'm not free?"

It took a lot to anger Wendall. Infinitely patient, he divided his time between his practice at Columbia and working gratis in a storefront medical office in the South Bronx. When he did get angry, he blew. "Get divorced. I don't have time for this shit, pal. This is my final statement on the subject. What a woman says and what she wants aren't necessarily identical. *Capisce?* The Samara I know loved you unconditionally. Sure she was hurt. It's understandable she didn't want to see you. Orchin, you're a prize jerk. I told you to marry her, but you insisted on waiting. You advised her to concentrate on her career. You made it easy for her to believe Solange's lies."

"Samara was in mourning. I wanted her to have every chance, not to tie herself down to me until she was sure."

Wendall snorted. "Look where that brilliant bit of strategy got you." Wendall slapped his palms together. "Asher thinks married couples sleep in separate bedrooms. He's going to grow up, move away, live his own life. Then what? You'll be a miserable old fart of a man. What would that accomplish? Do you enjoy punishment?" he asked.

Now Wendall repeated himself. He'd come to David's office after David phoned to tell him he'd heard from Samara.

"Stop dissecting her motives," he advised. "Count your blessings. Don't fuck up your opportunity. Don't look a gift horse in the mouth. Take your best shot. This is my last noble speech. Ask yourself why she stopped seeing Peter Watanabe. My guess is she still loves you. In another life, you and she were joined at the hip. You two need each other to breathe. Think about how you want to live the rest of your life, buddy. Where do you see yourself five years from now?"

David did think about it. All afternoon, on the drive home to shower, and while he changed his clothes. He ached thinking about Wendall's exasperating expertise of succinctly narrowing down his options. He wished he had a crystal ball to Samara's thoughts before he saw her tonight.

He couldn't bear the possibility of her marrying, having another man's child. If he let her go without telling her he loved her, he'd have no one but himself to blame. Nothing mattered except letting her know the truth of what had happened. He'd work out the rest—if she would give him a second chance. A big if. For the present he'd hang on to the fact that she'd asked to see him.

A blast of noise assaulted his ears the moment he arrived

home. Asher, with a child's keen hearing, let out a war whoop from the second-floor landing.

"Hiya, Pop. Spot me!"

In seconds Asher slid down the banister. David caught him. They exchanged loud kisses. Like his father's, Asher's hair stubbornly resisted a comb. "Turn down the volume on the TV," David ordered.

Undaunted, Asher announced, "You're just in time, Pop. Pepe's making popcorn. We rented *E.T.*" He skipped in front of him. "How come I never met Aunt Samara?"

David's hand loosening the knot in his tie froze. "Who told you about her?"

"Grandma Tessie phoned from Florida before Mommy left. She said Aunt Samara is Mommy's twin sister. Mommy grabbed the phone." In a fit of disgust, he stamped his feet. Eyes flashing with irritation, he thrust his tongue to the side of his cheek. "Mommy made Pepe take me in the kitchen. It's unfair. If Samara is Mommy's sister, how come I don't know her?"

David hid his surprise. Why had Tessie chosen now to tell Asher about Samara? He could imagine Solange's reaction. "Did you ask Mommy?" Asher nodded. "What did she say?"

"Samara lives in California, never comes to New York. Take me there so I can meet her. Mommy went to see Lou-Lou. She said to remind you to bring home more vitamin C."

"Anything else?" David asked.

"Mommy's coming home on Monday." Asher zipped around the room, imitating an airplane. "She left Pepe a list of stuff to do. I'm to have an ice cream. Seven scoops."

David caught him on the turn. He ruffled his son's hair. "Faker. The most you'll get is two."

"Five?" Asher begged.

"Two."

"Three?"

"Don't press your luck or you'll get one scoop, which is what Mommy gives you. I'm going out tonight, sport."

Asher couldn't care less. He flew to the kitchen to tell Pepe the good news. Upstairs, David twice cut himself shaving. He spied his mismatched socks as he was leaving his room and had to run back to find a matched sock. The fierce pounding in his chest warned him that if he didn't get a grip on himself, Samara would say hello to a blithering, hyperventilating moron.

Seated at the vanity table in her spacious Plaza suite overlooking Central Park, Samara let out a frustrated sigh. She gazed critically at her reflection in the mirror, approving of the sleeveless Oscar de la Renta black silk charmeuse dress she'd chosen. Its demure front—the neckline skimmed her collarbones—belied its sexy confident statement when viewed from the back, revealing a generous expanse of silken skin. Rhinestone bows clipped at the shoulders, another at the base of the vee, added a hint of naughtiness. A black silk-grosgrain hair bow, its saucy tassel swaying gently when she moved her head, completed the outfit. She portrayed the image of a self-confident, glamorous woman.

Who was she trying to kid? she reflected wryly. Her mouth was dry, her hands clammy. Her stomach housed thousands of butterflies. She slipped her feet into a pair of black silk pumps, decorated with tiny rhinestone bows at the top of the heels.

The two-room suite was filled with priceless art objects and antiques. The spacious bedroom and living room each had crystal chandeliers and white marble fireplaces. Duplicate armoires handcrafted of the finest rosewood concealed remote-controlled televisions and fully stocked liquor cabinets. She harbored no illusions. Seeing David tonight would be her ultimate test. No more hiding and avoiding New York. She settled down on the sofa to watch the TV news. Ed Koch, reelected mayor of New York for the third term, asked the audience, "How'm I doing?"

"Better than I am," she muttered, plagued by a fresh attack of nerves. From the street, the wail of a police siren pierced the night. A glance at the clock told her she didn't have long to wait. Either David would phone from the lobby announcing his arrival or he wouldn't. She'd give him until eight forty-five, then she'd leave.

A hard rap at the door had her jumping up, nearly knocking over a small vase filled with painted daisies that sat on a nearby table. With lightning-quick motions her hand flew to her heart, she wet her lips and took a deep breath. She opened the door.

David! He smiled down at her, and she thought her heart would melt. Clad in a navy wool suit, white shirt, striped blue tie, his coat slung over his arm, he filled the doorway. She gave herself a hard mental shake. Pride mingled with the pain of memories kept her from flinging herself in his arms.

"Hello, Samara."

For a moment she couldn't get her thick tongue to peel away from the roof of her mouth. Solange transformed them into strangers. "Hello, David," she managed to say.

A rush of emotion rivered through her. Her heart tripped. Her pulses quickened, but she stood erect, her chin held high, exactly as she had rehearsed it, locking gazes with the man who hadn't been out of her thoughts even for a day during their years of separation.

A sprinkling of gray hair added charm to his distinguished features. Tall, broad-shouldered, lean, and chiseled, he epitomized the rugged gracefulness of an athlete. The main difference was in his darker, more somber eyes. They held the look of a man whose life, like hers, stopped on one awful day, and was never the same again. Standing near him, trapped by his sheer physical size and the scent of familiar cologne, she felt her cheeks flush, remembering the touch and taste of his body. Under the searing impact of his intense scrutiny, studying her with the same open admiration, she nervously ran a hand down her hip, smoothing the line of her dress.

David gazed into her brilliant blue eyes. Dear God, how he had missed her, the years they'd lost. She wore her hair differently, pulled back, a bow to match the ones at her shoulders. She carried off the severity of the hairdo with dignity emanating from every regal pore. "I thought it might be easier if I came up," he said, seeking refuge in words.

He saw by the slight relaxing of her stance that his words helped ease the tension. The perfume was new—lusher, sexier, intoxicating.

When she turned, he glimpsed her creamy flesh and inwardly groaned. Only a confident woman could wear that dress. Outrageous, sexy, it invited his touch. He'd made love to her luscious skin, tasting every delicious inch. More than anything in the world, he wanted that right again. He tunneled his fingers through his hair to keep from making a fool of himself.

"How have you been?" she asked, barely recognizing her tinny, strained, unnatural voice.

His gaze lingered on her lush mouth, skimmed her breasts. He looked into her long-lashed eyes, telling the truth. "Marking time. And you?"

"Very well," she replied, wanting to scream just the opposite. "Gold's West is projecting a forty-nine percent increase. Mimi and Jules and I have a licensing partnership. Besides the lingerie, we've added a line of perfume." *Brilliant. I'm prattling nonsense.* "And your practice? How is the research coming along?"

David took a deep breath and let it out. "Fine."

That covers both our lives. "That's good. I'll get my stole. I made reservations in the Edwardian Room."

He stayed her arm, and his thigh brushed her dress. She jumped back, as if burned. "Samara, are you hungry?"

"Not especially," she admitted. A fork couldn't get past her mouth in her present condition.

"I'd rather you cancel the reservation so that we can talk in private. Isn't that why I'm here? To discuss the past. Isn't that why you phoned? Isn't it what you want, too?"

She could feel the pressure building in her chest, the electric current charging her body from his touch. Not trusting herself to speak, she led him to one of the blue-and-white-striped sofas in the living room. When she started to take a separate chair, he drew her down to sit next to him, taking her hand in his as if afraid she might bolt.

David wasted no time in getting to the point. "I've waited a long time to say this. I have never once knowingly made love to Solange," he said bluntly, referring to the day she had found Solange in their bed. "I have never touched her. Not once in all these years. Do you understand what I'm telling you?" He spoke quietly but firmly.

Her lower lip trembled. Tears misted her eyes, blurring the soft golden lamplight that delineated the rugged planes on his face. "I find it hard to believe you didn't know it was Solange, not me. *'I could find you in the dark,'* you said."

He drew a long, harsh breath. "She bragged later that she stole your perfume." His eyes grew cold with anger. "The special night shades you'd bought kept the room dark. If you recall, I had been at the hospital all night when Emmett died. In my sleepy state, I was vulnerable. She never said a word. Why would I think it *wasn't* you? I naturally expected it would be you. That's what I wrote in the letters Max and Wendall told me you tore up.''

Ignoring that, she asked angrily, "Why did you marry Solange? It was broad daylight. No one put a gun to your head. Did you expect me to listen to the messages you sent with my father or with Wendall? You're still married to her. It can't be that bad, can it?''

Her words stung at him. Thanks to him, she wasn't a trusting young woman anymore. Hurt had put new sharp edges on her. Edges that made her wary, mistrusting.

Tersely he recounted the scene in his office when he'd looked up to find Solange. "She demanded an abortion. She insisted I was the father. I made her undergo a medical examination. It confirmed her pregnancy. I offered to care for her, then find a good adoptive family.''

"And you believed her when she said the baby was yours?'' Samara scoffed.

"Yes. We hated each other too much for me not to believe her. She refused to give birth to an illegitimate baby. She demanded that I help her abort it or she'd find someone else to do it. She reneged on our agreement.''

"What agreement?''

"The marriage was supposed to be a mere formality, to legitimize the baby, to save its life. We were to divorce, and I'd raise the baby. There's no question that Asher is my son, even without the subsequent blood tests I took.''

Your son and Solange's! She gagged. Abruptly she yanked her hand away from his. "That answers why you married her, not why you're still married to her. Solange sent me the issue of *Time*. Pictures don't lie.''

"Damn her.'' He balled his fists. "Solange manipulated that. She came into the room uninvited, bringing Asher. She placed her chair in such a way that when I smiled at Asher, it appeared I was smiling at her. What could I do? Throw her out of her own home in front of the photographer?''

Samara sprang up and moved swiftly across the floor. "Why didn't you leave her after Asher was born?''

"I intended to, but then Solange latched on to her child as if she'd wanted him with all her heart. The truth was she wasn't faking it. When you refused to see me, I didn't care what happened to me. Hiring competent help to replace a mother is difficult at best. You know my hours. My concern was for Asher. When you're a new father, you look at this tiny helpless infant who needs care, whose mother is giving him care, and it shakes you up. Besides, she repeated her threat."

Samara studied his hard profile. "What threat?"

His face became grim, his body taut. He flexed his jaw. "To hide Asher where I'll never find him if I start divorce proceedings. When he was younger, I worried she'd poison his mind against me. She can't do that anymore. He's older. He knows I love him. She can't legally hide him from me. I'm determined to get a divorce. It's sad to think she'd rather endure a loveless marriage than allow me to be happy, if it meant letting you be happy."

She was appalled at the depth of her sister's malice. "What hatred Solange feels for me. Why? I've never taken or wanted what was hers."

"Whatever her problems, they're deeply rooted," he said, speaking more calmly. "Solange couldn't stand sharing Max with Maggie. You've seen how she treated Maggie."

"I certainly have," Samara agreed heatedly, recalling Maggie's stories. "Because of her, Maggie hasn't set a wedding date. She and my father love each other. He wants to marry her, start a new family, but until she becomes pregnant, she won't."

"The only way I've been able to keep myself sane is by trying to understand what motivates Solange. It's all I had." David spoke quietly with a sense of despair that convinced Samara she'd blamed him unjustly. Through the years, David had endured more than she. He lived with Solange.

"Go on," she said.

"The way I figure it, Solange suffered a severe shock when you arrived. Imagine learning her mother had been alive all these years and never contacted her. It didn't matter that the rest of the family showered her with love—she still felt discarded. Much the same reaction you had when you first learned about Max."

"But I got over that!" Samara bristled, leaping to Lilli's defense as well as her own. "I'm on good terms with everyone. Except your wife!"

"To your credit," David acknowledged. "I consulted a psychiatrist. Without the jargon, Solange's envy of you progressed rapidly to jealousy, then to obsession. She couldn't accept Lilli's choosing you over her. With Lilli dead, she focused the blame on you. Max, and your grandparents' love for you, fueled her desire for revenge. She cast about for the best way to exact it. We made it easy for her. She knew we were in love. She plotted to eliminate you the only way she knew how: by trying to destroy you through me. It didn't matter that she destroyed me in the process. I was the handy tool.''

''When it happened, Avrim said much the same thing. My God!'' Samara interrupted heatedly. ''It worked.''

David nodded grimly. ''Nearly worked. Haven't you wondered about Lilli's story? I have. Often. It never made sense to me that she would threaten suicide. Lilli upheld the sacraments. I can't see your mother breaking one intentionally.''

''Me neither. I've wondered about that, too, but then why the suicide threat?''

''Isn't it possible she wrote that for another reason?''

''Perhaps, but we won't know. Anyway, what difference does it make? It's old news. Maman's dead. I'm glad she isn't alive to see this. It would kill her.''

''If Lilli had left you with Max, not Solange, I'm convinced your twin would be a different person.''

Samara's lips thinned. She shook her head in rebuke. ''Don't start that psychological stuff with me. I won't buy it. Adults make choices. According to your theory, if your parent is a killer, you'll end up one, too. People overcome childhood adversity. I didn't let Max's rejection ruin me, did I?''

Unbuttoning his suit jacket, David stretched his legs. ''He didn't reject you. He wanted you, provided for you. Lilli set the rules. Max tried to see you personally and through Murray Leightner. My father and Jules were your substitute fathers. My mother was your second mother. You were loved.''

''Oh, pardon me for being loved,'' she flared. ''Is that supposed to excuse Solange's behavior?''

He shook his head. ''Not excuse it—explain it. If I didn't try to understand this, I'd have gone out of my mind long ago. There's more. You recall Avrim saying he and Solange had had an affair.''

Samara nodded. ''Maggie guessed as much.''

''The affair began when she was fifteen. It lasted for years.

She aborted his child. To this day he doesn't know. I only
learned it from Solange by mistake."

Samara gasped. Both she and David regarded abortion as
anathema, unless it was to save the mother's life, or if a woman
was raped and couldn't emotionally carry the child.

"I look at Asher," David said, his voice softening as he
spoke about his son. "This wonderful little boy wouldn't be
alive today if it had been up to her."

Samara rigidly asked, "Do you resent me for looking like
her?"

Her question drew a sharp protest. Jumping up from the sofa,
he grabbed hold of her wrists. "You crazy little fool. After all
we've been to each other. We have a lifetime of memories.
How can you believe such nonsense?"

A surge of resentment, of pure anger, rippled through
Samara. "Is she a good mother?"

David wanted to lie. It would have been easier to lie, to feed
Samara's wrath, to put them both in the position of outcasts, so
that together they could add being a rotten mother to the list of
Solange's faults. This was the most important conversation of
his life, but it had to be based on truth.

"Yes. She adores Asher. She's there for him, he loves her.
We don't argue in front of him. We take him to the zoo, the
museums, that sort of thing. But we lead separate private lives.
Until today I didn't care."

Samara stiffened. She hadn't let herself think of David
sleeping with other women. "That's over," he informed her
flatly, putting casual affairs behind him.

"I despise Solange," Samara said vehemently. "I wish to
God I had never come here. None of this would have
happened."

"I wish you'd stayed in Paris, too. By now we'd be an old
married couple."

Her hackles rose. The light in her eyes burned fiercely. "It's
not fair," she said. Pacing the room, she stopped in midstride.
"Solange is living my life. She's your wife. She's the mother
of your son. She's gotten it all. How could she be so evil? She's
stolen our lives." The ring of truth bounced off the walls, rising
and settling about them with a thud. She stood with her back to
him at the window, her arms wrapped about her waist, locking
him out.

Fear socked him in the throat, drained the blood from his veins. His heart skittered. Had he come here merely to help her write the last chapter? He had to make this right, or risk losing her forever. He couldn't—wouldn't—allow that to happen without putting up a battle. He circled his arm about her shoulders. With his other hand, he tipped up her chin.

He looked deeply into her eyes. "Solange knows I love you. You are as much a part of me as the air I breathe. Wendall knows I'm here. You should have heard him scold me. You'd be proud of him. He told me to ask myself where I want to be five years from now. I want to be with you. Since you left I've buried myself in work. Without you there's no joy. Except for Asher, my work is gray, colorless. Solange can only steal our lives if you continue to allow her to. Our future is up to you, Samara. Ask yourself where you want to be five years from now. If there's another man in your life, if you love him, there's nothing more I can do except to wish you well. I love you. That's what I came to say."

Her gaze fell to where his hands had fallen stiffly at his sides. This proud man wished her luck in the most agonized voice she'd ever heard. Had it not been for her, he never would have met Solange. He'd paid dearly for her decision to come to America. *Our future is up to you.* Her choice. Follow her heart or be practical and walk away from the trouble that Solange would surely cause. Acutely aware that he was her destiny, she couldn't imagine the rest of her life without David. The past was unchangeable, the future questionable, but the present was hers.

Samara put her hands on his arms and tilted up her head, smiling. "There is no one else, David. I tried. It didn't work." At the look of absolute joy on David's face, she grinned. "David, do you think you could recover from shock and kiss me?"

He swept her in his arms. "I won't let you be sorry," he said, bringing his mouth down to hers. He kissed her in a way that left little doubt how much he'd missed her. She had been terrified that they couldn't bridge the past. Samara felt all the old familiar longings rushing back. The world shrank to a tiny passion-filled space. His tongue found ready access to her mouth, tasting its warm interior. His hands began to glide all over her body. Her sigh when he touched her breasts, her pleased murmur when he cupped her buttocks, the satisfied kitten sounds she made when he insinuated his thigh between her legs—all raised the level of his arousal, leaving no doubt that he wanted her as much as she wanted him. "I'm shaking I love you so much."

She moaned as he pulled her hard and tight against him to feel how much he yearned for her. She leaned into his arms, clinging to his neck, returning his kisses with all the fierce longing she'd been denied, reveling in the freedom to touch. She could almost let herself believe their separation had been a figment of her imagination. She raised shining eyes to his, stroking his face with the back of her fingers. "I'm trembling, too. Poor Wendall. We've been giving him a hard time for years. I think it's time we took his advice. Darling, can you stay with me this weekend?"

A dazzling smile lit David's eyes as the full import of her invitation crystallized. "I'll phone Pepe later, tell her where to reach me."

For a moment they just held each other, stunned by being together at last. Then he began to kiss her. He trailed kisses down her face, touching her with adoration, kissing her eyes, her cheeks, her neck. Samara turned her face from side to side, giving David freedom to seek his pleasure and hers. He treated her as though she were a precious jewel, inspecting his treasure with his lips and hands. She tingled as his lips awoke pulse points.

"Oh, my," she moaned, dropping her head limply forward, letting him do with her as he pleased. His tongue trailed a path on her bare spine. Soft pleasure moans spilled from her lips. She shivered deliciously. "Oh, my, oh, my," she repeated in little gasps.

His mouth closed over hers again, continuing his sensual assault. His hands raced across her skin. He blew gently in her ear, eliciting a rapturous response. She turned her mouth to his, demanding to be kissed. With a groan of pleasure, he treated her to more worshipful ardor.

He shrugged out of his suit jacket, scooped her up in his arms, and strode into the luxurious bedroom that was fit for a queen. His hands roamed upward to capture her full breasts. Dipping his head, he took a nipple in his mouth, sucking and tugging gently at first one, then the other.

He spoke to her in French, in the language they had always used when making love. Trembling, she closed her eyes, yielding once again to the sweet ecstasy of hearing herself praised in her native tongue. Beneath her questing fingers she felt his hard, sinewy muscles. She leaned her fevered cheek against his shirt, listening to the rapid beating of his heart.

With an urgency borne of years of denial, they shed unwanted clothes. She kissed his chest, savoring the taste of his flesh. She possessively reacquainted herself with his body. A smattering of dark chest hair led to a long narrow line tapering to a curly dark nest, surrounding his rigid shaft. Her touch brought an immediate masculine reaction. His body jerked convulsively. With a cry, he crushed her lips to his, marauding her mouth, relentlessly igniting her fiery passion.

"Come to bed," he said, removing the bow from her hair. He buried his face in her subtle perfume. "Let me love you."

"Oh, yes," she gasped, soaring anew as he blazed kisses down her flat stomach. Whimpering with pleasure, she unfolded like a flower, urging his exploration to kiss, to taste, to touch. Except to concentrate on David, Samara lost contact with rational thought. His form bespoke masculine beauty, sculpted with biceps, muscles, and hard thighs. The sound of her heart thundered in her ears. Her hands tangled mindlessly in his hair. She buried her face at his neck, inhaling his fragrance, tasting the faint saltiness of his skin, clasping him to her, offering him the gift of herself.

In naked splendor, they lay on silken sheets, their magic carpet. Above her, David held her eyes with his midnight gaze, stroking her sensitive body. Her body took its cue, circling her hips in an ancient rhythm. David gazed down at her pink-tipped breasts, her porcelain skin, her ruby lips. Her hair shimmered on the pillow.

He felt alive and vibrant. His senses zinged. His heart sang. She seemed so delicate, his woman of strength, of valor. They became one again.

In body.

In spirit.

In love.

David lazily stroked her thigh. They'd phoned room service for a bottle of Chateauneuf-du-Pape and an assortment of fruit.

Samara snuggled in his arms, her box of candy on her stomach.
In the middle of a story about Tessie, she paused to give him
a kiss.

"You should have seen her." She chuckled. "Grandma
dragged me around the country, checking out the competition.
After a while, Neiman-Marcus looked like Nordstrom. I can't
tell you how many hotel rooms we stayed in. At night she'd
quiz me. First she'd tell me she loved me like her heart, then
wham! 'What's a spiff? A perk? Net back? Incentives?' She
made me convert square footage to departments. She drummed
chain of command in my head. 'You've got managers and
money men. It's your job to let them know that Gold's is an
image store. We are not a K Mart, Penney, or Sears. We
anticipate. We create an ambience of sight and sound and
smell.'" Samara giggled. "I knew how to drive her crazy.
Whenever I'd stand close to the air-conditioning unit in
whatever hotel room we stayed in, Tessie pursed her lips and
shook her head. She'd pat the bed, tell me I was going to catch
my death of cold if I didn't move. Invariably I ended up next
to her on the bed, which is what she wanted from the
beginning."

"You love her a lot, don't you?"

"Mmmm. Yes. I forgave her a long time ago for Maman."

"She phoned from Florida. She told Asher about you.
Tessie's trying to speed up the future."

Samara glanced up at him. "Are you upset she told him?"

He hugged her. "Are you kidding? It's time Asher knew his
gorgeous aunt. Would you like to meet him? He's anxious to
meet you."

"Another time," she said carefully. "When I'm here for
longer than a weekend."

Sensing her shift of mood, David drew her in his arms.
"Samara, you're going to have to face him sometime. No more
hiding in hotel rooms, no more shadows. The sooner you two
meet, the better."

"Suppose Solange objects?"

"Let me handle that," he said firmly, doing his best to break
down her resistance.

Samara stalled. "It's too soon."

"Whatever you prefer. Darling, he's a little boy. He can't
hurt you or me or us together. That's what I want you to see,

to understand. I know it's on your mind, sweetheart. Won't you give him a chance?''

Choices. She struggled with her choices. He wasn't forcing her, yet she really had no choice. To be with David meant accepting a part in Asher's life. If she refused, she'd hurt David. Whether she wanted to or not, she was forced to examine her feelings. Solange wasn't the reason she was reluctant to see Asher. The truth was she didn't relish meeting a walking, talking reminder of the awful night Solange and David made love.

"Honey," he said, reading her thoughts. "It's okay. Forget I said anything."

"It's not okay, and we both know it." If she didn't meet Asher, Solange would still be calling the shots. "Tomorrow will be ours, if you don't mind. Bring Asher on Sunday, darling. Tell him his aunt Samara would appreciate his company for brunch."

David rolled off the bed. From his wallet he drew out pictures of Asher and handed them to her. Samara studied them closely. It helped considerably that Asher looked like a miniature David.

"He's your image, David." *Thank God.*

"How long can you stay in New York?" he asked.

"Until Tuesday." She mentioned the pattern she needed to cut for Mr. Friedman to replace the damaged gowns. She explained that her busy schedule included a photo shoot that had been set up months ago. "We're cutting it close. Why don't you fly out to California? You're overworked. You could use a vacation. You'll see my house, meet my dog, Fred. She's a snob."

David wasn't in the mood to hear about a dog or see a house. His arms tightened about her. He noted with a high degree of satisfaction that Samara looked adorable with her lips swollen from *his* kisses, her hair mussed from *his* hands, her eyes sparkling from *his* lovemaking, her cheeks flushed, thanks to *him*. He didn't relish the idea of her leaving so soon.

"All right." He grinned. "I'm dying to see your house, meet your dog." She rewarded him with a squeal of pleasure. "I'm contacting a lawyer to get the ball rolling on the divorce. As soon as I can arrange my schedule, I'll fly out. We've got to make plans. Permanent plans. Phone me the moment you return,'' he said. ''This time I'm not taking any chances.''

''Don't wait too long to visit. I'm the impatient type. In the meantime, we still have the rest of the weekend.''

The next morning they awoke entwined in each other's arms, sublimely happy and well rested. Dressing quickly, they ate breakfast. Afterward David kept a promise he'd made years before.

Bundled beneath a blanket, they rode a hansom cab through Central Park. In the afternoon, they wobbled precariously around the ice skating rink at Rockefeller Center. Around five P.M. they dined on thick steaks at Gallagher's. With the hours ticking by, they decided against seeing a Broadway show, returning instead to their hotel room, hoarding each precious minute they could spend alone.

On Sunday morning while David was at the hospital checking on his patients before bringing Asher to meet her, Samara hurried along Fifth Avenue to St. Patrick's Cathedral to hear John Cardinal O'Connor officiate the mass. Fashionably trim in a wool-and-mohair tweed suit, mustard-yellow silk long-sleeved blouse, Samara found a seat in the front pew next to elderly female twins.

They fascinated Samara. In yellow woolen cloches, capped over brown curly hair and in yellow woolen dresses, they reminded her of two sunflowers blooming amid a field of drab wintery colors. As the mass began, she studied them covertly, amused and a little jealous that rather than proclaim independence, they flaunted their oneness.

As if on cue, both lifted their sturdy brown walking shoes from the footrests, tapping them up and down in perfect unison. At the same time they reassuringly patted each other's hand. They held their hymnals, and then their missals, in their left hands, turning the pages with their right hands. Each time John Cardinal O'Connor rammed home a point in his rousing sermon on the sanctity of the home, the sisters jabbed each other, tittered, and bobbed their heads in vigorous affirmation. Although Samara tried to pay attention to the cardinal, he lost to the merry twins. At the close of the mass, they erupted from their seats in precision, then rumbled up the aisle to receive communion.

Samara felt an overwhelming sense of loss—grief—that she

had been denied such obvious closeness. If only things could have been different between her and Solange, she thought sadly. For the first time the religious service failed to offer her solace. She received communion, flying down the steps to return to the suite to cut a pattern for Sammy Friedman before David arrived with Asher.

She dreaded meeting the boy. What would she say to him if he asked why he'd never met her? I hate your mother. I haven't spoken to her in over six years. Or, I'm the twin who should have been your mother. Darn it! Why did she agree to meet him? Why couldn't David leave well enough alone?

You know why, she answered for the umpteenth time, although it didn't help. She heard a knock at the door.

Asher's small exclamation of surprise gave her a chance to quell her panic. The little boy at David's side dropped open his mouth. He peered at her with the intensity of a scientist, making two complete circles around her.

"Wow!" Asher cried in wide-eyed amazement. "I think being a twin is neat."

David coughed, bringing Asher's head swinging upward. Silent communication flew between father and son. "Ooops, I nearly forgot. Daddy told me I had to give you this." Samara laughed delightedly at his honesty. David rolled up his eyes.

From behind his back, Asher produced a crushed red rose that seemed glued to his palm. "It's not much of a gift," he admitted, peeling the stuck petals from his hand to drop them one by one into hers. Staring at the flower's lifeless remains, he shook his head. "No good," he muttered. His face a study in consternation, his hand dug deep into his trouser pocket.

"Here," he said in the most reluctant little boy voice she'd ever heard.

"This is my favorite shooter marble. It's a glassie. I play with it every day. *Every single day,*" he slowly enunciated. "It's turquoise. I'll never find another turquoise glassie. You can have it."

He kept his fist wrapped tightly around his treasure. He wore his best suit, she assumed, courtesy of the small fry department. From the way his fingers fidgeted with his starched shirt collar, yanked at his tie, he made it clear he despised being confined. Glancing down, she hid a smile. Asher's right foot was doing a very efficient job of scuffing the shine off the top of his left shoe.

"If you're afraid you'll lose it," he said anxiously, "I'll keep it for you if you want. It's a good deal. The glassie is used to me."

She tried to keep a straight face. "What a grand idea. It's a very good deal. Thank you very much." She gazed into his eyes. His eyes were David's—intelligent, alert, flecked with streaks of amber.

"May I peek at your marble?"

Asher took a wobbly breath. Gnawing at his bottom lip, he gingerly cracked a sweaty fist. Samara looked down. The marble remained hidden. She cupped her hand over his. His tightened protectively around the glassie. There was no way the marble was leaving its owner. What had she been afraid of? Asher Orchin was David's flesh and blood. She wanted to wrap her arms about Asher, bury her face in the folds of his sweet little boy neck. He had been terrified she might take his treasure, yet he still made the offer.

"If I'm very careful, very, very careful, may I touch it with one finger?"

He nodded. He hovered over her, ready to pounce. Samara glanced at David, then back at Asher. It took all her willpower to maintain a straight face, for Asher was chewing his bottom lip exactly as his father was doing now.

Bending over his hand again, she saw a tiny sliver of the glassie. "It's beautiful. It's the nicest color I've ever seen. I know it's in good hands. Thank you for taking care of it for me," she assured him, soothing his anxiety. She nearly laughed aloud at the relief written on David's and his son's faces. What would they have done if she had accepted the marble? Like his son, David had been holding his breath.

"You're welcome," Asher said, obviously relieved that the horrible moment had passed.

"Asher, I believe if someone offers me a treasure, then I should offer a treasure of mine. Do you agree?" He eagerly nodded. "Do you like chocolate-covered walnuts?"

"Oh, yes." His eyes shone. Twin dimples creased his face. Taking his hand, she led him into the living room. Sitting down by his side on the sofa, she opened the box of delectable candy she'd purchased at Neuchatel Chocolates. Asher's hand made a dive for it.

"One," David cautioned. "You'll spoil your appetite." At Samara's scowl, he amended the count. "Two." She pursed her lips. His eyebrows lifted. "Three?" he asked, checking.

Asher, obviously a seasoned negotiator, closed ranks with Samara. He placed a hand on her thigh, bringing his face close to hers. "Four," he piped up.

Samara smothered a helpless grin. *Asher, you little devil, we're going to be friends. How could we not when we have so much in common. We both prefer comfortable clothes. We both love chocolate. We both love your daddy. I'd say that's a pretty good start.* With a little nudge from her, they exchanged conspiratorial winks.

Faced with two kindred spirits, two chocolate lovers, David shook his head. From the sunny smile creasing his face, it was evident that he'd never been so happy to lose.

"Those four are the largest candies," she whispered. "If I were you, I'd hurry up and take them before your daddy swipes them. Eat one now. Save the rest for later."

Asher flashed her an adoring smile, melting her heart. He wiggled closer, half leaning over her. The second he did, she lifted him fully onto her lap. "Do I get a kiss?" she asked, knowing that if he didn't kiss her, she was going to kiss him anyway.

With his mouth already filled with a first bite of candy, Asher threw his arms around Samara's neck. He nuzzled his face against her cheek. David beamed. Samara returned his son's kiss with a lingering embrace. A huge lump of gratitude swelling his throat, David ushered them out of the suite, before the two "negotiated" the entire box of candy.

Chapter Twenty-four

On Tuesday David drove Samara to Kennedy Airport for her return to San Francisco. Their euphoria of reconciliation had settled into mild depression based on the reality of their situation. That morning they had had a long talk, solving nothing regarding the impact on Asher when he would learn of his parents' divorce. David's concern for him endeared David to Samara more, if that were possible. He worried that the boy would be stunned, angry; he might blame himself and think he had done something wrong to make his daddy leave home, the way most children feel when parents divorce.

According to David, Solange shrewdly refrained from haranguing him in Asher's presence, delivering her threats in private. David carried the charade for Asher's sake, to give him the security of a stable home. He didn't doubt Solange would spitefully tell Asher his father wanted to discard his mother, to switch one twin for the other. It could devastate the boy and destroy Samara's chance of forming a good relationship with Asher. Samara and David tried not to dwell on it, but the subject sat between them, festering like a boil that needed lancing.

Samara felt like the other woman in a bad movie.

David steered the car off the Belt Parkway, following the signs to Kennedy Airport, onto the congested departure ramp.

She sought his hand on the wheel. "David, are you sure?"

There was a tense pause. "The only thing I'm sure of is that I love you and Asher. God, nothing is easy, is it? Good people end up getting hurt."

For most of the airplane ride she mulled over her situation. She and David had avoided speaking of where they would live.

The topic was too sensitive to thrash out at this early stage. She worked hard to establish a good life for herself in California. Even if she wanted to, which she most assuredly did not, Samara couldn't just pick up and move Gold's West. The thought of living near viperish Solange set her on edge. On the other hand, David would want to live close to Asher. She respected and agreed with his desire not to let Asher think he was abandoned. Marrying David would require a lot of transcontinental flying. When their own children arrived, his loyalties would be torn between two families. Then what?

When she got home, she called David's office. Since he had already gone for the day, she left word that she had arrived safely. Driving to Maggie's for Fred, Maggie greeted her with marvelous news. "Finally. It's official. I've missed a period. I'm pregnant. I haven't told Max. I want to see his face when I tell him."

Samara was thrilled for her. "Don't worry about Solange. She'll be too busy trying to make trouble for us when David tells her he's getting a divorce."

Samara was almost thankful for the crisis at the store that kept her too busy to watch the hours tick by waiting for David to phone. A truck carrying a shipment of merchandise overturned on the Pacific Coast Highway. Keyed to impending sales advertised in the area newspapers and on local television stations, she and her traffic manager spent hours locating a trucking firm willing to wait around to offload the shipment once the police and insurance investigators released it.

The next night David phoned. Samara asked him if he'd spoken to Solange about the divorce.

"Not yet, sweetheart. Solange has the flu. I love you."

Disappointed, she hung up. That night she awoke in a sheen of sweat, facing a question that plagued her. Why should Solange's flu override David telling her he wanted a divorce? She went into her kitchen to boil water for currant tea. She sipped the hot brew. No one said this was going to be easy, she chastised herself. If David wanted to pick the opportune time, he must have a good reason. Mimi, seeing a bleak Samara, cursed Solange.

The following week, Samara gleefully told Mimi that David had phoned. "He's coming in four days. That means Solange has recovered from the flu."

The night before his arrival, Samara whipped through her house, cleaning everything in sight. Although she could easily afford full-time help, she didn't like strangers underfoot, nor did she want a larger, more glamorous house. Cleaning and scrubbing helped work off her nervous energy.

Humming happily, she donned an old pair of blue slacks, a pink shirt that she rolled up at the sleeves, tied her hair back with a ribbon, and set out her baking ingredients. Several hours later, the house smelled like a bakery. The counter held David's favorites: chocolate mousse cake, a lemon meringue pie, cinnamon rolls, and vanilla cookies. Fred monitored the proceedings, begging for handouts. The doorbell rang. A large shadow fell across the porch. She lit the carriage light.

"David, you're early!"

She leapt into his arms. She was in heaven, feeling him hold her close. She burrowed deeper in his embrace. All her worries were for nothing. He was there, truly there in her home, with her. He couldn't stand the separation either.

He buried his face in her neck, inhaling her fragrance. "Don't move. Just let me hold you." He cupped her face in his hands, looking directly into her eyes. He thought she had never looked more enticing, with flour smudged on her nose, her hair coming loose from its band, her mouth rich, red, and desirable. "I love you."

Her gaze drifted over him. For the first time she noticed his weariness, his exhaustion, his bloodshot eyes. Tension lines furrowed his brow. "Darling, when we're married, you're going to keep regular hours. You work too hard. You're here now. I'm going to pamper you, feed you, make endless love to you. After you've had a good night's sleep."

"I can't stay. I'm leaving tomorrow. I'm needed in New York."

For a moment words failed her. A sense of foreboding made her feel as if she'd been dropped into a vat of ice cubes. The smile left her face. "You flew three thousand miles for one night."

He came inside, not seeming to notice the decor made more cheerful by a crackling fire on the grate in the fireplace, the vases filled with pink bud roses, or the marvelous aromas emanating from the kitchen. Distractedly he patted Fred's head when the dog trotted over to inspect him. He dropped onto the couch. "Samara, there's no good way to say this."

"Say what?" she asked, afraid to hear whatever it was.

"Solange is ill," he said raggedly. "She has acute myelogenous leukemia. There's a good possibility that unless she gets a bone marrow transplant, she will die."

"That's ridiculous!" Samara scoffed, blurting the first thing that came to her mind. "It's a trick! It can't be true. There's a mistake. Solange can't be dying. Only the good die young."

"It's true," he said. "Unless I can help her."

True! She was stunned. Shocked beyond belief. David had flown from one coast to the other to tell her Solange was ill when he could have told her on the telephone.

"Did you get a second opinion?" He read the doubt, the accusation in her eyes. She thought he'd changed his mind about wanting a divorce.

"Several. I should have known." His voice rang with harsh recrimination. "That night she returned home I was in the hall with Asher. He ran to her. She screamed at him not to touch her stomach. I wanted to examine her. She had classic flulike symptoms: fatigue, headache, sore throat, fever, pain in her joints. So when she refused, saying she had the flu, I let it go." Samara couldn't speak. In the agonizing silence that stretched between them, she saw her future die before her eyes. David buried his head in his hands. He drew a ragged breath.

"Asher told her he'd met you. She knew we'd been together. My happiness showed on my face. She didn't want any part of me when I asked to examine her. Solange pops vitamin C pills to cure everything. She's a devotee of Linus Pauling. I was concerned she might have strep throat and give it to Asher. The next morning I asked Pepe to take her temperature and call me at the office. She said it was normal. I thought she was on the mend then, that the flu was leaving her body. All I could think of was us, of asking her for a divorce, of being with you."

There was a roar as loud as the ocean's waves in Samara's ears.

"Solange hates doctors." David stared at the tiny fireworks shooting outward from a log. "She read the thermometer for Pepe. She lied. I became suspicious, especially after Asher quoted Solange saying she hurt. I insisted on examining her. Her spleen had enlarged. She had a temperature of one hundred four degrees. I admitted her to the hospital. She's been there all week, too weak to argue." His voice cracked. "We took a biopsy. There are two parts to it. We gave her the first part, then gave her forty-eight hours to rest before doing the second part. Solange prides herself on her looks. Her legs and abdomen are marked with purpura. She's bleeding in many places under the skin. There's a Hickman catheter in her chest. The diarrhea exhausts her. Her hemoglobin is low. Her white count is one hundred thousand—normal is five thousand. Her platelet count is also low." Samara tried to follow, but all she kept thinking was that Solange wasn't faking.

David leaned his head on his hands. "She hates hospitals. In the past week, she's been examined by a slew of doctors. She'll feel better when she goes into remission. It's a long process. Her red count should be maintained by multiple transfusions of platelets and red cells. We'll try to maintain an adequate platelet count by transfusion of platelets."

"Does Max know?"

"Yes. I thought a member of the family should be with Asher. Max is at the house. He's devastated but he's trying to hold up for Asher's sake. Asher wants to see his mother."

"Have you told her?" Samara dragged the question through a constricted throat.

"Yes, of course. I'm trying to get her to fight. She thinks it's a trick. Denial is common when a person is told a diagnosis of cancer. She's got to fight for her sake and for Asher's."

Samara's stomach churned. "Why didn't you tell me she was hospitalized?"

"She asked me not to."

Samara bit her lip. Her eyes flashed. How could she have been so stupid as to think David could ever be hers? "I see. Now she wants me to know," she said tightly.

"She's unaware I'm here. I came to ask if you'd consent to be matched as a bone marrow donor. You're her best chance."

Samara gave a sharp little scream. "You're asking me to save her life, is that it?"

"To try. If the HLA typing confirms that your white cells match, and if the red cells antigens match. With identical twins, it should."

She clenched her fists. "I read an article about this. Donating bone marrow is painful. Don't they take a lot of . . . aspirations?''

"Yes, I won't lie to you. They take the aspirations from the center of the hip bone. It's the largest bone.''

"That's what I read. Doesn't the donor walk with pain, perhaps need a transfusion since so much blood is taken out?''

David sighed. "Yes, but you're healthy. It's a chance to save a human life. I won't lie to you. None of this is easy. It's a long process. If Solange can be a candidate, if she doesn't die first, if she withstands the chemo, the hospital stay in New York, the four-to-six-week recuperation period, I'll fly her, Asher, and Pepe to Seattle to the Fred Hutchinson Research Center. You can appreciate the stress of waiting. There's always the danger of a relapse.''

"Why take everyone?'' Samara asked, trying to hold her temper.

"Family support is very important to the patient's recovery. It's a team effort. You'll be tested again there,'' he said, clarifying the role of a donor. "You'll be put up in a nearby apartment. Depending on your choice, you will either be given a spinal or a general anesthesia. Most donors opt for the general. You only hurt for a short time.''

Samara had a vision of that. She didn't like it.

He wiped his hand on his trouser. "We'll ask for you to remain for twenty-one to twenty-eight days for your new marrow to come back. In twenty-one days, Solange should begin to grow new bone marrow, too. You might be asked to stay. During this time you'll donate platelets for her, possibly white cells, too.'' Samara marveled that he sounded so calm when inside she was a roiling mass. "I want to assure you there's no additional risk of cancer for a twin.''

She listened with growing horror and aversion. Had she been asked to do this for someone she loved, she wouldn't hesitate. How generous David was with *her* blood, *her* bone marrow, *her* life! Had he dropped a bomb in her lap, she couldn't be more furious.

In one swift motion, she flew off the couch. Smarting with indignation, she lashed out. "You paint quite a vivid and most unpleasant description. Why should I live my life as a metaphor for second place? What has Solange done to deserve my help? She pretended to be my friend, my loving sister, yet she schemed against me the entire time. She mocked you and me, David. She didn't keep her promise to divorce you.'' He winced, but she didn't care.

"No. Solange broke the agreement. You said yourself she would do anything to keep me from being happy, even if it destroyed you. Before I entered the picture, she thought nothing of killing Avrim's baby. She's been rotten to Maggie. I assure you if the positions were reversed, she'd let me rot in hell! Well, she can rot in hell for all I care! How could you ask this of me, David?''

He looked wretched. "I can't consider my personal feelings. The truth is I haven't exactly been nice to her either.''

Samara's heart careened. She threw up her hands. "You haven't exactly been nice to her! You swore you couldn't wait to start divorce proceedings. Now you beg me to save her life because you weren't *exactly* nice to her! You want me to salve your conscience. That's rich! How about me? I gave up a decent kind man because I still loved you. What's my future if I do this lifesaving deed? Let me know,'' she bleated, flinging David's hand away.

Blistering mad, breathing hard, she stalked about the room, her arms jerking spasmodically at her sides. She couldn't deal with it. She'd been so deliriously happy. For five minutes! She suppressed an hysterical urge to scream. Sick or well, Solange called the shots.

"Solange accused me of being the good one. Naive stupid fool that I was, I didn't see her blow coming. David, I'm not wearing blinders now. Count me out!''

Fredrica, insulted at not being the center of attention, pawed her hand, wanting to play. "Leave me alone!'' she snapped. "I'm not in the mood for fun, you dumb dog.'' The dog, never hearing her mistress speak in anger, cowered in the corner.

Samara raced to her. How could she be so cruel? She loved Fred. She wrapped her arms about the dog, her tears wetting the animal's fur. *He knew before he came here that this means the end of us, that he'll never leave her. She would need years of care.*

"Samara, I've lived with guilt, knowing I've hurt you. This is different. I'm asking for Asher, for my son's mother. Solange loves him. He loves her.''

She crumpled in the corner, crying. Choices! Whatever her

answer, whatever her action, she put herself in a no-win position. If she refused, the whole family would resent her. Asher would come to despise her for not helping his mother. If she agreed, she would lose David, her future, any hope for children of her own.

"Go to hell!"

"I probably will," he raged. "I'm halfway there now. What's that expression? Man proposes; God disposes. Shit!"

Samara stood near the couch. "Just so you're absolutely clear that you know what you're asking, David. You want me to save her and kill us. Don't you realize this means the end of us?"

David faltered. "I'm not noble. Death is the absolute freedom. Given all she's done to me, to us, I wanted my freedom. How do you think it makes me feel to realize how low I've sunk? If I don't help her, I won't be able to live with myself, be a father to Asher, practice medicine, or ever hope to be your husband. I hate this as much as you do. That doesn't make it easier. Solange is suffering. She deserves the best medical treatment I can offer. She's given up. She needs you, she needs me. Asher needs his mother. It's that simple, that complex. That's why I flew here rather than ask you on the phone. Max offered to come. He would have, but he didn't know how to explain this to you."

She saw the awful despair on David's face, the emptiness in his eyes. She steeled herself against his entreaties. "Solange and I agree on one thing," she told him. "We don't want to see each other. You can't expect me to be a party to my ruination."

David rose. His shoulders slumped in defeat. An air of gloom permeated the room. Samara wrapped her arms about him.

"Maggie's pregnant. She's going to tell Max when she sees him. Poor Max. How hard this is for him." David yawned. His eyelids drooped. "Come, I'll show you to bed."

He let her help him undress. Drained, he fell back onto the bed. "I'm sorry, Sam. I'll always love you."

In the kitchen that still smelled so inviting, she put away the cakes she'd baked for David. Setting the timer for the morning coffee, she undressed and then soaked in the bathtub. After drying herself, she crawled into bed naked.

In sleep, David turned on his side, reaching for her. His hand strayed to her breast. She moaned and burrowed against him, curved in their favorite position. She closed her eyes and breathed in his scent. His smell was arousing: manly and clean, and she wanted him. She had expected Solange to try to make trouble, but not this, never this . . .

When David left, Samara felt as if their brief interlude in New York had been a dream. She threw herself into a frenzy of work, impressing everyone with her hectic pace, her single-minded dedication. Samara paid higher wages, so consequently she employed the best people. She knew every employee by name. In return for that, for her unfailing kindness, her little gifts of appreciation, her remembrance of their birthdays, her loyal staff transformed Gold's West into a celebration of Paris. They pulled out all stops in preparation for Jules LeClaire's arrival. Store windows displayed a retrospective of the master couturier's influence on fashion. Bay Area society, Hollywood luminaries, a sprinkling of European royalty, *Vogue*'s Leon Talley and Anna Wintour, *W* and *Women's Wear Daily*'s John Fairchild, plus fashion editors from other major fashion magazines, among them *Harper's Bazaar, Figaro,* and *Elle* accepted coveted engraved invitations. For the gala cocktail party, Samara had unknowingly selected the identical theme of French-American unity chosen by her twin when Solange debuted as Max's hostess.

She posed for the poster art. In one she modeled a curvaceous gown of clinging black silk lace cut high at one thigh to reveal a hint of red garter. In another, her hands at her hips, legs spread apart, she wore an open weave champagne cotton mini. For that shot her hair stylist wet her hair, messed it with his fingers, moussed, sprayed it to windblown perfection. For the last picture, she straddled a white wooden chair. The photographer caught her in profile wearing a backless, black lace bodysuit.

The days passed easily. At night she tortured herself with images of David. His sensitive, strong, sexy hands covering her body, awakening each erogenous zone. When she wasn't focusing on his hands, she fantasized about his mouth making love to her, of her loving him . . .

Jules arrived looking not a day older in his traditional garb: regimental British tie, Savile Row suit, Hilditch & Key shirt, Bally shoes. Being with Jules took Samara back to her carefree days. She and Mimi gave him a guided tour of Gold's West, of San Francisco, and Sausalito. Jules bestowed the two cities with his ultimate accolade. San Francisco reminded him of Paris with its stores, its neighborhood bistros, its parks, and its energy. Sausalito reminded him of St. Tropez on the French Riviera. "Sparkling water, gleaming yachts, and pretty women."

During a working lunch of Samara's version of American hot dogs ("haute dogs"—hot dog buns filled with crab salad, Bibb lettuce, diced tomatoes), Mimi reported the success accorded the test marketing and advance orders for the Samara fragrance line. Samara gave full credit to Mimi. "She's got a Midas touch, Jules." He read the figures and echoed Samara's praise. Mimi basked in her father's approval. She had truly moved out of his shadow into her own light.

On the day of the fashion show, a bright blue sky swathed the Bay Area, sweeping away the strong winds that had hit the previous night. "It's a good omen," Jules declared.

It proved to be. Liveried doormen welcomed guests with gifts of Samara's perfume. After Jules's spectacular bejeweled collection that mixed motifs and colors, the lights dimmed.

To the audience's delight, Samara Bousseauc Gold, clad in a slinky peacock-blue tube of shirred polysatin pleats, stepped into a single spotlight and raised her arms high above her head. In the twinkling of an eye, she put her tattered heart on hold. She had work to do. She owed everyone her best. At her signal the band switched to a bump and grind beat. She tossed her long hair, rolled her pelvis, and wiggled her hips. Bending forward, she grabbed the hem of her gown. She lifted it inch by tantalizing inch, to skim her buttocks. She strutted, treating the on-their-toes clientele to a strip tease. With her other hand, she coyly slipped the spaghetti straps off her shoulders. Smiling her world-famous smile that had graced countless fashion covers, she showed she could still own a runway. Photographers clicked furiously. Would the youthful head of Gold's West dare to take it off? Let everyone see her naked? The men prayed she would. She winked. The audience roared. She pranced. The audience clapped. She wiggled her derriere. Oh, yes, she dared!

A hush fell. The drumroll alerted the crowd. One more prance down the runway. A strut up. A dip. A turn. Another strut back. Suddenly the gown flew off. Samara flung it high over her head. It landed on the lap of a startled buyer. Giving a triumphant laugh, Samara scampered down the runway in a blue silk mini she had artfully concealed beneath the dress. The audience loved it.

Following tradition, she and Jules closed the show. Buyers scratched numbers on pads of paper, assuring a huge financial success. The next day Jules rocked on Samara's porch counting the boats sailing beneath the Golden Gate Bridge. Wind chimes, hooked to support beams, sang a light chorus. At the railings wicker planters offered a bonanza of herbs: thyme, rosemary, parsley, sage, and the scent of honeysuckle and roses twined on trellises permeated the breeze. For Jules's final night, Samara had invited Mimi and Maggie to share a private dinner in his honor.

Samara served rack of lamb, baby carrots, curried rice, and salad. Maggie announced she'd told Max about their baby, hoping to give him a ray of happiness. They made plans for a quiet wedding ceremony. Jules set down his flute of Cristal champagne.

"We all know how Solange's illness is affecting you, Samara. I love you, therefore I'm taking the liberty of giving you advice."

Samara folded her napkin. She gritted her teeth. "Jules, I wish you wouldn't."

"Isn't it possible Solange might feel the need to apologize to you?"

"I doubt it. If you're about to tell me to see her, don't. I'm much too busy."

"Excuses. The store didn't fold up when you went to New York. You have an excellent staff. Your grandparents are prepared to fly here to oversee things during the crisis. Mimi will mind our company. You're a phone call away. I'm not trying to put you on the spot—"

Her fork hit the table. "Yes, you are. You're trying to force me to go to New York."

"All right. I am. For your sake. Perhaps there are things you want to say to Solange, too. Don't be so stubborn. Don't be sorry later. I wish I had had the chance to speak with my brothers before they died."

"You loved your brothers. There's a difference."

His words gnawed at her. She did want to see Solange, but not for noble reasons. On the day she left, Fred lifted her tail, her snooty nose, and trotted up the path to Maggie's. Maggie squeezed her hand. "I'm in your corner, whatever you decide to do."

When she entered Solange's house, Samara felt like an interloper, a trespasser. David had said he considered the house Solange's. Decorated in shades of creamy white, the living room's massive black leather sofa, modern occasional chairs, ebony Kawaii baby grand, and abstract paintings were too modern for her taste. Near the Vermont stone fireplace, a Fred Bier sculpture of a woman stood on a black marble base. Samara preferred a cozy atmosphere, the clutter of pillows, piles of magazines, tables laden with flowers, the scent of simmering potpourri. She grudgingly appreciated Solange's taste, however, especially her whimsical touch in the kitchen. What appeared to be a bookcase lined with shelves of books above a work desk was actually wallpaper. The spines of the faux cookbooks quoted the titles of famous cookbooks.

Max held out his arms for a sad reunion. She asked him to tell her everything before Asher returned home from school.

"He wets the bed. He complains his stomach hurts. His kindergarten teacher says he's sucking his thumb. He wants to stay home." She promised to do what she could for Asher.

Within minutes Asher arrived home. Spying her, he flew into her arms. At the same time he managed to fling his Superman book bag off his shoulder onto the floor.

"Aunt Samara! I'm glad you're here." He kissed her.

"Grandpa, I'm taking Samara to meet my pets." He introduced her to Fluffy and Happy, a collie and a Yorkshire terrier; his hamster, Mabel; his gerbil, Frankenstein; his pet goldfish, Chuckles. "Come see my bed."

"My goodness!" Samara said, genuinely impressed by the Packard replica. "That's amazing. Do you drive the bed into the hall?" She tousled his hair. Max had said he rarely smiled. "How about if I read you a story?"

He found a book and without the least bit of shyness, he cuddled in her lap in the rocking chair. He asked her to read him the story twice.

"Are you going to see Mommy?" He wiggled down to put

away the book. She told him that she was. He put his hand under his pillow, bringing out his precious turquoise marble.

"The glassie will make her better." His mouth trembled. "I miss Mommy."

Samara kissed him and held him for a long time.

"Suppose you draw Mommy a picture. I'll take it to her with the glassie." Asher decided to start right away.

Downstairs, she congratulated Max on his good fortune to marry Maggie, on his impending fatherhood.

"You know, I've wanted to marry Maggie for years. When I start to feel happy about the baby, I feel guilty."

David called out that he was home. Her heart leapt at the sound of his voice. She wanted to run to him, but her feet stayed rooted to the spot. He came into the room, shrugging out of his navy coat, pushing his hair away from his forehead before he saw her. Then his eyes went soft. He came forward, his arm reaching toward her as if he couldn't wait for the rest of his body to catch up. "I'm glad you've changed your mind. We haven't been able to find a suitable donor. It's been hard. On Asher, too."

"I'm sorry if I raised your hopes. I came to see her. Please don't ask me for more. I'm staying at Tessie's."

David's face shuttered. "I see." He didn't, and they both knew it. Max interrupted before either could say more.

"We're all tense. Sit down, both of you. Please. There's something I've got to tell you." He slipped into the chair next to Samara.

"Thank you. First of all, I want you both to know that I think Solange's actions were inexcusable, hurtful beyond measure. It took me years to accept the truth, to remove the blinders. If she weren't ill, I'd support David if he made the decision to seek a divorce."

"Max, this is pointless," Samara said.

"Perhaps you'll change your mind after you hear what I have to say. I know why your mother left Solange with me."

Startled, Samara leaned forward. "What do you mean?"

In a steady voice Max recounted the story of Lilli's past. When David heard Frans Wurfel's name, his curses ripped the air.

Samara's head whipped around. "Who is he, David?"

"The fucking Nazi who ordered my relatives killed, who

nearly murdered my parents, who would have if the war hadn't ended. God!'' He slammed the table. ''I don't believe it, Max. Lilli was a good person. She wouldn't harm a fly.''

A cry of disbelief rose in Samara's throat. ''He can't be her father!'' Her father's nod confirmed David's shocking announcement.

''Lilli was an innocent victim, just as your parents were, David. Sister Jean gave Lilli a bogus identity for Lilli's protection. After the nun died, a priest found Stella's letter. Believing Sister Jean meant for Lilli to have it one day, he gave it to Lilli when he visited America. The note triggered your mother's memory. She lived her life paying penance for her parents' crimes, terrified of my parents' reaction if the truth came out. She thought we'd hate her, that she'd destroy my political career. It doesn't speak well for her faith in me, does it?'' he said bitterly. ''She loved me, and I failed her.''

Samara struggled to comprehend the enormity of her father's news. ''This is . . . incredible. Bella and Michel knew, didn't they?''

''Yes. She told them the day before she died. To their credit, they didn't blame her.''

Samara half rose from her seat. ''David, that's the night Maman took ill! The night she insisted on speaking with your parents.''

There was silence in the room, then Max said, ''The only satisfaction I can take in this is that Lilli unburdened herself before she died. She held that terrible secret for eighteen years.''

David added, ''Now I understand why my parents acted strangely when I went home for you, Samara. They're remarkable people.''

Awash with compassion for the Orchins, for her kind, gentle mother, the past became clear to Samara. ''I can't think of those despicable animals as people, as Maman's parents.''

''They had nothing to do with the mother you loved,'' Max said. ''Sister Jean raised her. The priests and the nuns were her family. Samara, when you and David phoned his parents to tell them I was going to run for president, they surmised you two were in love. They agonized over whether or not to break their promise to Lilli. They feared if reporters learned the truth, it would damage you girls. Otherwise I still wouldn't know.''

Samara measured her father's sacrifice. He'd given up his dream. "Then that's why you dropped out of public life."

He smiled at her. "How could I let your mother's sacrifice be for nothing? She loved you and Solange. Solange was a colicky infant. Lilli rocked her for hours. Your mother's desperation caused her to use the only excuse that kept me from coming for her and for you. Her suicide threat was merely a ploy to keep me off the trail."

"We never believed Maman's suicide threat. Now the pieces of the puzzle fit."

"Maggie's helped me to understand Solange's jealousy. Incidentally Maggie has known the truth ever since I found out. I made her promise not to tell you, but now the stakes are too high for me to remain silent. Samara, David asked you to be Solange's bone marrow donor for Asher's sake. I'm asking for my sake. I placed my career first. I'm to blame for Solange's behavior."

"If that is true, Maman shares the blame," Samara said gently, surprising herself by her admission. Her mother's well-intentioned lie backfired, causing far-reaching damage to her family and others.

A single memory, an image of the happy elderly twins she'd seen at St. Patrick's Cathedral, burned through Samara's mind. The ensuing stretch of time was deafening, yet its noise could have sparked a crowd to thunder. "Will you tell Solange?"

Max said no. "One day if—when—she recovers." He coughed, clearing his throat. "What's your opinion, David?"

David's dark eyes held Samara's when he answered Max. "I agree. Solange has more than enough to handle."

Ill at ease, Samara broke the eye contact, fidgeting with her hands in her lap, burdened by the knowledge that both men awaited her answer to Max's petition. From the top of the stairs, Asher screeched he was coming down. In seconds he crash-landed at Samara's side, proudly showing everyone the drawing he'd made for his mother.

Choices, Samara thought. *It all comes down to choices.* She'd see Solange. For now that was all she could manage.

Chapter Twenty-five

Samara stood in the doorway of Solange's darkened hospital room, trying to get over her shock. With the room temperature set high only a sheet covered Solange. Samara tiptoed in, careful not to awaken her or disturb the nurse who smiled a greeting as she worked at the bed. Her sister's bones pushed at translucent flesh. Hooked to machines, Solange resembled a bald creature from outer space.

The nurse's starched white uniform rustled with quick, efficient motions. She applied a ribbon of cream to Solange's dry lips, adjusted the IV, flicked two fingers at the tubing, and checked the Hickman catheter. Throughout all the fussing, Solange slept.

Samara hated the room on sight. The walls were a drab tan. Tied to the bed was a bouquet of balloons in need of air, their get-well messages struggling to float toward the ceiling. A basket of wilted painted daisies sat on the windowsill. A flaked bulletin board displayed Asher's cards that he'd signed with multiple X's and O's. She added Asher's drawing.

Samara sat down on a brown Naugahyde chair, its lumpy cushion shaped by countless previous users. Minutes ticked by. She thrust her legs out in front, noiselessly tipping the toes of her shoes inward and outward. Samara's stomach roiled. In another five minutes, she'd leave. Seeing Solange now made her see herself in an altered state.

Last night David phoned his parents from Tessie's apartment to tell them he had asked the Simon Wiesenthal Center in Los Angeles if they had news of Hans Wurfel. He'd learned that Wurfel had lived under an assumed name in South America but had died many years ago. He handed the phone to Samara, giving her an opportunity to speak with Bella and Michel, to heal the bridge of time. "I'm sure you wish you'd never met me," she said to David afterward.

He gathered her in his arms. "If that's the case, why am I wishing I had the energy to make love to you?"

Samara pulled her leg out of the nurse's way so the woman had room to scribble on the chart hanging at the foot of the bed before she left on noiseless rubber soles. Samara glanced at her watch. Four minutes. She'd stay four more minutes.

Solange cracked open an eye. "What are you doing here?"

Startled, Samara jumped up from the chair. Her hand flew to her throat. "I thought you were asleep."

"I wasn't. If you came to gloat, you vulture, get out."

Relief flooded through Samara at Solange's bitchy welcome. "David tells me you're not fighting this."

Solange lifted a ridge of skin where her eyebrows once were to glare at her. "By *this* you mean cancer. Why should you care what happens to me?"

"I don't. That's what I came to say."

"Bitch," Solange muttered.

Samara removed her red poncho, fluffed her hair, flicked a piece of lint from her tomato-red cashmere pullover, smoothed the line of her red woolen trousers, sat down, then crossed her ankles to reveal red leather Charles Jourdan boots.

"You look like a damn prostitute. You're lit up like a neon sign."

Samara's smile was unflagging, her nerves screaming. Suddenly she knew she couldn't turn her back on David, Asher, Max, or her Lilli. Or herself. Her future depended on her own moral code, not Solange's. She never really had a choice. According to David, Solange rarely spoke except to order people out of the room. Encouraged by her attention, Samara raised the venetian blinds. Dust motes danced in the air. "David adores me in red."

"Fuck you. Say what you came to say, then leave. Close those dumb blinds. This dump is ugly enough without giving it a spotlight."

Samara left the blinds up. She posed at the foot of the bed. She forced herself to sound breezy and bitchy. "Maman left another letter. It concerns you. Out of the generosity of my heart, with you in that sorry condition, I figured you ought to know.''

Solange eyed her suspiciously. ''Crapola. If Lilli had written to me, you would have told me years ago.''

Striving for an impersonal air, Samara nonchalantly said, ''Bella read it to me on the phone. You remember your in-laws. You were rude to them the one time they visited. It's too bad you're so dumb you couldn't figure out for yourself why Maman took me and left you with Max. Since you're not interested, I'm leaving.'' Samara slung her poncho over her arm.

''What letter?'' Solange rasped.

Samara disregarded that for a moment. ''David says you need a bone marrow transplant. Can you believe he asked me to donate my bone marrow?''

Solange licked her lips. ''I wouldn't do it for you.''

''Don't worry,'' Samara scoffed. ''If I did agree, it wouldn't be for your sake. I'd do it for Asher.'' She untacked Asher's drawing from the cork board. Bits of corking floated onto the floor. She bent down to pick them up.

''Leave it,'' Solange ordered. ''It adds character.''

Samara handed Solange the drawing and dug in her shoulder bag. ''Asher asked me to give you this, too.''

Their fingers touched when she transferred the marble to her sister's hand. Bones on flesh. Samara shuddered. Solange, not realizing her effect on her twin, emitted a soft cry. ''His glassie,'' she murmured, misty-eyed. ''It's his dearest possession. He sleeps with it.''

Samara kept her voice neutral. ''It's going to break his heart when I tell him you didn't love him enough to put up a fight for him.''

Solange sat the glassie on her chest, her fingers lightly touching it. ''What did Maman say in her letter to me?''

''She loves you, misses you. Mostly she wishes she could have seen you grow up.''

Solange's hand groped the air. ''She had a funny way of showing it.''

''Don't start that. A mother knows a child. She knew you. You needed more attention. She didn't have a lot of money, and she reasoned Max and his parents would provide for you. They did, too.''

"Crazy," Solange muttered, rolling the glassie between knobby fingers.

"That's what I thought. Until I got over my jealousy."

"You were jealous?" Solange sounded dubious.

Samara slid the chair next to the bed. "Do you think you have a monopoly on jealousy? But I'm smarter than you. I got over mine. You let yours eat at you. But that's not Maman's fault. It's entirely yours. You're responsible for your actions, no one else. Although," she added, "I concede Maman gave you the makings of a charmed life."

"Garbage."

Samara privately agreed with her. "Not when you compare our lives. I worked, you played. I wore hand-me-downs or handmade dresses. Yours were new, fancy. You played hostess for Max. The family catered to you. Pepe still does. You're a spoiled brat. Maman wouldn't approve of you."

Solange's hand wrapped about the glassie. "More crapola. Our father sent Lilli money. She could have spent it. Why didn't she contact me? Did she say?"

Solange might be ill, but there was nothing wrong with either her memory or her brain.

"Yes," Samara improvised. "As the years passed, Maman was afraid to write. She feared you'd reject her, but her fears were overshadowed by her desire to ask for your forgiveness. That's why she finally wrote. Maman loved you. You're a mother, too. If Asher hurt you, I'm sure you'd forgive him rather than lose him."

Silence.

Samara plunged on, fabricating. "On the other hand, I suppose it's just as well you two never met. You'd be a major disappointment. Maman thought she acted in your best interest. Of course, she was wrong, but poor judgment didn't make her an evil person. She was kind, gentle, religious. You're nothing like her. She acted out of love. It's obvious you're not fighting for Asher."

Solange twisted the sheet. Her toe poked through a rip at the side. "What's your game Samara? That's the third time you've said that about Asher."

"Is it? Well, forget I said anything. For myself, I'm delighted with the way things are," Samara replied airily. "I want you to keep up the good work. We're alone now, and I can be myself. I can tell you what an awful person you are. You see, it doesn't matter to me one bit that you're ill. I don't have to impress the family. With your brilliant do-nothing-to-help-yourself attitude, you're making this easy for me. So you see, even after all your scheming, I'll have the last laugh. I'm going to end up with everything. And I mean everything. Gold's New York. Gold's West. You can throw in David and Asher, too. I'll be there for your son when he's bar mitzvahed, graduates college, marries. Heck! You're probably going to make me a grandmother one day.''

"Like hell I will, you shit!" Solange snapped, her eyes burning fiercely.

Samara appeared taken aback. Her lower jaw dropped open. "I beg your pardon?"

Solange sent her a withering look. In one hand she clutched Asher's turquoise marble, with the other she rang her bell. "If you think I'm giving up, sister dear, you're living in an oasis of unreality! You're stupid for telling me what you did. No one takes what's mine! Put on my head scarf," she ordered the nurse when she came in. "Then tell my husband I want to see him." To Samara, she offered a typical Solange smirk. "When you come tomorrow, bring a new bathrobe and nightgown. I want to see my son."

Samara smoothed a hand down her hip. "You assume I plan to see you again. I don't. Besides, what happened to saying please? Did you lose the word when you lost your hair?"

"Comedienne. You'll return all right. You're keeping tabs. You wouldn't miss this for the world!"

"Say please," Samara repeated.

"All right! Please. Far be it from me, Saint Samara, to topple you from your exalted pedestal." The effort to speak showed in Solange's labored speech. Beads of sweat dotted her brow. Her hand fluttered over her chest.

"Since it's for Asher, I'll bring makeup and a wig. No sense scaring him," Samara said, growing alarmed that she'd gone too far.

She found David pacing the hallway, waiting for her. He took her to an unoccupied office and closed the door.

"She'll fight," Samara said.

Incredulous, he asked, "How did you manage that?"

She offered a typical Samara grin. "I'm five minutes older.

I practiced child psychology on her. Tomorrow I'll get a few things to brighten the room. David, I've decided to help. Solange wants to see Asher. I need a day to buy her a wig and makeup and to fix the room so Asher won't be shocked.''

David's eyes caressed her face. He smoothed back a lock of her golden hair. ''Have you any idea how much I love you? How much I need you?''

His words triggered wrenching sobs, as if a dam had broken. She couldn't stop. The minutes ticked by as David soothed her. She burrowed her face in his warm chest, her arms about his waist, his about her quaking shoulders. Emotionally drained, she felt as if she'd run a marathon race. With no guidelines, she had acted instinctively.

She wiped her eyes. ''It's a terrible shock. She's all mouth. Skins and bones and mouth. In a way her biting sarcasm helped me decide. So when I made the decision to help her, I pretended she was my patient.'' She cautioned David to perpetuate the lie she'd told about Lilli writing Solange a letter. ''Go on in. She's expecting you.''

With renewed purpose, Samara shifted gears. Leaving the hospital, she came out into the sunshine, breathed the air, relished the city's noises, and lunched at the Palm Court with Sammi Esterhelts, a cosmetician whose clientele included cancer patients. ''The right makeup can lift a person's spirits,'' she said, explaining the rudiments to Samara.

The following day, travel posters to Athens, Rome, London, and Paris covered the unattractive walls in Solange's hospital room. Floral bed linens replaced the stark white hospital sheets. The windowsills and dresser held vases of freshly cut red roses. Samara threw out the balloons.

She stepped back to observe her handiwork. She'd used a generous amount of blusher on Solange's cheeks, dabbing color on her forehead, even the tip of her nose to hide her waxy pallor. The thickly quilted rose bedjacket, under which she wore a long-sleeve flannel gown, added bulk to her thin frame. If Asher didn't look too closely at Solange's hair coloring, he might not notice the wig was a shade darker.

Solange snatched Samara's wrist. ''Watch it, dammit! You're poking my eye.''

''Then stop moving. How do you expect me to apply eyeliner if you wiggle?''

"Well?" Solange asked worriedly. "Will I scare Asher? I don't want to see him if I'll upset him."

"You won't. Whatever you do, don't act anxious. Kids pick up on that," Samara warned.

Solange fretted. "I have to gargle. My mouth tastes like iodine."

"You gargled a few minutes ago." She handed her a breath mint and a mirror.

Solange cackled. "To think before this happened I seriously considered a tushy and a tummy tuck if I ever gained weight. Well, at least I don't have to exercise."

"You should have considered zipping up your big mouth. Look at yourself. The wig's perfect. The blusher gives you color, right, Max?"

Seated near the window, Max braced his elbows on his knees. He made a temple with his fingers. "You look fine," he lied.

Solange grimaced. She gave herself a rueful once-over. "The wig covers a multitude of sins. The eyebrows aren't too bad." She caught Samara's arm. "Thank you," she muttered. "But this doesn't change anything. I accepted your help for Asher. Roll up the bed." Samara stood still. "Please, dammit! I want Asher to see me sitting up, not lying down dead."

Samara adjusted the bed.

"What do you think Maman would have thought of him?" Solange asked after a while.

Samara put the makeup in the dresser drawer. "She knows him. I'm sure she adores him."

Beneath the blusher, Solange paled. "What's that supposed to mean?"

Samara dried the sink with a paper towel and shined the fixtures. "Exactly what I said. Maman knows him."

"Hogwash. When you're dead, you're dead. Finis. Over and out. Insect munchies." In the corner, Max lowered his head.

"It's not hogwash," Samara said with conviction. "Maman and I believe in heaven. Study your Bible. I'm pretty sure Jews believe that, too. Don't they, Max?"

He shrugged.

"It sounds like horseshit to me," Solange said.

"Must you always curse?"

Solange made a sound with her mouth. "Samara, you're

unreal. I could be dying, and you're correcting my language. Your fucking priorities kill me!''

Asher, all cowboy in Levi's, shiny cowboy buckle, denim shirt, and brand-new cowboy boots with circles for spurs, bounded into the room. He stopped in his tracks, his serious little face finding his mother's. He looked past the wig and the makeup, into his mother's apprehensive eyes. ''Mommy?''

''Asher,'' she crooned, opening her arms. ''Asher,'' she said in her strongest voice, ''I love you this much.''

''Mommy, you're better! The glassie worked,'' he cried, leaping toward her, his face wreathed in smiles. He threw open his little arms. ''I love you this much, Mommy. When are you coming home?''

If Samara needed proof of why she'd agreed to be Solange's bone marrow donor, the sublime happiness on the little boy's face reaffirmed it. Witnessing the scene, she was stunned by another fact. Asher instantly transformed Solange. Beneath Solange's calculating exterior, Samara glimpsed a side of her sister's nature, the one she hid from everyone but her child. This was universal maternal instinct, the surge of tenderness, compassion, and overwhelming love that mothers all over the world feel for their children. With no need to compete, Solange blossomed. She gave. Glancing at the family scene of David hovering by Asher's side, at Solange kissing their child, Samara quietly left the room. Squeezing shut her eyes, she sagged against the wall, grateful for the reprieve. In a little while she'd resume her act for Asher.

Max laid a hand on her shoulder. ''Thank you,'' he said. She reached over to cover his hand with hers.

A half hour later, Asher skipped out of the room, his face aglow, his eyes shining. ''See you later, alligator,'' he chirped. At Samara's blank look, he giggled. ''You're supposed to say, 'After a while, crocodile.' ''

David paused long enough to thank her.

''I guess I'd better tell her and get it over with,'' Max said to Samara nervously. They strolled back into the room.

''Have a good visit?'' he asked.

''The best,'' Solange replied, smiling.

Max placed a gentle hand on her arm. ''Sweetheart, that

makes me happy.'' He sat down, an uncomfortable expression on his face.

Solange hadn't earned her stripes interpreting her father's facial expression for nothing. She was a past master at it. He looked guilty. Guilty for what reason?

"Daddy, spit it out. I can see you're ready to bust. What is it you want to tell me?"

He cleared his throat and fingered his collar. "I'm getting married. To Maggie. As soon as possible. She's pregnant.''

Solange stared at him as if he'd lost his mind. "You're marrying Maggie!" she sputtered. "You're having a baby at your age!''

Max flushed.

Samara spoke quickly before her father could reply. "Naturally you're surprised, Solange. I was, too, but isn't it wonderful? Age is a state of mind. Be happy for Maggie and Max. After all,'' she said pointedly, sending Solange a clear statement of fact, "there's nothing you can do about it, is there? Babies aren't returnable. You taught me that a long time ago.''

Their gazes locked. Message received. *If you want my help, shut up.* Solange nodded imperceptibly. Her thin legs shifted. She was in no position to bargain. *Maggie, you bitch, you won.*

"Daddy,'' she simpered, switching tactics. She kissed him as he held her. "You have my blessing, too. A baby is exactly what this family needs. Congratulations, Daddy. I love you.'' She smirked at Samara.

Proud of herself, Samara grinned.

Solange was in the middle of making out a list of things for David to do when she put down her pen, closed her eyes, and smiled. Yesterday's visit with Asher had gone better than she'd expected. The one blight on the day was her father's wedding announcement. A baby at his age! What would her friends say? His relief, when she'd congratulated him, was touching. Imagine sending congratulations to Maggie! Maggie would see through it. Women were smarter than men.

David. Poor man. The strain told on him. His eyes looked sunken in their sockets. They'd all be in deep shit trouble if he cracked. Alarm rivered through her at the thought. David must be strong for Asher. Her son couldn't ask for a better father, even if he had proven to be a lousy husband. Not that she'd been a good wife. She wasn't cut out for marriage. Motherhood, yes. Marriage, no.

She glanced over at David snoozing in the chair where he'd been for the last half hour, taking a break. She studied him with clinical interest. The touch of gray hair gave him an air of respectability. Females went gaga whenever they saw him. With his white coat off, his shirt strained over broad shoulders. She'd seen his muscular chest enough times to know it was lean, hard, and sexy. Sex. She wouldn't care if she ever made love again. If she did, she wished it could be with Avrim. Giving him up was the hardest thing she'd ever done. Just once she'd love to feel his arms about her, but that was wishful thinking. She rated that miracle equal with her recovery.

Why hadn't she been true to Avrim? If she knew then what she knew now . . . She'd been young, stupid, foolish. She'd thrown away the one man she ever loved. Tears stung the backs of her eyes. Loving Asher, she mourned for Avrim's child. What would it have been? Boy? Girl? A little girl. Somehow she knew they would have had a daughter. A perfect little girl. Mommy's girl. She'd have dressed her in frills, bows, laces. And visited her in college with presents others would envy. They'd have long mother-daughter chats on the phone. She couldn't quite see Avrim in the role of daddy. Not like David. Avrim's globe-hopping wasn't good for a child. A child needed stability.

David stirred, breaking her reverie. He yawned and stretched.

"Did you have a good sleep?"

He shook his head like a dog, then unfolded himself from the chair. At the sink he doused his face with cold water, combed his hair, and straightened his tie. "I could sleep for days. What's on your reminder list today?"

"Haircut for Asher. The barber cut it too short last time. Asher's waves are too adorable to snip. He's due for a dental checkup. There's a story I read to him before I take him to the dentist. You'll find it in his bookcase on the bottom shelf. Is he brushing his teeth every morning and night?" David nodded. "Molars, too?" He nodded again. "Trim his toenails. Don't let Pepe near him with her failing eyesight, she'll cut his skin. Damn, I'm forgetting something, I know I am."

David checked the time. He slipped on his white coat.

"David."

"Mmmm?"

"Thanks."

Thanks. His gaze swerved to the bed. He regarded her with keen brown eyes, stunned to hear the word. The wig softened the sharpness of her sallow face, its waves hiding the extent of her gaunt cheekbones. With lipstick, blusher, eyebrow pencil, wearing one of Samara's flannel nightgowns, Solange looked passable. At least she hadn't scared Asher. "What for?"

"For giving me Asher." She gave a little laugh, astounding him by appearing almost shy. "It's a bit late to say this since he'll be six his next birthday, but I want you to know I thank God for not aborting him."

Her voice had softened. Amazed, he came to her bedside. He didn't know what to say.

She bit her lip. "His glassie's in the dresser drawer. Take it home."

"He wants you to have it. You'll hurt his feelings."

"Take it home," she insisted. "Tell him it's the hospital rules. Tell him I'm only allowed to keep it overnight. If . . ."

He pocketed the marble. He'd never lied to her. She was in remission now. He'd be taking her home soon to continue her recuperation. "Solange, whatever else is between us, you're a good mother. Asher adores you."

Tears stung her eyes. "It's so unfair," she blurted. "Inside I'm screaming. Outside I don't have the energy to scream. I'm too young for this shit, but if it had to be Asher or me, I'm glad it's me."

David held her hand. "I don't want it to be either one of you."

She believed him. Despite their miserable marriage, the lies she'd told him, the hurt she'd caused, she believed him. "Does Samara resent Asher?"

David drew a deep breath. "Would you if the tables were turned?"

His question caught her short. "Probably," she admitted.

"I suggest you ask her."

"You should hear yourself whenever you talk about Samara. You love her very much, don't you?"

He withdrew his hand. "I don't think this is the time for that discussion."

Since she'd gotten ill, Solange had begun to think about her life. What it meant. Where she was heading. "Why not? I'm not making long-range plans. Not that I'm giving up, mind you. You've told me enough times I've stolen six years of your life. If I could be assured of having Asher, I'd do it again," she said with a touch of the old haughty Solange. "We've always been brutally honest with each other. Don't change now. I know how you feel about me. You're the only man I could never entice into my bed. Have you any idea what you did to my ego?"

David cleared his throat. "Solange, drop it."

She wouldn't. "No. Right now you have the same stubborn make-me-do-it pout on your face Asher gets when I send him back to wash behind his ears. Samara said Lilli never spanked her."

On safer ground, David relaxed. "Don't tell her, but I spanked her, more than once."

Solange pursed her lips. "How cloyingly sweet. Our first secret. It's comforting to know she wasn't perfect. She hates it when I call her Saint Samara. Was my mother a good cook?"

He blinked at the rapid change of topics. "I can't recall. Yes, I guess so. Why?"

"Samara claims she was. Samara bragged she's a good cook, too."

David rubbed his neck. "She is. Where's this leading to?"

"No place special. I'm gathering information. Don't bullshit me, David. Did you ask Samara to be my donor so the two of you won't feel guilty later?"

A rush of guilt swept through him. *Only at first.* He ran exasperated fingers through his hair. He bit back an angry retort—*Don't judge us by your standards!*—then he saw the tears glistening in her eyes, and he knew she spoke from fear. He wished he could be a magician—abracadabra, a cure.

"Would you do it for her? No bullshit, as you say. Would you save her life?"

"I told her I wouldn't."

"Talk is cheap. Tell me, now that you know how it feels. Would you help her?" he asked relentlessly.

He had to bend to hear her response. "I suppose so," she muttered. The flush of pink on her cheeks deepened. "David, you two are such a holy pair: you should have been a priest, and she should have been a nun.''

David laughed at her preposterous statement. He'd never felt holy around Samara. Heavenly, yes. Celibate, no.

"Solange, it was a lot easier when I hated you," he joked, then to his amazement realized it was true. Caring for her health, doing what he did best, let him set aside his animosity.

She laughed low—understanding exactly what he meant.

"Sorry for messing up your priorities. I believe this is the first time we laughed together."

David gazed out the window. Skyscrapers blotted most of the azure sky. He took a breath and let it out slowly. "I guess it is."

"Here's the list."

He folded the paper and stuck it in his breast pocket along with yesterday's forgotten list. Solange lived by organization. At home her desk overflowed with reminder lists.

At the end of the day Wendall caught up with David for a progress report. He'd taken it upon himself to be David's relief valve, knowing that no one could appreciate the tension David lived under more than he could. "How's the juggling act?"

David leaned back in his chair, pushing the front legs up off the floor and balancing himself against the wall. "One day at a time. Fred Marcus will look after my practice while I'm gone. Samara's HLA typing matched. We'll be in Seattle in six weeks."

"Is Samara returning to California to wait?"

"Yes. Mimi's in town. They've scheduled meetings. Also she's doing a promo for her new line of perfume. She sees Solange in the mornings, leaves the room white-lipped. Solange manages to get her digs in. Once I bring Solange home next week, there's no reason for Samara to remain, except for my selfishness in wanting her here."

Wendall didn't ask how they were going to solve their personal problems. They didn't know themselves. "Gotta go. Guess who's back in town after two years?"

"Who?"

"Maisy Daisy."

"Give her my regards."

Wendall punched his arm. "I'm going to give her a helluva lot more than that, pal."

Chapter Twenty-six

Solange made a mental note to ask David if the medication was responsible for the vivid dreams she'd been having lately. Last night—or was it this morning?—she'd heard her mother calling her. The gentle voice had to be her mother's. Who else would speak French to her?

Solange snuggled down on the pillow. She closed her eyes, hugging the dream to her bosom. In it she was four years old. She was with her mother in the kitchen in Paris. The breeze from the window carried the aromas of the lamb stew cooking on the stove. Solange climbed up on a stool. "Maman, can I cook, too?"

Her mother let her add herbs and spices. "Not too much garlic, darling," Maman cautioned, kissing her. Her mother wore her hair in a bun. They wore matching mother-daughter blue cotton aprons. Solange's shielded a yellow dress with a shirred bodice that her mother had sewn for her.

Her eyes drifted open as Samara sailed in. "Did Lilli own a lilac dress?"

Samara put fresh water in the vase, snipping the stems on the daisies. Solange's eyes were brighter, her color improved.

"Yes, a cotton jersey with scattered wildflowers. I gave it to her for her last birthday. Why do you ask?"

Growing excited, Solange clasped her hands. Her dream wasn't bunk! Her mother did communicate with her. "I saw her in it in a dream. My dress was yellow. We were in the kitchen cooking. I helped her make lamb stew. I saw it all, Samara. The long windows, the curtains, the white enamel stove, the hooks on the back of the door where she kept the aprons. Spooky, isn't it? What do you make of it? You're the believer in hocus-pocus.''

Samara tossed her coat onto the chair, smoothed her black hip huggers, and opened the top button of her white blouse. Each morning she arrived determined not to let Solange get to her.

''I can do without your sarcasm. I do not believe in chicanery and humbug incantations. Hocus-pocus! I've no doubt you owned every color dress, including every shade of yellow. As for cooking lamb stew with Maman, that's easy. It's not unusual to dream of recent events. Yesterday we talked about Maman's lamb stew. I described the kitchen in detail, as I did the rest of the apartment. There's a perfectly logical explanation for your dream.'' She dumped a clean blue nightgown in the dresser and slammed the drawer shut.

''Don't get in a snit. I was just asking.''

''No, you weren't,'' Samara charged, whipping around to face her. ''You were your usual snide self. One of these days we have a score to settle.''

Solange propped herself up on her elbows. ''Why not now?''

Samara looked at her sharply. ''So you can accuse me of attacking you while you're down? Forget it. When I let you have it, I'll choose the time and place.''

Solange was quick to note her sister's tight expression. ''Don't let a little thing like cancer stop you. I want to talk. Compared to the way I've been feeling, I'm having a banner day. Get it off your chest, sister dear. You've been wanting to for years. We might as well have it out. I can see you're dying to—no pun intended.''

''How do you do it?'' Samara snarled.

''Do what?''

Samara gritted her teeth, refusing to be drawn in by Solange. ''I'm leaving in a few days,'' she said, her tone cold and hard. ''We'll do this after the transplant. Or don't you want it? Is that why you're deliberately baiting me?''

Solange smirked. ''You missed your calling. You should have been a writer with your vivid imagination. Okay, go. Asher's going to miss you.''

''He's got you.''

Solange smacked her lips. ''And David. Don't forget him.''

Samara felt her shoulder blades tighten. *I don't need her bullying. I want to put a gun to her head, not help save her life.* "This visit is over."

"Sit down, for goodness' sake. I'm giving you permission to clear the air." She swallowed hard, choking over the next words. "I thought if you said your piece, I could apologize."

"Apologize! You?" Astounded, Samara's lower jaw dropped open. "This is how you lead up to an apology?"

Solange flopped back on the pillow. *Christ. Don't fuck up,* she told herself. *Apologize and get it over with. Asher might need Samara.* "Yes, dammit. I'm sorry. There. I said it. I'm sorry for a lot of things."

"Like what?" Samara pressed, the thin thread of her temper snapping. "Like trying to steal my life? Is that what you're sorry about? Or are you sorry you need me to save your life?"

Solange's eyes met hers unflinchingly. "I hurt me, too."

Samara stalked to the bed. She exploded. The overwhelming resentment of her sister's malevolence spilled forth like a broken dam. "Oh, really! Tell me. When did you become sorry? Yesterday? This morning? A year ago? Two minutes ago? Tell me. I'll pinpoint the exact moment. I don't know what your game is, Solange, only that you have one. David asked you for a divorce numerous times. I don't believe you're sorry for a thing, what do you think of that? Scheming is second nature to you. You're rotten. Selfish." Samara snatched her coat from the chair. She was almost out the door when Solange called her back with a surprise question.

"Do you hate Asher?"

"What's he got to do with this?" Samara stalked back to the bed, her chest heaving with indignation. "He can't help it if you're his mother. You hypocrite. How dare you continuously wrap yourself in the flag of motherhood after what you did to Avrim's baby! That doesn't absolve you."

Solange bit her lip. "I'm not the only woman who's ever had an abortion."

Now that she'd started, Samara couldn't stop. "We are not talking about other women. You want me to talk now? Fine. We'll air the whole sordid mess. What about my rights? David's rights? Why did you do it, you snake? Wasn't Avrim enough of a man for you? Weren't you getting pleasure from Max's and Maggie's heartache? Were David and I your kick for the week? Solange, you and I were nine-month-old babies when Maman left.''

Solange tugged at the sheet. ''How do you know how I felt?''

''You could have told me. I loved you, not Max. You. I hated you for cheating us. We could have been sisters, close friends, sharing secrets, helping each other. I wish Maman had taken you instead of me, although I'm sure if she had, you would have directed your hatred at Max, ultimately at me. You knew David and I were in love, that we planned to marry. How could you be so cold-blooded, so barbarous?''

Solange bristled. ''Stop yelling at me.''

Samara let out an explosive breath. ''You're responsible for years of our unhappiness. Avrim's lucky. He got out. You asked for this, and you're going to hear it. I've just begun to let you have it. The least you can do is lie there and shut up!''

''And give up David. Don't forget to add that,'' Solange said grudgingly.

Samara resisted the urge to smash the flower vase over Solange's head. ''There you go again. When will you realize that David was never yours to give up?''

''He wants Asher,'' Solange whined.

Disgusted, Samara thrust a finger at her. She'd tried. She'd honestly tried her best to view Solange as her patient, so as to make it bearable for her to forget for a little while.

''Asher isn't a spoil of war to be divided. He needs both parents. David's moving heaven and earth to save your misbegotten life. How would you like a woman to treat Asher the way you've treated David? Believe me, if it weren't for him, I wouldn't be here.''

''I wish I were loved the way he loves you.''

Except the one time prior to Asher's first visit, Solange had never shed her air of bravado. David had explained that her surliness helped her cope. Fear shot through Samara. Suppose she caused a setback? It wouldn't take much to push Solange over the edge. Seeing her worn-out twin, she took no pleasure in exacting her pound of flesh.

Solange wiped her eyes.

Just at that moment the medication nurse sailed in. Smiling, she bustled about the bed, checked the chart, and said to Samara whom she knew was leaving for California, ''I'm going to miss you. Anyone could tell you two are as close as two peas in a pod. Everyone says you're lucky to have each other.''

Samara and Solange exchanged harried glances. Without meaning to, they began to smile. It was the kind of smile that cavorted into a chuckle, gathered momentum, causing cloudbursts of laughter. As the twins rocked with merriment, the confused nurse drew a blank. Hysterical, Solange waved her hand in the air. Samara flopped down in the chair. ''Tell her, Solange.''

Solange gasped, ''No, you.''

Samara appreciated the irony of the situation. Giggles punctuated her attempts to talk. ''We . . . we,'' she gulped, pointing to her sister. ''We despise each other.''

The nurse knew twins loved to fool poor unsuspecting people. ''Oh, go on! I know when I'm being set up.'' Her reaction set them off again. Shaking her head, she gave up. ''I'll be back later, you two. You must have been a handful when you were kids.''

''I think we gave her an attack of apoplexy,'' Solange said when she got her breath back. Their outburst over, Samara resumed her glum expression.

''We don't look alike anymore,'' Solange said. Samara gazed at her twin's hollow cheeks and the frail body beneath the mint-green gown. ''Is it too late, Samara?''

Samara eyed her suspiciously.

''Get that leery look off your puss. I'm trying to apologize.'' Samara rose. ''Where are you going now?''

''To borrow a tape recorder.''

''God, you're a hard bitch. You're beginning to sound like me. Sit down.''

''Stop cursing. If Maman heard you, she'd wash your mouth with soap. I can imagine how you mortified Max.''

''What you said about me hit home. I do want more for Asher.''

Samara rolled her teeth over her bottom lip. ''Then set him a good example. Stop treating David and me as pawns on your personal score card.''

''If I did, then what?''

''I'm back in the picture, Solange,'' Samara said quietly. ''I'm not going away. Ever.''

Solange couldn't wait for Samara to leave. The specter of a dire future—of death—robbed her of delusions. She sincerely hoped it wasn't God's way of exacting retribution. Illness had transformed her into a pragmatist. She needed Samara's genuine forgiveness to guarantee fairness for Asher should Samara become his stepmother. Where to begin?

At the beginning, Avrim used to say . . .

Solange reached for the pad and pencil on the table near the bed. Her goal: to list every horrible deed, dating back to her earliest recollection. A tall order. Her school years alone took up pages. Her devilment of Mrs. Manfred, former cruddy headmistress of Regents Academy, brought proud memories. She'd do the old horror in again with no qualms. She blacklined those entries. Fanny Manfred could go to hell.

Her hand cramped. She flexed her fingers, taking a moment to rest. The more serious misdeeds in her memory's kaleidoscope surfaced readily. The fuzzier incidents required a more thorough dredging up. Eventually even the most distant capers flew across the legal pad. Some memories captivated the chronicler. She recalled vividly the first time she'd stepped out of Avrim's bathroom naked; the way his eyes narrowed, the slight flaring of his nostrils, how he walked over to gather her in his arms. She tingled at the memory of his hard body pressed against hers. Of his wicked tongue . . . If only she could turn back the clock.

"Well, you can't." She gave herself a mental shake, moving onward. Mother Maggie about to marry her father and have his child. "I still don't like you, Maggie," she muttered, listing her offenses.

Coming clean with one's slate of misdeeds seemed to her more like confessing to a psychiatrist or paddling a boat without oars through treacherous shoals than asking for God's grace. The mind meanders through circuitous routes. For Asher's sake, she left nothing out.

Abetted by Rabbi Cohen's statement that God is aware of His children's errant behavior, she scrolled her sins toward Samara before her eyes: how she hated the family's acceptance of her; the animosity she felt when Max asked her to sign the legal documents that would add Samara's name to the properties she'd owned solely until that time; heaving a Waterford crystal vase at her fireplace the day her grandparents inked

Samara's name to Gold's West; her envy of David's and Samara's steadfast love for each other; and yesterday, when Asher chirped how much he loved his aunt's peanut butter sandwiches, she'd felt a twinge of jealousy.

Even then . . .

But no more. She was through scheming, through lying. But oh, what she wouldn't give to see Avrim . . .

That afternoon she took a long nap. In her dream, her mother congratulated her for being such a good cook—and a good girl. When David came by to see her later, she had showered with the nurse's help and donned a clean peach-colored flannel nightgown and velour bathrobe. He found her seated in a chair by the window, her feet propped on a pillow, her legs covered with a blanket. Behind her the setting sun formed a halo of gold.

"You need a break," she said casually. "Take off tomorrow. Things will be hectic when I come home. The weatherman is calling for balmy weather. Go to the park. Invite Samara."

She was pleased by his astonishment. "Asher will invite her anyhow. He said she makes the doggiest peanut butter sandwiches. That's a compliment."

Unsure of her motives, David told Samara that night it was Solange's idea. "What do you make of that? Does this mean she's accepting the inevitable?"

Thinking back to their blowup, she hesitated to hazard a guess. Could it be Solange's apology meant she wanted to right the wrongs of the past? She wanted to believe it. "Can you take off?"

"I've got a couple of early-morning appointments. I'll play hooky from the lab."

They couldn't ask for more perfect weather. A January thaw replaced the grip of winter. Warm southwesterly breezes hinted of springtime. Manhattan took its pulse, then declared a holiday for itself. Central Park swarmed with bicyclists, joggers, bench-sitters, strollers, and loafers. On the Great Lawn, Asher, thrilled to have an unauthorized day off from kindergarten, flew his Superman kite. David and Samara cheered him on.

David's hand lightly rode Samara's shoulder. "You smell good," he said, sniffing her neck.

"At sixty dollars an ounce, I should."

David leaned over to softly place a kiss on her lips.

"It's good to get out," she said.

It was more than that. The reprieve soothed his jangled nerves. Samara's voice was music to his ears, and her smile filled his heart with joy. Like a miser, he stored up the rare moments.

He tucked her hand in his. "You'd better believe it. Uh-oh, Asher's tangled the line."

After David worked it free, they moseyed to Belvedere Lake to toss bread to the ducks.

"I'm hungry," Asher announced.

David took them to Rumpelmayer's on Central Park South. He and Samara shared a St. Moritz sandwich, piled high with turkey, ham, Swiss cheese, lettuce and tomatoes, and Russian dressing on rye bread. Asher ordered a hamburger. "With peanut butter."

"Are you going to eat that?" David asked, dubious when the strange combination arrived. Asher told him his aunt Samara introduced him to the treat. "That explains it."

While waiting for their dessert, David and Asher used the bathroom. "Daddy's dingle is larger than mine. We had a peeing contest. He shoots farther. Isn't that right, Pop?" Asher's voice carried to the next table, causing a ripple of laughs.

"Asher!" David said sharply. Samara managed to swallow without choking.

"Aunt Samara isn't interested. Are you?" he asked pointedly.

Samara whispered in his ear. "It's nothing to be ashamed of, darling. I mean, having a big dingle—"

He burst into laughter. "You're as bad as Asher."

Samara stole a thick glob of his whipped cream, then helped herself to more. "Make a straight face, Asher," she said. "Like Daddy." That cracked him up again. David reached down.

"Ouch!" Asher screeched, jerking his head up from his ice cream. "Who pinched me?"

Samara pointed an accusing finger. "He did."

David deadpanned, "Son, did I ever tell you your aunt Samara is ticklish?"

"David!" she protested.

"Aunt Samara, don't go to California. Stay with us. I love you," Asher gushed.

Next to him, David mouthed the same words. Her heart fluttered. *This isn't real,* Samara thought. *I'm having too much fun.*

Reality put her on a plane to California the next day in time for her to serve as maid of honor at Maggie's marriage to her father that weekend. Officiated by Murray Leightner, the ceremony was held in the chapel of Stanford University. Maggie's producer hosted the reception. In deference to Max, Maggie limited the guest list to family and close friends. As a wedding present, Samara gave Maggie a gown she had designed: prima taffeta and reembroidered alençon lace with shirred deco sleeves. Maggie glided down the flower-bedecked aisle, the perfect picture of a happy bride, her slightly rounded stomach hidden by the dress.

Solange phoned Samara daily, mainly to discuss Asher. She even asked for and accepted Samara's suggestion with regard to an appropriate wedding gift for Maggie and Max.

Solange sent Maggie and Max a unique gift—a commissioned portrait by a famous San Francisco artist. Mimi remarked that leopards don't change spots. The new Mrs. Max Gold agreed.

While she waited to be called to Seattle, Samara posed for an upcoming issue of *People.* She held a series of meetings with the president of an investment group who wanted to license her name on jewelry, bath products, accessories, leather goods, and linens. Intrigued by the opportunity to expand her licensing partnership with the LeClaires, Samara reserved her decision, pending an independent investigation. The last thing Jules, Mimi, and she wanted to do was push too fast in the wrong direction. They were in for the long haul, not the fast buck, associating her name with quality.

"Sam, I don't wish her harm, you know that, but between us, Solange is suckering you with her constant phone calls. What does David say?" Maggie asked.

"He says Solange is nicer to him than she's been in all the years they've been married." Her love for him touched her soul, nestled in the essence of her being, blinding her temporarily to the sympathy in Maggie's eyes. Maggie, who knew that Solange wouldn't appreciate seeing her, remained in San

Francisco ready to go to Seattle if Max called saying he needed her.

"Fredrica's going to throw a tantrum when you leave next week."

She did. On the day Samara left, the dog trotted up Maggie's path, refusing to lick Samara good-bye. Asher, on the other hand, flung himself at her when he and David met her plane at Seattle-Tacoma International Airport. "I don't like it here," Asher grumbled. "My glassie hates it here. We want to go home. *Today!*" he announced, skipping ahead to the car.

David brought her bags to the apartment. Stark white, the three rooms had none of the amenities that would help temper the turmoil and uncertainty of the days ahead. "It's fine," she said cheerfully.

Leaving quickly, they crossed the street to the Fred Hutchinson Research Center. Up the hill from Puget Sound, the Center bore the name of a former manager of the Cincinnati Reds. Samara noted that the display case to the left of the sliding doors contained baseballs signed by Major League Baseball players. Carrying her jacket, she strode across the parquet floor in sneakers, blue jeans, and a plum-colored sweater.

Having not seen her twin in weeks, Samara approached her room with trepidation. She found Solange tired but in good spirits for one about to undergo total body radiation as preparation for the bone marrow transplant.

"David played Asher a tape on Seattle," Solange said after they caught up on the latest news. "I'm going to be sedated, so there's nothing you can do for me. I'd appreciate it if you take Asher out of everyone's hair."

"You're so calm," Samara stammered.

Solange glanced at David. "Samara, if we can face the fact I may die, it would help me if you face it, too."

Samara shook her head. "I'm here. You'll be fine." Despite her initial reluctance, she felt an integral part of a team effort. Her hatred of her sister was gone. In its place she carried the knowledge that they'd started life together, that she alone could save her.

Solange lay quietly watching her. Clasping her hands tightly, she squeezed her eyes shut. "There are no guarantees," she said quietly. "I know about graft versus host disease and cytomegalovirus pneumonia."

"I don't want you to think that way," Samara protested. "You must be positive."

"Are you sure you're older?" Solange asked. "Sis, when you don't have the luxury of time, you can't squander it. In New York you laid it on the line. You didn't paint a pretty picture of me."

Samara bit her lip. "I shouldn't have hit you when you were down."

"Are you sorry for telling the truth?"

"No," she answered. "Only for the timing."

Solange grinned. "Spoken like my twin. I probably would have been a lot harder on you. When they told me Maman had died, I was too young to understand. Then you came along, all grown up, telling me I had a mother all those years. To put it mildly, I was furious she abandoned me. David, stop fussing. He's sending you frantic eye messages not to upset me. Go take a break, David. You're driving me crazy."

Some of the fire came back into Solange's eyes after he left. "It wasn't entirely my fault that I was rude to his parents. Bella and Michel never passed up a chance to let me know how much they loved you. I'd like David to take Asher to France. He should know his grandparents better."

"Solange, why didn't you agree to the divorce? You don't love David. You never have."

"It suited me to stay married to him. The truth is, if I could rewrite the script, I would tie Avrim to me, never let him go. You do know that Avrim's found someone else. She can never make him feel the way I did. We were special." She lapsed into silence.

Samara looked down at the frail hand in hers. Poor Solange. She was still her own worst enemy.

Solange's lower lip trembled. "Oh, shit! Who the fuck am I kidding? I'm petrified. I'm very grateful for your bone marrow, twinnie. I have one request. If . . . you know . . . please accept Asher in your heart. Promise me you'll love him like your own son. He needs a mother's love. I know what it's like without it. Please promise me you won't resent him."

"How can I resent David's spitting image? Promise me you'll get well. We'll work out the rest." Solange's gratitude nearly did Samara in. Impulsively she kissed her cheek. Then she fled from the room.

Solange's eyes drifted shut. As he had so often lately, Avrim took center stage. Treasuring the past, she dreamed of them in his bed, making love . . .

"Cut it out, Solly," she heard Avrim groan. *"Cut it out or we'll never make it to the bed . . ."*

The February weather was cold, a blustery thirty-eight degrees. Samara dressed warmly. With Asher in a bright red ski suit, waterproof boots, they set off to tour Emerald City's pier district. During the next few days, they visited the Museum of Sea and Ships, the Space Needle, the Seattle Children's Museum, ate fish and chips at Fisherman's Terminal, wandered through the downtown area, and even went bowling. One night David took her aside. "It's tomorrow, Sam."

She gulped.

After Samara was admitted to Swedish Hospital, everything happened steamroller fast. With a team of physicians from France and Italy congratulating her in their native languages for donating her bone marrow, she counted backward for the anesthesiologist.

"I'll never complain again about anything," she groaned, doing the Hickman shuffle when they discharged her the next day. "How's Solange?"

"She's receiving your bone marrow now. In twenty-one days or so, she should grow new bone marrow."

"I'm glad I did it," Samara said, jubilant despite her temporary discomfort.

David kissed her. "Sam, I know you hate being congratulated, especially since we both know you're a first-class A number-one coward." She swatted his arm. "I want you to know how proud I am of you."

"It better work."

Samara switched battle plans. Leaving Asher with Max and Pepe, she sat near Solange. Talking herself hoarse, she recounted stories of her childhood in Paris, repeating them over and over. Aware of Solange's interest in their mother's cooking, she recited Lilli's recipes, then altered the ingredients to elaborate the list. She raised her voice over the noise from the machines monitoring Solange's progress. While her twin slept, sedated by morphine, Samara regaled her with tales of how she plagued David to do her homework, especially her spelling. She described in detail the "thrones," the chipped gold-leaf-painted chairs, discards from Jules's showroom. She acted out scenes of Mimi and her holding court. She brought a smile to David's and her father's faces, who were in the room at the time, when she admitted that she and Mimi purposely kept the adults in a dither, requiring permission from them to speak, then regally refusing to grant it.

Samara tacked up pictures of Asher who offered his glassie as the best medicine his mother could have. David gently told his son that his mother had expressly requested he keep the glassie safe.

"You'll meet my best friend, Mimi," Samara rattled one afternoon to a sedated Solange. "I have to warn you. Mimi doesn't like the old you. You'll have to be extra nice to her, convince her you're changing. She's good at spotting phonies."

David put a hand on her shoulder. She hadn't noticed him come back into the room. Startled, she jumped. "Samara, you're wearing yourself out."

"Tell me the part about the throne room again," the voice from the bed rasped.

"You're awake!" Samara shrieked. Solange opened her eyes. "You're better. Look, David. She's alert."

David moved to Solange's side, relief flooding his features. He held her hand. "Good girl, Solange."

"Good girl, nothing," Solange smiled. "Who could sleep through all her yakking? She hasn't shut up in days. What right do you have to add lemon to Maman's lamb stew?"

Samara punched David's arm. "How about that! She heard me."

"Over and over," Solange groaned. "You're a broken record." She reached for her hand. "Thank you. This time I mean it from the bottom of my heart. How's Asher?"

Samara yawned. She stretched her stiff muscles. "He misses you, but he's fine." It wasn't true. Left mainly with Pepe, Asher moped and complained he wanted his mother.

"He's lucky to have you for an aunt. You're off duty. You look worse than I do. Go home, get some rest. David, sit with me for a little while."

"I'm glad she's gone," Solange said when they were alone. "She's so . . ." She groped for the word. "Committed."

David slouched in the chair and rubbed his chin. There were no secrets between them now. "She's always been that way."

"That theatrical?"

"Always."

Solange smiled. "Asher takes after her in that respect. I'm glad he's got part of her in him."

David could feel the backs of his eyes sting with compassion for her plight. He stroked her hand, saying more with his gesture than with words. He came home to a celebratory ice cream party. With Asher in tow, Samara had purchased five flavors of ice cream: vanilla, mocha fudge, chocolate chip, pistachio, and coffee, as well as assorted toppings. Max, Asher, Pepe, and Samara gorged themselves on ice cream. David didn't have the heart to ruin their euphoria. He looked at his son's shining face and prayed for the best . . .

Six days later, David's beeper went off at one A.M. He dressed quickly, dashing across the street in the rain.

"Her blood gases went down suddenly," her doctor said. "There was no warning. She's got hypoxia. We're pumping antibiotics in the IV. She's on the respirator."

David wanted to scream at him to do more, but he knew it was impossible. What he feared most had come true. If Solange wasn't exchanging oxygen, she would die of pulmonary congestion.

David's tormented eyes flew to the bed. She had no defenses. The new bone marrow never had a chance to grow. Death lurked in the room. He smelled it, tasted it, felt it.

"Leave us alone, please."

He picked up her featherlight hand. His finger skimmed the wedding band she'd bought for herself, so loose it was a wonder it stayed on her finger. Their wedding had been a farce, their marriage a disaster, yet together they'd made a fine son. A boy who would grow to manhood, do them both proud. He would never forget Solange, the precious gift she'd given him.

His finger caught on something misshapen. Peering at the ring, he noticed the Scotch tape wrapped around the inside as a ring guard. "Images," he said aloud. "You believed in keeping up appearances. Solange, don't do this. You've got to live. You have a son. You've been so brave. I never expected it of you. Why now, dammit?'' he railed. Her chest heaved with the exertion of breathing. It infuriated David.

"What should I tell our son?" He swiped at his nose. *Get up,* he wanted to scream. *Get up and stop playacting, you spoiled brat.*

Seven hours later, he remained at his vigil, summoning every ounce of his willpower to stay awake, refusing entreaties by the staff to take a break. He sat by her bedside, his face drawn with fatigue, praying for her as she slipped into a coma. He asked the nurse to phone Samara and Max.

Samara's eyes went wide with disbelief as they settled on the still form of her sister. Bewildered, she stared at the nurse. The nurse gave her a look of pity.

"Ohmigod! No! David, the bone marrow—"

"She has pneumonia." Max uttered a cry. "Max, I'm so sorry."

"No!" Samara ran to the bed to stand by her father. This was her twin. They were just becoming friends again. She shouted at Solange. She clapped her hands near her twin's ears. "Wake up, Solange. Wake up this minute, do you hear me! Don't you dare let go now. Think of Asher. He needs you."

Outside, lightning crackled jagged bolts, flickering the lamplight near the bed. A great drumroll of thunder rumbled in the heavens, rattling the windows with sheets of rain. Solange's eyes flew open. David gently closed his dead wife's eyes.

"She knew," Samara wept. "She knew she wasn't alone."

David urged them into the hall while the nurse removed the tubation and shut off the monitors. They returned for a final good-bye. Samara was struck by the eerie absence of noise. David's head bowed. He would honor Solange's memory, use her love for her child to guide their son. They stayed for a long time, as though by remaining with Solange they could put off the sad task of telling Asher.

"David," Samara said, "Solange regretted Asher not knowing your parents. Now would be a good time to take him to France."

He agreed. "Yes. We spoke about it. Solange knew that Asher would need time to work through his grief, to be able to see you for yourself, not as his mother's double. We'll be gone for as long as it takes, Samara. It could be months."

She embraced him. "I'll be here for both of you when you return."

Max blew his nose. "There's a saying, 'For every life that's taken, one is replaced.' It's not true," he said sadly. "You can never replace the person you've lost. You can only move on."

They rode silently down the elevator and walked out into the street. Cars pushed puddles of water nearer the curb. The air smelled of the sea: salt-fresh and new. Overhead, the sun drew back the curtain of gray gloom to bathe the sky in watery sunshine.

Asher insisted that his glassie be buried with his mother. "So she'll know it's me when we talk." David requested that donations be made in Solange's name to fund research for organ transplantation.

Father and son flew to France to begin the healing process. Samara did what she did best in times of crisis.

Work.

Chapter Twenty-seven

Paris, 1987

Avrim Leightner instructed the cabdriver to take him to the Jardin d'Acclimitation in the Bois de Boulogne. Once there, he paid his admission to the children's park and handed his ticket to the collector at the main gate. He spotted David playing ball with a boy in blue jeans and a San Francisco 49ers sweatshirt. The boy ran, caught the toss, and whipped it back. *The kid's good,* Avrim thought.

Then the boy rattled something off in French. French!

Solange's son! Speaking French. Brown as a berry, the kid bore a strong resemblance to his father.

Avrim stepped forward. "David, hello. I was in the neighborhood. Your parents told me where to find you."

David shook Avrim's hand. "It's good to see you, Avrim. Asher, you remember Uncle Murray and Aunt Ceil Leightner. Mr. Leightner is their son. Say hello to Avrim Leightner."

Asher tossed the ball in his hands. His feet danced pebbles into the air. "Are you the television son?"

Avrim laughed. "'Fraid so."

Asher's face grew solemn. His hands grew still. "Did you know my mother?"

Avrim glanced at David. "Yes, son. From the time your mommy was a little baby."

Asher craned his neck, tilting up his head. "She's in heaven with her mother. She wrote me a letter. Whenever I feel bad, I read it. She's always with me."

"I'm sure she loved you very much," Avrim said.

"Yeah, she did." Asher squirmed out from beneath his

father's hold. He dropped the football and skipped off to collect horse chestnuts that had fallen from the trees.

"What brings you to Paris?" David asked, keeping an eye on his son.

Avrim sat on the bench next to him. "I figured it's time to stop running. I'm going home for good. I couldn't before. I meant to write."

David understood. "Me, too. I should have written to you when Solange died. She wore the pin you gave her until she took ill. She never stopped loving you. As a matter of fact, you're the only man she ever did love. She told that to me and to Samara. Yours was the last name she mentioned before she slipped into a coma. I hear you're getting married."

Avrim shook his head. "That's over. My fault, I guess. Felicia couldn't handle my addiction to Solange. I tried and failed to get over her. Felicia did us both a favor, tossing me out. How about you? How long are you staying in France? You've been gone a long time."

David smiled. "A year. Asher started school here. I've been doing some work at a local hospital. The main thing is my parents got to know Asher. They've helped tremendously."

"He speaks French like a native."

David grinned. "So Samara says. She's been taking care of Asher's menagerie. They speak constantly."

Avrim cocked his head. "David, you're more relaxed than I've ever seen you. You're okay now, aren't you?"

"Yes. Asher and I are ready to go home. Max sold the house for me. We put the money in Asher's account. He had it rough, especially at the beginning. Asher blamed me for not insisting that Solange take his good luck marble. She was afraid he'd place too much importance on it. He was an angry little boy. He had a very special relationship with his mother."

Avrim tried to picture Solange in that role. It didn't fit his image of her. "At least he's got Samara. When he sees her, he sees his mother."

"That's the main reason we've stayed away this long," David said. "He needed time. Now when we return, he'll love Samara for herself, not as a substitute. He starts his new school term in Sausalito. I'll open an office in San Francisco."

"I'm happy for you, David," Avrim said, meaning it.

"Thanks, Avrim. Life's a circle. I was with Lilli when she

first met Max right here in the Jardin d'Acclimation.'' David repeated the rest of the story of that fateful day.

Avrim understood. He'd come to tie up loose ends, too. "My father was Max's conduit to Lilli. Now her grandson plays in the very same park where his grandparents met. You and I were fated to be part of their daughters' lives. I'm glad it's worked out for you." Avrim cleared his throat. "I spoke with Maggie. She's thrilled with motherhood. She designed a gold 'Super Stud' pin for Max's lapel."

David laughed. "The Golds are a dynasty. Their strength comes from each other. Tessie and Barney are still going strong. They've purchased a home not far from Max and Maggie's. Samara's won the Femme Award given by the Under Fashion Club. The Femme's the equivalent to an Oscar in the lingerie business."

Avrim grew serious. "Samara's a winner. In her own way, Solange was, too. I loved her even when I tried not to. Does that makes sense?"

David nodded. "It makes perfect sense. Don't forget, I'm addicted to Samara." It was good to pick up the threads of their friendship.

Asher ran back with a pile of horse chestnuts. He wiped his dusty hands on his jeans.

"How do you feel about attending weddings?" David asked.

Avrim grinned. "As long as I'm not the groom. When's the happy day?"

"Next weekend at Maggie's. A priest and a rabbi will officiate."

Avrim laughed. "You're not taking any chances, are you?"

"Damn right I'm not."

"Uncle Wendall and I are going to be the best men," Asher said. "Whatever that is. Only I can't go on the honeymoon. It's not fair. They get to have all the fun."

Avrim struggled not to laugh. He took a stab at the unfamiliar role of wise old uncle. "Who would look after the animals if you tagged along on the honeymoon?"

"The vet," Asher snapped back, dashing off to chase a squirrel.

Avrim roared. He could get to love that kid.

A bundle of nerves, Samara paced up and down her office.

In three days, she was getting married in the heirloom lace bridal gown she'd wanted David and her mother to see her in years ago. Her staff had thrown a massive bridal shower for her. Friends and family feted her with luncheons, teas, and dinner parties. "Anything could go wrong," she wailed to Mimi. "It's been ages since David and I have seen each other."

Mimi's commiseration fluctuated between "Gimme a break, Samara!" and "Enough already!"

"Suppose David changes his mind?" Samara cried to her grandmother.

"Oh, please!" Tessie retorted, then went off to tell anyone within hearing distance how delighted she and Barney were that the fashion world hailed Samara's sequined bustiers, gold-and-silver-trimmed slips, and her daytime pajama look as lingerie's trendiest statement. "Of course *I* recognized her talents immediately." She bragged that Samara's collection, modeled by a dozen leggy Hollywood starlets, had created a sensation and skyrocketed sales.

Samara corraled Maggie. "What if David has stopped loving me?"

"When the polar cap melts!" Maggie replied, kissing her son Sammy's chubby neck.

Samara locked herself in her office. She *knew* no one would understand!

She pressed the intercom button. "No calls, Noki," she ordered. "I can't speak to anyone."

Her secretary called back. "Boss, there's a man out here who wants to see you. He doesn't have an appointment."

"Tell him I'm busy!" Samara shouted. Her stomach lurched. She'd been to the bathroom so often, she hurt. She had just gotten over her period. She had limp hair and four chipped fingernails. David would take one look at her and run.

"He refuses to leave," Noki drawled into the intercom. "He says he's too busy to come back later."

Samara grew incensed. "Tough! No meetings. Nobody."

"He insists on seeing you, boss. He says he only needs a minute of your time. He promises to make it worth your while."

Annoyed, Samara's hand crashed down on the desk, scattering papers onto the floor. "You heard me. No one."

"Okay, but he says you'll be sorry."

Samara grew livid. "Noki, come in here!"

With her head down to retrieve the fallen papers, Samara started scolding her secretary as soon as she heard the door open. "Now see here, Noki. How many times do I have to tell you I want to be alone? What's getting into you?"

"I hope me," a deeply masculine voice said. Then she heard a deep chuckle.

Samara's head shot up. She screamed in disbelief. "Oh, God! David! Oh, God! I look awful!"

David strolled into the room, grinning.

"Oh, God! What are you doing here?" she cried delightedly. She leapt into his arms, kissing his face over and over. Her eyes swept over him. The year had worked wonders on his looks. Tall and strong and deliciously sexy, he took her breath away. "Oh, God, it's you!"

"I'm glad you recognized me," he teased, his eyes roaming over her lovingly. His hands moved possessively over her body, touching her in ways she'd spent nights dreaming about. "Asher and I couldn't wait. We caught an earlier plane. He's with Tessie."

He wrapped his arms about her. She was everything he'd dreamed about, more if possible. He couldn't concentrate when she directed those big blue eyes at him. So he contented himself by giving her a slow, burning kiss. His lips scorched hers with all the pent-up passion he'd been holding back for months.

Samara wound her arms about him, giving as well as receiving. She sighed rapturously. All her fears vanished.

He looked into her eyes. "I love you, Samara. I always have. I always will." With his arms about her, he told her about Asher, about seeing Avrim. "His engagement's off."

"I wish we all could have a happy ending, but that's not the way real life works, is it? When I think of Solange, there's no hatred, only sadness at the waste. Maggie's helped Max tremendously. The raw hurt's passed. The grief comes in waves when you least expect it. We talk about Maman and Solange."

Before she knew what was happening, he grabbed her hand, dragging her out the door, past a beaming Noki.

"Where are we going?" she asked, running alongside him in the hall as executives popped out of their offices. Not caring who saw them, he stopped long enough to give her another fiery kiss, letting it last until they both ached and everyone clapped.

"Home," he said in a voice husky with desire. In her bedroom, they undressed quickly, falling together onto the bed. They reacquainted themselves with the pleasures of the flesh, the pledges of their hearts, the promises of tomorrow. Their long wait over, David settled between her thighs. He kissed her. "I love you. I'll never leave you again."

Samara guided him home . . .

The sundial in Maggie and Max's backyard pointed to noon. The guests milled around the grass. Near the latticed canopy—the *chuppa*—adorned with lilacs, Rabbi Feldman and Father Ignatius finished their white wine and remarked on the beautiful weather. Seated at the rented piano on the brick patio, Wendall played Brahms's "Lullaby" for the third time. One of three songs in his repertoire, he was saving the "Wedding March" for the ceremony and "Chopsticks" for afterward when the party got going. At a signal from Pepe, he raised both hands high, then solemnly switched to the opening chords of the "Wedding March."

The guests hurriedly sat.

Asher, his hair slicked back and wearing his first tux, began the procession by muttering, "I hate this dumb monkey suit."

Snooty Fredrica, wearing a pink bow and a scowl, prissed down the aisle in back of him.

A radiant Samara, her luminous blue eyes shining like stars, her platinum hair cascading down her shoulders and back—David insisted she wear it loose!—glided down the aisle on the arm of her father who looked ready to burst with pride.

Jules left his seat to check the long bridal train. His wife pulled him back.

Tessie, Barney, Pepe, and Vittorio wept.

Ceil and Murray linked hands.

Maggie bounced a drooling Sammy on her knee.

Mimi and Noki hugged each other.

Bella and Michel threw kisses when they weren't clutching their hearts. Avrim felt a pang of longing for the twin who wasn't there.

Samara joined her handsome groom at the flower-bedecked

chuppa. Wendall stopped playing the piano to assume his duties as one of the best men. David heaved a sigh of relief.

The guests tittered when Wendall dropped the rings twice.

"Let me do that or we'll never eat," Asher hissed.

Father Ignatius spoke of family and eternal love.

Rabbi Feldman looked first at the happy groom and then at his glowing bride. The couple didn't look as if they needed his lecture, but he'd give it anyway. He spoke of the custom of the groom's smashing of the ceremonial, napkin-wrapped wineglass, and that it counsels us never to forget the plight of Jews in history. The rabbi glanced at Father Ignatius, who nodded as if to agree with him that from the way David and Samara were lost in each other's eyes, he might as well be telling them that Egyptians smashed clay pots with their enemies' names written on them. But, the rabbi thought, he was getting to the good part. He had an idea he'd get their attention with this. Another glance at Father Ignatius, who knew what he was going to say, confirmed it.

"David, Samara, on a day as auspicious as today, we remember the first positive commandment of the Bible: *Be fruitful, and multiply.*"

David grinned at his bride. She winked. Then he smashed the glass with religious fervor.

The entire assemblage said a loud "Amen" at the conclusion of the service, retained for posterity on videotape—courtesy of Avrim, who knew damn well he was going to love Solange's kid.

Jules unhooked Samara's long bridal train. He packed it away, praying he'd see his daughter wear it one day.

Mimi caught the bridal bouquet.

David raised his glass in a toast. "I love you, wife."

"I love you, husband." They linked arms. Leaving the festivities for a moment, they strolled away from the others.

The warm wind caressed her cheek. Suddenly she stopped. As if she were standing next to her, she heard her mother's loving voice.

Solange and I are happy for you, Samara. David and you and Asher belong together. We love you.

"They would approve, wouldn't they?"

Knowing she meant Lilli and Solange, David nodded. "I'm

sure of it, darling.'' Their love had been tested, tempered like steel.

Asher bounded over to them, joy written on his shining face. Judging from the marks around his mouth, he'd obviously been delving into the chocolates. David scooped him up. Asher wrapped an arm around Samara's neck. ''I loved getting married to you.''

She kissed her new son, tasting the chocolate. She remembered the first time they'd met, how he'd negotiated sweets from a nervous David. ''I loved getting married to you, Asher.''

''Hey, what about me?'' cried David.

Samara and Asher exchanged glances. The two born negotiators relayed silent messages. Turning to David, they chirped in unison, ''You, too.''

Grinning happily, all three were in perfect agreement.